THE WALKER'S DAUGHTER

Janet Allison Brown

Firedance Books

First published in the UK by Firedance Books in 2012.

This edition published in the UK by Firedance Books in 2014.

Copyright © 2014 Janet Allison Brown

Cover photograph copyright © Chaoss/Shutterstock.com

Cover and book design copyright © 2014 William Sauer

ISBN: 978-1-909256-33-0

Firedance Books

firedancebooks.com

To Kevin and our children:
Four clovers forever.

Chapter 1

FROST. THERE WAS FROST SPARKLING round me on the icy doorstep. Like diamonds. *Breathe.*

'Where is she?'

'The ambulance took her to St Mary's in Paddington. You didn't answer your mobile. I came straight here.' Sue leaned down to lift me from my knees. 'We have to go, Cora. I'll drive you there.'

I raised my eyes to her blanched face.

'Cora. Get up, please,' she pleaded.

Reality flooded back to me. I jumped to my feet, grabbed house keys from the hallway and slammed the front door. 'Let's go,' I said, running towards Sue's car.

I stared out of the window as we pulled out of Gregory Square into Finn Street and a line of slow-moving traffic.

Too slow. Too slow.

'Can you speed up?'

'I really can't, Cora. There's too much traffic, and this ice. You'd think they'd have gritted the roads.' Her voice broke.

'How bad is it?' My own voice sounded eerily calm.

'I don't know. We were outside the school gates heading for my car. She was running ahead. Dancing, actually. You know Grace. She couldn't wait to get out of there. The van mounted the pavement — there was nothing I could do.' Her hands shook on the steering wheel.

'Of course there wasn't,' I said.

'She wasn't moving when they put her in the ambulance. But she wasn't dead — God, no Cora! She was unconscious. She was breathing and everything.'

I curled over, my arms around my stomach, willing myself not to hear the thud of metal against my daughter's soft, yielding body, not to see her flung into the air.

'Cora—'

'It's okay. Please, just get me there.'

You can get there quicker.

No! Where did that thought come from?

You could be there right now. You know how to do it.

I gripped the edge of the seat, feeling the gorge rise, willing myself to concentrate on *being*. It took forever, an endless white purgatory of not knowing, of having to sit still.

Finally we pulled into the car park.

'Go, go,' urged Sue and I leaped out of the car and ran through the ice and slush.

It was like dream running — working my legs as fast as I could, but getting nowhere. A revolving door, a help desk, long white corridors and signs, voices and questions and finally, finally a large room, a curtain, a cubicle — and a child on a bed.

The world shrank to a pin-point: this time, this place; this child.

Grace.

I laid my hand on her unblemished forehead and stroked back her brown curls.

A tired voice came from behind me. 'Are you the mother? The doctor will be in shortly to talk to you.'

My eyes were busy examining Grace's face. 'Has she woken at all? Did you give her something?'

'She'll wake when she's ready.'

'Should she be unconscious? Is this normal?'

I heard the sound of creaking shoes as the nurse shifted her weight from foot to foot. 'Everything looks fine. The doctor will be here soon.' She might as well have said, 'How should I know? Accidents happen everyday.'

I turned now and met her disinterested eyes. 'What do you need from me?'

'The school's given us all her details. We need you to confirm them, but we can do that later. Talk to her. Let her know you're here.'

She turned and left us.

Grace's arm shook under my trembling hand. 'Shush,' I said, more for myself than her. I felt utterly helpless.

You're not helpless. Get on with it.

I was aware of sweat pooling under my arms. I looked at the strip lighting; no windows. It was already dark outside but in here it could have been any time at all.

I squeezed my eyes closed and took in a deep breath. Grace. 'I'm coming, baby.' I withdrew my hand and went to draw the cubicle curtains tightly shut, leaving no chinks. Then I pulled a chair to the bedside, sat down and laid my head against Grace's body for support.

'Oh God,' I said. 'Oh God.'

Before I could go any further, the curtains parted and Sue came in.

I clapped my hand against my hammering heart. 'You made me jump.' Grace hadn't moved; the machines went on beeping.

'Sorry. How is she?' Sue's mascara was smudged and her eyes were red.

I nodded towards the machines with a mute shrug. Sue sat down on the other side of the bed and took Grace's free hand.

'Do you want me to call someone?'

'No. Thanks.'

'I could call your sister.'

Just what I needed. 'No. I'm fine. Really. Sue, you don't have to stay.'

'I would never leave you alone!' she said in horrified tones. She was hunched in her chair, buckling under the weight of her guilt — because she'd been the grown-up in charge; because she was relieved it wasn't her daughter lying here.

It was all I could do to stay polite. *Go away! I can't do this unless you leave us alone!*

She wouldn't. Nor would anyone else. Grace was like Eros in her own Piccadilly Circus, with a troupe of uniformed staff whirling around her. They took her pulse. They gave her injections and measured her blood pressure. They raised her eyelids and shone lights into her eyes. They pressed her tender white belly so that the breath came out of her mouth in little gasps.

The pain in my chest made it hard to breathe; every breath made the room around me swim.

Excellent. Pass out, Cora, why don't you? That'll help. You know what you have to do.

'Shall I find us a hot drink?' said Sue.

I nodded vigorously. 'Yes, please. That's exactly what I need.'

Sue left, happy to be useful and, grasping the chance to be alone with Grace, I clutched the arm of a hovering nurse. 'Can you give me some time with my daughter?'

'I'll be done in a minute,' she said, ticking something off a chart.

'No, I need a few minutes of privacy now. I need to talk to her.'

This nurse smiled kindly. 'She looks a lovely little girl. How old is she — eight? She's going to be all right, you know. You'll have plenty of time for all the things you want to say.'

'No. Now. Right now. Can you do something?'

The nurse put her hand on mine. 'It'll be okay. You should go with your friend and get a cup of tea. Take a break.'

The minute she'd gone, Sue returned, followed closely by a doctor. I clasped my hands tightly and bit another hole in my lip.

'Ms Bloux?'

'Yes?'

'We're fairly sure there's no internal bleeding. Everything seems to be okay, only a few cuts and bruises. Which is why...'

'Yes?'

'We're surprised she's still unconscious. There doesn't appear to be any damage to her head, but we can't rule out concussion. Or even coma, although that's unlikely...'

I don't know what else they told me. I don't know who else came and went, or when we were moved into a tiny room off a larger ward. I only know it seemed like hours before everything quietened down, Sue went home, and we were alone.

This room had a window. Despite the streetlamps illuminating the hospital grounds outside, darkness pressed up against the glass as if it had noticed us.

Get on with it, coward. No one's looking.

My fear for Grace was a living, breathing thing inside my heart, clawing at me. In comparison, my other fear — the driving fear of my life — paled into insignificance. I hadn't *walked* for twenty years. Most of that twenty years had been an agony of not walking, yet here I stood, on the threshold, feeling as if I were about to die — wanting to die if Grace didn't wake up.

I peered into the ward, quietly closed the door of our little room, and then sat down and popped — *at last!* — leaving my body in the chair, half-lying across Grace's body.

It had been so long, but this was like breathing — no practice required. I hovered over Grace.

Baby. Are you in there? Grace? It's me.

Nothing. No flutter of the eyelids, no stir of a Self behind her face.

Are you there?

It didn't look like anybody was home but I knew nothing about serious injury. The machines wired to her chest said her body was still alive, but where was the rest of her? I would have to go in and look.

I slid a tentative hand into Grace's shoulder, leaned over her face and sank against her — then pulled up sharply, chilled, terrified.

Grace was absent. Her body was as empty as mine.

I shot up to the ceiling in confusion, looking down at the two of us, her neat and wired to the machines that showed her beating heart, me slumped over her like Raggedy Ann.

She's dead. I'm too late.

The chart at the bottom of the bed flew up and slapped onto the floor, the pages fluttering at the lash of energy created by my despair.

I would disappear. I would leave my body with hers and I would dissolve...

Did it work like that? Could I simply vanish?

Grace, I wailed. *Come back!*

The air around me chilled as my mind focused, sharpened into the point of an icicle. She couldn't be dead. No. She wouldn't be breathing. I would have known. *I would know.*

I snapbacked into my body and lifted my head as Sue came into the room.

'I thought you went home.' My voice, raspy and harsh, sounded as torn as my heart.

'I did but I couldn't sleep knowing you were here alone. Won't you let me call your sister? How are you holding up? Did something happen?'

'I don't want Rebecca. Nothing's changed.' *Go away!*

'She hasn't woken up yet?'

I shook my head, my mind beginning to race. *She isn't dead. But she's not in her body. Is it possible — ? She can't be. Can she?*

'Don't cry, Cora,' said Sue, beginning to cry herself. 'This is a very good hospital. They'll do everything they can for her.'

I should have hugged her; we should have traded small words and gestures of comfort. But I couldn't let my guard down, so I found a blanket instead and laid it over her, ignoring her protestations. Then I sat staring at Grace's empty face as the machines ticked over and Sue dropped into exhausted sleep amid the background clatter and stress of the busy hospital.

And then, quiet as a whisper, gentle as a kiss, Grace slipped into the room.

CHAPTER 2

GRACE LOOKED DOWN AT ME with a half-smile, a little embarrassed. Then she registered my face and the machines plugged into her body, and she snapbacked and sat up in bed, fully awake, fully alert.

'Mum?'

For an eyeblink we stared at one another and then I snatched her into a fierce hug.

'Oh my God,' I whispered. 'You were gone. I thought you were dead.'

'Sorry.'

'Are you okay?'

She shifted her body experimentally. 'A bit stiff.'

'What happened?' I glanced at Sue, whose breathing was heavy and deep; I didn't want her waking now. I laid a finger on my lips. 'Keep your voice down, darling.'

'I've been—' began Grace, with downcast eyes.

'Not that. The accident.'

'I saw the van coming and I couldn't get out of the way in time,' she whispered. 'I thought it would hurt less if I wasn't there.'

'You popped *before* it hit you?' I asked.

A series of emotions flitted across her face: relief; disbelief; and then confusion. 'You *know* about popping? Why didn't you tell me, Mum?'

I swallowed hard. 'I didn't think I'd ever need to tell you.'

Grace was frowning at me. 'I popped as the car hit me. It seemed like a good idea.'

That's why there was so little injury; her body was limp and yielding to the impact. God looks after drunks and idiots — and Grace.

I looked into her blessed, perfect little face. 'It was a good idea,' I conceded. 'It was a very good idea. And how long have you been popping, Grace?'

'A while,' she said, her brows still furrowed. 'I didn't think you knew about it.'

Relief took over again. I pulled her head onto my shoulder and stroked her hair. 'You're safe,' I said, through tears. 'I thought I'd lost you for good.'

'Mummy,' she began, raising her head.

'It looks like we have things to talk about,' I interrupted.

'Well I should have told you about the popping,' she admitted. 'I wasn't sure what you'd say. But you should have told me, too — why didn't you? Do you pop?'

Oops. 'All babies pop,' I said, stalling. 'Do you remember popping as a baby?'

She raised her head. 'Ouch, my head hurts. Really, I popped as a baby? Wow, clever baby. Can *you* pop?'

'All babies pop. Then they grow out of it.'

'Why?' She was searching my face. I couldn't avoid eye contact, but I could at least avoid blinking too much.

'That's how it's supposed to be.'

'Will I grow out of it?'

I pursed my lips. 'I thought you grew out of it long ago.'

'So why am I still popping?'

I shook my head. 'I don't know, Grace.'

Her eyes narrowed. 'You didn't grow out of it either, did you Mum?'

'I never pop,' I said. 'Never. It's incredibly dangerous. You must never do it again, Grace.'

She opened her mouth to object but we hadn't been quiet enough; Sue stirred and then sat up abruptly. 'Grace? Oh thank God.' She burst into tears and ran to Grace's side. 'Are you all right? Does anything hurt?'

We called a nurse, and there was another lengthy round of activity. They wouldn't let me take Grace home; there would be more tests in the morning. But they confirmed that, physically at least, everything was fine. Which meant that Sue, at least, could go home and resume a normal life.

'Thank you, Sue.' I hugged her.

'I feel so bad.'

'Accidents happen. Everyone knows that. I'll give you a call when we're home.'

'I'll understand if you want to change things. If you want to stop sharing lifts—'

'Don't be silly. I'm just going to keep her home for a day or two. Will you tell her teacher tomorrow? I'll call you.'

Sue touched Grace's cheek for the umpteenth time. 'It's so good to see you smiling. Honestly, Grace. I haven't known you long but if anything happened to you I'd... Ruth will be so relieved. You should take a week off school. A month. It's not like it would hurt you, you clever little girl.' She caught Grace into a hug and cried all over again. 'I just love you, Grace. I'm so happy you're all right.'

Everyone loved Grace. She was that kind of a child: stupid-pretty, full of joy, wise beyond her years. People engaged more fully in the moment when she was present. She was life personified.

She's a walker.

My heart crashed to my knees as the full truth hit me. I smiled tightly and waved Sue off. I knew Sue found me a strange contrast to my daughter — all pointy edges to Grace's rounded openness.

Grace did a victory jig in the bed at the prospect of a day or two off school. It was maddening how unaffected she was by the events of the last few hours, whereas I —

You were considering suicide, idiot.

When things had quietened down again, I slipped into bed beside Grace and she fell asleep, her head on my shoulder, her little bunched fists in my hands, and I thought I had never been so happy, so absolutely, perfectly happy as at that moment.

She'd been hit by a moving vehicle and she'd survived. She'd been walking, but she'd survived that too and I would make sure it never happened again. *I* had survived walking again, after all this time.

There was a lot to be happy about.

****

We were at the bottom of the house in what the estate agent had called the 'family room' but we called the kitchen — a huge space with a kitchen at one end and a fireplace at the other. The new sofas either side of the fireplace were still in their plastic wrapping.

'I miss Dad,' said Grace, tearing a hole in the plastic.

'I miss him too.'

'Aunt Rebecca says he was too young for a heart attack. Is that true, Mum? He never seemed that young to me. Not like you.'

My heart gave a dull thud that should have been grief, but was more like guilt because a year later I was here, starting a new life without him.

'You'll get used to it, Grace,' I said, rocking back on my heels in front of the last packing crate.

'I am used to it,' she said, attacking the plastic with gusto. 'I miss Dad but I like it, just you and me in London.'

'Doorbell,' I said, without raising my head, and a second later the doorbell sounded.

I froze, realising what I'd done. Then I raised my head very slowly, to find Grace staring at me in delight. 'I'll get it,' she said and she skipped out of the room, returning a second later with mail in her hand. 'So, Mum, you can do it too?'

'Do what?' I said as casually as I could manage.

'The doorbell thing. Knowing someone's there before it rings.'

'It's called intuition,' I said with a shrug. 'Everyone does it sometimes.' I used to do it all the time. Before I stopped walking. I hadn't done it for years.

I shook my head. It was just a doorbell.

Yes, but it was just one walk. What else has been re-activated? Scared yet?

There was a sudden bang from upstairs. Cora dropped the mail and leaped to my side. 'What was that?'

'I don't know.'

'Why are you whispering?'

'I'm not.' I coughed. 'I'm not. Let's go and investigate.'

Grace clung to my arm. 'Mum, no, don't go.'

'Don't be silly, Grace,' I said, shaking her off. 'Something's fallen over. There's still stuff everywhere.'

'What if this house is haunted?'

I raised an eyebrow at her. 'And we believe in ghosts, do we?'

She insisted on coming upstairs with me, gripping my hand tightly in her own. In Grace's new bedroom we found books scattered on the floor and a shelf that had clearly collapsed under their weight.

'I've just tidied up in here!' wailed Grace.

'I'll fix the shelf. You'll just have to put less on it.'

We left the mess and returned to the kitchen, where I made sandwiches. Through a mouthful of ham and cheese, Grace said, 'When I heard that bang, I thought there was another spirit person in the house. You know, a popper like us.'

'What?' I carefully laid my sandwich on my plate. 'Listen, honey. There are no others. Only babies pop, remember? There are no other poppers, as you call them. There's just me. And you. And we are never going to do it again.' My voice sounded monotonous and clipped; I had never lied to Grace before. It was a code of honour between us.

But she wasn't remotely perturbed. 'Okay Mum,' she said, spraying bread. Her eyes were gleaming. 'If you say so.'

Chapter 3

THEY SAY YOU SHOULD TREAD LIGHTLY with children, so instead of laying down the law, I tried to keep everything as normal as possible — in a new house, a new city, a new life. It wasn't easy, pretending all was well with fifty internal alarm bells going off at once.

Two days later, Sue came to pick Grace up for school again. I waved them off and ran upstairs to my studio at the very top of the townhouse that was our new home. I hadn't painted for days and I was longing to get back to work.

My current project was a reproduction of *Above the Town*, the Chagall painting of a smiling couple floating over a folksy village. I loved the way the man held the woman, the natural way they flew. I was painting them huge, much larger than the original. This copy was destined for the foyer of a German automobile company. Most of my commissions were museum reproductions, but working for commercial ventures was more lucrative, and left more room for creativity.

The doorbell sounded for the second time that morning, but this time it wasn't Sue's light touch, not a press and release; it was a press and hold and press again. Only one person would ring my doorbell like that. I screwed up my face and braced myself to face my sister.

By the time I'd got downstairs, she had rung at least five more times.

'Rebecca!' I said in mock surprise.

She wasn't amused. 'About time,' she snapped. She stepped over the threshold and paused. 'You haven't finished unpacking. You're still living out of boxes.' She nodded towards a solitary box still standing in the hallway.

'Peter's clothes,' I said.

'I'll deal with them.'

'I'll do it.'

She looked at me with distaste. 'You're not dressed. Is Grace even up?'

'Grace has gone to school,' I said, and when she looked down at my pyjamas in horror I added, 'A friend picked her up.'

'I'm glad to hear you have friends in the city. Is that the one who let Grace get run over?'

'Rebecca!' I took a moment. 'You know perfectly well it was an accident. It could have happened to anyone. And anyway, you remember Sue. We were at school together.'

'Sue Johnson? From Yorkshire? Well I suppose that's a small mercy. I didn't know she was in London. And I don't remember the two of you being such great friends at school.'

'We weren't. We're not. But she's nice, and her daughter Ruth is in Grace's class.'

Ruth had dyslexia, dyscalculia and a debilitating stutter; Grace had read most of the classics and talked like an intelligent adult. As a result, they both had a decidedly off-beat view of the world, and therein lay the basis of their friendship.

We went into the kitchen and I ignored Rebecca's loud tut at the breakfast dishes still on the table. I started to fill the kettle as she took off her smart belted mac and gingerly pulled back her sleeves. 'Shall we?' she said, beginning to stack dishes.

'Rebecca,' I began, and then more forcefully: 'Rebecca, stop it!'

She paused halfway to the sink. 'Do you really want to live like this, Cora? Do you want Grace to live like this?'

I took the bowls from her hands. 'I'm fine. We're fine.'

'You should be at home.'

'I am home. This is my home.'

Rebecca sat down heavily on one of the high stools at the kitchen counter. 'No, *I'm* home. *I* live in London. You live in Yorkshire.'

'Not any more. Don't worry, I won't bother you.'

'You're my sister. Of course you'll bother me.'

'I'll make us a coffee,' I said. 'I have got clean cups, honestly. Look.' I opened a cupboard and was grateful to find a complete set of cups and saucers neatly stacked on the shelf. 'See?'

She wasn't done. 'I don't know what possessed you. You were happy there.'

'No, you were happy I was there. I'm happy here.'

We drank coffee, keeping to safe topics, and then I proudly showed her over the four floors of my new home. My house. My choice. Mine.

'What do you think?' I asked at last.

'Your old house was bigger. And you had a garden.'

'I have a garden here.'

'You mean that patch of lawn and trees in the middle of the square?' Rebecca sniffed. 'It's a shared space, Cora. It's not your garden. In Yorkshire you had four acres of orchard.'

'No, Peter had four acres of orchard. I just lived there.'

'I could have kept my eye on you there,' she said. 'I always knew where you were and what you were doing. How will I know now? The city's a big place. Peter would have hated it.'

'Peter would have liked this house,' I said.

'Yes,' she said, conceding at last. 'He would. But I can't look after you here.'

'Rebecca,' I said, gritting my teeth. 'I'm a fully grown woman. I don't need looking after anymore.'

****

Privacy and independence: that's what I wanted from my life. God knows it had been a long time coming. First there was Rebecca's mum. Then Rebecca. Then Peter, my insanely handsome, rich, easygoing husband. All of them dedicated to keeping me safe. Because, as Rebecca so often said, when your mother's been murdered and the killer hasn't been found, you really can't be too careful.

I was only six when I arrived in England, lonely and terrified of the new person I had to become. A non-walker. Because that's what my mother had made me promise: that I would never walk again. *Walking is bad. It's a bad, bad thing. Cora, you must never walk. I was wrong to let you. Terrible things will happen to you if you ever walk again. Do you hear me?* Getting bullied and bossed and half-killed with kindness — frankly, I scarcely noticed any of that. I was too busy making sure I stayed inside my body *so that my mother's killer would never find me.*

Not that Rebecca knew anything about that. Walking was as far removed from her realm of imagination as a picnic on Pluto. But she was an only child and naturally dominating; a little sister to take care of was her idea of manna from heaven.

And here she was, at it again.

****

'Do we need a housekeeper?' asked Grace tentatively.

'Aunt Rebecca thinks we do.'

'She'll be just like Aunt Rebecca,' predicted Grace. 'She'll boss us around and tell us what to do all the time.'

'You'll be at school,' I said. 'You probably won't even see her. Lucky you.'

'Mum, you're not giving in, are you?'

I stirred the gravy while Grace kicked off her school shoes. 'Rebecca loves us,' I said. 'Helping us makes her happy.'

'It makes you unhappy.'

'Well a housekeeper won't make a scrap of difference to me.'

Grace rolled her eyes. 'When is she moving in?' she said in the world-weary voice that usually made me smile.

'Moving in?' I shook my head. 'She's not moving in.'

'All right,' said Grace in a tone that meant: good luck with that. She disappeared upstairs to change out of her school uniform. When she came back down she said, 'I'm glad you and Aunt Rebecca are so different. Why is that?'

'Because we're not blood-sisters,' I said without thinking. 'We're just *very* distantly related cousins.'

'You and I aren't blood-family at all, and we're way similar.'

I had an uneasy feeling I knew what she was getting at, and it wasn't her adoption. I busied myself serving dinner onto two plates.

'For example,' continued Grace, 'there's no way Aunt Rebecca is a walker, even though she's blood-related to you. But I'm not, and I'm one. So it doesn't run in families, does it?'

Here we go. 'My mother was a walker,' I said carefully.

'Cool!' said Grace.

'No,' I said, more sharply than I intended. 'It's not cool at all. Walking is forbidden. Do you hear me?'

Her silence surprised me. I risked a glance at her face and saw rebellion in her eyes.

'Why? It's lovely.'

It *was* lovely. She was right. It was incomparably wonderful and giving it up had been the greatest struggle of my life. But fear had done its work, and I'd never succumbed to temptation — until the day of Grace's accident. But now... Now I was facing the struggle all over again, and asking Grace to do the same, to deny who she was, to submit to normal.

Fear. I had to make her afraid.

'Grace, people aren't meant to walk. Your Self — your spirit person — is supposed to stay inside your body where it belongs. We're designed that way. And when you walk...' I hesitated because I realised how ridiculous this was going to sound, and how cruel. 'When you walk, bad people can find you and bad things can happen.'

She closed her eyes, frowning. 'What bad people?'

Flash of silver. Silver and black. I sat down abruptly at the kitchen counter and put out my hand to draw Grace to me. 'You're too young and I shouldn't be telling you this. But you've been walking and you have to understand why you must stop. My mother and I were walkers. My sister too — my Canadian sister, not Aunt Rebecca.'

'The one who stayed in Canada?'

'Magda. Yes.' I hesitated. I almost never mentioned my sister's name. It made me uncomfortable; it threatened to dredge up feelings I didn't want to know. 'Walking isn't good for you,' I persevered. 'It's ... it's like smoking. You have to learn to give it up.'

'What if I can't?' said Grace defiantly.

'It's really bad for you,' I said, and then, with a heavy heart, I added, 'Adults who walk are generally bad people.'

'The man that killed your mother — was he a walker?' she asked in a small voice.

I couldn't speak, so I nodded.

'Why did your mother walk, if it's so bad for you?'

I folded my hands. 'Because she was young and there was no one to teach her better.'

Grace took one of those leaps of logic that made her such an extraordinary child. 'Will your mother's killer find me more easily if I walk?'

'He's not looking for you,' I said, and I smiled, trying to lighten the mood. 'Why would he be looking for you?' But my heart was hammering, because she was exactly right.

'But he's looking for you?' said Grace, peeping at me from under big eyes.

'No. Maybe. All I know is that even if he were looking for me, he wouldn't find me because I'm not a walker. And neither are you. Got it?'

She nodded, troubled. We began to eat our dinner in silence. 'Mum?' said Grace. 'Walking doesn't *feel* bad. It makes me feel like I'm really me, only better. And the colours... I know things when I walk. I forget them again when I'm in my body.'

Cruel to be kind. Cruel to be kind. 'That's why it's so addictive,' I said steadily. 'No one would do it if it felt horrible, would they?'

Stupid logic again, but she let it pass. She poured herself a glass of water. 'You popped,' she said suddenly.

'Sorry?'

'At the hospital. You popped and came to find me.'

'That was an emergency,' I said. 'It won't happen again.'

'Yes,' she insisted, 'but if he is looking for you, he'll find you now, won't he?'

Chapter 4

I SAT UP IN THE MIDDLE OF THE NIGHT, out of breath, my heart pounding in my ears. *Flash of silver. Silver and black.* I hadn't had this nightmare for a while. I turned on my bedside light and sat still, waiting for recovery, waiting for the blood to slow in my veins.

The craving was acute, as always on nights like these. In my dream, I walked and it was glorious — like floating; like flying. I swam through the air, perched on treetops, listened to the interweaving strands of music generated by the wind and all the living, growing things in the night. And then he came: a flash of silver, and he was right there, perched on the branch at my side, smiling. White teeth and poker-straight silver hair —

I put my hand to my chest. *Calm down, calm down.* I got out of bed and drew back the curtains. With an effort of will I quieted my mind and tuned in to what lay outside my window: the still, ice-spiked air; the energy of a million busy lives rising from the city around me; the bare branches and twigs at the top of the trees, that stirred under the growing weight of frost. On this hushed winter night the stars were steely and motionless. The moon and Mars had risen together, and now stood bright and bold in the vast, glittering sky. Seven of the twelve brightest stars shone down like searchlights. I picked them out one by one: Sirius, Capella, Rigel, Procyon, Betelgeuse, Aldebaran, Pollux.

Good God. I remembered this. *I remember this!* The acute sense of being, the infinitely precious and unbreakable connection between things. It was back. All the old ways of being. I was a child again, walking with my mother, laughing at the stars.

Go on. Walk. You could slip away.

The still night was like an invitation, a drug.

You'll be back before Grace even notices.

I took a deep breath and my Self fluttered in me. I closed my eyes, opened my palms and let myself go, smiling at the familiar delight of separation.

The temperature dropped by another degree and outside the night became heavier, darker. All was silent and still.

A small movement flashed. Something outside, on the other side of the glass. A Self — peering in. Not at my window. At Grace's.

A Self was staring into Grace's bedroom.

I jerkily snapbacked and the Self sensed me. It turned. The air between us pulsed and darkened and a wave of panic rolled off me. I leaped to my feet and raced out of my bedroom and into Grace's, my breath stuck in my throat.

Her curtains were open but only the stars peered through. I glanced quickly at the bed but the bedclothes rose and fell to steady breathing; she was safe. I went to the window, and leaned against the glass, trying to see what had become of the Self.

The street was empty.

But beyond that... The trees in the garden square in front of the house reached up to the height of the bedroom windows on the third floor. In the very tallest, sat a figure.

I cupped my hands around my face on the glass. This was a different Self. I couldn't see very well but I could *feel*, and the feeling was very clear: from him, at least, there was nothing to fear. As I stared across, the Self slowly raised a hand, as if to tell me all was well, and then it rose from the branch and drifted off into the night.

I slid down the window and the wall beneath it onto the carpet of Grace's room, and sat there listening to Grace breathing, like I used to do when she was a baby.

My mother's words echoed in my head: *Terrible things will happen to you if you ever walk again. Do you hear me?*

****

Amy moved in a week later. She followed Rebecca into the house, long legs loping, blonde hair swinging, all smiles and sincerity. The air seemed to shimmy around her.

'Hello?' I said.

Rebecca took off her gloves and sat down, inviting the girl to do the same. 'This is Amy Banister,' she told me. 'I got her from an agency. She's ready to move straight in.'

'Move in where?'

'Now don't be silly, Cora, we've been through all this.'

'You said a housekeeper. I was thinking a couple of hours a week.'

'Yes, well, the more I thought about it, the more I realised that what you really need is an au pair.'

'Grace is eight.'

'And very precocious, yes, I know. That's why I said an au pair and not a nanny.'

'And the difference is...?'

'I do housekeeping and babysitting,' said Amy brightly. 'And anything else you want me to do. And I'm planning to go out to work during the day, so I won't get in your way at all.'

'So really you're a paid lodger. Look, Rebecca—'

Rebecca was smiling, thoroughly pleased with herself. 'You wanted change.'

This wasn't what I wanted, not what I planned. This was more of the same, and I minded terribly. And yet... Looking at Amy sent clichés dancing through my head. A breath of fresh air. A new broom. A problem shared, a stitch in time, a thing of beauty. Things were unfolding as they should.

There wasn't time to be certain, because Rebecca had started talking and Rebecca had an extraordinary ability to kill my instincts. But Amy, right here in Gregory Square looked — felt — *right*.

And Grace would love her.

I frowned, and felt bold. 'I might choose this.'

'It's already chosen,' scoffed Rebecca in her my-good-woman voice.

'Do you have any references?' I asked Amy, ignoring Rebecca, working hard to keep my own voice flat and professional.

Now Amy scoffed, but it was a very different sound. 'I'm nineteen. I've been at school all my life.'

Grace is going to love her.

'So where are you from? Why are you here?'

Rebecca tapped the table. 'Bright lights, big city, why does any young girl come to London? You'll be a safe place for her and she'll be a Godsend for you. Although as you can see, Amy, you'll have your work cut out.' She looked expressively around her; my house was only marginally tidier than last time she'd been here. 'Cora is newly widowed and, rather than stay in familiar surroundings, she has moved her entire life to live among strangers.' She gave me a tight smile.

'I moved to be near you, Rebecca, dear,' I said.

Amy cracked a wide grin, revealing two rows of perfect teeth. 'New starts all round then. I'm good in the kitchen. And handy with a vacuum cleaner.'

'I suppose I could offer free board and lodging in return for mucking in.' What was I saying? What was I *thinking*?

'That sounds like a very good deal to me — for me, I mean.'

'There's a one-off agency fee,' said Rebecca. 'I settled it for you, Cora — here's the receipt.'

I took it absently; this was moving too fast. My brows came together in a worried frown but my mouth went on talking. 'How long do you think you'll stay — Amy, was it?'

'Oh I'm making it up as I go along. Life's going to happen whether I plan it all out or not. I wanted to live in the city, I registered with an agency, Rebecca found me. I like your house.' She looked around. 'I can lie if you want me to: I'll stay for about a year. What do you think?'

'Is your case heavy?'

'Weighs a tonne but I can manage. Upstairs, is it?'

Rebecca looked smug. 'I'll let myself out,' she said.

****

'This wasn't your idea, was it?' said Amy later, when she'd taken her case to the spare bedroom and the kettle was on. 'Having me here.'

'No. But that doesn't mean it's a bad idea.'

'Don't worry. I saw from the start that this was all about Rebecca. But now I've met you — look, I'm all yours, okay? I'll only do what you ask me to do.'

This was a surprise. I looked at her speculatively. 'As opposed to — ?'

'As opposed to what Rebecca has asked me to do.'

'Ah. Let me guess. Keep an eye on me and ... ring her once in a while

... every week ... *every day*? Rebecca told you to ring her every day?'

'See! I didn't even have to tell you! We're going to get along fine.' She lowered her hands, which had been directing my guesswork. 'This doesn't have to be forever anyway. You could let me stay for a few weeks and help you. That'll give me time to find my feet and start looking for a place of my own, and it'll keep Rebecca happy. What do you say? Please?'

I poured boiling water into the teapot and I couldn't think of a single reason — a real, tangible reason — to say no.

CHAPTER 5

GRACE LOVED HER. Amy had an easy presence that made us feel we'd known her all our lives. She wasn't domineering like Rebecca, or over-protective like Peter. She didn't patronise or invade. She was like sea grass, happy to sway this way and that with the tide of events, yet remain firmly rooted in her own reality. It would be good for Grace to have her around in case —

In case Grace was tempted to disobey me and go walking again. In case I was unable to resist walking myself. In case something happened to me. At least with Amy around there was another adult to keep an eye on her.

The night after the Self at the window, I started sleeping in Grace's room. Her bed was easily big enough for the two of us, and she had no objection; it was cosy, snuggling at night and telling each other stories. But it was getting hard to keep her close without transferring onto her any more of my fear than was necessary. It was a difficult balance: just enough fear to stop her walking, but not enough to ruin her life. Why didn't children come with a handbook? Especially *walker* children...

For myself, I didn't know what to be afraid of, so I was afraid of everything. Who *was* that at the window? A random passer? Why Grace's window, why not mine? There was no logic to it. All I knew was that I had walked, just once, and all my certainties had been swept away.

Perhaps worst of all was the re-activated craving to do the thing I most needed not to do. I wanted to walk so badly that sometimes I had to sit on my hands, or sing at the top of my voice, or run very fast — anything to stop my Self from rising out of me and taking flight. I wanted to walk when I was sad, or lonely, or missing Peter; I wanted to walk when I was happy, or surprised, or relaxed. I wanted to walk.

I wondered if Grace was suffering in the same way, but there was no outward sign of it and I didn't like to ask the question for fear of planting the idea in her head.

****

I was carrying clean laundry to her room one evening when I heard her and Amy talking. I paused outside the door.

'When did he die?' Amy was asking. Her voice had none of the phoney sympathy that made Grace and me squirm.

'About a year ago. A bit more.'

'You must miss him.'

'I do. But not like I'd miss Mum if she was the one who died.'

'No,' said Amy. 'Mums are special, aren't they?'

'Mine is,' said Grace. 'Mine is especially special.'

I quickly entered the room. 'Time to get ready for bed. Brush your teeth.'

Amy left us to our nightly ritual. When Grace was tucked up in bed, I leaned over her. 'Gracie.'

'Oh Mum, you know we're going to tell her.'

I frowned. 'Until recently I didn't even know you knew, and suddenly we're telling everyone?'

'Amy isn't everyone. She's here to help.'

I gazed at my daughter and she gazed back at me, peaceful and trusting. 'What do you mean?' I asked.

Grace shrugged. 'She's here to help. You know she is.' Then she lowered her voice and whispered, 'There's one planet and one bright star visible tonight.'

'Which ones?' I whispered back.

'The planet's Saturn. The star's Regulus.'

She was right. I closed my eyes as a wave of newly recovered memory washed over me. I had been in this scene before, only last time round I was the child and it was my mother leaning over me with kisses and complicity.

'You're right,' I said.

'I like being a walker, Mum.'

'So do I, Grace, but remember—'

'I don't see what harm it would do.'

My heart jolted at the memory of the watcher at the window. 'No walking.'

Grace giggled and wiggled down into her bed. 'Night,' she sighed.

I kissed her forehead. 'Night Gracie.'

Amy was downstairs in the kitchen, lounging on a sofa with a glass of wine.

'You must miss your husband,' she said. It was brave and direct, qualities I would come to know and love about Amy.

'I did,' I said. 'I do. But he travelled a lot. Grace and I were quite used to being without him. That's been a bit of a blessing, really.'

'Were you happy?' She sat up and poured a glass for me.

I looked at her carefully and then I said, 'I wasn't unhappy, but Peter deserved better.'

'And now you feel guilty?'

'Don't hold back,' I said.

She grinned. 'Sorry. I don't know any other way to be. Let's make a deal. I get to say anything I want, and you get to tell me when to shut up.'

****

I opened the last box, the one that held all of Peter's clothes. On top was his green jumper, the one with the small hole on the cuff, which he'd worn to go shooting with Rebecca's husband, Hugh. I'd been wrong to worry about this task. There was nothing of Peter here, only bundles of cloth. Very well-cut cloth, expensively put together, but just a bunch of threads in the end. Lots of shoes that were just crafted leather. They could have been anybody's things. I put everything back into the box and called a local charity to come and collect it.

It was done, the final hurdle cleared. My new life had begun.

About time, too.

Amy had gone to sign on with a temp agency, so I put on the kettle for a solo celebratory cup of coffee. When the doorbell rang I thought it would be the charity coming to collect, but the dusty young man on the doorstep was already carrying a heavy box.

'Vegetable delivery,' he said and then, when I looked blank, he added, 'Your sister sent me. I deliver vegetables to her also.'

'Vegetables?'

'Seasonal. Grown by yours truly.' It was a nice smile, shy and unassuming. 'I'm Imtiaz.'

'Come in,' I said, pulling back the door.

He followed me into the kitchen and set the box on the counter. Then he stood awkwardly moving his hands over and over his stomach until I nodded him towards a high stool.

'How much does it cost and how often do you deliver?' I asked.

'This is a £10 box, but I can make it smaller or bigger, as you wish. And I can come weekly or fortnightly.'

I looked into the box.

'It's exactly the same as Rebecca's box,' Imtiaz assured me. 'Nothing bruised, nothing unfamiliar.'

'Of course,' I said. I caught his eye and we exchanged smiles. 'Weekly I think.' I reached for my purse to pay him. 'Look, the kettle has boiled. Do you want a coffee? It's cold out there.'

When he smiled, his eyes lit up. 'Coffee would be very nice. I don't need your money today. Your sister has already paid me. She said it was your ... your housewarming? You have recently moved here?'

Good old Rebecca.

We drank our coffee and I kept up a flow of easy chatter, asking him about his business, growing and delivering, working with his hands, with the soil. He answered obligingly but his politeness was an impervious barrier between us. I had the impression it got in his way; he seemed lonely.

Amy came home as he was leaving. I introduced them on the doorstep, but Amy, in thigh-high boots, tight sweater and a scarf, was obviously too much for Imtiaz; he practically ran away from us.

'Chatty man,' said Amy, swinging her bag in the door ahead of her. 'Have you been making new friends?'

'Rebecca sent him. He's our new vegetable delivery man.'

'Oh God,' said Amy, with a guilty look. 'I haven't rung Rebecca yet. I better make a full report this afternoon. He's quite intense, isn't he?'

'Who, Imtiaz?'

And then it struck me. Imtiaz wasn't any old delivery man. He was a walker. That strange motion of his hands, like a wounded man trying to scoop his spilling guts back into his stomach... He wasn't intense, he was desperate, with loneliness, with a desire to belong, with the need to contain the great SOS that was leaking out of him.

Imtiaz was another walker in hiding. Like me.

Yes, but he's in denial. You're just a coward.

I went upstairs and sat on my bed. Nothing for years and suddenly there were walkers coming out of the woodwork: the watcher at the window, the Self in the tree, and now Imtiaz. Either my brief walk the day of Grace's accident had cleared my eyes to what had always been around me or *it had attracted these walkers to me.*

And then there was Amy.

Wait. Wait. I tried to clear my head, slow down, wait. Amy and Imtiaz were both sent by Rebecca, and Rebecca was just doing what she always did: taking care of me. So there was nothing sinister in either of them. If Imtiaz was a walker — well, that was a coincidence. An odd coincidence, and one that I wouldn't even have noticed if I hadn't popped so very recently, but still. The appearance of Amy and Imtiaz had nothing to do with my having walked.

The walker at the window, and the one in the tree, on the other hand? Those I was responsible for. When I walked that night at the hospital, I might just as well have sent up a flare into the sky: here I am!

I didn't know what to do. Everything had changed. Something was coming; I felt it, deep in my Self.

Relax. So some Selfs saw your trace and were curious. So what? No one's looking for you.

I came downstairs to find Amy on the phone, reporting to Rebecca. She winked at me. 'No, she's fine. No, she seems perfectly happy. Honestly, Rebecca, she's very happy. Yes, she's eating well. So is Grace.'

I could have minded; I could have been furious. But I knew better. Rebecca wanted the best for me. I didn't like her methods, but I liked her intentions. Sometimes you had to accept people the way they were.

Amy hung up and went to put on the kettle. 'That should keep Rebecca at bay. She really worries about you, doesn't she? By the way, who's Mercury?'

'Who?'

'Mercury. Grace told me this morning that Mercury was leaving.'

'Oh.' I hesitated. 'Mercury's a planet.'

Amy looked blank.

'It's, um, leaving the night sky. Tomorrow night, actually.'

'The planet Mercury is leaving the night sky?'

'Yes. We won't be able to see it any more. With the naked eye,' I added, growing wary at the sight of her passive face. I began drawing silly elliptical patterns in the air with my forefinger.

'Grace is into astronomy?'

'Always has been,' I said.

'Oh.' Amy shrugged. 'Cool. Tea?'

I exhaled. How would I ever explain that Grace collected facts about the natural world *empirically*? She sensed Mercury leaving; felt it, because her Self was connected to it. *Like the tide and the moon*, I thought, and was pleased with the analogy: a walker's Self was connected to the natural world like the tide was connected to the moon.

All Selfs are connected to the natural world, idiot, not just walker Selfs.

Which was true, of course, although almost no one I'd ever met acted like they knew the fact.

Good grief. I was even thinking like a walker these days.

CHAPTER 6

I BEGAN TO THINK that the peepers at my window had been cosmic warnings not to step out of line, to keep faith with my mother and live the normal life she wanted for me. Grace had settled in her new school as much as she ever would settle at a school, I was busy at work and Amy was very close to being the kind of sister I'd always wanted.

The only *problem* with Amy was that she was difficult to resist.

'Oh come on, Cora. You know you want to. And you owe me a favour, too.'

'I do?' I said. 'What for?'

'For being so cool about Rebecca. Come on. You'll have a good time. I promise.' She batted her long, silky lashes at me.

'You can't possibly promise that. All right, I'll come. If — and it's a big if — you can get a nice, reliable friend to sit with Grace. You, after all, are supposed to be the babysitter.'

She'd never find anyone; she hadn't been here long enough to make reliable friends.

Amy kissed me resoundingly on the forehead. 'I'm going out on the town and Cora's coming with me,' she sang, dancing around the kitchen.

'Only if you find a babysitter before this evening.'

'No problem.'

'And I don't want to go too far away.'

'The bar on Finn Street has a live band on Saturdays.'

Finn Street was around the corner. There was nothing I could object to.

At five-thirty I came downstairs. 'I'm ready,' I announced. 'I need to meet this sitter of yours. What time is she coming?'

Amy was in the kitchen feeding Grace hotdogs. She looked me up and down and raised an eyebrow. 'It's not that you don't look nice,' she began. 'It's just, you don't look any different.'

I pointed to my face.

'Okay, apart from the make-up. The smoky eyes are good. Really nice, actually. But do you *ever* get out of jeans and a white top? It's a classic look, I grant you, and … it kind of suits you. That shirt *almost* rocks.' She fingered my shirt, then resumed her lecture. 'But don't you want a change, since we're going out?'

'No,' I said. 'I'm very happy.'

'Come on.' Amy headed for the stairs. 'Let's check out your wardrobe.'

'No!' I said, chasing after her. 'I shall start calling you Rebecca if you mess with my room.'

Grace trailed us upstairs, hotdog in hand, giggling. I had to admit, even at this moment, that Amy had brightened our lives considerably.

She flung open my wardrobe door and froze.

'Oh. My God.'

'What's wrong?'

'I've never seen anything like it.'

'It's tidy,' I said.

'It certainly is. Tidy and clinical. Good God, Cora, when did you last go shopping for clothes?'

I tried to look at it through her eyes and, honestly, I began to see what she meant. On the left hung eight or so pairs of dark jeans. On the right hung a variety of white shirts and tee-shirts in various styles and fabrics. And that was it, apart from a small assortment of jackets tucked right over on one side, and a single plain long dress.

'Did this happen by accident?' asked Amy, in awe. 'Do you keep walking into clothes shops and choosing the same thing again and again without realising it?'

'No,' I admitted. 'It was a plan. It never seemed like an odd plan until this minute.'

Amy snorted. 'It's completely barking. Although also … kind of … classy in a twisted way. It's as if you're an alien trying to pass for a normal human being and almost getting it right.' She cocked her head to one side. 'Don't you get bored?'

'No, I don't have to think about it. That was the whole point.'

She ignored my tone. 'Did you dress like this when you were married?'

'That was a different life,' I said defensively.

'But you're still alive, Cora!'

I tried again. 'Dressing like this is completely normal for most people, Amy.'

'What is this obsession with *normal*?' said Amy. She caught sight of my expression. 'All right, all right. Put this jacket on.' She reached in for a short, bright pink jacket and handed it to me.

The doorbell rang and Grace flew down ahead of us to get it. 'Aunt Rebecca!' I heard her say.

'You called *Rebecca*?' I hissed at Amy. 'Are you crazy? Now she'll think I can't manage my own life!'

'She thinks I'm going to introduce you to some nice new friends,' admitted Amy. 'She's very pleased with me.'

'You *lied*? To *Rebecca*?'

'Who says I lied? We might make some nice new friends tonight.'

'In a bar? Are you crazy?'

Amy sailed downstairs and hugged Rebecca as if they were old friends.

'Can I go to bed late?' asked Grace, who was hanging onto Rebecca's hand.

'About eight-thirty — that's quite late enough,' said Rebecca.

'Nine,' I said firmly. 'It's the weekend. Will you be okay, Gracie?'

'Of course,' she said.

'Rebecca, this is seriously kind of you.'

'Isn't it,' she said, kissing my cheek. 'Don't worry. Hugh was home tonight anyway, and you've spared me an evening of watching him watch re-runs of old sitcoms. Are you really going out in those jeans?'

'Yes, I am. How are the girls?' Rebecca and Hugh had a teenage daughter at boarding school and four-year-old twins — a surprise that delighted Hugh and wearied Rebecca. Grace adored them.

Rebecca closed her eyes as if her children's antics were too manifold to mention. I grinned.

'Hurry up,' said Amy.

I ran upstairs to fetch my bag and Grace followed me. 'Did you know that Mercury's back? In the morning sky now. Along with Venus, Saturn and Jupiter.'

'I know Mercury's back, smarty-pants.' I tweaked her nose. Then I hesitated. 'You know it doesn't actually vanish, don't you?'

She rolled her eyes at me.

'Sorry. Just checking. Remember not to say things like that to Aunt Rebecca. She'll think you're weird.'

'I said them to Imtiaz today. He didn't think I was weird.'

I stopped dead in my tracks. 'When did you meet Imtiaz?' I asked, playing for time, wondering why I felt so sick.

'When I was out with Amy this afternoon. He was walking in the park with some woman.'

'And you talked to him about Mercury?'

'He's a walker, Mum.' She looked as if it were the most obvious thing in the world.

I stared at her in amazement. 'Grace—'

She held out her hands. 'I can't help knowing, but I was very careful. His friend and Amy didn't hear me.'

I stared at her for a moment longer. 'I'm sure he's trying to give it up,' I said.

She rolled her eyes again. 'Why do you think his vegetables are so great? I bet he knows exactly when to plant things.'

Not so in denial as I'd imagined, then.

Rebecca was in the kitchen chatting with Amy.

'At last — time to go!' sang Amy as I came in. Somewhere between organising Grace, Rebecca and me, she'd changed. I was amused to see that she wore jeans too, although any comparison between the two of us stopped right there; she looked completely gorgeous.

'Have fun, girls,' said Rebecca.

We walked around the corner, past the shuttered newsagent, the grocer, the butcher and the deli, and into a crowded bar with a stripy awning out front. Inside, the air was warm with bodies and noisy with chatter and music. Within minutes Amy had bagged us a table in front of a cleared floor space where a band was performing later in the evening. Then she disappeared off to the bar to get us a couple of beers.

I looked around nervously at the room full of strangers, wishing I had never allowed myself to be persuaded into this. I might as well have landed on another planet. I pulled anxiously at my fringe.

No one's going to look at you, idiot.

No one did. Everyone else was there with a purpose, chatting, drinking, relaxing with friends — doing normal.

For God's sake, get over yourself.

I felt so utterly displaced that my Self itched to get out. I sat on my hands and began reciting *Life on Mars* in my head. Then I saw the brighter side; if any of my old Yorkshire friends could see me here, in jeans, in a bar, with a really cool friend — well, they'd have apoplexy. Which was a nice thought. I began to relax.

Amy returned to my side, not with drinks but with a man with drinks. 'Cora, this is Andrew. Andrew, Cora,' she said. 'Thank you, Andrew. You're a star.' She flashed him a megawatt smile and he blushed and retreated.

'You're shameless,' I said.

'So I'm told,' said Amy. 'Can I help it if men fall over themselves to help me?'

She was so utterly without vanity, it was funny. She knew perfectly well how gorgeous she was, and she wasn't above enjoying it. But she attached no value to it, and in that she was as natural as a daisy.

'When does the music start?' I asked.

'Around ten. Don't worry about the time. I told Rebecca we'd be late.'

'One day you'll have to tell me how you got her wound around your little finger.'

Amy shrugged. 'No point. It wouldn't work for you. You're Rebecca's mission in life.'

The beer was warm and malty. Amy was sipping hers and looking around, and I did the same for a while. The music was too loud for idle chat and besides, there was plenty of time for idle chat at home. I looked around some more and after a while I began to wonder why people ever came into bars at all, because everyone was having to shout into each other's ear anyway. Then I noticed how nicely the women and girls were dressed, how they were eyeing up the men and boys, who were doing the same thing back, and after that I forgot about myself and enjoyed the spectacle.

'Have you heard of this band?' I yelled into Amy's ear. 'They seem very popular. Lots of people here.'

'A girl at work said the lead singer was cute.'

Right on cue, a slim man with spiky brown hair came through the door, struggling under the weight of a huge black case. He dumped it on the floor in front of us and straightened up, stretching his back. He caught my eye and his face cracked into an irresistibly crooked grin and I realised he wasn't cute at all; he was impossibly cool. He wore his masculinity in a timeless way that made something in me ache, not for him, but for the idea of a hundred shades of him — the intoxicating essence of unreconstituted male. It gave me a jolt, as if I were rising through another level of sleep towards consciousness.

'Hi, how are you,' he said with an unmistakeable Spanish accent; like he needed any more ammunition.

I was confused. I was sitting next to the most gorgeous girl in the bar, and he was saying hello to me?

'Hi,' I said back. And then, because he was so close and I didn't know what else to do, I stuck out my hand. 'I'm Cora.'

'Raul,' he said, taking it, and then he saw Amy, and his smile froze for a fraction of a second.

'I'm Amy,' said Amy. She did not proffer her hand. She knew, as I clearly didn't, that you don't shake hands in a bar, for God's sake.

'Raul,' repeated Raul, blinking rapidly. And that was that; he was smitten. 'I have to get the rest of the stuff,' he apologised. 'I'll be back. Don't go away, okay?'

'I bet he's with the band,' said Amy dreamily.

Raul went back out into the street, and three more band members came in lugging equipment. One was thin and sandy-haired. One was older, black, with a fabulous afro. And the other was huge, thick-set and —

My blood froze, and then it began to gallop through my veins; the jerk of my heart almost made me throw up. The huge man had silver hair. Straight, shoulder-length silver hair, and he was dressed in jeans and a polo-neck — both black. *A streak of silver. Silver and black.*

I stumbled to my feet.

'Are you okay?' said Amy.

'I'll be right back,' I yelled.

The silver-haired giant was blocking the doorway so I headed deep into the bar, as far from him as I could get, barging through groups of people. The ladies' toilets were back there, so I dived in and locked myself in a cubicle.

I was shaking so hard I could hear my teeth chattering. I leaned against the door, my mind rattling.

Could it be him? Could it possibly be him? Had he found me?

CHAPTER 7

I TOOK A DEEP BREATH.

Stop. Think about it. That man was your mother's age. This one is barely more than a boy. It can't possibly be the same person.

But I couldn't stop shaking and, in my panic, I did the unthinkable: I popped, leaving my body propped up in the cubicle, and went to take another look.

I hovered near the back of the bar, not daring to go any closer. But it was impossible to see from here, so I slowly advanced over the heads of the people who were beginning to press forward to hear the band.

There he was. He'd strapped himself into a fancy painted guitar and was running through some chords. He wasn't cool like Raul, and he wasn't as relaxed as he'd like people to think. But he was — I could feel it — decent. He was a decent person.

Silver-haired or not, this wasn't my demon.

I was about to turn and snapback when I noticed a curious thing. The man with the afro, who was also holding a guitar, appeared to be looking at me. I shot backwards, astonished, but of course he wasn't looking at me; he was looking *through* me into space while he tuned his guitar.

I snapbacked and went to the sink to splash some water on my face. When did I get so jumpy?

How often do young men sport long, straight, silver hair?

I stared into the mirror. My pupils had virtually disappeared into my dark irises; I looked strange. I pulled at my spiky hair and applied some lipstick, but that made me look even less like myself.

'You are very cool,' I told my reflection. 'You are in a bar in London with a good friend. Perfectly safe.' I turned away and then turned back: 'And you are Grace's mother,' I said severely. 'Man up, Cora.'

I stood for a moment with my hand on the door. Of course there was more than one man in the world with long silver hair. It wasn't common, exactly, but anyone could dye their hair. I opened the door and went back to Amy.

Raul, it transpired, was the band's lead singer — of course. What also quickly became clear was that Amy Banister, newly arrived in London, had snagged the super-cool, Spanish lead-singer in a band. I laughed under my breath and felt a spike of — what was that? *Life blood. Life lust.* After the horrible fright I'd just had, this felt warm. It felt *good.*

Raul introduced the audience to each member of the band, and I had plenty of time to stare at them when the music began. Joe-afro, on guitar, was the oldest — older than me — and the most experienced member of the band. It was him the others looked to for the start and finish of each song. Ken the drummer was visibly the youngest. Sandy-haired and slight, he was like one of those very distant stars in the night sky, glinting quietly in the corner of the eye, becoming almost invisible when you looked at him straight on. And then there was Reese of the silver hair, who sang backing vocals as well as playing guitar, and who was, now I could see past his height and colouring, spectacularly ugly, but in the manner of a troll, not a monster. (Was my demon ugly? I tried to remember and couldn't.)

The music was clever and interesting, with intelligent lyrics and persistent rhythms. On stage, Raul's arrogance was justified. He had a gravelly, compelling voice, full of sentiment and promise. There was a palpable line of communication between him and Joe, who would regularly sweep over the melody with a crashing metallic guitar line that made the hair on my neck stand up and my Self almost pop spontaneously.

There was constant movement around us as people shifted between the tables and the bar. In between songs, I rose to get more drinks, and when I returned, someone new was sitting at our table with Amy.

The man was probably in his late twenties. As I sat down he half-rose and tried to say something, but the next song had started and with a shrug and a smile he gave up and turned his attention to the band.

He was connected to them; the charged line of energy between Raul and Joe triangulated to include him. Throughout the next song, I noticed Raul watch him, and he responded with a smile, a raised eyebrow, a thumbs-up. I took in his striped shirt, dark, untidy hair, and wide shoulders. When he turned to smile at me, I saw he had very pronounced eyebrows and narrow, slanted eyes; they were bright and intense in a way that belied his languid frame. He was a curious hybrid, a man until he smiled, and then he was all boy. Older than Raul; much younger than Joe.

It's not like you to notice so much.

It wasn't. I generally noticed only the distinguishing features of a person, passing over the fine detail except in terms of how it affected me or the people around them. This man's physical being filled my eyes so completely that I found myself staring.

The band took a break and Raul and Joe pounced on him. 'So? How do you like the new arrangements?'

'Not bad at all,' he said, cheerfully slapping Raul on the back and shaking hands with Joe. 'I like that bridge you played, that thing with the slide. It really worked.'

'Have you met Cora and Amy?' asked Raul. 'Ladies, this is the band. Joe, Reese, Ken. And this is Charlie Tam. He's our songwriter and honorary member.'

Everyone nodded or waved a greeting except Reese, who enthusiastically kissed Amy on the cheek, earning a punch from Joe — 'What did I do? It's good manners!' He moved to embrace me too, but I shrank back.

Charlie shook our hands good-naturedly. 'I only write some of the songs,' he told me. His voice was deep and confident.

'Charlie here is our musical consultant,' said Joe, pulling a chair to our table. Raul followed suit, seating himself close to Amy.

'Yeah, one of these days they might earn enough money to pay me,' said Charlie. 'What are you boys drinking?'

I didn't need to join in the conversation. There was plenty going on, and I could sit back quietly and listen in. I would have liked to be invisible, but Charlie kept turning to include me and, in the end, manners required me to respond and even contribute a little. I wasn't comfortable, exactly; but I didn't feel as disconnected as I had felt earlier in the evening.

Charlie turned to me again. 'So, what do you think of the band?

Have you heard them play before?' He looked me straight in the face, a little shy but unflinching. He was attractive, and not just to my eyes.

I shook my head. 'No, this is the first time.'

'How did you hear about them? Or did you just happen to be here tonight?'

'We live around here,' I said. 'Amy and I. And my daughter.'

His look politely requested more information, but I didn't give it. 'So,' he said at last, 'have you lived here long?'

To be heard over the chatter, he had to lean close and talk straight into my ear. I willed my hair to be smelling nice. I quickly discovered that whenever I pulled back and looked into Charlie Tam's eyes, I couldn't look away. It was embarrassing. I decided to look only at his mouth.

'Have you lived here long?'

'Grace and I moved in after Christmas. Amy's only been here a few days. She's my au pair. And my friend.' *Damn. Information.* I gazed at his mouth and realised — *damn again* — that he was saying something. *Oh for goodness sake.* I gave myself a sharp mental slap, looked up, and instantly drowned in his eyes again. He didn't look away.

'Pardon?'

'I said,' he said, and his breath was warm in my ear, 'where did you live before?'

Our faces brushed as we shifted position so I could lean into his ear — *oh my God, he smells delicious.* 'Yorkshire.'

'Do you listen to a lot of live music?'

I shook my head. 'I don't get out much.' And then I felt compelled to add, 'My daughter's only eight.'

He nodded as if he understood how that must be, although of course he couldn't possibly have understood anything about my life. And then he said, 'Child bride.'

I was used to this type of comment: how can a woman your age have an eight-year-old daughter? I ignored it. 'Is that what you do for a living — write music?' I asked.

'Yes.'

'For the band?'

'No, not just for them. That's for fun. I write mostly commercial stuff.

Adverts, video games, incidental music for documentaries. Anything that pays. I teach a couple of classes at a sixth-form college, too.'

'Do you work for yourself?'

'Part-time for a small company. It's too expensive to work alone all the time.'

'Expensive?'

'The trouble with musicians these days,' said Joe, turning away from teasing Reese about something, 'is they use a lot of fancy-pants technology. Synthesisers. Computers.' He made them sound like rude words. 'Luckily Charlie here is more than a technical whizz. He's a real musician too, and that's what sets him apart. He's an authentic.'

'Joe's highest form of praise,' said Raul, knocking his beer bottle against Charlie's pint glass.

'What does it mean?' Amy asked Joe.

'Authentic? It means the real deal. Most people most of the time pretend to be something they're not. To get a job or a mate or to fit in or look good. Then you get the rare few who don't have to pretend, who are what they are. They're the authentics. Charlie's one of them.'

Charlie looked away, embarrassed. I wondered how they were going to sing again after all this shouting. Then I looked at my watch and wondered how Grace was getting on with Rebecca.

'You can't leave now,' said Raul, looking alarmed.

'I'm going to make a phone call,' I yelled.

'Oh no you don't,' said Amy, grabbing the mobile out of my hand. 'She'll be fine. Have a little faith.'

I thought about arguing, but instead I shrugged in defeat. 'Okay. Since I'm already on my feet I'll visit the Ladies. Excuse me.'

I was halfway to the loo when I remembered this was my second visit in less than an hour; they were going to think I had bladder issues.

When I was making my way back to the table I heard Raul say, 'Her husband died?' in horrified tones, and they all looked up as I pulled back my chair.

I tried to pretend I hadn't heard, but I suspect my face gave me away. Oh dear. Now everything would change. No one except Charlie had particularly talked to me before but now they would all struggle to find something to say to me, and it would be false and horrible and no one would breathe easy until I left and they could resume their carefree conversation. My evening was over.

But nothing changed. The conversations continued much as before and I was neither more nor less included. Once, when I looked at Charlie, our eyes tangled, but there was neither pity nor cold curiosity in his, only friendliness and — something else I couldn't place.

Was it interest?

Could this lovely oriental-eyed man find me *interesting*?

We left after eleven-thirty, leaving Charlie, Raul and the band packing away their gear. Outside, our breath came out of our mouths in a stream of white bubbles. Amy sang all the way home, holding Raul's phone number inside her glove.

'What a fantastic evening,' she murmured. She gave my arm a little squeeze. 'Thank you for coming with me. Did you like it?'

'I had a great time.' I meant it, too. 'Amy, do you want to stay with us? Indefinitely, I mean.'

She looked at me in delight. 'Really? I can stay? Really?'

'We love you,' I assured her. 'Grace and I. We want you to stay. If you want to.'

'I want to!' she wailed, and I smiled.

'Good. That's settled then. In which case, my home is your home, and you should invite anyone home that you want to. Anyone, any time.'

'Raul?' she asked.

'Especially Raul. Hell, invite the whole band if you want to.'

She smiled and returned to her reverie, humming under her breath. Then she said, '*You* invite the band,' and it didn't even sound like an afterthought.

Grace was asleep when we got in, and Rebecca was dozing on the kitchen sofa. I was in the house and had called for a taxi before she even knew we were back.

'I must say, Cora,' she said, putting on her coat, 'this is a very comfortable house. You've done a good job. And Grace is surprisingly good company.'

'High praise, Rebecca,' I said, kissing her cheek. I was grateful she didn't ask how my evening had gone.

'Off to bed now,' she said. 'You look peaky. Good night, dear.'

Later I stood by the window, gazing out onto the dark garden in the centre of the square, and I made a snap decision; seconds later I was soaring over the city. It had been so long — so long! — since I had done this! The lights were bright, the city hummed. There were dark spots, of course, areas where the energy flared into red, even black. But I gravitated to the yellow and ended up on top of Marble Arch, gazing across to the relative peace of Hyde Park, watching the traffic swirl into Park Lane and the snatches of Arabic music float over from Edgware Road.

It was all there, waiting for me. All the old connections safely in place — the spirit of everything, calmly existing beneath the weight of physical reality. It was glorious.

I drifted back to my bed and fell asleep.

I woke in the morning with a headache, wondering what had come over me, feeling a deep sense of shame. Here I was, telling Grace to control herself, and look at me! It was like an alcoholic telling someone else to step away from the bottle.

CHAPTER 8

GRACE HAD NO INTENTION OF LISTENING to me anyway. On Monday morning I came downstairs clutching her PE shorts, to find her sitting on the sofa neatly dressed in school uniform, brown curls tied back, shoes fastened, totally vacant.

Given my own recent escapade, I didn't know whether to laugh or cry. I glanced at my watch. 'It's eight-fifteen, Grace. Sue will be here in about three minutes.' I knew the Grace in front of me could neither see nor hear me, and the one that could was nowhere in the house. I glanced out of the window and into the treetops. No sign of her in the bare brown branches. I checked my watch again. Only a few minutes to go; Sue was never late.

There was nothing for it. I put my arms around Grace's inert body and tried to lift it, which was no mean feat because my daughter, at eight, was nearly as tall as me. I heaved her up and carried her clumsily towards the door. And then she was back; her head lifted and her legs reached for the floor and she was giggling into my neck.

'What are you doing, Mum?'

'What are *you* doing, Grace?'

She looked at her feet. 'I can't stop, Mum, I can't. When I don't walk I feel kind of — sick. And awkward. I don't feel like me.'

I knew what she meant. 'It's so dangerous,' I began.

'It isn't dangerous! It's natural. And beautiful. It's like breathing. I can't not do it!' She looked at me beseechingly, and then frowned. 'Were you going to carry me out to the car?'

'No, I was going to carry you to your room so Sue wouldn't see you like that if she had to come in and wait.'

'She'd think I'd fallen asleep. It'd be no big deal if she saw me.'

'Normal little girls don't sit unconscious on the sofa between breakfast and school,' I said. 'With their eyes open.'

'Well she'll be pulling up any minute. I saw her turn into Finn Street. I raced her up the street.'

'That's not funny, Grace. Where have you been?'

She shifted from one leg to the other. 'Just out. I couldn't help it. I'm going to have to sit still now for hours and hours.'

'I'm going to permanently ground you one of these days.'

She refocused, interested. 'Can you do that?'

'No.' I stroked her fringe out of her eyes. 'We're going to have to take this very steady, Grace. There are risks.'

She clapped her hands together; she knew I was yielding. Then she started to run towards the door but I caught her arm. 'Wait until it rings.'

So she stood with her hand on the door-knob, and threw open the door at precisely the moment the bell rang.

Sue took a step backwards. 'Morning, Grace! You're eager today.'

I kissed Grace goodbye, gave her a warning glance, and watched her join Ruth in the back seat of the car.

****

I came home late the next night after a dinner party with Rebecca and her husband Hugh. It had been a horrible evening. Rebecca had lined up not one but two prospective new husbands for me. Both of them worked in finance and earned fabulous salaries; Rebecca made sure I knew that.

'Rebecca,' I told her when everyone had gone home. 'I don't want a new husband and if I ever do, this time I'll choose him for myself, thank you.'

'What's that supposed to mean? I didn't choose Peter.' She smoothed her skirt over her ample hips.

I looked at her affectionately. 'You bloody did. You and Peter sorted it all out between you, and I was too young to know better.'

'You were very happy with him.'

'I was happy enough, but I was too young, Rebecca. Peter knew that. He was my schoolgirl crush — he should never have been my husband.'

'He gave you Grace. And he kept you safe. You know that was everything back then, especially when Mother became sick and couldn't watch you properly.'

We'd never talked so openly about the past. 'I know,' I said, as gently as I could. 'You did the right thing, and I was perfectly happy with Peter. You've always taken care of me, and I'll be grateful till the day I die. You're my family, Rebecca. But I'm an adult now. The danger is long past and I don't need looking after anymore.'

'Are you sure about that?'

No. I'm not at all sure. But I'm not going to live in the shadows any more.
'Quite sure,' I told her.

Amy was still up when I came through the door. 'Charlie called,' she said, by way of greeting.

'That's nice. What did he want?'

'He wanted you.' Amy was grinning.

I frowned. 'About what?'

'Well gosh, Cora, now let's think. What could Charlie possibly want?'

'I have no idea.' I was surprised at her tone. 'Have you?'

She cocked her head to one side. 'I suspect he wants to ask you out, Cora. You know, a date.'

I raised both eyebrows and felt them disappearing high into my hairline. 'Yes, I'm sure you're right,' I said at last.

'Well, why not?'

I frowned some more. 'I'm Grace's mum.'

'You're Grace's single mum,' said Amy. 'You've been alone for more than a year now. I think you deserve a date.'

My eyes narrowed.

'Look, Charlie rang for you; it's nothing to do with me. Here's the number.'

I waited until midday the next day before returning his call, and his answer phone picked up. 'Um, Charlie, this is Cora Bloux. I'm returning your call. Thank you.'

Thank you? *For what?* Oh good grief.

He called me back a few minutes later. 'Hello, Cora? It's Charlie Tam.'

'Um… hi Charlie.'

'Are you okay?'

'Yes, thank you. How are you?'

'I'm fine.' There was a pause. 'Do you mind me ringing you?'

'No, of course not.' I grimaced. What do I say next. *What do I say next.* 'I'm glad you called.'

'Good,' he said, and his voice warmed up. 'I'd like to see you again. If you want to. Shall we go out somewhere?'

'Where?' I asked stupidly.

I could imagine him smiling, his Chinese eyes narrowing to dark horizontal lines. 'Well, how about the cinema?'

'Why? Is there something good on?' I started racking my brain. Had we talked about the cinema? Was there something showing that one of us had expressed an interest in? Was he following up on some hint I didn't remember making?

Charlie laughed. It was a good-natured sound. 'Are you trying to make this hard for me? You can say no and I won't ask again. Well, not for a day or two.' He laughed again. It seemed like his confidence was growing in inverse proportion to mine.

I took a deep breath. 'I'm not trying to make it hard. I'm glad you called. But you're not asking me *out* out … are you?'

He sounded puzzled, cautious. 'Is that all right?'

Was it *all right?* Let's see. I had left Yorkshire, my hiding place for two decades, and moved to the big, unknown city. I had discovered my daughter was a walker. I had started walking again myself. I had no idea what I was doing and what was going to happen next. Was anything in my life all right any more?

I said, 'Um,' and there was silence at the other end of the phone. 'Sorry. I married the last man that asked me out, so I don't have much practice at this.' *Dear God, no — did I say that out loud?*

Charlie laughed again, and I did too, as if I'd made a joke even though it was completely true. 'If it's too soon after your husband,' he began.

'No! No, it's been a year. It's probably exactly the right time. There's only one problem.'

'What's that?' He didn't sound worried.

'My sister Rebecca, who generally arranges these things for me, won't let me date anyone who doesn't work in the City and earn a six-figure salary.'

'Well,' said Charlie. 'I think your sister should get used to disappointment.'

I was overcome with panic. This wasn't funny at all. I had no experience whatsoever with men or boys either, for that matter. I had only ever been out with Peter. I was assailed by a sudden memory of Charlie's scent, and how it had made me feel. 'Would you mind very much if I get back to you on this one?' I asked.

'Of course,' he said. 'By all means go and ask your sister for permission. Remember to tell her I'm a penniless musician — that should go down well.'

He was joking; I think he was joking.

'It's just — I have to go. I will call you back, I promise.' I hung up, blushing furiously. Then I lifted the phone again, because it was about to ring, but I was too fast and the call hadn't connected so I hung up again and waited, hoping it would be Charlie.

It wasn't. It was Rebecca. We chatted, about nothing in particular. All I could think was: I just got asked out. Charlie Tam just asked me out!

All I had to do was call him back.

****

Amy came home late the following day, brimming with news about her temp job. 'I've been out for drinks. They took me off reception and put me into the director's office,' she said. 'I answer the phone to famous people — talented, glamorous, interesting people! Can you believe it?'

Grace was flat out on the sofa; she'd been to Ruth's house for tea and had come home exhausted.

'I'll take her up to bed and change. You're in tonight, right? Because I'm going out — with Raul. Hurrah!'

Grace was asleep in bed and Amy had just left when there was a ring at the door. It was Imtiaz, without vegetables.

'Is everything all right?' I asked him. He looked very different; he wasn't grubby from carrying boxes of vegetables. He wore a smart coat and shoes, not trainers. And he wasn't alone.

'Everything is very good,' he said and then, with bashful pride, he stood aside to reveal his companion. A striking woman with a mass of stylishly untidy brown hair stepped out from behind him into the light of the front porch. She was flamboyantly dressed in a velvet coat and a multi-coloured scarf. For a beat I did not know her, and then I looked into her eyes.

'That didn't take you long,' she said. 'Hello Cora.'

I took a stumbling step backwards. I felt my mouth opening and closing, and fireworks went off in my head. Then I threw my arms around my sister's neck.

'Magda!' I cried.

Chapter 9

I HUGGED HER FOR A LONG MOMENT, until it finally occurred to me that she wasn't hugging me back, and then I stepped away and stared at her some more.

There was no mistaking her. I hadn't seen her since I was six — just before I came to England. But I knew her, beyond the shadow of a doubt.

She was staring back at me with a look of amused detachment. As the rest of the world filtered back into my peripheral vision, I saw Imtiaz vibrating with excitement. 'She said it would be a good surprise!' he said. 'I hope you don't mind.'

'Mind?' I cried. 'Come in! Come in out of the cold!'

Magda stepped over the threshold and I led them into the kitchen.

'I don't believe it.' I was breathless, babbling. 'How did you find me?'

Magda flashed me a grin. 'Chance,' she said. 'And Imtiaz.'

'Magda is my new girlfriend,' said Imtiaz. His excitement and pride were touching.

'That's … amazing,' I said. 'I can't believe it's such a small world. Magda!' I snatched up her hands in mine. 'Tell me everything! Where have you been, how did you get here?'

She smiled again and I registered that she was significantly less excited than I was. But then, she'd come to me; she'd had time to get used to the idea of seeing her sister. I was taken entirely by surprise.

'You've done very nicely, I see,' she said, looking around. Her Canadian accent was strong. 'Very nicely indeed.'

'And you? Do you have any family?'

'Just me,' said Magda.

'And when did you leave Canada? How long have you been here?'

'I've been here a while. Not as long as you, of course.'

The words were loaded; they hummed in the silence that followed. I was the one sent to England, furthest away from danger. What had happened to her?

'Well, this is great,' I said at last. 'I can't believe you're here. You must stay for dinner. And you, Imtiaz, of course.'

'No,' said Magda. 'I can't stay long.'

'Coffee then. Or tea?'

Nearly twenty years and here she was. My sister. And I was offering her a cup of coffee. 'There's so much to catch up on,' I said, becoming confused at the enormity of what was happening and my inability to get a grip on it.

'Isn't there,' said Magda.

'Tell me a little about your life. What happened to you?'

She gave me a funny look and I was suddenly aware of my Self banging around inside my head and legs. It wanted to get out; it wanted to flee. What was I afraid of?

And then, as I began preparing coffee, a memory came to me. It appeared in my head fully formed, as if it had never gone away.

I was four years old and it was my first day at kindergarten. Magda, two years older than me, was at another school across town. I was standing scared and lonely in the middle of the playground, separate from the hive of noise and activity going on around me, missing Mum, wishing I could be home with her. And my sister's spirit came to me.

I thought she'd come to comfort me and, for a moment, I was delighted to see her. I called out a greeting and the other children stared at me because, of course, they couldn't see her. But Magda didn't smile. She didn't speak either — not that I would have heard her if she had, without popping myself — but her lips didn't move at all. She just stared at me. It was a look of such resentment and dislike that I backed away in distress. Then she'd disappeared.

I stared at the Magda who was now sitting in my kitchen, drinking coffee from one of my mugs. 'You came to me in the playground,' I said. 'On my first day at school.'

'Oh I came more than once,' said Magda. I stared at her hands wrapped around the mug. She was lighter-haired than me, and much taller, but we had exactly the same fingers, long with tiny fingernails.

'Did you?' I said. 'I don't remember.'

'You look like Mum.' Her lips thinned and whitened as she scrutinised me.

'I hardly remember what she looked like. I remember her smell.' My Self was shrinking now, pressing against the back of my head and spine, edging away from my sister. I was struggling to find conversation; this wasn't a reunion I could have imagined. 'So how did you and Imtiaz meet?'

'We met *walking*,' said Imtiaz, and then he looked around swiftly, as if alarmed that he'd said it out loud.

'You walk?' I said to my sister, aghast.

'I never stopped,' she said.

I cleared my throat. 'We were told not to.'

'I was never very good at doing as I was told.'

'But it did you no harm?' I was striving for a light note, but my voice sounded strangled and false.

Magda spread out her arms. 'As you see. The bogeyman never hurt me.'

With that casual gesture she dismissed my past. The painful resolution never to walk, the never-ending effort at playing normal — all for nothing, because Magda never followed the rules and nothing bad had happened to her. Our mother's killer hadn't found her.

'You met Imtiaz walking,' I said, grasping at the first thing that came into my head in an effort to appear unconcerned. 'So how did you find each other afterwards?'

'*I* found *him*,' said Magda. 'You know how it is, Cora; some of us look like our Self and some of us don't. Imtiaz and his Self are exactly alike.' She watched me closely. 'Like you and yours,' she added.

'You can't remember that,' I said. 'We were children.'

She leaned closer towards me. 'I remember everything.'

Another devastating wave of memory swamped me, only this time there were lots of different images, rolling through me like waves, crashing against my heart. Magda in the playground; Magda in the corridor; Magda in the classroom. I would be going about my normal day and suddenly, silently, there was her Self standing at my side, too close for comfort, so close that sometimes *I had to pass through her.*

It was a hideous thing for a walker to pass through a Self. She must have known that. It must have been hideous for her, too, yet she forced it. Again and again. I had to pretend to ignore it, to hide my shock, my fear, the nausea that crawled up my throat from my stomach. I started feigning illness to avoid school. I started wetting my bed. It went on for several months. I never told Mum, because Magda would have beaten me if I'd told tales about her.

Magda had ruled my earliest childhood. I'd been terrified of her — so terrified that I'd buried her beyond the access of normal memory.

Imtiaz glanced quickly at his watch, but Magda was watching me as if she could see inside my head. She laughed quietly and started to hum *Me and My Shadow*. What was it about her, precisely, that could still make me shake and quake inside — and how could I hide it from her?

'So,' she said, 'what have you been up to these last two decades? You haven't changed much. Apart from the fancy new accent. Very English. I hear you have a daughter.'

My Self stilled. I went cold from the inside out.

'Yes, and I heard you were a widow now,' she said. 'I'm sorry. Well, hasn't this been nice? I have to go now. But I'll come again.'

I walked numbly to the door. 'Where do you live?' I mumbled. 'I don't have your number.' I clutched at her hand. 'You're my sister.'

'I'll come to you, don't worry,' she said, shaking me off.

I watched them leave, walking off down the street arm in arm. Then I ran upstairs and was violently sick in the toilet.

How could I have forgotten? How could I possibly have forgotten how different my sister was to me, how thoroughly unpleasant she'd always been, how afraid of her I was? For years all I'd remembered was that she existed. I'd even begun to romanticise a little, imagine how different my life would have been if Mum had sent us away together. I always wondered why she didn't. Looking at it now, from an adult perspective, the reason was suggesting itself only too clearly: Mum separated us because she knew I would keep my promise and Magda wouldn't. At least one of us would be safe.

And then ... and then ... I was sick again at the realisation that I'd been sent to a foreign land to be guarded by distant family I'd never met before for *nothing*. Magda had stayed in Canada, had continued to walk, and had remained perfectly safe.

My whole life was pointless.

How can you say that when you have Grace? And it's not as if you were neglected or hurt. If you were lonely and bullied, that was your own fault.

I threw up yet again.

Amy, coming home near midnight, switched on the hall lights and jumped when she saw me sitting on the stairs.

'You were sitting there in the dark? Cora, what's wrong?'

'My sister came to visit me.'

'Rebecca? Has she upset you?'

'Not Rebecca. I have another sister. A blood-sister. I haven't seen her since we were children.'

'Well that's a good thing, right?' said Amy, helping me to my feet.

'Probably not,' I whispered.

Chapter 10

I WAS IN THE KITCHEN a few days later, chopping pistachios and rosemary to make biscuits, when I felt a commotion upstairs, and then Amy gave a loud cry: 'Cora! Cora, come quickly!'

I dropped the knife and raced up the stairs. Amy was on the floor of Grace's bedroom, cradling Grace's prone body. My daughter's Self stood on the bed, looking wide-eyed and guilty.

'I found her like this,' sobbed Amy. 'She's breathing but she's not moving.'

I took a deep breath and addressed the bed. 'Gracie Bloux, you snapback this minute!'

Amy hugged Grace's body closer and stared at me, shocked.

'Now, young lady.' My eyes narrowed. 'Don't make me come and get you.'

Grace obediently jumped off the bed and back into her body. 'Ow,' she said, waggling her jaw from side to side. 'I hit my face when I fell.'

'Get into bed,' I said in a voice shaking with the anger that often follows fear.

'What — ?' said Amy, releasing Grace abruptly.

'We'll talk about this in the morning, young lady.'

Grace stood up looking disgruntled and a little ashamed.

'Bed!' I ordered. I put my hand out to raise Amy from the floor, and then I led her down the stairs. In the kitchen I opened a bottle of wine and handed her a glass.

Amy was frowning and staring at me, clearly troubled. 'What happened?' she said. 'I don't understand.'

I searched my head for an excuse to give her, some plausible explanation. Epilepsy, narcolepsy — any epsy would have done. But in the end, I settled for the truth. 'Do you believe in spirits?' I asked.

'You mean like ghosts?'

'Not really. Well, sort of. But no.' On second thoughts, I poured myself a glug of wine too. 'I mean the part of you that isn't your body.'

'Go on.'

'There are people that can separate their spirit and their body at will. They can — how can I put this? — come out of their bodies.'

'Like ghosts?' She didn't sound as sceptical as I expected.

'Well, it's complicated. Most regular people can't see spirits, and the few that do generally think they've seen a ghost. Very occasionally you do get the spirit of a dead person hanging around, but most spirits have got living bodies somewhere—'

'Grace?' prompted Amy. So far she was taking this better than I expected.

'Is a spirit-walker. She's not supposed to do it. I've told her not to. That's why I was so angry with her.'

Amy's eyes never left my face. 'So when you were talking to the bed—'

'I was talking to Grace. Grace was playing on the bed when you came in.'

'And her body was—'

'Empty.'

Amy was silent. 'Why couldn't I see her?' she asked at last.

'Because you're not a spirit-walker.'

Amy stared at me. 'But you could see her.'

'Yes.'

'Right,' said Amy. 'Let's start again. A spirit-walker can separate her spirit from her body?'

'Yes.'

'And Grace is one, and so are you.'

'Yes.'

'Who taught you?' she asked, incredulous, as if that was the most surprising part of the equation.

'No one. We're all born walkers. You were once a walker too.'

'Was not,' said Amy emphatically. She took a long gulp of wine and swallowed it audibly.

I grinned. 'Were too. You chose to stop, that's all.'

'I never chose. What are you talking about?'

'It's nothing to feel bad about.'

'I don't feel bad. I don't know what you're talking about.'

'Everyone's born a walker. You attach yourself to the physical world around the time you start talking. The process of naming things connects you to this reality and that's when you stop walking.'

'So why didn't you and Grace stop?'

I shifted uncomfortably, more than a little embarrassed. 'I thought Grace had stopped, but apparently I was wrong. I stopped when I was about six but I, um, recently started again. I'm trying to stop. We're both trying to stop.'

'You sound like me,' said Amy, draining her glass of wine in a series of gulps and holding it out to be refilled.

'Well,' I said. 'We're supposed to stop. Humans are made for the material world. Walking is an aberration.'

Amy looked surprised. 'I'm not saying I believe you, exactly. But if I could separate my spirit from my body, well hell, I'd go out flying every day of the week.'

I rolled my eyes at her. 'Trust me, it's not a superpower.'

'It sounds like a superpower. What can you see in this invisible world?'

'Everything.' I waved my hand lamely. 'The spirit of everything. I can see time — well, not time itself, but the way it speeds up and slows down according to the human bustle within it. And the colour of different energies. I can see the way everything on the planet is connected.'

'Energy has colour?' She drained the wine bottle into her glass, opened another bottle. 'So why can't I remember that, if I was once a walker. Oh, wait, because I was only a baby then?'

'Everyone kind of remembers,' I said.

And I really did think that, that everyone — *everyone*, in every culture and every time — knew that walking, by whatever name it was known, wasn't a fantasy. They made a rock of the physical world and then broke themselves upon it trying to regain access to the spiritual one. Angels, ghosts and demons; pantheism, animism, monotheism — people endlessly tried to recreate the experience of the spirit world through stories and religions. Because deep down they all remembered that, once, they'd seen it, it was real, and they hoped their stories would lead the way back.

'You can feel it sometimes,' I said, 'in music and art. A yearning, a memory you can't place. Homesickness for somewhere that you don't remember living.'

'The artist is remembering what it was like to spirit-walk?' Amy was incredulous.

'They're snatching at echoes. Either that, or they're actually walkers.' It had been a mistake drinking the wine. I had never, ever talked about such things out loud. 'I used to play this game with myself, where I tried to guess which composer or painter was just taking a stab in the dark, and which was the real deal.'

'Is it easy to tell the difference?'

'No. Walkers can be tricksters.'

'So the trick to recognising them is to know whether the clues are deliberate or accidental?'

I smiled. 'Yup.'

Amy leaned forward. 'Could I choose to be a walker, now I know about it?'

I shook my head. 'You're asking the wrong person. I really don't know. But once, at a piano recital in the Brighton Pavilion, I saw an elderly woman in the audience pop out of her body for a second, without warning. She wasn't a walker but the music just drew her out. The woman was astonished; it was clearly her first time and she had no idea what had happened to her.'

Amy began giggling. 'Fill me up again,' she said, holding out her glass. 'Will I wake up in the morning and find this conversation was all a dream?'

'Absolutely,' I assured her.

Chapter 11

I WOKE UP WITH A HEADACHE and an uncomfortable pain in my chest. When Grace had gone to school and Amy had left for work, I took a shower and I was still in my dressing gown when I felt visitors at the door. It was Imtiaz with my vegetables — and Magda.

The pain in my chest grew sharper.

'Hello, Cora,' said Imtiaz, with a wider smile than usual. Magda was carrying the vegetable box, which surprised me, as the box was dusty and she was wearing her nice velvet coat.

'Come in,' I said, widening the door. 'Go on through. I'll just get dressed.'

Three adult walkers in one house. Again. And again one of them was *Magda*. I got dressed quickly and hurried downstairs, my wet hair laying slick against my cheeks and tickling my neck.

Imtiaz was on the sofa. Being with Magda seemed to have given him a strange release, a rather unexpected insouciance; he was lounging.

Magda had made herself at home in my kitchen and was pouring boiling water into the tea-pot. She seemed to be watching Imtiaz closely.

'Do you often help Imtiaz?' I asked her, mostly for something to say.

Imtiaz made a sound curiously like a snort. 'Just today,' he said and he laughed as if something amused him. 'What about you — are you having the day off? I wouldn't have expected to see you in your dressing gown at this time of day.'

This was not a side to Imtiaz I'd seen before, and I didn't much like it.

'You just caught me by surprise,' I said.

'I'll bet,' he said. 'It's not everyday your sister turns up out of the blue. Delivered to your door by your very own vegetable man, too.'

His behaviour was all wrong. He was showing off for his new girlfriend. My sister.

Magda quietly put a mug of tea down in front of me and then passed one along to Imtiaz. 'Should I help you put your vegetables away?' she asked.

She was much gentler this time and I reminded myself that everyone changes; just because she'd been a troublesome child didn't mean she'd be a troublesome adult. She might have been edgy last time she visited, but wasn't that to be expected? It's not every day you meet your sister after a twenty-year gap.

They stayed for a while. We chatted, about nothing in particular. I suppose we hung out, spent time. We skirted around anything personal; we talked about London, and my new house, and what was on at the cinema. Magda was chastened and polite. Imtiaz, on the other hand, grew more assuming and bizarre with every moment. I wanted to smack him, but I also didn't want to embarrass him in front of his new girlfriend. The Imtiaz I'd met before was modest and gentle and entirely unassuming. I guessed he hadn't had a girlfriend in a long time — if ever. But he was trampling on my time with my sister, and I was irritated.

When they finally left, I breathed a sigh of relief. I went to work on the Chagall canvas; but a growing sense of unease was creeping over me and after a while I stopped for fear of ruining the picture.

****

To make up for my recent distractions, I put my head down and worked through Wednesday and Thursday evening. Grace wasn't impressed.

'I know I've got Amy too now,' she grumbled. 'But that doesn't mean I should have less of you.'

I caught her into a ferocious hug. 'You'll never have less of me,' I promised. 'And if it feels like it now, it's only because I've got a lot on my mind.'

'Work things?' she asked, eyeing me challengingly after I released her.

'Yes, work things,' I said. 'And other things, too.'

'Raul's coming over tomorrow. He's Amy's new boyfriend.'

I looked up, surprised but pleased, too. 'That's good,' I said.

'Amy should invite her friends here. I'll tell you what. Have you got any homework? Because if not, we could bake some biscuits for tomorrow.'

This was one of the things we did, Grace and I: we made biscuits. It started in the days after Peter's death, when friends kept arriving with pot dinners and advice, and Grace and I quickly discovered it was all much easier to handle if we were actively busy. Plus, of course, each batch gave us something to offer to our guests and helped convince them that we were not wasting away; homemade biscuits being a universal symbol for abundance and well-being. We went through every recipe on our bookshelf and then we progressed to the Internet. We rated each recipe out of ten and only repeated those that scored eight or higher.

I had never finished the pistachio and rosemary biscuits I'd begun the evening Grace had terrified Amy, so I pulled out that recipe again.

'They're called *biscotti*,' scoffed Grace.

'That's because they're Italian and biscotti means biscuit.'

'I think I guessed that, Mum.'

She weighed everything out and began sifting the flour, while I turned on the stove and greased the trays. In less than an hour we had thirty-two slices of Italian-style biscuits cooling on the rack.

Grace raised her head and sniffed the air. 'Is there an eclipse coming?'

I put down the washing-up sponge and concentrated. 'Lunar eclipse. It won't peak until after three and no, you may not stay up for it.'

These things must have been going on in her head all the time, but she was able to take on the idea that I was a walker too and just run with it, share her secret world without breaking her stride. I leaned over and kissed her cheek. 'I love you, Gracie.'

'Mum,' said Grace. 'Why are you always sleeping in my room? Are you scared at night?'

'Of course not,' I said. 'Mums don't get scared. I thought you might be scared, with this new house and everything.'

'So you'll sleep in your own bed tonight? Only, you move round a lot. It wakes me up.'

'Okay.'

Shit. I wanted to keep Grace as close by me as possible. But she was right; she was much too old to have me coddle her like this and I needed to keep everything normal, for my sake as much as hers.

Before going to my own bed that night, I went to tuck Grace in. As always, she was too hot. I pulled the duvet lower down and stroked the wet tendrils from her sweaty forehead. Then I kissed her, inhaling her mouth-watering scent and feeling my stomach flutter with pure, unalloyed adoration. Was there ever anything in the world like having a daughter, *this* daughter? She was so — precious.

And in that second several things flashed into my consciousness and stuck there, screaming.

Magda was back in my life.

Magda was dangerous.

Magda must not be allowed anywhere near my daughter.

And there was a good reason why Imtiaz and Magda had seemed so strange the other morning.

I hurried from Grace's room as if even thinking bad thoughts in there might have an adverse effect on her. In my own room I flung open the window and stuck my head out, breathing in the damp night air as if I'd been suffocating inside. There was someone in the garden; I could see the tip of a lit cigarette and hear the sound of quiet talking. Normal life was still out there, outside my window. In here, everything was in turmoil.

Because Imtiaz had been Magda and Magda had been Imtiaz. They had swapped bodies.

I should have seen it in their eyes. I could see it quite clearly now, in retrospect. Was I completely stupid that it had taken me so long to work it out?

Body-swapping. *Is that even possible?* And if it was, if two walkers could swap bodies, from now on I would never know for sure who was who. And my demon could come for me in any shape he chose. The silver hair might, after all these years, turn out to be a red herring.

If he's coming for me. If. Just come and get this over with! It was the not knowing that was killing me. The not knowing had always killed me.

I found myself on the floor, rolled into a ball, while the cold air streamed in through the open window above my head.

Chapter 12

A T SIX THE NEXT EVENING I heard the front door open and a kerfuffle in the hallway. Then Amy stuck her head around the kitchen door.

'Um, Cora, do you remember you said I was to treat your home as my own? Well, I hope you meant it, because I've brought some friends home with me.'

I grinned at her. 'You already told me Raul was coming over, Amy. Of course it's all right.' And I called out, 'Hi Raul, come on in.'

Raul stuck his head around the door and I gulped at the waft of pure testosterone he brought with him. Not my type but still; *gulp*. 'I brought a friend home, too,' he said. 'You don't mind?'

They made a show of it. Joe was next to stick *his* head around the door, announcing in his extraordinarily deep and happy voice, 'I brought one too.' Then Reese: 'Me too!' And finally Ken, who smiled apologetically.

They piled onto the sofas, nudging one another, making themselves comfortable.

'I'm Grace,' said Grace in a loud voice and each of them shook her hand in turn, except Joe, who kissed it.

'Would you like to touch my hair?' he asked, lowering his afro to her height.

'Yes please,' said Grace. 'Oh! It's soft! Is your skin soft too? I've never met anyone with such black skin.'

'I'm sorry,' I said, mortified. 'She's lived a horribly ... sheltered ... life.'

'Culturally or just ethnically?' asked Joe, clearly enjoying having his hand and arm stroked by a rapt Grace.

'You have no idea,' I said.

'Be careful, eh? You might catch something,' said Raul, and Grace turned her attention to him.

'Are you English?' she asked. 'No, wait, I'll tell you.' She closed her eyes and screwed up her face in concentration.

'Grace…!' I began, stepping forward to grab her.

'I'm starving!' said Reese, who was taking up more than half of the sofa he was on, so that Ken had to perch on one arm. His silver hair still unnerved me; it would take a while to undo the habit of a lifetime.

'You're so rude,' Raul told Reese. 'Grace, did you guess where I'm from?'

She creased her forehead. 'It's somewhere hot. I thought France at first, but it's further south. Spain?'

I thought the band was rather cool about Grace's incredible perception, but Amy was gratifyingly astonished. 'That's amazing, Grace! How did you do that?'

'He's got Spanishness hanging all around him,' explained Grace with a pantomime air of mystery.

Amy was busy unloading bags of shopping, and then chopping onions into a frying pan.

'Charlie should be here,' said Reese. 'Everyone's here but Charlie. We should call him.'

'Hold your horses,' said Joe, reaching out and taking the mobile out of Reese's hand. 'You can't go round inviting people to Cora's house.'

My heart was kicking at my chest. Did they know he'd asked me on a date? And that I'd never called him back? 'That's okay,' I said, as casually as I could. 'Go ahead and ask anyone you like.'

Reese went off to a corner and rang Charlie. After a moment, he called over, 'Cora, Charlie wants to know if it's you inviting him.'

I blushed to my roots, then turned quickly away. 'Tell him I'd like him to come,' I mumbled.

I helped Amy make dinner while the guys messed around with each other and Grace. I managed to stop Grace opening the door too early when Charlie arrived and then I held my breath as he came into the kitchen and was loudly welcomed by his friends.

'I brought provisions,' he said and set a box of beer onto the counter. 'Can't have you lot drinking Cora out of house and home.'

I had to look up some time. 'Hello, Charlie,' I said.

'Cora,' he replied. Under his voice, he added, 'This isn't quite the first date I had in mind, but it's original.'

I gave him an apologetic look. 'I think you know everyone.'

'I think I do. Thank you for inviting me.' He was being overly formal and polite; he was laughing at me.

I hesitated. 'You're welcome,' I said. He was dangerous; he seemed to tip me off my guard and with everything that was happening with Magda, now wasn't a good time to be defenceless. Perhaps a warning showed in my face; he turned to his friends and was absorbed into their conversation.

I looked over to see how Grace was doing. She was sitting on the floor next to Joe, looking from face to face, quietly taking it all in. She looked happy.

'Hey, Ken,' said Reese loudly, 'sing us a song!'

Ken mumbled a refusal.

'Oh go on,' said Reese. 'The girls would love to hear you sing.'

'Yes they would,' agreed Joe. 'Go on, Ken. Show them what you're made of.'

Ken was such a skinny, self-effacing little boy; I wondered if his parents knew where he was. I was curious to hear whether singing transformed him the way drumming did. Charlie was leaning against the kitchen counter with a grin all over his face.

'Shame we don't have a guitar with us,' said Joe.

'Mum's got one!' said Grace. She ran out of the room; there were several resonating thumps from the staircase and then she made a triumphant entry with my guitar in her arms.

'You play guitar?' said Reese, pulling a face.

'I know two chords,' I said with a grimace. 'And I've forgotten those.'

'It works, but there's something wrong with it,' began Grace, handing the guitar to Joe.

He wrinkled his nose and began to strum it loudly. 'Nylon strings — ugh!' he cried. 'This is a good guitar, Cora, and you're making it cry. What were you thinking of, stringing it with this shit?'

'Metal strings cut my fingers.' I shrugged.

'Get over it!'

'Give it to Ken,' commanded Raul. He'd been notably quiet so far, as had Amy. While dinner simmered on the stove, they were sitting side-by-side, squished up because Reese occupied the larger part of the sofa. They looked like an advert for designer perfume, just ridiculously beautiful.

Ken took the guitar and began to strum through a series of chord changes, while the others sat forward in anticipation and I set the table.

Ken began to sing and it quickly became apparent that this was an old joke. His first problem was pitch; he had none. His second was that his voice was still breaking; he couldn't hold a note, even when he found it. Again and again he cleared his throat and restarted. I was quickly overcome with giggles and had to hide my face. The others showed no such discretion.

'I love it when Ken sings,' guffawed Reese, wiping his eyes on his sleeve and sitting upright at last. 'Thank God he can play the drums.'

'Is he any good at that?' asked Grace.

'Best in the city,' said Joe.

Grace now felt free to enjoy the spectacle of his humiliation. 'Play again!' she suggested.

'Nothing wrong with being tone deaf. I'm tone deaf,' said Amy.

'Yes, but you're not masquerading as a musician,' Reese pointed out.

'Grub's up,' announced Amy.

It was the noisiest gathering Grace and I had ever seen in this or any other house we'd ever been in. Nothing in our tradition-bound country life with Peter had prepared us for a rock band in our kitchen. These boys had probably never seen the inside of a boarding school. They neither knew nor cared when the shooting season began; they'd probably never held a golf club. All the secret codes of family and class were absent here. It was as refreshing as a blast of cool air, and as welcome.

The boys — they were men, of course, but together they acted like boys — needed neither hosting nor entertaining; they were their own entertainment, and ours, knowing each other as well as they did, and they absorbed the rest of us with good-humoured generosity. The dynamics between them were interesting. Joe was the big daddy; he naturally took the lead, reminding the others of what was due to me as their hostess, directing the conversation, modifying opinions where necessary and mostly because of Grace's presence. It wasn't only because he was the oldest of them. It became clear as the evening progressed that his seniority was due to his being the best and most experienced musician among them.

'No, but I've played with lots of people who are,' he told Grace when she asked if he was famous.

It was hard to judge what Raul was. It was hard to get past the testosterone, the face, the beguiling accent. He was by far the coolest and best-looking member of the band, and he was outwardly easygoing, but I noticed that he did not like to be shouted down during the noisy and often heated exchanges that regularly erupted around the table.

Reese was that generic entity in any male group: noisy, childish, boisterous; loyal. And ugly. He was quite fascinatingly ugly, with a sharp nose and bony cheeks and lively eyes that seemed to live independently of his face. I couldn't yet like him, but it was getting harder and harder to be afraid of him.

And there was more to Ken than met the eye. He was a boy and a drum-hero; self-effacing and entirely confident. He smiled in the face of a world of teasing, but he was no pushover. I'd been surprised, at first, to find him in such noisy company. I was beginning to understand that he could more than hold his own.

Charlie was one step removed from them. All of them, even Joe, treated him with a healthy respect. Or maybe my own point of view was colouring my perception. The more I watched him, the more dazzled I became; the more dazzled I became, the more wary I was of who or what he was. There was something ... something about him that I couldn't put my finger on. Something I recognised...

Is this love? Is this what it means to fall in love?

When I handed the plates around the table, Charlie's fingers brushed mine and the touch was like a kiss, warm and promising. When the noise in the room was at its loudest, I began to laugh and caught Charlie's eye, and he held it, and laughed back at me.

Once, I caught him watching me, searching my face, a frown between his eyes. Then he smiled, caught, and the whole room stilled.

'Music isn't about fame,' Raul was insisting, as Joe and Ken hooted him down.

'A bit of fame might be nice,' grumbled Reese. 'I wouldn't exactly *mind*.'

I busied myself with Grace. We had no dessert, so after the pasta she served the Italian biscuits and she took a pencil and paper to record everyone's votes. The recipe scored a unanimous ten out of ten. Grace was suspicious. 'You don't have to be nice to me,' she said. 'I've made lots of biscuits before. You can tell the truth.' But no one would amend their score.

I took her to bed shortly afterwards and Amy came with me.

'Are you sure this is okay?' she asked as we came back down again.

'Of course.'

'I would have given you warning, but it evolved.'

'I'm having a good time,' I said. 'You and Raul — ?'

She smiled and raised crossed fingers. 'Charlie's nice,' she said, knowingly.

'Don't be ridiculous,' I snapped.

Amy gave me a calm smile. 'You should watch that prickly manner, Cora. Not everyone is as impervious as Rebecca.'

I bit my lip. 'You're right. I'm sorry.'

'It's not me I'm worried about,' she said as we went back downstairs.

Raul had the guitar in his hands and was picking out a tune I recognised from the night in the bar. Joe began to sing softly and, to my surprise, Charlie joined in with a harmony that, at first, sat quietly over the top and then began to weave subtly in and out, like a spell. Without the metallic blur of the electric guitars and the drums it was a completely different sound. It was mesmerising. I'd watched boys at school mucking around with guitars; this was nothing like that. Charlie and the band were, beneath the humour, genuinely talented musicians.

They were pretty proficient drinkers too, judging by the growing collection of empty beer bottles, but no one seemed the worse for wear.

Some time after midnight everyone left together. Amy and Raul lingered on the doorstep while I turned out the lights in the kitchen. Halfway up the stairs I heard Reese and Joe calling Raul to hurry up, to get a move on. By the time I reached my bedroom door, Amy was coming up behind me.

'Thank you,' she said simply and put her arms around me.

'No,' I murmured. 'Thank you. I wasn't sure how to make a new life. You've kind of — done it for me.' I tried to sound light-hearted, but I don't think I fooled her.

CHAPTER 13

A FEW DAYS LATER I WAS WORKING in my studio when the doorbell rang. It was Charlie.

Crap. He was wearing a tee-shirt with an open, checked shirt over the top of it, jeans, trainers, and one of those stupid, shapeless, woollen beanie hats. He looked about twelve years old, apart from the dark growth on his jaw.

I was so used to adjusting my own life to Peter's, that I habitually thought like a forty-year-old; maybe that's what was making me so conscious of Charlie's youth.

I was panting with the effort of having run down three flights of stairs. I willed my heart to slow down to a normal pace.

'Raul sent me. To fetch the guitar? I left a message on your mobile.'

'Oh. Sorry, I never answer my mobile. Come on in. A guitar?'

'He left it last time he was here with Amy. I was passing so I said I'd pick it up.'

He was breathless himself, clearly in a hurry, so I led him straight upstairs, self-conscious in my tatty jeans, and horribly aware that I smelled of paint and turpentine.

'What are you working on?' he asked.

'A copy. A Chagall.'

'I only know *Above the Town*. You know, the one with Marc flying Bella across the sky.'

'That's the one,' I said. I went into Amy's room, where the guitar was conveniently lying on her bed.

'You're copying it? From the original?'

'I don't have the original upstairs in my studio, no.'

'Well, no,' he said. 'Obviously. You might be going backwards and forwards to a gallery, though.'

'The original's in a private collection. But I have a lot of digital images. You can get amazing clarity and colour-match these days.'

'Who are you copying it for? Can I see it?'

'A German corporation,' I said, leading the way up to my studio. 'The image represents their product, apparently. Or rather, they've based their advertising around it.'

We were in my studio. The pale sun streamed in through the skylights onto the chaos of my workspace and the large canvas perched on its easel. I was less than half-finished, had only blocked in the image and scarcely begun the colour matching, but Charlie smiled broadly as soon as he saw it. He looked at the digital images on display on several screens around the room, and compared them to my painting.

At first his scrutiny looked like enthusiastic interest. Somewhere in the silent minutes that followed it turned into something more ... disturbing.

'You've really caught them,' he said at last. 'But not like a copy. Like the real thing, like Chagall is painting it from scratch all over again, for the first time.'

I was pleased, but something was wrong. He was speaking slowly and very, very cautiously. It scared me. 'Thank you,' I said.

'You might almost say that you've caught the spirit of the picture,' he said.

'That's a nice compliment.'

'Don't you feel that sometimes? That some things have an essence that has nothing to do with what the eye sees.'

I looked at him in alarm, but he was still staring at the canvas.

'I think everything does,' I said. 'That's what Chagall is painting.'

'Explain,' he said, turning to me at last.

'You don't think Marc and Bella can actually fly, do you?' I said with a forced laugh.

'Then what's that up in the sky?' His voice was low and searching.

I gulped. 'It's their happiness. It's their joyful spirit.'

'You mean it's their joyful spirits. It's their spirits that are flying.'

I backed away, my eyes wide with fear. 'You're a walker,' I whispered.

He shook his head. 'No,' he said. 'But you are.'

'How do you know that if you're not one too?'

He sighed. 'I have walker friends.'

'Like Reese!' I said, my voice rising. 'Oh my God. I was right. The silver hair.'

I wasn't right. I couldn't possibly be right. But another walker … another one, so soon after Imtiaz and my sister. And that head of hair…

'Silver hair?' said Charlie, and his manner suddenly changed completely. 'What are you talking about?' he asked roughly, swiping the beanie off his head. His dark hair was crushed close to his skull; he ran a frantic hand through it. 'What about silver hair?'

'Have you come for me?' I said, sinking to the floor.

'What?' He took a step towards me but, seeing me flinch away, he halted. 'Cora, I'm not going to hurt you.' He crouched down to meet me at eye level. 'Tell me what's wrong.'

'What's wrong with you?' I whispered. 'You just ran me to ground as a walker and now you're acting like a thousand pennies are dropping in your head. Do you know who I am?'

'Tell me what you mean,' he said gently. 'I won't touch you — look, I'll stay right here.' He sat back and held his hands up. 'I won't move.'

'I don't want to … talk to you. Just do whatever it is you've come to do.'

His eyes widened and he looked astonished. 'Who on earth do you think I am? Who do you think I think you are?' When I didn't reply he said, 'You're going to have to talk to me, Cora.'

'We were walkers,' I said. 'My mother and my sister and I—'

'Slow down, slow down,' said Charlie. He closed his eyes, blanked all expression. 'It's okay. Take your time.'

I took a deep breath. 'He killed my mother,' I said. 'There was a walker, when I was a girl. There was my mother and my sister and I, and we used to walk together. And then my mother met this — this man with silver hair. And he ruined everything. He had a bunch of walker friends. They thought it was funny to tease non-walkers.'

'Tease how?' said Charlie. His voice was gentle, as if he were talking to a child or an animal.

'They'd play ghost — move things, create noise. They took Magda on a trip once and she came back — different. She popped all the time after that. Mum never knew where she was.' I paused, slightly awed by how much I had forgotten; how much I suddenly remembered. 'My mother changed when he came. She was happy at first ... and then she wasn't. She wanted to run away, but he wouldn't let her go. She managed to send us away in secret, my sister and me. Just before he killed her.'

'Shit,' said Charlie softly.

'Mum said I must never walk. She made us promise. She said if we walked, he would find us. And I didn't walk for twenty years. But then ... Grace had an accident and I walked to find her ... because she's a walker too.'

'And now I turn up asking if you're a walker, and you think it's connected?'

His face was so sad, so sorry, it was impossible to be afraid of him. 'It's not just you,' I said. 'Two minutes later I find out my vegetable man is a walker. Then I meet Reese and he's got silver hair. Then my sister turns up.'

'But that's a good thing, finding your sister again, isn't it?'

I wrung my hands. 'With my sister it's complicated.'

He nodded but I had the distinct feeling his mind was suddenly elsewhere. He was silent for a moment, and then he came back to me. 'Cora,' he said, 'when you walk, you send out certain ... signals ... to anyone that can see them.'

I raised an eyebrow. 'I'm out of practice. I'm not stupid.'

He smiled. 'I know you're not stupid. I'm just trying to explain. That's why you're seeing walkers again. They're attracted to you, and you're attracted to them.'

'That's what my mother said. That's why I don't walk.' I winced. 'That's why I didn't walk. And why I won't walk again.'

'I wouldn't worry too much about that,' he said. 'It was all a long time ago. I'm sure no one's looking for you.'

'What about Reese?'

Charlie shook his head slowly. 'Reese's hair is a fashion statement. He's not your guy.'

He was trying very hard to comfort me, and I wanted to be comforted... 'What about you?' I said abruptly.

'What about me?' He looked me straight in the eye and something leaped between us.

'Why did you say you're not a walker?'

'Because I'm not.'

'Then how do you know so much about it?'

'I told you, I have friends.'

I shook my head slowly. 'Not good enough. I can feel it. You're lying.'

'I'm not a walker,' he said in a way that pronounced the subject closed.

When people want to convince you of something, they generally overdo it — eye contact, sincere expression, persuasive voice. Charlie's face was deadpan, his voice flat. He was talking automatically; his mind was busy with something else. He suddenly rose to his feet and turned back to my painting. 'Well, at least we've solved the problem of your amazing artistic abilities,' he said in a newly light tone.

I stood up, too. 'We have?'

'You've painted the spirit of the picture. Literally.'

I looked at my painting and tried to smile. 'Yes I have.'

'I don't think I've ever seen spirit-walking put to such good use. You're marvellous.'

He was flirting now, but only with his words. In ever other way, he had detached himself from me completely. I knew with savage certainty that he wouldn't be asking me out again, that whatever might have been between us was now strictly off-limits.

I just didn't know why.

'I've noticed you refer to your painting as work,' he went on.

'It is work,' I said, blinking at last. 'It's my job.'

'You could call yourself a painter. Or an artist.'

'Those terms carry baggage. They imply I'm some whimsical creature who wafts around waiting for inspiration to strike. There's no mystique. It's a job — a great job — but a job, with deadlines.'

He gave me a mocking glance. 'No mystique? The way you do it?'

'You could call yourself a composer, but you don't,' I countered. If he could do empty flirting, so could I.

'No,' he said, smiling. 'For all the same reasons. Except with me there's *really* no mystique.'

He's lying.

I stared at him openly. He *was* lying. Everything about him screamed mystique and it compelled me, burned me. I wanted to consume him, claw at the essence of him.

Back away. Back away.

I was shaking but he didn't seem to notice a thing. He was wandering around the studio, looking at everything but touching nothing. I looked around at the chaos — pin-boards full of clippings, sketches and postcards, feathers and fabric swatches, stacks of cotton canvases against the wall, fanciful colour wheels, endless tins of pencils and brushes, and dozens of tubes of Blockx oil paints — and wondered what it looked like from his perspective. I realised, too late, quite how much of me was on display.

'Do you have time for coffee?' I asked, to distract him. 'I've got some coconut biscuits, too. You could rate them for Grace.'

He started, as if his mind had been elsewhere. 'No, I'm in a bit of a rush. I've got a meeting.' He glanced at his watch. 'And I'm going to be late.'

Our moment had passed. He was just an odd, gawky man with Chinese eyes who happened to know about walkers. I was completely confused and disarmed.

'What's your meeting about?'

'I'm looking for a studio to do some recording. I've been working on the soundtrack for a video game and for once I've got the budget to work with a real orchestra.'

'What do you usually work with?'

'A keyboard and a lot of computers. I'll show you some time if you're interested.'

'That would be nice. I've got a meeting today too, actually. But mine's tonight.'

'That kind of meeting,' he said, raising his eyebrows.

I thought of my client, Klaus Hundertmark, with his glasses and his earnest kindness. 'The client for *Above the Town*.'

'Oh.' Charlie frowned. 'Isn't Amy out with Raul tonight?'

'Is she?' I wailed.

'I'm sure that's what he said. Don't worry. I can babysit.'

'You can't babysit,' I objected.

'Why not? I'll babysit. Around seven? I'll be here.'

'No,' I said.

He put his head on one side. 'What will you do, then?'

'I'll think of something.'

'Don't you trust me?'

No. Absolutely not.

But I did. That's what was so unsettling. Charlie made no sense to me at all, but I trusted him.

'No,' I said.

Charlie followed me downstairs, Raul's guitar in his hand, and at the door he said, 'See you later.'

'No,' I said. 'You won't, because you're not babysitting.'

He smiled and was gone.

Chapter 14

Y FRIENDSHIP WITH SUE had no life of its own outside the lives of our daughters; we shared the school run and our daughters had become best friends. So I was surprised later that afternoon when, instead of dropping Grace off outside the house and watching her in, she turned off her engine and came to the door.

I invited her in and automatically put on the kettle, while the two girls ran upstairs to Grace's bedroom.

Sue shook her head. 'I can't stay, but I need to talk to you about something.'

'Everything okay?'

She frowned. 'Mrs Eldridge called me in when I picked up the girls. Apparently Grace was ill today — or something.'

I felt a lurch in my heart. 'She looked okay just now.'

'No, don't worry, she's fine. It was just at lunchtime.'

'What happened? Why didn't they ring me?' *Why did they tell you instead of me?*

'That's the thing, Cora.' Sue looked uncomfortable. 'They really weren't clear what was wrong. They said Grace, um, fell asleep. But her eyes were open, so they couldn't be sure. They were quite clear it wasn't a fit or anything serious like that.'

'Did they call a doctor?' I asked very quietly.

'No, it was over very quickly. They don't really seem to know what to think. She's very clever, of course, which would be intimidating if she weren't such a completely joyful little thing. I think' — Sue took in a deep breath and looked at me warily — '*they* think that Grace is going through some kind of grief thing. For Peter.'

'A year later?'

Don't sound too sceptical. You might need that excuse.

'I'll be frank, Cora. Eldridge was asking questions I didn't like. Does Grace seem happy to me. Do I know if she's sleeping properly. Do I think the move to London has unsettled her.'

My eyes widened in disbelief. 'You're joking! Why ask you? Why not ask me? It's not as if they don't see me, or have my number.'

'That's what I said. I told her I wasn't comfortable talking to her about it and she should talk to you if she had any concerns. I did say that Grace was a perfect child with a very happy home life,' she added apologetically.

I realised it would look better to appear more worried about Grace's health than my reputation as a mother. 'Thanks Sue. I'll talk to Grace and book an appointment with the doctor. She was a bit feverish last night, but she seemed fine this morning.'

'No problem. You okay for tomorrow?' She turned to call for Ruth.

I stood at the door after they had left, thinking about how to handle things.

Don't panic. She's not you — no one is looking for her so it's probably perfectly fine for her to walk.

But it didn't feel fine.

'What's wrong, Mummy?' asked Grace, skipping down the stairs behind me.

'You,' I said. 'What's this I hear about you popping at school?'

She looked amazed. 'That's what they told you?'

'They *told* me you fell asleep.' Grace continued to look at me innocently. 'With your eyes open,' I said.

She gave up. 'Oh Mum, I was so bored! I know I shouldn't have done it. I wasn't gone for long. But I hate it there. I have told you before. Didn't you ever pop when you were at school, just to get away?'

A shot of acid hit my stomach but I kept my voice calm. 'What exactly is so boring about it?'

'It feels — like I can't breathe. I read everything they give me, but they make me sit there and wait until everyone else has read it too. But when I get stuck, like in maths, which I really don't understand because numbers make no sense, nobody ever waits for me.'

'I find that hard to believe,' I said, for want of anything more intelligent to say.

'I've been reading about the Masai tribesmen in Africa.' Grace was still talking, justifying herself. 'They don't understand yesterday or tomorrow. They only understand now. So if you put them in prison, they die, because they can't imagine ever being free again.'

I paused, imagining a group of Masai running across an open plain, moving inside a perpetual bubble of *now*. 'And that's how you feel in school,' I said. 'I do understand, Gracie. There's nothing I can do about that. But you are going to make life very difficult for yourself, and for me too, if you start popping at school.'

'Sorry.' Small voice.

'Don't do it again.' Pretend-stern voice.

'Okay Mummy.' Smaller voice.

I was about to call Klaus to cancel our meeting, when Amy came in. 'Don't worry,' she said. 'We don't have to go out. I'll get Raul to come here instead.'

'Really? Would you mind?'

'Not a bit. Don't worry, Cora.'

****

I met Klaus at a gallery in the West End, for the opening of a new exhibition that his company was sponsoring.

'These things are easier now, yes?' said Klaus. 'Now you are living in London you must be seen in public. It will help your career.'

'You already take very good care of my career, Klaus,' I reminded him. *Above the Town* was the fourth commission he'd given me in as many years.

We mingled for half an hour, and then got into conversation with a young and arrogant art critic. 'Ah yes,' he said, looking down at me. 'You're the copier. Tell me, do you ever come up with your own ideas?'

'If people wanted mere copies, they would use a photocopier,' Klaus told him. 'Believe me, Mr Henry, what Ms Bloux does is not copying. If it were, we wouldn't be paying her so much. We are looking for the spirit of the original, not merely a reproduction.'

Did Klaus — calm, Teutonic Klaus — *wink* at me? Is it possible he was ... he was...

Of course not, Cora. Good grief, everyone's a walker now. Relax.

It wasn't late when I got home. I came in noisily; Grace would be in bed and I didn't want to take Amy and Raul by surprise.

I went up the stairs to the TV-living room — and froze. Grace wasn't in bed. And Amy and Raul weren't at home.

'Charlie,' I said.

'Hiya, Mummy!' cried Grace, flinging herself on me. 'We've had popcorn, we've watched movies, Charlie and I wrote a song, we've—'

'Grace, go to bed.'

Grace pulled away from me. 'Aw, Mum.'

'Go to bed, Grace.'

She looked into my face, saw I was immoveable, and trailed reluctantly out of the room.

'It's not her fault,' began Charlie, a smile of welcome sliding off his face.

I cut him off. 'What are you doing here? Where's Amy?'

'Raul had a last-minute gig. Amy went with him.'

'You knew I wasn't happy about you babysitting. You knew that.'

Charlie's face suddenly split into a wide, confident grin. 'You'll get over it,' he assured me. 'See, Grace is fine — she's a great girl by the way. We had a fine time.'

I was incandescent with fury. 'How dare you,' I began. 'You knew, I told you why, why things aren't safe, and yet you waltz in here against my wishes—'

Charlie reached out and took me by the shoulders. 'Cora, it's okay. Calm down. You don't have to worry about me. I'm not the enemy.'

I wanted to slap his face; I wanted to cry against his shoulder. 'Go away!'

'Really?' he said, studying my face. 'You're throwing me out?' He saw that I meant it. 'I will go,' he said. 'And I'm sorry you're upset. I really thought you'd be fine with this. Cora, you should save your energy for the things you really have to worry about. I'm not one of them.'

'What do you know about the things I have to worry about?'

He let me go and turned to pick up his sweater from the floor. It was then I noticed the state of the room. There were cushions all over the floor, and three or four loose DVDs lying by the television. There was a jigsaw open and half-finished, and my guitar was taking up the sofa. Two bowls held the remnants of a popcorn feast, and two half-full mugs of hot chocolate sat on the coffee table.

'You've been playing,' I said.

'That's what you do when you babysit eight-year-old girls.' His voice was gentle.

I said, 'What do you know about eight-year-old girls?' but I wasn't angry any more.

'I have a cousin three years older than Grace.'

I pulled a face. 'You have a cousin the same age as my daughter?'

'Three years older. From my aunt's second marriage.'

'That makes me feel weird.'

'You were the child bride,' said Charlie. He was perfectly relaxed.

'I'm sorry,' I said and sat down abruptly. 'I wasn't expecting you.'

'Perhaps it was a liberty,' he admitted. 'I didn't exactly plan it, after what you said. But Amy wanted to go with Raul and I didn't think you'd mind quite as much as you obviously do.'

He was picking cushions off the floor and putting them back on the sofa; he was collecting up the DVDs and putting them back into their boxes.

'I should go and say sorry to Grace. Will you stay and have a drink with me?'

I didn't wait for an answer. I went to Grace and kissed her and tucked her in, and then I ran back down. The living room was tidy again. I offered Charlie wine but he preferred to re-heat his hot chocolate and made me one, too. We sat in the kitchen.

'Go ahead,' he invited.

'Go ahead what?'

'You're trying to feel me out to see if you can trust me. Go ahead. I won't faint.'

'I don't pop,' I said.

'Why not?' he said, a little too casually. 'I've been thinking about this. If this guy is still after you — and I don't for a second think he is — but if he is, then he's going to find you. You've walked; the damage is done. The best thing you can do is learn how to be a good walker.' He smiled beatifically.

'You're just incredible,' I said. 'Breathtaking. Who the hell are you to encourage me to walk? To tell me whether I'm safe or not safe? You know nothing!'

My anger didn't phase him at all. 'I know it's hard for a walker not to walk,' he said amiably.

'Well you should know,' I retorted.

'I'm not a walker.'

I rolled my eyes.

'Go on then,' he said. 'Suss me out. I know you're dying to.'

That evasive flirting again. I popped, leaving my body sitting on the sofa.

I leaned towards him. He smiled and closed his eyes. I put my hand close to his face so I could feel his energy. It was intoxicating. I moved closer, right up against him now. He was easily the calmest, most gentle human being I'd ever encountered. But I knew I wasn't seeing the whole picture; he was only releasing what he wanted me to know. Still, it wasn't possible to fake this...

'All right?' he murmured. His eyes opened and suddenly we were face to face, eye to eye, and a jolt of something new went through me. I backed away, shocked, and snapbacked immediately.

A person can't see a Self. Unless he's a walker. Charlie had just looked directly — hungrily, searchingly — into *me*. Charlie was a walker.

And therefore a liar.

'Cora,' he said, reaching out to me. 'It's all right.'

'What was that?' My body was panting, even though it hadn't been involved.

He sat down; I immediately stood up, wringing my hands.

'I'll go,' he said.

'I think you'd better.'

I followed him to the door. 'I'll babysit for you any time,' he said.

'Charlie, what are you doing?'

'What?'

I squeezed my hands into fists. 'Are we going to be friends or what? Because your mixed messages are beginning to piss me off.'

He put a hand on my arm and was suddenly serious. 'I'm sorry, Cora. We're going to be friends. I'd like to be friends.'

I couldn't help myself, especially after what had just happened. 'Just friends?'

He squeezed my arm.

'It's the walker thing, isn't it?' I said.

He grimaced apologetically. 'It kind of freaks me out. I'm sorry.'

'I freak you out?' I said.

'Not you personally. The whole walker thing.'

I took a step backwards and closed the door in his face.

It wasn't until I was lying in bed that night that I thought, *It was mutual attraction. I don't have to be embarrassed. It was mutual, whatever he says.*

CHAPTER 15

I COULDN'T SLEEP. Hour after hour I lay in bed going over the evening in my head. Charlie was right. Mum would never have wanted me to spend a lifetime being someone I wasn't. I was a walker. That's what I was. And walking wasn't bad, any more than living was bad. There were good walkers and bad walkers, like everyone else. It was a choice. Magda and her body-swapping — all it really proved was that here, as in regular life, there were choices to be made. You didn't have to be a walker to choose to be an idiot.

And on that thought, I popped. I hung by the window for a moment before ghosting outside and drifting over to the trees in the central garden. For a while I gazed at the stars and played around in the branches, and then I grew braver, and I flew across the city feeling the wind speeding by me, watching the light flickering below me.

Eventually, as I picked up speed, the light fell away behind me and I was in open countryside. I could see several threads of motorway vibrating across the landscape in different directions. Once, I sensed a haze of furious red energy and went lower to investigate. A very young man was at the wheel of a black Ferrari, intoxicated by the road and the power at his fingertips and beneath his pedal foot. He drove recklessly, fearlessly, far too fast, without thought.

He's going to crash.

I was in the seat beside him, watching his face. He shook his head, blinked rapidly, and lifted his foot from the accelerator.

I was back in the sky. A tiny movement indicating cattle in the fields below me. A pink glow where two houses nestled like lovers between tall trees. I wheeled around and headed back to the city, fast and faster and faster.

I was going to go home, but the closer I got to the city, the more I felt a strange tugging at my Self. It took me a moment to realise something was calling me. It wasn't the impersonal pull of a universal joy or a tragedy sending a giant flare into the world. This was a pure imperative, not a beacon but a tangible path I had to take; it was unique and personal to me. Something was calling to my Self.

I had no idea what to expect, and I took no decision; I simply followed the path, closer, closer to London, over the river, down over streets, houses, in at a window.

I was in a large, very male room dominated by a sleek black baby-grand piano. There was a leather sofa, and a silver floor lamp that made a high arch across the room. A silver Rolls-Royce angel the same size as me stood in one corner. Behind a screen was the kitchen, and at the back of the room were stairs leading to a mezzanine with black armchairs and piles of books.

There was sound pealing around the room, pouring from the piano, rippling out of the fingers on the keyboard.

Charlie's eyes were closed. His Self was contained within his body, but it had such resonance, was so much the larger part of him as he immersed himself in his music, that it seemed to burn through his skin.

It wasn't the music that had called me to his side across the city and the sky. It was the fierce desire of his Self.

His eyes didn't see me — they remained firmly closed — but his Self knew I was there. The music changed, gentled, morphed into a rippling melody that might have broken my heart if I'd brought it with me.

He was so beautiful, dazzling, real. *He knows I'm here.* But he seemed lost in the music, and for a while I stayed there, lost in him, awed by the way he'd called to me. I had a hazy idea that he'd be able to call me from across the world if he chose to.

At last I floated away, back into the sky, catching the gusts and eddies caused by chimney stacks and the differing roof heights of the buildings.

I came in at Grace's window, hovered over her for a second, then went to my own room and snapbacked.

****

I had intense dreams for several nights in a row. I dreamed I was flying. The flying dream.

Flying dreams were the non-walker equivalent of walking. Walkers didn't need to *dream* about flying; it was completely stupid. And yet here I was, every night in my sleep, one minute running down the street, the next minute leaping into the air, straining for height, reaching, reaching, grasping and finally lifting clear off the ground into the treetops.

No sexual tension there, then.

Grace had been counting down the days to a pyjama party — a sleep-over, she called it — with Ruth. Amy, too, was on a sleep-over, although of a very different kind. She and Raul were going to see a film and, she told me that evening, she was taking her toothbrush, a condom and a clean pair of knickers in her handbag.

I was nervous. 'Are you sure?' I asked.

'Listen to you! You're clucking like a mother hen.'

I sighed. 'I'm sorry. Think of me as your big sister. Are you sure about this?'

'It's my first time,' Amy admitted.

'Well that makes it even more important that you know what you're doing.'

'I do,' she said dreamily. 'Honestly, Cora, I know I'm only nineteen, but if Raul isn't *it,* the real deal, then there's no such thing in the world for me.'

I fervently hoped Raul was as pure and sure as she thought he was. But she was Amy; her instincts were good.

Alone in the house, it occurred to me that the way to snap out of my sleepless nights and strange dreams was to keep walking. With the evening stretching ahead of me and nothing to look forward to except another restless night, I decided to go flying again instead of dreaming about it.

The sister I'd missed and longed for over the years was completely irresponsible, even dangerous. And yet... Something in me had changed. I was a walker again and there was something exhilarating about that. I was through hiding. I wouldn't live in fear any more.

I waited to hear what my Self had to say. Something sardonic, probably, a pot-shot at my fragile courage. But it was silent and ... content. I felt whole.

I popped, did a quick tour of the house and then went out into the street. I took my time. I walked along the pavement, my feet on the ground as if I were in my body, and passed through the railings and into the garden, which hummed invitingly. I was connected to the trembling of eager new shoots, the rustle of birds and scurry of mammals. As in my dreams, I jumped up towards the branches of a tree, reaching, grasping for height. I rose towards the treetop, gained a high branch, perched on it and then, for sheer pleasure, stood on it, leaned backwards and fell into the cradle of air that moulded itself around me.

For a while I drifted along with random currents that fluted me in spirals around the garden, up and down and around with the breath of the plane trees in the little green square. I twisted over onto my belly and did the breaststroke, little froggy movements that created eddies of energy around me, rustling the leaves at the very tops of the trees and throwing out phosphorescent sparks into the night air.

I jacked my body into a surface-dive, leading downwards with my head — a child's slide; a knife through butter — following through with my shoulders, hips, knees and feet. Then I shot upwards, a cork heading for the surface, spiralled horizontally — a corkscrew now — and I giggled. The sound flew out of my mouth in a stream of pure, deep blue.

Calm and happy, I drifted home again and snapbacked.

Or rather, I tried to snapback, but instead of rejoining my body I slammed into a wall of nothing that sent my Self reeling.

My body wasn't on the bed. My bedroom was empty.

Chapter 16

THE SHOCKWAVE THAT BOLTED FROM ME sent the bedcover, books and papers flying through the air.

Where's my body? Where is it?

It was one thing to *choose* to walk, but quite another to find myself walking because I couldn't snapback. I searched the house in a frenzy. Nothing. This was ridiculous. I was wrecking my home: pictures were flying off the walls as I passed, ornaments were smashing into walls and ceilings. Thank God I was alone in the house.

I had to calm down. I flew to the studio and gazed at my copy of *Above the Town*. There was Marc, flying through the sky with his Bella. It was so peaceful, my panic began to ease. Where was he taking her, I wondered for the thousandth time? Where had someone taken me?

No, stupid, not where. Who.

Magda of course. I couldn't snapback because Magda was in me.

What does she think she's doing? What would she do with me? And what was I supposed to do without my body?

The painting started to rattle on its easel.

Calm down! Calm down and think.

Inside my body, Magda would have access to my residual memories. Where would they lead her?

I tried to concentrate. I tried and tried and then goose-bumps crawled up my spine: what if ... what if Charlie and Magda—

Hadn't he encouraged me to walk?

You're being an idiot. There's nothing to tie Charlie with Magda. Magda's being irresponsible and disturbing. But Charlie? He's only ever been nice to you. You like him; you like him a lot.

Once again, my Self was talking at me like we were disconnected. And so we were; but not with my permission.

There was only one way to be sure about Charlie and Magda. The moment I thought it, I was in his flat.

And there they were, the three of them together: Charlie, Magda — and my body. Magda *in* my body.

They were sitting on the piano stool side by side. He was playing something classical, non-committal, in a stilted manner. She was trying to sidle closer to him, impeding the movement of his arms. Soon he wouldn't be able to play at all.

A flash of anger engulfed me and a wind rushed through the room. *Don't let them know I'm here!* I thought and vanished up to the mezzanine.

Charlie stopped playing. 'Did I close the windows?' He rose and briefly disappeared behind the curtains.

I slipped down to the stairs where I could watch them, expecting one of them to sense my presence at any moment.

'Come and sit by me again,' invited Magda.

Charlie looked at her closely. 'Have you been drinking, Cora?'

'I'm such an idiot,' said Magda. The voice might have had the same pitch as mine, but it sounded nothing like me. Not by any stretch of the imagination. And Charlie, surely, had imagination.

Unless he already knows it's Magda in there and not you.

'Forget everything I've ever said,' Magda was purring. 'I just want to be here with you.'

If she was pretending to be me, she'd taken my nascent feelings for Charlie and made too many assumptions. I'd never given Charlie any come-on signal.

Ah, there it was, the sign I'd been hoping for: Charlie looked confused. Not mistrustful, not worried; but definitely confused.

He isn't part of this!

For a moment I was so relieved that my other, more significant problem — the fact that my sister had stolen my body and was pretending to be me — sank into the background. It quickly resurfaced. If Charlie wasn't part of some nefarious scheme with Magda — *honestly, what was I thinking?* — then he had no way of knowing Magda wasn't me. In which case, I was about to be appallingly embarrassed by my sister.

Magda got up from the piano stool and draped herself languidly across the black leather sofa. 'Did anyone mention a drink?'

Charlie frowned. 'I've got a bottle of white in the fridge. I'll be right back.' He went behind the screen into the kitchen and stood still for a moment, his brow creased up. Then he took a bottle of wine from the fridge.

When he turned around, I was behind him — me, my Self. He took a startled step backwards and my finger flew to my lips: *Shush!* I shook my head and looked significantly towards Magda.

Charlie stopped dead. His eyes grew wide and flicked involuntarily between the back of her head — *my* head — and me.

Shush! I gestured again.

Charlie walked deliberately back into the living room and Magda obligingly turned to look at him as he approached. 'Is white all right?' he asked her. 'I've got a bottle of red, too, if you'd prefer.'

'White's just peachy,' said Magda.

I watched him hesitate. 'Right,' he said. 'I'll be back.'

He came back to the kitchen, eyes watching me intently. How could I explain what was happening? He knew about spirit-walking but had he ever come across body-stealing? I'd never heard of it myself until now.

That's not me, I said. I pointed at Magda, shook my head and pointed back to myself. *That's not me, Charlie.*

'Cora?' he breathed, looking intently at me.

Yes! I said. *This is me!* I pointed at myself nodding and then repeated the pantomime to show him that the person sitting on his sofa wasn't me.

'What's going on?'

I shrugged. I couldn't begin to explain that to him without a voice. The stress coming out of me rippled his hair.

Keep calm. Keep calm!

I pointed towards a tower of speakers and a CD player on the bookshelf and Charlie immediately put on some music, taking his time, exchanging small talk with Magda before returning to me.

'We need help,' he said in a low voice, reaching for his phone.

Oh for goodness sake. Who was he going to call — the fire service? Ghostbusters?

'What's that?' called Magda loudly from the other room.

Charlie glanced quickly at me and I shook my head furiously.

'I just remembered something,' he called back. 'A phone call I have to make. Will you give me a minute?'

'Don't be long,' she grumbled.

Charlie looked back at me. 'I don't know who that is out there,' he whispered, 'but it's not you.'

I was flooded with warmth. Charlie wasn't fooled by my sister. Charlie knew the difference between us. He wasn't an enemy at all. Probably.

I wondered again who he was calling. He flipped open his mobile and dialled. 'Joe? I've got a problem — your line of business. I need you here now. Right now.'

My hopes sank. Joe-afro? What could he do to help us?

Charlie hung up. Then he opened the fridge door and whispered, 'Cora?'

I nodded and tried to give him a reassuring smile.

'Who's that on the sofa?'

I mouthed Magda's name, but perhaps he'd never heard of her; I made a gesture of helplessness.

His lips set into a hard line.

Without warning Magda came into the kitchen. Fortunately the fridge door blocked me from her line of sight; I vanished back to the stairs.

'You're taking a long time,' she complained.

'Sorry. Here we are,' he said and drew the cork.

They came back into the living room with the bottle and two glasses. Charlie waited until she sat down and then placed himself opposite her.

'You're too far away.' Magda pouted.

'I can see you better from here,' said Charlie. He couldn't take his eyes off her; I knew now he was studying the differences rather than falling for it.

'Well,' said Magda. 'Isn't this cosy? I don't think we've ever done anything like this before.' She paused and I knew she was searching through my memories. 'Well well! She's not as cold-blooded as she looks,' she said maliciously.

'What?' said Charlie. 'Who's cold-blooded?'

'Nothing,' said Magda. 'How much do you know about me, Charlie?' There was a glint in her eye.

'Enough,' said Charlie.

'Oh, I bet I could surprise you. Did I ever tell you I had a sister? Magda. Dear old Mum sent me to England to be raised by a lovely rich family. I had a great childhood. Magda, on the other hand, was left behind in Canada. She grew up in a children's home.'

A children's home? Magda was sent to distant relatives, as I was. What was she trying to do?

Charlie was saying, 'No, I didn't know you had another sister.'

'Another sister? Oh, you mean what's-her-face. Rebecca. She's not real. Magda's real.' There was an edge to her voice. 'Little old Cora, little old me, I was the special one, of course. But Magda exists alright. In fact, I have a feeling I'm going to be seeing her pretty soon.'

'Really?' said Charlie. 'How do you know that?' He was making conversation, but a thought suddenly dawned on his face. Perhaps he'd guessed who was inside my body.

'Our mother abandoned Magda,' said Magda with mock sorrow. 'It only happens in stories, right?'

'You don't have to tell me anything,' said Charlie.

'Oh but I want to! Our mother was pretty young herself, you see, and she couldn't look after us.'

He did not reply.

'Magda was in a dozen or more foster homes,' Magda went on, a gloating satisfaction in her voice. 'No one would keep her because she's — well, she's a little bit out of the ordinary, my sister. One foster family after another.' She lowered her voice and said, 'Some of the dads in those homes... Well. Magda was always a looker.'

It was hard to stay quiet and listen to this. Her lies were so cruel to our mum. I couldn't think what she hoped to gain by telling them.

Charlie glanced upwards and, because of where he was seated, he saw me sitting on the stairs with my head in my hands.

'Don't tell me any more,' he said roughly. 'I don't want to hear it. Shall I play for you again?'

'If you like,' said Magda, pouting again.

Charlie went back to the piano and began to play, thumping out rolling jazz with an angry energy. Then, as he relaxed, the music slowed down and rippling melodies began to echo around his flat. Magda was captivated despite herself, and so was I.

The doorbell rang. Charlie stopped playing mid-flow and jumped to his feet. He opened the door and Joe stepped inside. Raul was right behind him.

CHAPTER 17

'YOU'RE HAVING A PARTY,' said Joe when he saw Magda. 'Hello there, Cora!' he added, and I watched closely as his eyes narrowed.

Joe sat down immediately next to Magda and kissed her cheek. It looked for a second as if he sniffed her at the same time, but that made no sense. Raul sat too, on Magda's other side. Magda looked a little startled.

'Nice to see you, Cora,' said Raul and I thought he sounded ... amused?

What is going on? I thought. *Why does Charlie think Joe can help?*

They had brought cans of beer with them, and for a while the three boys sat around, comfortably chatting and drinking. I had the awful suspicion that, while she appeared to watch them, Magda was rummaging through the thoughts in my head to see what she could use in this situation.

There was something swirling under the surface of the scene, something I couldn't put my finger on. Every now and then Charlie's gaze flicked up to me, and once I thought Joe's eyes turned my way too — which was impossible.

The evening grew late. Joe, Raul and Charlie were flattering Magda now. They weren't quite flirting, but it was close. She grew lax and careless under their attention. Her Canadian accent was coming through.

Joe leaned close to her and took her hand. 'Cora,' he said insinuatingly. 'You've been holding out on us. Now tell me the truth.' He licked his lips. 'You're a walker, aren't you?'

And before her eyes, and mine, Joe popped. His Self slipped half out of his body, enough that there could be no doubt it had happened, and then he snapbacked. He looked smug.

Magda gave a low whistle. 'Well, fuck me,' she said.

'There are other possibilities,' said Joe, leaning in so he was breathing into her ear, 'that might be just as much fun. The question is, are you one of those trembling stargazers, or are you up for it?'

Magda shook her head in amazement and gave a rough laugh. It was a disturbing sound, coming out of my mouth. 'I had no idea Cora had such interesting friends!' she said, and didn't seem to care at all that she'd blown her cover.

'You're not Cora?' said Charlie. He was pretending to be shocked but I sensed it was no great effort; even I felt a fresh wave of horror wash over me.

'Of course not,' she sneered. 'Like Cora was ever half so interesting. Although I have to say again: who knew she had such interesting friends?'

'Well, she doesn't know *quite* how interesting we are,' said Joe, and they laughed together.

'What about the cool one?' Magda turned towards Raul. He smiled slowly, and then his Self peeped out of the top of his head.

'Damn!' cried Magda, slapping her knees. 'You?' she demanded, jerking her chin at Charlie. He shook his head and she made a dismissive gesture. 'That figures. She likes you best.'

'So, you're not Cora,' said Joe. 'Well whoever you are, you've got guts, I'll tell you that. And I can see you're up for it. So what about it then?' His voice was seductive, hypnotic.

'What about what?' asked Magda with interest.

'Another swap?'

'Oh I didn't swap.' Magda's eyes were unnaturally bright with pride and malice. 'Swapping's fine, in its place, but I prefer to snatch.'

My eyes flicked to Charlie in response to his sharply indrawn breath. But Joe gave a soft laugh.

'Oh you are good,' he said. 'Just found an empty body and snatched it?'

Magda snorted. 'It wasn't quite that opportunistic. I was waiting for Cora and she didn't disappoint. She's a trembler, a stargazer. Always was, even when we were children.'

'You're Magda,' said Charlie with a catch in his voice.

Magda giggled.

'You'd be doing me a great favour if you'd do me a swap,' said Joe. 'We've all had fantasies about getting inside Cora.' He threw Charlie a lascivious grin.

'A fellow junkie!' said Magda with genuine admiration.

I had no idea what was going on. I was still reeling at the discovery that Joe and Raul were walkers. The rest made little sense to me. I glanced at Charlie; his face was very white but otherwise impassive now. Magda paid him no attention at all; she was completely fixated on Joe.

'So,' said Joe, leaning back. 'Want to do it?'

'Oh yes!' said Magda. 'Now?'

For answer, Joe's Self stepped out and stood two feet from his body. In the moments before Magda followed suit, before she would be able to hear him, he said, *Don't move until I say. We're almost there*, and I knew he was talking to me.

Magda stood up and then popped, carelessly letting my body drop half on the sofa, half on the floor.

Ladies first, Joe said to Magda, indicating his body.

Magda's Self snapped into Joe. I heard a curious sound, like a seatbelt fastening, as if she were clicking into place.

'Your turn,' said Magda in Joe's voice, pointing to my body, which Raul and Charlie were lifting carefully onto the sofa.

But Joe's Self didn't snap into my body. It stood there, looking at Magda in Joe's body.

'Feeling chicken?' mocked Magda, but her voice wasn't sure of itself.

Still Joe didn't move.

'She's all yours!' said Magda. She stretched experimentally, as if Joe's body didn't quite fit. 'There's not much room in here,' she complained.

Time to come home, Cora, said Joe, and with a flood of relief I snapbacked.

She'd hurt my body, dropping it like that, and the pollution was so bad I felt sick. But still, I was *me* again. Two pairs of hands helped me to right myself, and then Charlie was on his knees before me, looking anxiously into my face.

'Are you okay?' he asked, urgently stroking the hair from my eyes as Raul propped a cushion behind my back.

'I'm okay,' I breathed, and I let my forehead rest against his, for balance.

'What are you doing?' asked Magda. 'Where did you come from, Cora?'

'You're not very bright for an experienced junkie,' mocked Raul, standing up to let Charlie sit down beside me. 'You should have felt the presence of another Self immediately. We did.'

'She was here all the time?' said Magda. It was funny how different Joe's deep, impeccable voice was now she was using it; it was creepy how wrong it sounded.

I lay back against Charlie; he was holding me close, encircled in his arms as if he were protecting me. I wanted to tell him Magda couldn't hurt me now I had my body back; then I thought better of it.

Something was going on between Joe and Magda. They were staring at each other intently, and I realised she was trying to move and somehow he was stopping her.

'Let go!' she said awkwardly, as if her lips wouldn't work properly. Her arms twitched; she was trying, and failing, to shift them. Joe's whole body jerked and a horrified look crossed its face. 'Stop it!' said Magda. 'I don't like it.'

'But you like other people's bodies,' said Raul. 'What's wrong?'

'I don't like this one,' she said. 'Let go of me!'

Joe's Self watched her with a harsh smile.

'What's he doing?' I murmured.

'I don't know,' Charlie replied.

It was horrible to watch. I felt sorry for Magda. Almost.

'He's still in control of his body,' said Raul with satisfaction.

'With her in it?' I breathed. 'How is that possible?'

'It takes practice,' said Raul. 'Joe's a master.'

Something new was going on now. Magda's eyes stared out of Joe's body with real terror in them. 'Let me out,' she squealed. 'I want to get out.'

'Why the hurry?' said Raul. 'Don't you like it in there?'

'Let me out!' she screamed. 'I don't like it. Let me out!'

Raul leaned towards her and said very distinctly, 'Listen carefully, junkie. If you ever touch one of our friends again, we will make sure you are very sorry. You might think you know a few things but believe me, you don't want to mess with my friend Joe. You're lucky I'm here tonight. Do you understand?' He seemed to remember she couldn't move, because he glanced at Joe's Self and grinned. 'Blink twice if you understand.'

Magda blinked furiously.

'Let her go, Joe.'

Before he'd finished talking, Magda was out of Joe and gone. Joe snapbacked and sat up.

'Yuck, she leaves residue,' he said with distaste, flexing his body and wrinkling his nose.

CHAPTER 18

I ALLOWED MYSELF A FEW MORE MOMENTS in Charlie's arms before disengaging and sitting upright.

'Someone is going to have to tell me what's going on,' I said dazedly. 'What happened?' And then I turned to look directly at Charlie. 'You've got some explaining to do.'

Charlie laughed; it was like the sun bursting through the clouds after a thunderstorm. 'I did tell you I knew other walkers,' he said. 'I just didn't tell you they were the band.'

'The band?' I said, feeling faint. 'You mean, the whole band?' I turned to Raul. '*All* of you?'

'All of us,' said Raul, and he seemed to think something in my face was funny.

'Did you know I was one?' I demanded.

'We've seen you before,' said Joe gently.

I frowned. Something stirred in my memory; a figure in a tree. 'It was you,' I said. 'You were watching from the tree. Was it Magda peeking through my window that night?'

'Not Magda. We haven't seen her before. But there are some mean walkers out there. We heard they were looking for someone so we were watching them.'

'They were looking for me?' I said in a tiny voice.

'Some story about a walker looking for her sister. I take it Magda's your sister?'

'Yes.'

'Well,' said Raul. 'She's playing with a seriously bad crowd. You need to watch out for that lot.'

I stared at Joe and Raul. 'Are you *angels*?' I asked, and I sounded exactly like Grace.

Apparently this was a very funny idea, and they seemed to enjoy it out of all proportion to any humour I could recognise in the circumstances.

'We're walkers,' said Joe at last. 'Same as you, baby.'

'Not quite,' I said. 'Until recently, I hadn't walked for twenty years. I'd never heard of body-swapping or body-snatching. Or that horrible remote-control thing I just saw you do.' I shuddered. 'Tell me again why you were in Gregory Square that night?'

Joe was perfectly calm. 'Walkers are like everyone else,' he said. 'They come in all flavours. It's never a good sign when a group like your sister's goes after someone so openly.'

'You're right. She is after me,' I said at last. 'If she were just looking for me, she wouldn't be stealing my body now that she's found me.' I gazed around at them in something that felt very like panic.

'Why was she looking for you in the first place?' asked Raul. 'Did you lose touch?'

I briefly explained about my mother, and why she'd sent Magda and me away, and how she'd been killed.

When I mentioned the silver hair, Joe and Raul stared pointedly at Charlie. He shook his head almost imperceptibly.

'What is it?' I said, and my stomach lurched.

'Straight silver hair like Reese's?' said Joe.

'Like Reese's,' I said. 'He scared me to death when I first saw him in that bar.'

Joe smiled, but it didn't reach his eyes.

'Reese is safe, isn't he?' I asked, gulping. 'He's a friend, right?'

'Reese?' Raul gave a rough laugh. 'Reese would love you to think he was a mysterious assassin.'

'Trust me,' said Joe. 'He's as safe as houses.'

'You're sure?'

'Quite sure,' said Charlie, turning at last, with the same unconvincing smile that was on Joe's face. 'Cora, think. Why would your sister try to hurt you?'

I shrugged awkwardly. Then I said, 'And you, Charlie?'

'What about me?' He was holding my eye too steadily; his smile was too fixed. Once again, his mind was busy on something else.

'He's safer than any of us,' said Joe quietly.

'I just thought,' I began. 'Things started happening as soon as I met Charlie. And he encouraged me to walk.'

'You should walk,' said Raul seriously. 'A walker that doesn't walk? That'll kill you every time.' He glanced at Charlie.

'I don't think I was in any danger of dying,' I said. And then I stopped because the truth was, a part of me had been dying — had died. I'd been living a half-life for most of my life.

Another thought occurred to me. 'So you, all of you, became my friend to protect me?'

'Hell no!' said Raul. 'We became your friend because we wanted to spend more time with Amy.' He and Joe exchanged a hearty high-five.

'And Grace,' said Joe. 'Don't forget Grace. Although we quite like you, too, Cora.' He put an arm around me. 'We only hang out with people we like. We're not do-gooders, for God's sake.'

'Well, we are,' objected Raul. 'Kind of.'

My mind was working in fits and starts, as though it were throwing off cobwebs. 'What if I hadn't walked into the bar that night? What if Amy hadn't persuaded me to come?' I stopped abruptly. This was beginning to feel like a set-up. 'Does Amy know you guys are walkers? Is she part of this?'

Raul shook his head. 'Amy doesn't know about walkers at all. What? You told her?' He gave a yelp of delight. 'Hell, my life just got a whole lot simpler!'

'But she knows nothing about this?' I persisted. 'You didn't tell her to bring me to the bar?'

'Pure coincidence,' said Joe soothingly. 'We'd have kept a look out for you anyway. You walking into that bar just made things easier. Becoming friends is a bonus.'

'Where is Amy?' I said. 'I thought she was with you, Raul?'

Several expressions crossed Raul's face in quick succession, before he settled on a swaggering nonchalance. 'She's asleep, at my place,' he said. Then he flashed me a smile and a wave of his heady testosterone assailed me. 'I left her a note in case she wakes up while I'm gone. I should get back.'

'You might want to learn that — what did you call it? — that remote-control thing,' Joe told me. 'Your sister Magda is a true-blue junkie. I've seen her type before.'

'And of course,' added Charlie, looking at Joe, 'she has friends.'

I felt a chill down my spine. 'You make that sound like you know who they are.'

He gave me another dead-eyed smile. 'Junkies always have friends.'

'What do you mean by junkie?' I asked. 'What is she addicted to?'

'Danger. Kicks.' Joe looked grim. 'I was one, so I know what I'm talking about.' He shook his head at me ruefully. 'Not all walkers are stargazers, Cora. The wonders of the universe aren't enough for some people. They need the adrenaline rush.'

'And how do they get it?'

'Some do the body-snatching thing, your sister's little party piece. Others learn to control their body from a distance.'

'That was quite something, Joe.' I shuddered. 'Quite terrifying, actually.'

'It is terrifying,' said Joe seriously, 'because one thing leads to another. An undisciplined walker is a serious hazard, and not only to other walkers. And' — he turned to frown at Charlie — 'there are more undisciplined walkers around right now than I've ever seen before.'

'How are they a hazard?' I asked, my stomach knotting.

'Lots of ways,' said Joe.

'Charlie will explain,' prompted Raul.

'No he won't,' said Joe, glaring at Raul.

Charlie rolled his eyes.

'Charlie?' I asked, shifting round to look at him. 'What happened?'

'I once had a problem with a — a walker,' he said. 'Reese and the boys helped me out.' His voice was calm, smooth even, but his lips were tight.

'But you're *not* angels,' I said to Joe, raising an eyebrow.

'Have you ever heard of a junkie angel?'

'He likes to think he's repaying his debt to society.' Raul stretched again and yawned. 'You, my friend,' he said to Charlie, 'are a magnet for trouble. How many times are we going to have to save your butt?'

'I think you'll find that, technically, it was my butt you just saved,' I corrected him.

'Same thing,' said Raul carelessly.

'So,' I began again — there was so much here to understand — 'you two, and Reese? And Ken? You're all walkers. And you formed a band because — ?'

'We like music,' said Joe.

If I'd been less tired by now, I would probably have got the giggles. As it was, Raul's yawn reminded me how late it was, and how sleepy and plain confused I felt. I didn't know how Magda had got my body here, but I was going to have to get it home again.

Charlie said, 'If Amy is at Raul's — yes, thank you, Raul, I got that — then where's Grace?'

'She's staying overnight with a friend,' I said.

'Then there's no one at home. You should stay here tonight, Cora. You're exhausted.'

I searched his face but there was nothing particularly personal in it. He was making a practical suggestion. Nevertheless, my heart began to race.

'And we must be going,' said Joe, rubbing his hands briskly together and rising to his feet.

I rose unsteadily and embraced first him and then Raul.

'You can return the favour by telling Amy how wonderful I am,' suggested Raul.

'I suspect she knows by now,' I said, punching him on the arm.

'On a more serious note,' said Joe, 'you might want to think about protecting yourself. We might not get Magda out so easily if there's another time.'

I shuddered. 'I don't understand what she wants. I need to talk to her.'

'You need to protect yourself,' warned Joe.

'I'll stop walking,' I said defiantly. 'I've done it before.'

'I'd say it's a little late for that,' said Raul.

'It would be stupid to stop walking,' cut in Charlie. 'You have to become a better walker. Better than them. That's the only way you'll be safe.'

'What do you mean?' I stuttered in a small voice. I waved a hand at Joe and Raul. 'How much safer do you really think I need to be?'

'What I really think is that it's time you stopped hiding and started taking responsibility for who you are.'

My throat felt hoarse and I could feel my eyes welling up. 'That's not fair,' I began.

His voice softened. 'Who's talking about fair?'

We were staring at each other as if there were no one else in the room. Joe and Raul hovered awkwardly for a moment and then Joe said, 'Come on, it's not that bad. Charlie just means a walker should be prepared. You know, like a boy scout. Be prepared.'

'You were a scout?' mocked Raul.

'You think black boys can't be scouts?'

'I think idiots can't be scouts.'

I could have kissed them for creating a diversion, however nonsensical. I saw that Charlie, too, was smiling.

'Well,' I said, trying to sound brisk. 'None of this makes any sense. Magda and I were both supposed to be hiding from Mum's killer. I wasn't supposed to be hiding from her. But if that's the deal, anyone have any suggestions about what I do next?'

Charlie nodded towards Joe. 'He can teach you. He taught the others.'

'But not tonight,' said Joe. 'Tonight we sleep.' He threw an envious glance at Raul. 'Or not. See you tomorrow.'

He left, taking Raul with him.

Chapter 19

WHEN THEY WERE GONE, I sat awkwardly on the sofa. 'Thank God you can see Selfs,' I said, scared of the silence. 'And thank God you know Joe and Raul.'

Charlie looked down at me. 'I wouldn't have mistaken her for you for much longer anyway. She didn't sound or feel right.' He grinned. '*She* was all over me.'

'Charlie,' I began, sitting up, feeling embarrassed.

He shook his head, calm and business-like. 'Not another word,' he said. 'I'll take the sofa, you take the bed — shut up, Cora. I'll go and change the sheets.'

I closed my eyes while he was gone, trying not to think. When I opened them again, I was still alone in the living room, and I realised how edgy I was. Every corner held a shadow; every shadow potentially held a Self waiting to leap into my body...

I jumped a mile when Charlie came into the room. He looked intently at me, and then made me a mug of hot chocolate, and toast with Marmite. He told me stories about the college where he taught, and how strange it felt to walk into the staffroom and be a teacher, not a student. He told me the kind of excuses the kids came up with for not doing their homework. He made me laugh, and he stopped me thinking.

And then, when I was completely dozy and relaxed, he led me into his bedroom and pushed me gently onto the bed. After a moment's hesitation he lay down and put his arms around me.

It was good to be small, so I could be cradled like this. We were shoeless but otherwise fully dressed, and Charlie pulled the cover over us and I was warm and cosy. And then I felt his body close to mine, and his breath in my hair, and suddenly I wasn't sleepy at all. My brain disengaged, my heart tripled its pace, my spirit soared ... and then it was quite literally soaring, several feet above our heads, and poor Charlie was left holding what was left of me, a motionless deadweight in his arms.

'Cora?' he said, a note of panic in his voice as he shook me. He looked up instinctively and saw me shooting around the ceiling.

'I'm so sorry,' I said, snapbacking the instant I realised what I'd done. 'Charlie, I'm sorry, I'm so sorry!'

'It's okay, it's okay,' he reassured me. 'Shush Cora, shhhh. Everything's fine.'

'No,' I said mortified. 'I'm an idiot with about as much self-control as ... well, *much* less than Grace.'

He laughed and tightened his arms. And then he stopped laughing and let go of me. 'Sleep, Cora. I'll be on the sofa. Call if you need me.'

He got out of bed, pulled the covers over me and left the room. Astonishingly, I slept.

****

I knew exactly where I was the second I woke up. I tiptoed across the room in case Charlie was still asleep, and then the smell of coffee and toast guided me to the kitchen.

Charlie looked relaxed. 'How did you sleep?' He handed me a mug of coffee.

'Deeply.'

'Good. Do you want to talk about yesterday?'

I was wary. 'Which part of yesterday?'

'Magda nicking your body? Joe and Raul being walkers? I would have told you about that, by the way, but it wasn't my secret to tell.'

I considered for a moment. 'I'm still sorting through it,' I admitted.

'Look,' he said. 'I'm sorry I know, but since I do: Magda said some pretty uncomfortable things about her childhood.'

I pulled a face. 'She was lying. Mum sent both of us to people she knew could be trusted. They were distant family, but they were family.'

'Why were you separated?'

'I always assumed she thought we'd have more chance that way. Her killer would be looking for two girls, not one.'

'And she was sure he would be coming after you?'

'Us,' I said. 'She was very sure he would be coming after us. That's why she told us never to walk, so that he'd never find us. But Magda did walk. She told me when she turned up the other day.'

Charlie went white. 'She walked?'

'She never stopped.'

'And this man with the silver hair didn't find her?'

'She isn't dead, is she?'

He turned away. He was shaking.

'Charlie?'

'Blood sugar,' he said. 'I need sugar in my tea.'

'He never found her, but I just walked once and she found me.' I closed my eyes in despair. 'That's all it took, Charlie. My life was completely walker-free. One brief pop and everything changed. My mother was right to stop me walking all those years ago.' My mind went back into a knot. 'I'm tired,' I said. 'I need to get back to Grace.'

Charlie took a step towards me and then hesitated. 'Do you trust me?' he asked. There was a flash of something on his face, the unhappiness I'd seen before. But there was also a resolution.

'I spent the night alone with you in your flat,' I assured him. 'I think I must trust you.'

'Good. Because I promise you, I'll do everything I can to keep you safe.'

That earnest promise scared me more than anything that had happened so far.

CHAPTER 20

BACK AT GREGORY SQUARE, I took the opportunity to get some concentrated work done. I was in my studio painting feverishly when Amy came into the house, and she took the stairs two at a time to find me. We met on the landing and she threw her arms around me. When she pulled away I looked into her face; she was glowing and happy.

'Hmm. I can see you're okay,' I said.

'I am more than okay! Can I come into your studio? I want to tell you everything.'

I frowned. 'Gory details?'

'Of course not gory details. Well, maybe a few.'

It was strange to realise we'd both just had significant, albeit very different experiences with Raul; Raul had had quite a night. I felt a little uncomfortable, wondering if Amy knew what had happened while she was asleep. I decided it was safer to say nothing for now.

'Cora, I asked him over this evening, and he's bringing the rest of the band. Charlie too. Is that okay? I've bought food, I'll cook.'

My heart gave a leap that had everything to do with Charlie coming. I checked my watch, trying to look casual. 'Sue's dropping off Grace in about half an hour. I'd better get cleaned up.'

Amy went downstairs while I cleaned my brushes and changed out of my work clothes. I looked at myself critically in the mirror and smiled at the sight of my hair, which had spiked around my neck so that I looked like a startled sea anemone. I felt so different these days, so alive. I *ought* to look different.

Raul and the band arrived before I was downstairs, and before Grace came home. By the time I came down, they were in various attitudes of repose around the kitchen, looking as if they had grown organically from the furniture. Two guitars in cases leaned against the radiators.

They rose one by one to embrace me and it was as if I'd known them all my life. Amy was already at the stove; Raul was making salad dressing.

'Charlie will be along shortly,' said Joe. 'He got held up.'

I scanned each of them surreptitiously to see if they looked any different to me now I knew they were walkers. But there was no difference, nothing obvious I'd missed, no signs, no clues — that I would know to look for, anyway.

I was helping to put away the last of Amy's shopping when Grace came running in. I was rather astonished at her *lack* of astonishment at finding her house crowded like this. She absorbed change faster than any person I'd yet encountered. She hugged me tempestuously and then flew to Joe.

'Joe! We're in the Bible!'

'We are?'

'Didn't you know? Really? Let me show you.'

I'd been piling beer bottles into the freezer to speed up the cooling process. I slowly straightened up and stared.

'What is it, Mum?'

Where would I start? 'We?' I said, and my voice was unnaturally high-pitched.

Grace clicked her tongue. 'Mum, I know they're walkers.'

'Who—' I cleared my throat. 'Who told you?'

Joe flashed me a grin. 'I'm not sure your daughter needed telling.'

'That's not fair,' I grumbled. 'I needed telling.' I remembered something and shot a worried look of enquiry at Raul.

'I told her,' he said, smiling possessively at Amy.

No more secrets. A whole roomful of people and everyone knew who *was* and *wasn't*, and everyone was cool about it. It was a miracle.

'So, where did you find us?' asked Joe, looking back to Grace.

'Right at the beginning.' She pulled a piece of paper out of the bag she'd dumped on the coffee table. 'I wrote down chapter and verse. Mum, can I fetch the Bible?'

'You know where.'

She was back within minutes. Curious, I perched over the back of the sofa as Joe thumbed through the opening pages of Genesis to find Grace's reference.

'There!' said Grace. 'Look.'

Joe read. '"Unto Adam also and to his wife did the Lord God make coats of skins, and clothed them."' He had a satisfied beam on his face. 'Clever Grace.'

But she looked disappointed. 'It doesn't sound right. It meant something different last time I read it.'

'You got the flash!' he congratulated her.

'The what?'

'Sometimes an idea leaps off the page and jumps into your head. Once it's in your head, you can't see it on the page anymore.'

'What about the next person that comes to that page?' frowned Grace. 'Isn't there anything left for them?'

'Of course there is. The words are still there, and they still mean the same thing. And maybe the flash will happen again for someone else and maybe it won't.'

'Is it a walker thing?'

'No baby, it's a human thing. Tell me what these words put into your head.'

'Well, before Eve ate the apple, she and Adam were naked. And after they ate the apple, God gave them coats of skins.'

'Yes?'

'Skin,' said Grace, with emphasis. 'Coats of *skin*.'

'What?' said Reese. 'I don't get it.'

Neither did I.

Joe was enjoying himself. 'They were just Selfs before the apple, before they gained knowledge. Once they gained knowledge, they actuated in the physical world. And God, feeling merciful and kind, gave them bodies — skin — to protect them. Because, you know, a naked Self without a body isn't much use to anyone.' He turned back to Grace. 'Did I get it right?'

'You made it sound complicated,' she complained.

'Sorry.'

'Good grief,' I said.

'They were walkers,' Grace was patiently explaining to Reese. 'Before they ate the apple. You told me that, Mum, that everyone starts out as a walker before their bodies claim them. Or they claim their bodies, whichever.'

I was distracted by the doorbell. Well, no, that wasn't quite true. I'd been listening to what was going on with mounting interest. Apart from my mother and sister, I'd never been among walkers who talked about it openly. But at the same time more than half of my entire being was on hold, listening out for Charlie's arrival.

'I'll get it,' said Grace.

He was through the front door and talking to Grace, in the hall, removing his jacket and laughing with her, and then he was across the hall and through the door and finally he was here and I tried *really* hard not to drop the Bible, which had been passed to me for safekeeping, and fly, fling myself on him.

I turned slowly and our eyes locked and then he was talking to someone else, Raul, and I busied myself with the groceries that hadn't yet been put away, delirious just to be in the same room with him. *Oh good grief. I'm acting like a teenager.*

'Look,' Grace said, grabbing the Bible again. 'There's another one too. Isaiah, chapter 62, verse 6.'

Again, Joe looked it up, and read, '"I have set watchmen upon thy walls, O Jerusalem, which shall never hold their peace day nor night: ye that make mention of the Lord, keep not silence."' He raised his eyebrows. 'And you think that's about — the watchers?'

Grace's face creased into a frown of concentration. 'I'm not sure. That one doesn't seem quite right, although it's kind of familiar. Are watchers the same as walkers? Because I'd like to be a watcher.'

'You can't be a watcher, Grace,' said Reese. 'You've got a body. And you're nice. You make people happy. Look up *pointless* in the dictionary and you'll find *watcher*. Anyway, watchers aren't born, they're made.'

'At first I thought they were angels,' said Grace, wisely ignoring him and addressing herself to Joe. 'But then I looked again and realised they were like us. Is it us?'

'Well,' said Joe. He was shifting around in his seat and I looked up to listen to whatever it was that made him feel so uncomfortable. 'You're a walker, baby, not a watcher. Watchers are a bit different. Having said that, most people, including most walkers, think watchers are a myth anyway.'

'They should be a myth,' snorted Reese. 'I mean, what's the point of watching if you can't change anything?'

'Don't they at least influence their environment?' I asked. Then I raised my eyebrows and smiled.

'What is it?' asked Charlie.

'I was remembering,' I said. 'Walker mythology. My mother told us the stories every night before we went to sleep.'

'You never told me,' said Grace, frowning. She'd taken up residence beside Joe, with her hand on his knee, as if they were family.

'Let's tell her now,' suggested Ken.

I looked at him in surprise; I'm not sure I'd ever heard him talk before.

'Ken likes the old stories,' scoffed Reese.

Chapter 21

'In the beginning,' said Joe, 'God created the heaven and all the worlds. The worlds were without form, and void. And everything was peace and harmony.'

'That's the Bible,' objected Amy.

'Close,' said Ken, 'but not quite.'

'Shush,' said Grace, listening intently.

'But even heaven gets dull, and all things need context. So God created time, and matter, and he incarnated a whole universe of wonders. He made light and darkness, and the deep blue waters and the great blue sky. He made land, and grass, and animals, and finally he made people.'

'But he didn't incarnate the watchers,' said Ken eagerly.

'He couldn't be bothered,' said Reese. 'They weren't worth the trouble.'

'No,' said Joe, ignoring Reese, 'he didn't incarnate the watchers. He kept them as spirit creatures and gave them a special job: to watch over the development of humans and make sure they stayed safe.'

'What does incarnate mean?' said Grace, wide-eyed.

'It's the same magic as the skins,' said Joe. 'It means giving spirit things a material form.'

'Like my spirit incarnated into this body when I was born,' said Grace, and I felt faint because I'd never told her any of the stories, and yet she understood everything.

'So the watchers did their job,' continued Joe. 'For a while. But it was hard to just watch. Because once they entered the physical world, humans forgot how to do any of the clever stuff. They went stumbling around the place with no clothes and no tools, babbling and living like the animals. So eventually the watchers reached out and gave them a hand. They taught them all sorts of valuable things like painting...'

'And killing each other,' said Reese.

'...and poetry...'

'And killing each other,' said Reese.

'... and pottery and tool-making and — shut up, Reese — the really big one. Know what it was?'

'Fire!' yelled Grace.

'Clever girl,' said Joe.

'Ten minutes 'til dinner,' said Amy, who had been listening as she stirred and chopped and clattered pans.

'And that's the story of the watchers,' said Joe, and there was instant uproar.

'And the rest!' yelled Reese, drumming his fists on his knees. 'She deserves to know the rest!'

'Cora?' said Joe.

I shrugged; the stories were better when my mother told them to me, but Joe wasn't doing a bad job of it.

'Well,' said Joe, 'human women can be pretty attractive, Grace. Look at you. One day you're going to be a cracker.' Grace hid her face in the cushions. 'And don't think the watchers hadn't noticed how cute human girls were, because they had.'

'So,' said Reese, butting in, 'not only did they disobey God by teaching us all the stuff we were supposed to work out for ourselves, but then they started bonking our womenfolk.'

'Mating!' shouted Joe. 'For God's sake, Reese, Grace is eight. Mating, Grace. You know what that means, right?'

Grace giggled. 'Of course I do. What, so the watchers started mating with human women? Ooh.' Her eyes grew wider. 'Did they make babies?'

'Yes they did,' said Ken, as if the story had finally reached the punchline he was waiting for.

'How?' said Grace. 'If watchers weren't incarnated, they had no body. So how do they mate? And what would their babies be like?'

'It's a story, remember,' I cautioned.

'Of course it's a story,' said Joe. 'Don't worry about the details. So the watchers mated with the cute human girls and a new race was born. The nephilim!'

I finished laying knives and forks and had started out on the glasses when I noticed that Charlie had been very quiet. He looked preoccupied. 'Do you know these stories?' I asked him. 'Have you heard them before?'

'Once or twice,' he said, smiling tightly.

'Nephilim,' repeated Grace. 'What does that mean?'

'Giants,' said Joe. 'Watchers are huge, Grace. They're long and thin and they can be as tall as trees — mountains, even, if they feel like it. So when their offspring were incarnated inside human women, what do you think happened?'

'Giants!' yelled Grace, and she began dancing around. 'Giants like Goliath!'

'Really?' said Amy, who was energetically mashing potatoes. 'I've heard of Goliath. Get to the table, everyone. Grub's up.'

There was a rumpus as Reese and Ken raced for the table. Joe lifted Grace over one shoulder and, under her direction, deposited her in her usual seat. The rest of us squeezed in around her. Amy started passing Charlie bowls heaped with food, which he put onto the table, and Raul handed round plates like he was dealing cards. For a while the story was lost in a frenzy of passing dishes and filling plates and mouths.

'Yum,' said Raul, with his mouth full. 'You're a good cook, Amy.'

She was; it was one of her many charms.

'I love you, Amy,' said Grace, also through a mouthful of food; she glanced at me surreptitiously, knowing I couldn't tell her off for it without telling Raul off too. 'I think you should stay with us forever and ever.'

'I think so, too,' I said.

'I think so three,' said Reese, 'and we'll come for dinner every night.'

'What's wrong?' said Charlie, watching my face, and for a moment I was caught in the undertow created by his proximity.

'Mummy?' demanded Grace, protective and worried at the same time.

'Nothing, sorry.' I shook my head.

'Are we making too much noise?' asked Reese, looking unapologetic.

'I love the noise,' I assured him. 'I was thinking how different this is from the way I grew up — no, don't misunderstand. I love this. This is what all mealtimes should be like. No manners, lots of noise—' I broke off, feeling I'd been rude.

'It's all right,' said Charlie.

'Our parents were elderly,' I said. 'And everything had to be properly done. It was all a bit rigid.'

'Sounds awful,' said Reese and Joe thumped him.

'It was fine,' I said. 'But this is more fun.'

'I want more stories,' said Grace. 'What happened to the giants? Where did they go?'

'Oh, they're still around,' said Ken and Joe gave *him* a thump.

'Stop it, Joe,' I said. 'Tell the stories.'

'I don't like these stories,' said Charlie.

I turned to him in surprise, but his face was curiously composed. 'Why not?' I asked.

'They're sad,' he said. 'I find them sad.'

'Well,' said Joe firmly. 'Every walker should know their own myths. Listen up, Grace. The nephilim went round the earth and caused a lot of trouble, because they were bigger and wilder and noisier than other humans. There are lots of stories about the trouble they got up to. But the real problems began when they had lived out the normal course of their lives. You see, their mothers were human but their fathers were watchers — spirits, remember? And spirits don't die.'

'Watchers live forever?' asked Grace. 'Forever and ever?'

'Too right they do. And the nephilim had watcher dads and human mums. So their bodies grew old and died like everyone else's, but their spirits went on forever.'

'Also like everyone else's,' put in Ken.

'Sure, but the nephilim spirits were bound to the earth, because of what their fathers had done.'

'So they were left on earth, but without bodies?' breathed Grace.

'Yup. Half-human, half-watcher, unable to die. Pretty scary huh?' said Reese.

'It's a story, Grace,' I reminded her.

'Of course it's a story,' said Joe. 'It's the mother and father of all stories. This is where all the other stories begin.'

'What other stories?' asked Amy. I had a strong suspicion she and

Raul were holding hands under the table.

'Well, ghost stories, to start with.'

'See, Grace,' I said. 'I told you there was no such thing as ghosts.'

'I don't see why a giant without a body is any less scary than a ghost,' said Grace pragmatically.

'And vampire stories,' said Joe.

I frowned. 'Vampires? How does that work?'

'Well, when the spirits of the nephilim had outlived their own human bodies, they started stealing bodies from living humans.'

'And I think that's where we wrap it up,' I said, rising abruptly. 'I must say, guys, my mother never told me that kind of story. I think you're making it up.'

'Of course we are,' said Joe.

We cleared the table and Amy served generous dollops of ice-cream for dessert.

'So, I understand the nephilim are just a story,' said Amy. 'But what about watchers? Are they real?'

'They're both in the Bible,' said Ken. 'The giants and the watchers.'

'Really?' she said. She turned to me. 'Is that true?'

'Oh well, if it's in the Bible it must be true,' scoffed Reese.

'Don't look at me.' I shrugged. 'I only know the walker myths as bedtime stories. I don't know the Bible at all.'

'So why do you have a copy of it in the house?' asked Reese.

'Everyone has a copy of the Bible,' said Amy.

'I don't.'

I noticed a dumb show going on between Joe and Ken. Both of them kept glancing warily at Charlie but in the middle of everything, I noticed they were watching *my* reactions really, *really* carefully.

'The watchers are real,' said Ken at last.

'Well,' said Joe. 'Only technically. Only in so far as a watcher watches. That's his job.'

'Yeah, like they ever stuck to *that* job description,' snorted Reese. 'That was the whole problem in the first place.'

'How do you know so much about them?' asked Grace. 'Are you one?'

'Hell no!' said Reese indignantly, as Joe and Raul fell about laughing.

'Look, I've got a body. That's your clue, Grace. Although—'

'Enough,' said Charlie.

'I think I believe in watchers,' said Grace. 'They sound real. What are walkers for? A watcher watches, but what does a walker do?'

'A walker walks,' said Charlie. I had to swallow hard every time he looked at me. I did it now, and instantly diverted my attention to my glass, relieved no one could see inside my head. 'Why?' he asked Grace. 'What did you have in mind?'

Grace shrugged. 'We should have a purpose. A special area of responsibility.'

Again, there was a subtle exchange of glances between the boys. 'What's going on?' I said.

'Nothing's going on,' said Reese with a yawn. 'The boys are about to come over all righteous.'

'I think Grace is right,' said Joe. 'No point in flying unless you fly awake.'

'I wish I was a watcher,' said Grace, her eyes going from face to face, watching for a reaction.

'Ah, but what would you watch for, if you were a watcher?' said Reese, wiggling his eyebrows up and down.

She giggled at him, but answered earnestly. 'I would watch because that would be my job. I would notice everything important that happened in the world. Someone has to notice it and if that's not a watcher's job, whose job is it?'

'That's really good logic,' said Ken.

Reese stood up. 'Oh shoot me now. Can I leave the table?' He stood up and resettled his bulky body in my suddenly tiny-looking sofa. 'Enough already. I walk because I can. That's it. Apart from that, I'm a regular bloke. I play guitar in a band, for God's sake. There's no job description to being a walker.'

'Which is why you—' began Raul.

'Don't!' said Reese loudly. 'I patrol with you guys because you're my friends. That's it.'

'Uhuh,' drawled Raul and Grace giggled again.

'You *patrol*?' I repeated, startled.

'I told you, Joe's the man who can,' said Raul. 'The rest of us just do as we're told.'

'I'd like to see *that*,' retorted Joe.

'What do you patrol? Who do you patrol?' I demanded; and then I remembered Joe in the tree outside my house.

'We deal with trouble where we find it,' said Joe smoothly. 'Just like you told Grace.'

'We hunt adrenaline junkies!' gloated Reese, his eyes lighting up.

'What's that?' asked Grace.

There was a sudden hush around the room.

'Not all walkers behave as they should,' I said.

'How do they behave?' She had her persistent face on.

Joe looked at me and I shook my head. He pulled a face that meant she had to know sometime, but I shook my head again. I needed to navigate the mysterious world of rogue walkers properly myself before I was willing to pull Grace into it.

'I'm sorry Amy,' I said, catching sight of her face across the table. 'All this talk about walkers. You must be bored stiff.'

'Oh I am,' said Amy. 'This is all I hear, day in and day out, walking walking walking. Don't you have any other conversation?'

Reese gave a shout of laughter. 'She's funny, your girlfriend,' he commented to Raul and then added plaintively, 'How come I never get a girlfriend?'

We cleared away the table, with everyone helping, and then Raul and Reese picked up guitars and we sang Beatles songs until I noticed Grace fast asleep against Charlie's shoulder.

'May I carry her up?' he offered.

He lifted her gently, as if she weighed nothing at all, and I led the way to her room. He put her on the bed and leaned over to give her a peck on the forehead. Then he straightened and looked at me, and I felt him as if he'd reached out and stroked me on the cheek. The breath caught in my throat and it was a relief when he turned and left the room. Grace stirred as I helped her into her pyjamas.

'Mum?'

'Yes, honey-pie?'

'I'm glad you like Charlie.'

'Of course I like Charlie. I like all of them.'

'But especially Charlie. He likes you too.'

'And what makes you say that?' I asked, trying to sound casual.

'You both go pink when you look at each other.'

Was she talking about my flaming face or my aura — or, indeed, the colour of the words I spoke to him? I didn't ask, and she didn't offer. *She said he went pink too.*

'I like Joe and the walkers,' she said drowsily.

'Me too.'

'And I love Amy.'

'Me too.'

'Our life is better now, isn't it? I'm glad we're walkers, Mum. And I like being with other walkers.'

'Me too,' I said.

'I wonder why Charlie wants us to think he isn't one,' she said groggily.

'Because he isn't one,' I said. 'He can see Selfs, that's all.'

She gave me one of her infuriating, wise looks, and then I laid her back down and covered her over.

'Night night Mum,' she mumbled. 'Fly awake.'

Downstairs, the bright light of the kitchen made me blink. 'Does your band have a name?' I asked Joe.

'We've never found a good one. Up to now we've called ourselves The Band.'

'Grace just called you Joe and the Walkers.'

Joe beamed but there was a chorus of disapproval from the others.

'You mean Raul and the Walkers!'

'That would be Reese and the Walkers.'

'Why Reese? Is that even a proper name?'

'Guys,' I said, 'Grace loves you all being here. Me too. Neither of us wants to wait around wondering if you're ever going to turn up again. Would you, um, do you want to come over for dinner every week? Well it doesn't have to be *every* week. Or even Saturdays. It could be any evening. If you want. It's not an obligation or anything...' My voice trailed off, leaving me thoroughly embarrassed.

'Sounds great!' boomed Reese.

Ken nodded vigorously.

'Excellent,' said Joe, looking hugely satisfied. 'You have no idea how nice it is to hang out in a proper home, for a change.'

'You don't live in proper homes?' I asked.

'Not even close,' said Raul. 'Charlie's the only one of us that's got his act together in that department. The rest of us live like bums.' He sounded proud.

Joe took up one of the guitars and began to pluck out a tune. 'Apart from pure pleasure,' he said, 'we have to start teaching you how to take care of that unpleasant sister of yours.' He glanced at me quickly. 'Sorry.'

I shivered at the thought of Magda.

Reese picked up another guitar and strummed a background rhythm to Joe's plucking and Charlie began to sing. At the sound of his voice I shivered again, in a different way.

One minute you're half asleep, moving from one day to the next like a deaf mute; and the next you're bolt upright, surrounded by new friends and the possibility of a whole new way of looking at life.

I shook my head in wonder.

Chapter 22

'NOW YOU'RE SURE YOU'RE HAPPY with this,' I said fretfully.

'Why wouldn't I be?' Charlie sighed.

'You'll be bored.'

'The only difference between this night and any other is that you'll be sitting beside me while I read.'

'Do you want me sleeping?'

He thought about it and then nodded with a little grimace. 'Yes please. I don't fancy the vacant staring-eyes thing.'

My stupid heart gave a flutter at his smile. 'Okay, okay,' I said, pretending to be grumpy. 'I'll close them. Grace is asleep and she isn't likely to stir.' I still stood there, fidgeting. 'Are you sure you're up for this?'

'Cora, really, what's the worst that could happen?'

'I don't know,' I said bleakly. 'Magda kind of catches me off my guard. I don't know what she's capable of, but if I feel her inside me again I swear I'm going to vomit. And if she hurt you or Grace and I wasn't here—'

'How could she possibly hurt us?' he asked. 'Grace is completely in control of her walking. You said so yourself. She won't drift off while she's sleeping. And Magda can't hurt me because I *don't* walk. So stop worrying. I won't let anything happen to you, Cora. Now get on with it.'

He took my hand and led me to the sofa. I sat down beside him, and he kept my hand firmly in his. It felt wonderful. Skin against skin, a perfect fit.

'Shall we sit here instead?' He sounded amused.

I shot him a look, closed my eyes, and popped.

'Good luck,' he said, and I was gone.

****

I was having my first lesson with Joe and the band. Amy had gone home to visit her family but even if she'd been there, Joe had insisted that only Charlie could stand as my guard, because at least he would see Magda coming.

'Yes, but he can't do anything about it!' I'd objected.

'Not the point,' said Joe. 'Magda will know she's been seen, and that should be deterrent enough until we can get you trained up.'

Which is why Charlie was sitting in my house minding Grace and my body.

Joe, Raul, Reese and Ken were waiting for me in the shadow of some trees on Primrose Hill. It was twilight and would be dark soon, but the street lights along the path that traversed the hill were already on.

'Hi Cora. Bang on time. Well done.'

Joe popped and came towards me. I was interested, and secretly rather appalled, when his body remained standing with the others. To a spectator, they were a group of four guys having a chat.

How do you do that?

That's what you're here to find out.

But I left my body with Charlie.

You don't need your body this time. This time I want to show you a few things.

Raul popped. There was no outward change to the group of four.

Hi Cora!

You make that look easy, Raul.

Raul chuckled and, for added effect, his body moved in time with his laughter.

Now you're creeping me out.

Ken came next.

'How come I get to play bodyguard?' grumbled Reese.

Hello Cora. Did you see what I did?

No. Did I miss something?

Watch again.

Ken snapbacked and then popped again, very slowly rising out of his body through his head.

Watch closely, murmured Joe.

No. I don't see anything special.

Again, Ken. The fingers, Cora. Watch the fingers.

Ken did it again and I watched his fingers and this time I saw it. There was a thin stream of energy, like a thread from a spider's web, hardly visible even in the spirit world. It joined Ken's two halves; his body and his Self were holding hands via this tiny silver thread.

I adjusted my eyes, my expectations, and sent my senses out to the space between Joe and his body; there was the thread. Same with Raul.

Got it!

That was fast, approved Joe.

'She got it already?' wailed Reese. 'Shit. It took me hours.'

Raul grinned. *It took you so long because you're a moron, Reese.* He stuck out his tongue.

'Don't forget I'm guarding your body, man,' said Reese, smiling sweetly

I was shocked. *Can Reese hear us? Can you teach me that?*

There are some things that can't be taught, Cora, said Joe. *Reese is just guessing from our faces. Sound travels into the spirit world, not from it. Now, concentrate, fellas.* Joe drifted slowly away from the group under the trees. The thread stretched. *Watch my body.* His body lifted its arm and waved at me.

I don't like it!

Focus, Cora. I'm not doing anything unnatural. It's just a different level of control. Now watch. I'm going to stand behind this tree. Watch my arm.

Again, Joe's body lifted its arm, but instead of the slick, natural movement of earlier, this gesture was sluggish; Joe looked drunk.

What's wrong?

I've lost the direct line. Can you see? The thread has to go through the tree to connect me with my body, and that slows things down — interrupts the signal, if you like.

Can't it bend around the tree?

No. The thread can only travel in straight lines. It has to go through anything that comes between you and your body.

It's easiest to keep the line uninterrupted by staying above, said Raul darting above his own head and waving his arm at me furiously. *But look, if my line's interrupted, I can't move at all.* His Self shot behind the treetops. I watched his body; there was no movement, scarcely even a gesture of the fingers, let alone the whole arm.

So how come Joe can do it and you can't?

It takes time and practice, said Joe easily. *With most walkers, the connection will break completely if something comes between the body and the Self. Even an experienced walker can be separated if you take him by surprise.*

Who showed you?

My dad.

Your dad was a walker?

Most walkers come from walkers, Cora.'

Your dad never told you it was dangerous to walk, and you should stop?

Why would he tell me that? Joe pulled a face.

Don't think every walker can do remote control because they can't, said Ken. *Joe taught me everything I know. I was a trembler before I met him.*

What does that mean: trembler? I asked. *I've heard you use it before.*

Trembler, said Raul in a mocking voice. *Also known as a stargazer. They're the walkers that spend their time gazing in wonder. They believe it's their job to witness. You know, a falling tree makes no sound unless there's someone there to hear it.*

Technically they're right, said Ken. *The sound waves don't actuate until they hit an ear drum. Tremblers believe the earth can't properly actuate unless it's properly witnessed.*

They're bonkers, in other words, said Raul.

It's a loose term, said Joe peaceably. *Mostly a trembler is someone who doesn't put their walking to any practical use.*

So Grace was right, I said, ignoring Raul's attitude. *We're supposed to have a purpose.*

There's no right or wrong about it, said Joe. *Walkers have no more or less responsibility for the wellbeing of the world than any other human.*

'Are you about done?' whined Reese. 'I'm bored and it's getting cold.'

We're not finished, are we? I said, panicked. *You haven't shown me how to do anything yet.*

Relax. This is only the first lesson.

But how do I make that silver thread thing happen?

You'll work it out. Can you wiggle your ears?

My ears? No! Why?

Can you curl your tongue?

Yes.

Can you tell me how you do it?

Um. No.

That's how we make the silver thread.

I had to consider this. *You mean it's instinctive?*

I mean, once you know about it, you think it into existence.

That sounds easy, I scoffed.

It just takes practice.

When?

We'll have a go at your house. I'll give you a call.

Okay. Thanks, Joe.

Hang on. One more thing.

I noticed that Raul and Ken immediately snapbacked and, with Reese, turned towards us expectantly, broad grins on their faces.

What? I asked suspiciously.

Stay very still. And don't be scared, okay? Joe drifted towards me. *Don't freak. It's as natural as breathing.*

He came up in front of me. Very cautiously, with a small smile on his face, he leaned his head towards me. Our Selves were almost touching … they were touching. I felt an extraordinary sense of Joe deep in my Self, a calm, authoritative kindliness. It was like a kiss, the kiss of a father, or an older brother. There was no electricity. It wasn't like my body touching Charlie's, for example. I'd touched Grace's Self, of course, but Grace was a part of me whether we were separated or not. This was different. It was odd … but nice.

See you tomorrow.

'Aw. I thought she'd go crazy,' grumbled Reese.

'That doesn't mean you should ever try it,' cautioned Raul, thumping him.

'She likes me as much as she likes Joe!'

'No one likes you as much as they like Joe.'

I flew home, grinning, taking my time — and fell back in shock the moment I entered the kitchen. My body was still on the sofa where I'd left it, still holding Charlie's hand, but my eyes were wide open and watching me.

Chapter 23

F OR THE SHORTEST MOMENT I was so cold and scared I began to dissolve. *No!* I screamed and the air stirred up my body's hair and Charlie's.

'It's okay, Mummy,' said my body, half rising, and at the same time Charlie leaned across it like a shield crying, 'It's Grace, it's Grace!'

Grace in my body? Where was hers? I rippled with fear.

My body's eyes closed and Grace separated. *Hang on a minute, Mum.* Her Self shot up through the ceiling and a moment later she came down the stairs and into the kitchen, her hair tousled and one cheek red where she'd been lying on it. 'See, I'm here. Everything's all right.'

'Do you fancy joining us?' asked Charlie, holding his hand towards my body like an invitation, and I realised I hadn't moved.

I snapbacked. When Magda had been inside my body, I'd felt tainted, physically sick and unhappy. This time it had been Grace, and all she left behind was warmth and love. But still, someone had been in me; it felt odd.

'What on earth has been happening here?' I demanded.

Charlie gave me a warning frown; I sounded hysterical.

'Grace,' I said, in a calmer tone. 'Come here darling and tell me what you've been up to.'

Grace cuddled up beside me. 'Magda came,' she said, yawning. 'We couldn't think of what else to do.'

'I don't understand,' I said slowly. 'How did you separate and get into me in time? Weren't you sleeping?'

Charlie said, 'I managed to delay Magda for a while, before clever Grace came to my rescue.'

'He was popping, Mummy!' said Grace giggling. 'You should have seen Magda's face! Charlie was magnificent.'

'You *walked?*' I said, raising my eyebrows at him in astonishment.

'Told you so,' said Grace triumphantly.

'I was going to jump in and save you,' said Charlie in a self-mocking tone.

I felt sick. 'You were going to jump into me? That would have left *your* body open for Magda.' My voice cracked as I reached the end of the sentence.

'Yes, I know that now. At the time all I could think about was stopping her getting into yours. And then Grace came in like the cavalry.' He ruffled her hair.

'It was quite funny,' said Grace contentedly, snuggling into my shoulder. 'Magda was standing there watching, and Charlie's Self couldn't seem to make its mind up. It kept peeping in and out of his body like hide and seek. In-out, in-out. Magda couldn't take her eyes off him.'

'I was doing my best,' said Charlie.

'And Magda just stood there and watched?'

'I think your charming sister was enjoying the spectacle.' There was a hard note in his voice now.

'I knew she wouldn't get in *my* body,' said Grace. 'So I stepped into yours while she was distracted.'

I hugged her tightly. 'You're so clever. Both of you. You're so clever.' There were tears in my eyes, and I looked over Grace's head and mouthed 'Thank you' at Charlie.

He held my gaze and all I could think was: he walked to protect me. He changed his whole way of being — or tried to — in the twinkling of an eye, without thinking of consequences, to protect me.

I took Grace to bed; she was asleep before I'd finished tucking her in. I sat beside her for a few minutes, watching her peaceful face, marvelling at her presence of mind and her courage.

When I came back to the living room, Charlie put a glass of whisky in my hand.

'I really don't drink whisky,' I told him. 'I only have it in the house for when Hugh visits.'

'It'll do you good. You should take a sip.'

It burned all the way down, but it braced me too, as he knew it would.

'Magda doesn't drift, like you do,' he said. 'She displaces — one minute there, the next minute, poof, gone. It's not nice.'

'Did she cause any trouble?' I looked around for any disturbance.

'No, nothing. It was as if she enjoyed what Grace did. She and Grace stared one another down. Magda smiled when she realised she was beaten.' He pursed his lips and frowned. 'Grace was absolutely confident Magda wouldn't take her body.'

I took another sip of whisky; it really was horrible stuff, but useful. 'There are some rules you understand without being told.'

'Rules?'

I was still grimacing over the whisky. 'It's a visible restriction. Children's energy is different. Seriously. Breaking into a child? That's pure evil.'

'And she isn't?'

'No,' I said. 'I don't think Magda has ever been evil. She's just angry. She was an angry child, too.'

'I don't think you should count on rules like that,' persisted Charlie.

The last drop of whisky was vibrating in the tumbler in my hand, and I realised I'd started to tremble. *Shock,* I thought. *What have I got to be shocked about? I've done nothing brave tonight.* Nevertheless, I was trembling more and more violently. I put the glass carefully down on the table.

'It's okay,' murmured Charlie. He seemed to be struggling with himself, and he sat on his hands. But still, I felt his intention, his wish to comfort me; it wrapped itself around me despite his wilfully incapacitated arms.

We were safe for now, but the enormity of my problem was beginning to make itself very clear. Now she'd found me, Magda wasn't going to leave me alone.

'If I walk,' I said out loud.

'If you walk what?'

'Magda can only hurt me if I walk.'

He gave up sitting on his hands and put an arm around me. 'We'll work it out,' he said.

Our sides were touching and I was warm and heavy with whisky. I turned my face towards him and he turned too, and then I leaned in and his lips were there, waiting for mine. It was the softest, sweetest, most exquisite *touch* in the world. Neither of us moved, and then, as I gave a sigh and my lips parted, he pulled away.

My eyes flew open, probably revealing my disappointment, but he'd already turned away. 'I'm sorry,' he said. 'I have to go.' He couldn't get out of my house quickly enough.

It was mutual. I knew it was mutual. *Maybe I'm doing something wrong.* Was I doing something wrong? I knew I wasn't good at inviting people in, but it wasn't as if I hadn't made my feelings obvious.

I ate chocolate, lots of it, and drank coffee, and lay awake half the night feeling faintly ridiculous.

Chapter 24

I RANG JOE THE NEXT MORNING and told him what had happened with Magda.

'Wow.'

'I know.'

'It's like she's trying to attract as much walker attention as possible. What did you do to make her so angry.'

'I have no idea,' I said.

'I'll come over. Show you a few more things.'

'Tonight?'

'Yeah. I can do tonight. I'll see who else is free. You don't need all of us.'

I rang Charlie.

'Are you okay?' he said, immediately on the alert. I wished I could tell him that his concern for my safety made me feel worse.

'I'm fine. We're having another session tonight.'

'Is Joe worried?'

'He thinks I should know how to protect myself.'

'Can I come too?'

'I was ringing to ask if you would,' I admitted.

I heard his low laugh. 'I'll come straight from work.'

Now I was worried. 'Am I stopping you from doing anything else?'

'I shall have to cancel a date. It's no problem.'

I felt sick. Charlie. On a date. With someone else.

What do you think — he never goes out with girls? Idiot.

'I'm sorry,' I mumbled.

'Cora, I'm kidding. See you later.'

And then I felt stupid.

****

Joe arrived at five and sat with Grace while I made dinner.

'This is pretty advanced stuff,' he told her, turning over her copy of *To Kill A Mockingbird*.

'I know,' she replied matter-of-factly. 'But *this* is what I have to read at school.' She held up a copy of a children's book, a reader with large font. 'I told Mrs Eldridge it's the spring equinox tomorrow morning, and this is what she gives me to read.'

Joe gave a yelp of laughter. 'Got any more homework?'

'I've got some science.'

'Bring it on, baby.'

I brought him a glass of wine. 'Thank you for helping her.'

He snorted. 'She doesn't need my help.'

Amy arrived with Charlie five minutes later.

'Look who I picked up on the underground,' she said, coming through the door. She kicked off her thigh-high boots and then kissed us all.

'Is anyone else coming?' I asked, before serving up.

'Ken might swing round later.'

'Raul's on his way,' said Amy.

After dinner Amy stacked the dishwasher and took Grace to watch television upstairs, and Joe and I got down to work, Charlie quietly observing from a stool at the kitchen counter.

'Right,' said Joe. 'Sit beside me.'

I sat on the sofa beside him and he immediately popped, beckoning me to follow suit.

Look.

I looked at the silver thread in his hand; my own hand was empty.

Snapback, and then try again. Really concentrate.

But I don't know what to do.

Think really hard about what you want to achieve. The key is to remain attached to yourself. Leave, but don't leave.

Right. That's logical.

I snapbacked. I closed my eyes and concentrated on the idea of a silver thread. I popped. My hands were empty.

Again, I snapbacked, concentrated, popped.

I repeated it three times before I felt even the smallest difference. This time, although there was no silver thread in my hand, I felt something, a reluctance to separate completely, the beginning of an attachment.

I snapbacked yet again and glanced over at Charlie. He was concentrating as hard as I was.

'You can do it.'

'Can you see it?' I asked, frustrated.

'I can see a little strand between the two Joes. Is that what you're aiming for?'

'Yes but I can't do it.'

'How does Joe do it?'

'Apparently he *thinks* about it,' I growled.

Charlie smiled sympathetically. 'You'll get it.'

My eyes tangled with his; as if this wasn't already hard enough. I took a deep breath.

But the distraction turned out to be exactly what was required. When I tried again, preoccupied with the awful *aching* after Charlie that had taken over all of my senses, I found my Self standing beside Joe, firmly grasping a silver thread.

Hey! I cried. I held my hand up to show Charlie, who applauded.

Well done, approved Joe. *Again.*

****

The curious by-product of the sessions with Joe was a general sense of being more in tune with myself. When I was whole, now, I was more whole than ever before.

The first time I succeeded in moving my fingers remotely, I snapbacked instantly in shock, and it was several minutes before I could separate again. We were in my kitchen — we hadn't practised outside again after the last time Magda had invaded my body — and Charlie had handed me a glass of whisky to help calm me down. I was beginning to develop a taste for the stuff.

The advantage of being able to remotely control my body, explained Joe, was that a controlled body could not be possessed as freely as an unconnected body. I'd already seen how uncomfortable Magda had been inside Joe.

Our sessions began to develop a routine. We practised my walking techniques, we shared meals, and the band practised their music or jammed for pleasure. Reese and Ken began to drop by more regularly the more proficient I became.

'She's getting better at it than I am,' grumbled Reese.

'That's because you don't practise,' said Raul.

Reese sniffed and shifted his bulk on the sofa.

'Quite comfortable?' asked Joe.

'I could use more cushions.'

'Do you guys still ... patrol?' I asked.

'We do enough,' said Joe.

'And what do you do, exactly?'

'I'll tell her,' volunteered Reese, sitting up. 'I'll tell you. We do two things: the dull stuff and the fun stuff. The dull stuff is a clean-up job. You know, when the bars and nightclubs empty and things are getting rowdy. We calm things down.'

'How, exactly?'

'In the same way you would if you saw a crisis,' said Joe.

'In spirit form?'

'Well I don't think we'd make very good peace-keepers with Reese whole, do you?'

Reese was contorting himself to scratch an itch in the middle of his back; the sofa virtually disintegrated beneath him. 'Got it,' he sighed, ecstatically rubbing his back against the hard arm of the sofa.

No, the sight of him wasn't likely to make anyone feel especially peaceful.

'What else do you do? Do you work together or separately?'

'Joe thinks we have more impact together,' said Reese. 'You know, in case we need to start getting *physical*. Throw things around a little bit.'

'Because you're so good at doing that,' said Ken, adroitly dodging the cushion flying his way.

'We also help the poppers,' offered Raul.

'Who are...?' I prompted.

Reese snorted. 'People that get themselves so high they pop *by accident*. Druggies, drunks, that sort of thing.'

'You have a problem with empathy,' observed Joe.

'What's empathy?'

'Does that happen a lot?' I asked, slightly horrified.

Raul shrugged. 'It happens.'

'So what do you do?'

'Well it scares the hell out of them, as you can imagine. We help them snapback. It isn't hard. They don't resist because they don't know what they're doing anyway. They're mostly not walkers.'

'And then there's the fun stuff,' gloated Reese. 'At first we just trawled the city, looking for negative energy spikes. And it was all fairly random and boring. But then we started noticing other walkers hanging around waiting for the poppers. And *then* these spectators started jumping into the bodies before we could help them snapback.'

'That'll do,' said Joe lazily. 'Cora's got enough on her own plate.'

'We even began seeing—'

'Enough,' said Joe.

'Is it getting worse?' I persisted. 'You make it sound like things are getting worse.'

'It's shifted up a notch,' said Ken.

'It's Magda, isn't it?' I demanded.

Joe frowned rebuke at the others before answering me. 'She's attracting attention,' he conceded.

'Won't work,' sang Reese. ''Cause he ain't going nowhere.'

'Who?' I said sharply.

'Reese,' said Joe. 'Reese is going nowhere because I'm going to beat the crap out of him.' My questions were lost in the ensuing cushion fight.

Chapter 25

'WE'RE SUPPORTING WHO?' asked Raul. Charlie named a band I'd never heard of.

'Number *thirty-two*,' said Reese.

'Not bad,' said Raul, and Reese snorted.

'Where?' wailed Amy, echoing my thoughts.

Charlie reeled off several major English cities.

'And we're the warm-up act?' Reese remained unimpressed.

'The opening act,' said Charlie.

'Do we get paid?' asked Ken.

'We'll do it,' said Joe.

'It's very short notice,' grumbled Reese, playing an irritating riff on his guitar.

'Do you want to be in a rock band?' I asked him.

Charlie grinned at me. 'It's short notice because their regular opener let them down.'

'How?'

'I don't know, Reese, and I don't care, and neither should you.'

'When did you become our agent?'

'Someone I met through work. Blame Joe — the guy I spoke to is a fan. He heard him play years ago and learned to play the guitar as a result.' Charlie reached over and took the guitar away from Reese.

'How *old* are you, man?' Raul asked Joe, while Reese gestured a finger down his throat.

'We're going to need a name,' said Joe.

'I already gave them one,' admitted Charlie. 'I told them you were called Spirit Walker.'

There was a surprised silence while everyone considered this.

'Isn't that a bit of a give-away?' asked Amy uncertainly.

'Yeah, because *everyone* knows what a spirit-walker is,' said Reese, helping himself to another white-chocolate biscuit.

They would be gone for days and days, which was bad enough. Worse still, without the excuse of the band and our practice sessions, I was unlikely to see Charlie. I glanced over at him; he was studying the floor. He was increasingly distant with me. Twice now he hadn't come over with the others. I wouldn't ask what he'd been doing instead. I had no claim on him whatsoever. All I could do was be grateful when he came, and carefully hide how I felt about him.

****

We were three again: Amy, Grace and me, a normal, female household. Grace went to school, Amy went to work, and I painted and kept house. *Above the Town* was progressing and Klaus was happy — I'd sent him digital photographs and he'd visited once — but I was loathe to make the finishing touches and relinquish it. The impending separation from my new friends unsettled me, and my disquiet showed in the painting.

I doubted it was anything visible to the naked eye. Bella's dress and Marc's shirt were the perfect shade, her arm flew out as it should, and his hand lay over her right breast. The birds on the ground were complete in every detail and the buildings below were faithful renditions. But there was more movement, somehow, an infinitesimal swirling of the air around them, and an intensity in their embrace. Marc's eyes looked back at something other than Bella; their universe was disrupted and there was urgency in their flight.

There were no more training sessions. The band was madly practising its music, finalising the playlist, checking equipment. Raul came once, and stayed over; I saw him only briefly.

And then they were gone. A week passed, then two days more, and this was life without Charlie: I worked, I raised my daughter, I cooked, shopped and cleaned.

I hardly slept, I hardly ate and sometimes I had trouble breathing. I wanted Charlie so badly, the touch of his hand, a glimpse of his smile, the sound of his voice, that sometimes at night I popped and hovered inches away from the bed just to take a break from my body. Not that the spirit-ache was any easier to bear — quite the opposite, in fact — but at least it had a certain purity, and released me from the tortuous *physical* longing.

I was in love; there it was. *Stupid, stupid!* How could I have allowed this to happen? It wasn't like anything I'd ever experienced before. It was exactly what it sounded like, and just as dumb: totally devoted, unexpected, inescapable, wholly committed, life-changing, head-over-heels in love. And my only hope was that he'd never know.

Because, for whatever reason, Charlie had disengaged from me. Even when he was present, that part of himself that had, briefly, been mine for the taking, was now withheld.

The world around me continued its steady course. Grace and I rose before dawn one morning to watch the Lyrid meteor shower, when Earth passed through the dust trail of a comet, an event that had faithfully announced the arrival of spring for over two-and-a-half thousand years.

And then the phone rang.

'Hello Charlie,' I said carefully before I even heard his voice.

'Cora,' he said, and then there was silence. I pressed the phone to my ear, imagining him doing the same, trying to feel him over the line. I would have sent my Self soaring to his side except I knew he would see me.

He cleared his throat. 'How's everything with you?'

'It's fine. Thank you. You?'

'Good. Busy.'

'Good.'

He gave a chuckle and it was such a lovely sound that tears sprang to my eyes.

'We're being awfully formal here. You are the Cora that jumps out of her body at the smallest invitation?'

'That would be me.' My voice sounded watery and small. *Get a grip.* 'Have you heard how the boys are doing?'

'Isn't Amy filling you in?'

'Amy's in mourning. She spends all her time in her room on the phone to Raul. I think she sleeps early so she can wake up when his gig's over and talk to him all night.'

'Nice. Shall we put her out of her misery and take her to see him?'

'How?'

'Do you fancy going to a gig?'

'Really?'

'Why not?'

It had never occurred to me. 'When?'

'Tomorrow? They'll be in Nottingham. I'll drive. If we leave around 4pm we'll be out of London before the worst of the traffic and we should get there in plenty of time. We can see the boys afterwards, and get back home in time for a few hours' sleep before work the next day. The only thing I haven't planned for,' he admitted, 'is Grace.'

'I can probably arrange a sleep-over for her. Let me make some calls. I'll get back to you.'

I rang Sue to see if she would have Grace, and then I rang Amy at work.

'Yippee!' she cried. 'Really? Tomorrow? Wait till I tell Raul! Or shall I make it a surprise?'

'You choose,' I said. 'Are you sure you can take the afternoon off?'

'Are you kidding? I'm a temp, Cora. If they make a fuss I'll quit.' She lowered her voice. 'And they love me here — they'd freak if I threatened to leave. Did I tell you they offered me a permanent job this morning?'

'Again?'

Chapter 26

NEXT DAY, CHARLIE RANG THE BELL a little before four. Amy opened the door and I pretended to be busy with my bag, but it didn't help. When I looked up, there he was, not looking at me, kissing Amy on the cheek, laughing at her gleeful anticipation, dazzling as sunrise. The breath caught in my throat, so that I gave a little choke and they both turned to me.

'Hello Cora,' he said. 'All set? Let's hit the road before the traffic starts.'

I sat in the front, Amy in the back. I would have had it otherwise, but she insisted. Then she yawned widely and promptly fell asleep, and there *we* were, speeding out of London, the only people in the only car on the only road in the whole wide world. We didn't speak but the car positively vibrated with our lack of conversation.

Finally, as we reached the M1, Charlie asked, 'How's Grace?'

'She's fine. Apart from school.'

'What's wrong at school?'

'I think she sometimes pops.'

He glanced at me. 'That doesn't sound very sensible.'

'It isn't. I think she's bored.'

'Make her stop,' said Charlie sharply, killing the conversation for another half-hour.

At last the silence became too heavy to bear, and I searched around for something innocuous to discuss. 'Your surname,' I said, trying to sound casual. 'Charlie Tam. That sounds Chinese.'

'My grandfather was from Shanghai. Long story. I never knew him.'

'Do you have a large family?'

'Why do you ask?'

I turned my head towards him, surprised. This was a tone I hadn't heard before. Charlie did happy; he did curious and laconic and gentle and kind and sometimes sceptical. He never did unfriendly; at least, not until now.

'I don't know anything about you,' I said. 'I'm just making conversation.'

'Sorry.' He shook his head. 'Sorry Cora. I don't have much family left. Mum died when I was little. I grew up with my Dad. And I have a brother.'

'You never mentioned him. Does he live in London?'

He hesitated. 'He lives with Dad some of the time, and some of the time he lives in London with me.'

'You must bring him over. Grace and I would love to meet him.'

'Right,' said Charlie.

He was uncomfortable — no, he was miserable. I wanted to put my hand on his shoulder, or in his hair. I wanted to ask what the problem was. Instead I went on making small talk. 'Do you get along?'

'My brother and I? We used to get along. But not now. Now we're very different. He's older than me.' Charlie laughed; it wasn't a nice sound.

'Much older?'

'*Much* older.'

'Looks like we both have difficult siblings,' I said.

He gave a grim laugh. 'It certainly looks like it, doesn't it?'

I had a feeling we were talking about different things. 'Charlie, what's wrong?'

'Nothing.' His eyes were back on the road. 'Nothing at all. How old did you say you were, Cora?'

'I'm twenty-six.'

'And how old is Magda?'

'She's twenty-eight.'

'It must be interesting to suddenly have two sisters in your life.'

'It is strange,' I said. 'To be honest, neither of them feels much like a regular sister. I grew up with Rebecca, and she's a darling, but she's ten years older than me. We are related, but only distantly; our grandmothers were second cousins. In many ways she's more like a young aunt than an older sister. She's always taken care of me.'

'Was it strange for you coming to a foreign country, joining a new family?'

'Not as strange as it sounds,' I said. 'It was never very real. I always had the feeling I was playing a game, waiting for my real life to begin.'

He shot another glance at me. 'Even when you got married?'

'Especially when I got married.'

'Why did you get married, then?'

'You have to understand,' I said. 'I was like a package that had to be guarded at all costs. That's what it felt like, from the minute I arrived in England. My new parents were quite elderly — more like grandparents. My father died when I was twelve, and Mother was never very active, so Rebecca took the brunt of it. And she took it very seriously. When the time came for her to marry Hugh and leave Yorkshire, she was afraid to leave me alone. So she married me off to her nearest friend and neighbour, and Peter took over where she left off.'

Charlie looked appalled. 'And you went along with it?'

'All I'd ever wanted was a normal life. A home, a family. Why would I resist?' I shifted in my seat. 'It sounds bad.'

He shrugged. 'It doesn't sound like you.'

'It was a bit like sleepwalking,' I began, but luckily Amy chose that moment to wake up.

'Are we there yet?'

We reached the outskirts of Nottingham and navigated our way into the city centre. Leaving the car in a multi-storey car-park on Talbot Street, we joined a long queue outside Rock City.

Charlie eyed Amy's suede platform boots. 'Do you have anything more comfortable to change into? We'll be standing all night.'

'Are you kidding?' Amy clicked her tongue. 'I'm going to surprise my boyfriend. I'd rather walk on pins than wear flats for this occasion.'

'At least you're in sensible shoes,' approved Charlie, looking at my feet.

'Cora always wears flats,' snorted Amy. 'Heaven forbid she should look like a proper grown-up.'

Charlie and I exchanged a smile and for a moment it was like being parents with a petulant child. I put my arm around Amy's waist; she was shaking with excitement.

'Well, you might surprise Raul, but I made a few calls in advance so we're not completely unexpected,' said Charlie, as a youth in a black tee-shirt waved at us from the door. 'Thank goodness. Let's go.'

I was embarrassed at walking past the curious, slightly outraged glances of those ahead of us in the queue. Amy was not. 'We're with the band,' she loudly told anyone that cared to listen, smiling beatifically. *Of course she is,* I thought; looking like she did, of course she was with the band. I was happy to follow invisibly in her and Charlie's wake.

The youth and Charlie greeted one another with mutual thumps on the back, and then we were in a large penumbral room with two disco balls and banks of lamps on girders hanging along the ceiling, and a floor whose colour was designed to hide spillage. There were only a few people inside.

We found the toilets, and when we emerged Charlie had staked us a claim at the barrier two feet in front of the stage. 'We can get seats inside the barrier but that will ruin your surprise, Amy — the guys will spot us before they get on stage. We can move later.'

The place filled up behind us, bodies gently pressing us forward. Without a word or look, and without touching me, Charlie made me a cage of his arms. Amy needed no such protection; her natural presence and increasing agitation ensured no one got too close, whereas I felt I might easily be — well, stepped on.

I'd been looked after all my life, and Charlie was following the trend. I wanted to slap his arms away and tell him I was *awake* now, I could take care of myself. But I also wanted to pull his arms closer, wrap them tightly around me. I stood awkwardly, not moving at all. Then after a while I started to watch the crowds building around us. There was a growing buzz of excitement and glamour, and I realised that this is how my teens should have been spent; I should have been hanging out in nightclubs and bars with people like Amy and Charlie, not married and keeping house. *But then you wouldn't have Grace,* I reminded myself and I felt a kick in my chest at the thought of life without Grace. *There is no life without Grace.*

It was too noisy to talk. Men in black tee-shirts were on stage now, positioning guitars, talking into microphones, checking plugs and sockets. The stage was a mess of cables and black boxes. At last, one of the men made an exaggerated clapping motion above his head, prompting the audience to welcome the opening act.

There was Ken! He shuffled onstage, virtually invisible in jeans and a top, and hid behind the drums, followed closely by a Reese I scarcely recognised; he looked bigger than ever on stage, and had teased his shoulder-length hair into a pony-tail, a look I'd never seen on him before. It made him look more than ever like a benign troll-monster.

Joe and Raul came out together, and the level of applause rose in response to their swagger. There was something intoxicating about them, without them having to play a single note. Even I fell half in love, and I knew their less-than-glamorous real selves pretty well by now.

They strapped on guitars, rock gods with attitude, and launched straight into a song I'd never heard before. Their catchy brand of indie-folk-rock flooded the room and the overhead lights on girders began to twist and flash. I turned to see the reaction of the people around me, but the movement brought me forehead-to-chin — my forehead, his chin — with Charlie, and I quickly concentrated on the stage again.

It was only then I noticed something funny. Although they all looked different from each other, the band was wearing a uniform: jeans and white tops. Reese's was a ripped tee-shirt with black writing on it; Ken, a demon-drummer now, sported a vest; Joe had a collared shirt with the sleeves ripped out; Raul wore a romantic, flowing shirt with pleats in the long sleeves and turned-back cuffs. I turned delightedly to Amy and pulled at my own white shirt. 'I know!' she yelled, although I only saw her lips moving; I couldn't hear her above the heavy strum of guitars and Raul's throaty yell.

I half-turned to Charlie and saw that he had noticed me noticing; he was laughing.

And then Raul saw Amy, and pretty soon he'd taken in Charlie and me too, and he was gesturing to the rest of the band. One after another, their eyes found us, and they were playing and singing through huge grins.

The song ended and Raul pointed a hand at Amy and yelled, 'Hello baby!' and the crowd roared. Two security men helped to haul Amy over the barrier. Joe began to strum, and Ken beat out a mounting rhythm on the cymbals as Raul leaned over the edge of the stage to give Amy a full-on, open-mouthed kiss. The crowd went wild; it couldn't have been rehearsed better.

Charlie hugged me quickly from behind, and just as quickly loosened his grip. I hugged myself, as excited as anyone there. And then Raul was back in the music, and I recognised a song I'd heard them all, including Charlie, singing in my kitchen. Right on cue I felt his breath on my cheek, and then he was humming the weaving descant close to my ear. It was like a secret, something precious and thrilling.

It was hard to see how the main attraction of the evening could follow this. A wild kind of symbiosis sprang up between stage and audience, a raw energy that made me imagine myself in love with Joe and Raul and Reese and Ken as well as Amy and Charlie and probably everyone else in the room. I was close enough to see every chord change, every expression on their faces, every drop of sweat that flew from Reese's brow.

And then I saw something else. Reese and Joe were shoulder to shoulder, wielding their guitars like — well, honestly, like parts of their anatomy — and Ken was beating a hailstorm of short, sharp strokes, and out of the corner of my eye I suddenly noticed several unnaturally tall people in the room. And *then* I realised they weren't tall people at all; they were Selfs, hovering above their bodies. People in the crowd were spontaneously popping.

CHAPTER 27

M
Y EYES FLEW TO THE STAGE in amazement, in time to catch a silent exchange between Joe and Raul; the slightest widening of the eyes.

They had seen it.

Did they make that happen?

Joe caught my eye. He smiled sheepishly, shook his head at me, his hands never breaking contact with the strings of his guitar.

I turned to Charlie, seriously disturbed.

'What's wrong?' he yelled into my ear. I shook my head and turned my attention back to the audience. The Selfs had disappeared. I had an instinct that the people concerned had no idea what had happened, had simply been carried away by the music.

It was over in less than five seconds; it was easy to imagine it had never happened. Three more songs and the set was over. To wild applause, Spirit Walker left the stage, Raul making frantic gestures at Amy, who was still on the other side of the barrier from Charlie and me. A security man took her arm; she turned to point at us, and it was our turn to cross the barrier, although we walked around the side instead of being hauled over the top. We were led to a room behind the stage and into the arms of the band. There was much hugging and back-slapping.

'What's with the outfits?' I said accusingly to Joe.

'It's a good look, baby!'

'You look like one of us,' said Reese, putting a huge arm around my neck and fingering my white collar.

'No, you look like one of me,' I corrected him.

'You were fabulous,' squealed Amy, disengaging from Raul long enough to quickly greet the others.

'Nice job, mate,' said a spiky-haired blond in ripped skinny jeans and a huge, blousy shirt.

'Lead singer of the *other* band,' said Charlie in my ear.

'Let's get a drink,' suggested Reese.

'You can help with the gear first,' said Joe, heading to the side of the stage where roadies had begun to stow equipment to make room for the main event.

We were directed to a bar around the corner, and Charlie, Amy and I headed there to wait for the others.

'How are you doing?' I asked Amy.

She pointed to the tears in her eyes, the smile on her face; she was too happy for words.

And I was, too. The others arrived, and we dissected their performance, and drank beer — all except Charlie, who drank coffee because he was driving — and slowly the young rock-gods morphed back into the familiar friends from my kitchen in Gregory Square. I was quiet, enjoying the noise and the camaraderie, the sense of belonging.

This feels like family, I thought, and hugged myself, wishing Grace was with me, and then laughing inwardly at the idea of Grace in a Nottingham bar late at night.

We broke up finally at midnight. Raul walked us to our car and Charlie and I climbed discreetly into our seats and took time strapping ourselves in to give him privacy and time to say goodbye to Amy. There was no need; they were oblivious anyway.

'Crap,' I said.

'What is it?'

'I forgot to ask Joe something.'

I was about to tell Charlie about the Selfs at the concert, but Amy slid into the backseat at that moment, and she was crying.

'It's all right, darling,' I said, turning to take her hand. 'They'll only be gone a few more days.'

'I know. I'm happy, that's all.' After she'd wiped her eyes, and we were bowling through the dark streets of Nottingham heading back to the M1, she said dreamily, 'Aren't I the lucky one? The lead singer of a band. And he's Spanish. Raul.' She sighed again.

Shortly afterwards Charlie looked in his rear-view mirror and jerked his head towards the back seat. 'Junior's passed out again. I think it's all the excitement.'

I turned to look at her; she was curled up on the seat, fast asleep.

'Are you okay driving?'

'Fine, thank you.'

'I can take over if you like. I didn't drink much.'

'It's okay. Why don't you tip your seat back? Get some sleep.'

I leaned back my seat and my head so I could watch the side of his face surreptitiously under my eyelashes.

Long fingers on the wheel; narrow eyes on the road. It was such pleasure, such peace, to just ... stare. But after a while it was troubling. I closed my eyes but I couldn't sleep.

'Charlie, would you mind?' I asked, pointing out of the window.

'What? Oh you mean ... sure. I suppose Magda's unlikely to find you speeding along the motorway late at night.'

I was out of the window in an eye-blink. The air was cold; it rushed past me as I flew beside the car, keeping close to my body, only the glass and some metal between us. I rose briefly towards the full moon, above the snake of traffic with its multiple feelers of light. Then I plunged back down and waved to Charlie through the window. For a moment I struck a pose on the bonnet of the car; I heard Charlie's indrawn breath, sensed his surprise as he adjusted his vision to see through me to the road ahead, and then felt the ripple of his delight as he recognised me as the living incarnation of his Rolls-Royce angel, posing on the bonnet of his mint-green Peugeot.

I flew above the car for a few moments more, and then snapbacked into my seat.

'Very funny,' he murmured. 'Are you cold?'

'No.'

He glanced quickly at my face. 'You looked beautiful.'

'I wish you could see what I see,' I said impulsively. 'If you think a Self is beautiful, you should see the things a Self can see.'

'I said *your* Self was beautiful,' he said, and quickly added, 'Tell me. What did you see?'

'The sun is up now. It won't set again until September.'

He glanced out of the window. 'It's dark. It's night.'

'Not here. Up north. Above seventy degrees latitude. They'll have non-stop sunshine now for the next few months. Twenty-four hours a day.'

'Above seventy degrees latitude,' he repeated, smiling.

I ignored him. 'Jupiter's rising. In a couple of nights you'll see it alongside the moon. Mercury's getting closer to the sun; a few more nights and it won't be visible any more, at least not to the naked eye. The bees are busy. The salmon are turning.'

'You can tell all that from one short flight?' He sounded hungry, like he wished he could see such things himself.

'It's a cycle, Charlie. It happens every year. You don't have to pop to know these things.'

'But you saw them all tonight.'

'I *sensed* them all tonight.'

'What else?'

I hesitated. It was hard to put into words. 'Things are generally … in balance.'

'Which means?'

'There's good and bad out there but overall the universe is in kilter tonight.'

'Have you ever seen the universe out of kilter?'

'Oh yes. But this is *this* universe, of course, and I'm a human, which means I get to exercise free will. If I don't like the overall picture I can choose to limit my view to the psychic weather in a particular location. And the other way around.'

'And which do you choose?'

I shrugged. 'It depends on my mood. The overview is usually more peaceful. It's easy to get very worked up about the currents and fluctuations over an individual town or street.'

'And do you think it's possible to interfere?'

I frowned, suddenly annoyed. 'Do you?' I demanded.

Charlie smiled. 'The boys certainly think so, or they wouldn't go out patrolling. What do you think?' He snapped on his long-lights; there was less traffic on the road now.

'You can't actively change anything,' I said, 'because everyone has free will. But you can sometimes effect a mood change, which can influence behaviour.'

'Do you believe the walker myths?'

'Believe them?' I said, taken by surprise. 'You mean do I believe they're literally true? Are you serious?' He was; I could see it on his face. I tried again. 'They probably work like most myths: they're a vehicle for the truth.' I raised my eyebrows at him. 'Will that do, Herr Professor?'

'Let's hope so,' he said.

'Why are you asking me all these questions?'

'It's important to know what you think.'

I gulped. 'Why is that important to you?'

'Not to me. To you. You need to be very clear in your own mind what you do and don't believe. It will make things simpler for you in the future.'

I stared at him for a moment longer and then shook my head. 'You do know you make no sense at all?'

'That's probably just as well.' His smile didn't reach his eyes.

Chapter 28

THE TOUR WAS OVER — the regular support band had returned. There were high hopes for more touring but in the meantime we returned to our regular Saturday nights in Gregory Square.

Reese and Ken had gone home, Grace was upstairs asleep, Amy, Raul, Charlie, Joe and I were in the kitchen, and I'd just succeeded in walking my separated body from the bookcase to the oven and back. I was so surprised at myself that I snapbacked and stood, astonished, next to Joe, blinking rapidly.

'Brava!' applauded Raul.

'It feels ... *wrong*,' I said, shivering.

'Anyone want a coffee?' asked Amy. She was in tight jeans and a tee-shirt with a heart on the chest; Raul could hardly keep his hands off her.

'Tell me about the music,' I said to Joe, remembering and coming to myself.

'What music?'

I narrowed my eyes. 'Your music. At the concert. The bit where you called out the Selfs.'

Joe and Raul exchanged nervous glances.

Charlie leaned forward to concentrate. 'You did what?' he said, frowning.

'What did you see?' Joe was trying to look casual. He pulled a hand through his unruly afro.

'I saw several Selfs, but they weren't walkers. I don't think the people even knew they'd popped. I know it wasn't an accident, Joe. I felt something tugging at me, too.' When he still didn't answer, I said, 'What did you do?'

He sighed. 'It's called charming.'

Raul threw him an incredulous, warning look, but Joe shrugged. 'She saw it, man. There's no point in hiding it. She'll find out soon enough.'

'Why will I?'

'Because Magda and her friends can probably do it. They're already actively seeking out poppers. Any minute now they'll get tired of waiting for it to happen and start *making* it happen.'

'You've been watching Magda?' I asked breathlessly.

Joe shrugged. 'She's hard to miss. She and her playmates are throwing out beacons all over town.'

'Explain charming,' I demanded.

Raul sighed. 'Don't listen to this, Amy.'

'If it affects you and Cora, I should know about it,' she said, offended. 'Even if I'm not a walker.'

'Aw baby, I didn't mean to insult you.' Raul threw his arms around her. 'I don't want you mixed up in this stuff, that's all.' He turned to me. 'It's like snake charming. We didn't know for sure that it was possible until recently. It's one of those things walkers don't talk about. It's not exactly ethical, you know?'

'How does it work?'

Charlie had been listening in silence. 'It's dangerous,' he said now. His voice was quiet, but it had an edge. 'We shouldn't mess with it.'

'You can talk,' said Joe.

When Charlie didn't answer I said, 'Why can Charlie talk?'

Raul was grinning. 'Because we found keys in a couple of his songs.'

'Rubbish,' said Charlie, a little too calmly.

'What are you talking about?' I was almost stamping my feet in frustration.

'Charming,' Joe told me, 'is when you draw the Self out of a person. In theory it works on walkers and non-walkers.'

'Why would you do that?' I asked, horrified.

'Well, we'd heard the stories, and we've seen the results, but we didn't know how to do it. Until now.'

'Could you do it to me?' asked Amy with real interest.

Raul shuddered and Joe shook his head emphatically. 'It's not something you volunteer for. It's an attack mechanism.'

'Oh my God,' I said. 'You charm out the Self and then invade the body. That's it, isn't it? That would be bad enough if you did it to a walker. But at least a walker would know what had happened. If you do that to a non-walker — what on earth happens to them?'

'It depends,' said Joe. 'If they're lucky the invader doesn't stick around for long and they snapback and imagine it was all a dream, or an illness, or that they drank too much or smoked something bad.'

'And if they're not lucky?'

'Sometimes an invader hangs onto the body for a while and the Self is left hanging around and *it* becomes the problem. A dislocated Self can generate some really negative energy. You know — so-called poltergeist activity and the like.'

'It's horrible enough being invaded when you know what's happening,' I said grimly.

'Why would anyone want to do that to someone else?' asked Amy.

'For kicks,' said Raul darkly. 'Charmers are generally not good people.'

'*How* do they do it?' I asked.

'There are ways to remind the Self of the spirit world,' said Joe.

Of course there were. I saw that Amy didn't understand. 'Do you remember I told you that all babies walk?' I reminded her. 'Everyone carries a memory, however deeply buried, of the spirit world. There are things that can evoke those memories.' With a sudden jolt I remembered something I'd read. 'Psychic shock,' I said, nodding slowly. 'It's what Marc Chagall said he tried to achieve in his painting — a psychic shock, a fourth dimension.'

Joe flattened his afro with his hand again. 'Music, art, literature, landscape, a certain taste or touch — there are lots of reminders that can unlock the right memories. Some of them are unique to the individual but there are universal keys to the lock. Charmers discover or create keys and use them deliberately to draw out Selfs. All you need is one person to respond.'

'I saw it happen once at a piano recital,' I said, remembering again the incident in the Brighton Pavilion all those years ago. 'But I don't think the pianist was a walker. At least, I didn't see his Self attack anybody.'

'It happens by accident all the time,' confirmed Joe. 'Sometimes it's drugs or alcohol. Charmers use the keys deliberately; with them it's not an accident.'

'It's your game,' said Amy.

All eyes were suddenly on me. 'What game?' said Joe.

'Trying to guess whether the artist knew what he was doing. Whether he was a walker or not,' I said. Cold fingers spread themselves around my neck. 'And you write this stuff deliberately — for fun?' I raised my eyebrows at Charlie. 'Even though you're not a walker?'

If anyone is capable of compelling a Self out of a person, it's him.

My stomach sank like a stone. The non-walker who could see spirits, the innocent who knew all about charming. The ambiguity in Charlie was beginning to kill me.

Raul screwed up his face. 'We only found keys in two of his songs. And we only tried one of those songs out at the concert. As we discovered, it didn't work on everyone.'

'You risked the possibility of popping an entire audience?' Even Charlie looked dumbfounded.

'We weren't planning to invade,' said Raul defensively.

'Of course not,' soothed Joe. 'And we guessed it would only work on a few — if it worked at all. Which it clearly did.'

'Why did you do it?' I asked.

'To stay one step ahead of the renegades. To help us patrol more effectively.'

'Is there an antidote to a key?' I demanded. 'Is there a way to resist?'

'We don't know that much.' Joe didn't like this confession. 'But now that we're all being so open: Charlie?'

'What?' said Charlie. He stared at Joe, who coolly stared back.

'You wrote the keys,' said Joe.

'They're just love songs,' said Charlie. 'They're supposed to be moving.'

'Moving, yes. They're not supposed to move Selfs out of bodies,' I said witheringly.

Charlie switched his gaze to me. 'Of course they are. The lover seeks to transport the soul of his beloved with music. It's a time-honoured tradition.'

I couldn't look away.

Joe interrupted the awkward silence. 'We're not certain we've ever seen a deliberate attack. But we need to prepare ourselves because right now, we're batting in the dark.'

'You seem very sure there's trouble coming,' said Amy.

'There's no trouble coming,' said Charlie, dropping his eyes from mine at last — but not before I'd seen his Self seething inside him. 'As long as everyone stays calm and does their job.'

Joe looked at me sympathetically. 'We're not sure if there's trouble coming,' he said. 'You used to get a renegade here and there, and suddenly there are more of them and they're better organised.'

'Are we talking world-wide?' asked Amy, looking horrified.

'No, just around here. I only patrol my own territory. I reckon if every walker takes care of his own territory, the world will take care of itself.'

'Is it something to do with Magda?' My voice sounded small and unhappy — which is how I felt.

'Of course it's something to do with Magda,' said Raul impatiently. 'She's deliberately drawing the attention of every walker on the planet. Jeez, Cora, wake up!'

I stared at him. 'You mean that man — the man that killed my mother? Why would she do that?' And then I said, 'If she does that, he'll find me. And Grace.'

'We won't let him get anywhere near you,' said Joe, thumping Raul hard.

I turned on Joe. 'What? What did you say?' I blinked furiously. 'You know who he is!'

There was a moment's silence.

'Do you know?' asked Amy in a small voice. She looked at Raul. 'Tell me.'

Joe shook his head, tried to smile. 'Of course not,' he said. 'No! Of course we don't know. How could we know? But we have your clue, don't we — silver hair?'

He wouldn't look at Charlie. His eyes went everywhere, except on Charlie. Raul was furiously concentrating on the floor.

'Charm me,' I said suddenly. 'Do it now, with one of Charlie's songs.'

Charlie began to say something and then gave a loud cough, as if to cut himself off. Raul looked horrified. But Joe raised his eyebrows speculatively. 'It's not a bad idea. We could do a run-through with you and Raul.'

'You didn't you think to test yourselves and each other before you took it to the concert?' asked Amy. She swiped Raul across the back of the head. 'You guys are unbelievable.'

Joe and Raul looked at one another and shrugged. 'Not really,' said Joe. 'We know it doesn't work on us when we're the ones playing the music, but that's about it.'

'But you said you were batting in the dark,' I prompted. 'See if it works on me now. Try it on Raul too — play the music yourself.'

'And we could start coming up with ways to resist it,' added Raul.

'Will it hurt them?' asked Amy, looking faintly alarmed. Joe shook his head.

I brought my guitar from upstairs and handed it to Joe.

'I'm having nothing to do with this,' said Charlie. 'Come on, Amy. We'll go watch TV upstairs.' He was pretending to be bored by the whole thing. I wanted to thump him the way Amy had just thumped Raul.

'Sit with me, baby,' invited Raul, making eyes at Amy. 'I don't want you going anywhere.'

'No,' said Joe. 'You need to concentrate. Good idea, Charlie. We'll call you down when we have something. Cora, you said you felt something pulling on you at the concert? That's what you're looking for, then. Relax, and when you feel it, let it happen as if you weren't forewarned. Later on you can start trying to resist.'

Chapter 29

J OE STRUMMED A FEW CHORDS and then began to sing. It must have been the second song Charlie had written with a key in it, because it wasn't the song I'd heard at the concert.

Raul found it hard not to join in, but Joe stopped him: 'It won't work on you if you're singing.'

I forgot the exercise and was lost in the lovely song, when I felt a pull at my heart, a piercing jolt, sweet but sharp, and then I was above myself; and so was Raul.

It feels good! he said, and I agreed. We snapbacked. Joe followed us with his eyes without breaking the song.

This happened a few more times and then Joe put down his guitar.

'Interesting,' he said, sounding satisfied with himself. He wandered over to the fridge and pulled out several bottles of beer he'd put in there earlier in the evening. He put his head outside the kitchen door and quietly called the other two down.

'Progress?' enquired Charlie.

Joe handed a bottle to him and one to Amy. 'I've got them swinging in and out of their bodies like a pair of yo-yos,' he said.

'You mean Charlie has us swinging in and out of our bodies like a pair of yo-yos,' said Raul. He looked as light-headed as I was feeling; I caught his eye and we both narrowly avoided a fit of the giggles.

'Interesting,' said Charlie, looking from one to the other of us.

'What does it feel like?' asked Amy.

Again Raul and I exchanged knowing glances; Raul snorted.

'Like that, huh?' said Joe knowingly.

Charlie's eyes narrowed.

'Cora?' prompted Raul.

I held up my hands defensively. 'Knock yourself out. I'm not giving details.'

'Well.' Raul drew in a breath. 'It's a little bit — a very little bit — like—'

'Like sneezing,' I cut in, and Raul exploded into laughter.

'Like scratching an itch,' he spluttered, and we fell about helplessly on the sofas.

'What?' said Amy.

'Orgasm,' said Charlie drily.

'Orgasm? Like — sex?' Amy looked blank and then furious. 'You're sitting down here having sex with Joe and Cora while I'm stuck upstairs with Charlie?'

'Orgasm is totally overstating it,' I said, to defend Raul. 'Let's think of another analogy.'

'Right,' said Raul quickly. 'It's like the moment of falling asleep when you're very tired.'

'Or drinking water when you're dead thirsty.'

'Or peeing when you're bursting.'

'Yes, thank you, children,' said Joe. 'It's a release. I think we get the general idea.'

I stole a look at Charlie; he wasn't laughing, which for some reason made me even more lightheaded.

'Okay, well you've both been keen enough. Now let's see you trying to resist it,' said Joe.

We pulled ourselves together. Raul gave Amy a loving kiss and then she and Charlie disappeared back upstairs and Joe pulled the guitar back onto his lap. 'Let's go.'

He played the first song again. *Here it comes.* A subtle key shift, an unexpected note that nudged an exquisitely painful nerve... I was ready for it; out I popped and Raul popped beside me. We grinned at one another and snapbacked.

'Try, guys,' said Joe.

'It's too nice,' protested Raul.

Joe played again; again I saw it coming and tensed, but the pulling at me was irresistible.

Now I see why they're called junkies, these renegades, I said to Raul. *I look forward to it every time.*

I concentrated hard, but either I was becoming too fond of being charmed, or Joe was getting too good at charming; I popped every time, and so did Raul. Suddenly I didn't feel so lighthearted about it.

'Just a minute,' I said. 'If I'm so affected now, how come I wasn't affected at the concert?'

'You must have been resisting,' said Joe slowly.

'How? I can't resist now, and I'm trying.'

There was a moment's silence as we each considered this.

'Something must have been different,' said Joe at last. Again he put his head outside the door and called Charlie and Amy to join us.

'Cora didn't separate at the concert, did she Charlie?'

'She didn't.'

'I already told you that,' I said.

'Yes, but it might have happened without you knowing. We're not sure precisely how this works, remember. We need to work out what was different then and now so we can work out how you resisted.'

I ran through the scene in my mind. 'I was standing in the crowd. I felt the pulling, just once, when I noticed the Selfs. But I didn't pop.'

'Maybe it was the crowd,' suggested Amy. 'Maybe the proximity of all those people kept you grounded.'

The truth dawned on me then, bringing with it a tide of red blood into my cheeks.

Proximity. And probably not just to anyone.

'Amy,' I said, being very careful not to look directly at anyone else until my blush had subsided. 'Come and sit next to Raul. That's it. Hold his hand. Joe, try that key again.'

'Amy's not a walker,' protested Raul. 'It'll be horrible for her if she's forced to pop.'

'If I were susceptible, wouldn't I have popped at the concert?' said Amy. 'Anyway, I'm tone deaf, remember? Music's probably not my key.'

We all looked at one another. 'Sounds reasonable,' conceded Joe.

Amy snuggled up to Raul and Joe sang the song again. I popped early, unwilling to be charmed out this time.

The key came and went and Raul's Self did not appear.

'I felt the pull but then — nothing!' said Raul. He was excited.

'Come back Cora and explain,' said Joe.

I snapbacked reluctantly. There was no way out of this, but I could delay it.

'Charlie, can you sing the song now? Amy, could you leave the room a moment? I'll call you back in. Joe, come and sit beside Raul. You don't have to hold hands, but touch him.'

They all protested, but did as I asked. With Charlie's voice twining around the tune the song was completely transformed. The charming effect on me was ten times more profound but I'd already separated, very deliberately, before Charlie even began. It was painful; for the first time, walking felt *unnatural*. Then Raul popped, right on cue — and so did Joe, which surprised and, I thought, rather embarrassed him. I looked at him in amusement for a moment and enjoyed the idea that he'd thought himself immune when we were not.

'So I charmed a Self,' said Charlie. 'Can I go now?' He wasn't pleased.

'Two Selfs,' I corrected him.

'It would have been three if you hadn't cheated,' he said, and I blushed again.

'So what have we proved?' said Joe. 'That Raul can stay for Amy but not for me?'

The truth hit him as he spoke the words and he began to nod excitedly. 'Of course, of course! Raul can stay for Amy but not for me! Which is why you didn't separate at the concert Cora, because you were—' He caught my frantic look and stopped immediately, but it didn't matter; everyone got it.

I hadn't separated at the concert because I was standing right beside Charlie. A Self in close proximity to its beloved could *choose* to walk, but couldn't be charmed away by anything — other than the beloved himself, I thought, remembering my Self dancing around the ceiling when Charlie had put his arms around me that night in his flat.

'And we're done,' cried Joe, creating a bustle by putting away the guitar and collecting empty bottles for the recycling bin. Everyone joined him in tidying up, and in a surprisingly short time Amy and Raul had disappeared upstairs and I was standing outside on the pavement seeing off Charlie and Joe.

Joe gamely went off ahead of Charlie, leaving us a moment of privacy.

'I can protect you?' said Charlie bluntly. 'Me? I'm the one?' He sounded resentful.

'So it would appear.'

He took in a deep breath. 'That's not fair. That's just not fair.'

I was deeply hurt — and, which was worse, I couldn't express it without revealing myself more than I'd already done.

'Fucking hell,' said Charlie.

'Nobody asked you to protect me,' I said, my voice rising several notches. 'I never asked you to!'

I turned to storm back into the house, but he grabbed me by the arm. 'Cora,' he said, and there was a real bleakness in his face. 'I can't help how I feel about you, but it doesn't mean I have to like it.'

'How you feel about me?' I said.

'I wrote those songs for you,' he said roughly. 'They were meant to transport you, not ... *charm* you. The keys were a by-product. I can't protect you from me!'

I took a deep breath. 'Charlie, I don't think you understand what happened. Raul didn't resist the key because Amy loves him. He resisted the key because he loves Amy. I resisted the key at the concert because ... well, not because of how you might feel about me ... or not.' I faltered. 'Joe got it. So did Raul and Amy. It's only you that thought it was the other way around.'

I watched the penny drop behind his eyes. 'It's about the way you feel?' he said.

I exhaled and closed my eyes. 'Yes, Charlie, it's about how I feel. I'm in control of it, not you. You're the unhappy recipient of my current affections. And don't think I wouldn't change it if I could, and I will, but I need time—'

'Shut up,' he said, and kissed me.

Joe had walked on discreetly. He stopped and waited. He turned. He walked back to the house. Finally he went inside, presumably to wait for us in the comfort of my kitchen.

I stood on the pavement caught tightly up against Charlie, clinging around him as he kissed up a storm in me, a whirlwind, then stilled the storm with an agony of touching, of fingers on cheeks and lips, and shared breath. And then he pulled away and broke my heart. 'I can't,' he said, one hand still on my cheek. 'And I can't tell you why.'

'You have a wife and five children,' I said, feebly trying to smile.

'I have a brother,' he said. 'And that's all I can tell you.' Then he turned and walked quickly away. 'I'll probably see you tomorrow, Cora.' He waved without turning.

I went inside, stirred to the point of madness. Joe rose, kissed my cheek and hurried after Charlie. I turned out the lights and stumbled upstairs.

I paced my bedroom floor, sat down on the edge of the bed, stood up, paced some more. Charlie loved me. That's what he'd said. *Isn't it?* But he wasn't going to do anything about it. Because he had a brother.

What?

My emotions see-sawed between euphoria and despair. Euphoria won. Charlie loved me. He'd said so. He wrote love songs for me!

Eventually I flung myself on my bed and, fully dressed, drifted to sleep on a wave of happiness; and woke in the morning to the cold light of reality.

Charlie would never be mine. He'd said that, too.

Chapter 30

C HARLIE RANG ON SATURDAY, when Grace and I were sitting in the sunshine on the Embankment watching the boats going up and down the river.

'Where are you?' he asked.

'By the river, near the South Bank Centre. What is it, Charlie?' I was struggling to keep my tone even, to revert to my manner of the days before I'd effectively told Charlie — *oh dear God* — that I loved him.

Charlie appeared to be having no such trouble; his tone was the same as ever. 'I'm at a bookshop on The Strand,' he said. 'Can I join you? I need to talk to you about something.'

'Are you walking? We could meet you halfway.'

'No, stay there. I'll be very quick. I'll call you again when I get close and you can tell me exactly where to find you.'

We were still on the bench when he arrived, out of breath, bearing ice-creams.

'Charlie!' squealed Grace, hugging him around the waist with one hand, reaching for an ice-cream with the other.

'Cupboard love,' he accused her playfully. He greeted me with a kiss on the cheek, like every other time; most other times.

Grace stood up to try and out-stare a performance artist sprayed gold from head to toe.

'What's up?' I said, as lightly as I could. I was trying to avoid looking him full in the face.

'My brother,' he said.

'What about your brother?'

'My brother's in a wheelchair, Cora. He's quadriplegic. My Dad and I share his care.'

'I'm sorry,' I said, frowning. 'Was it an accident?'

There was the smallest pause before he answered. 'Yes.'

'That's a big responsibility.' In a flash I understood what he thought he was telling me. 'You have a big responsibility. You already have someone to take care of, and you think I'd be a burden.' I looked at him properly for the first time. I was furious. 'You think I'd be a burden, that you'd have to look after me all the time, like Peter did, like Rebecca still does?'

'No,' he said, fidgeting awkwardly. 'Well, yes. And no.' He threw his half-eaten ice-cream into a rubbish bin and rammed his hands in his pockets. 'It's not that you'd be a burden, Cora. Why would you be? And it's not that I don't... Well, I think I've already made my feelings pretty clear.' He gave me a tight smile. 'I can't have relationships, Cora. I don't have time. When Michael is with my dad I live like there's no tomorrow. I met you in one of those periods. I didn't expect to... You took me by surprise. The rest of the time — I don't go to clubs and hang out with friends. I go to work and I come home and I take care of Michael. He's a full-time job.'

'And you think I...' I hesitated and rephrased: 'And you think no woman would be willing to share that load with you?'

'I don't share,' said Charlie.

'So that's it?'

He tried to grin; it didn't reach his eyes. 'Of course not. We're friends, Cora. I'll see you sometimes. But not when Michael is with me. I don't want you to think... I don't want you waiting for me.'

'I wasn't planning to hang around waiting for you, Charlie.'

'Well that's okay then.'

'Fine.'

'Good.'

We were both out of breath, glaring at one another, panting. Another second and I would have reached out and devoured his parted lips, sucked the last of his breath into my mouth. Luckily Grace interrupted us.

'I made her move!' she sang. The gold artist was shifting, slowly and deliberately, as if she'd planned it.

'Well done,' said Charlie woodenly.

Grace cocked her head and looked thoughtful. 'Antlers growing,' she said.

'Antlers?'

'Moose antlers. But only on the males. They started growing again. Last night. It happens each spring. Did you know, antlers are the fastest growing animal part in the world?'

'Really?' said Charlie, looking, to his credit, only mildly bemused.

'They grow about six feet across in three months.' Grace looked bashful for a moment and then confided, 'I know when things happen because I feel it, but sometimes I have to look up the details on the internet.'

'Quite right.' Charlie laid a hand on her shoulder.

We walked slowly up the Embankment, each of us holding one of Grace's hands. At first I was too frustrated and angry to say a word. I stared ahead of me and hardly noticed anyone or anything. But slowly, slowly my anger seeped away, and I began to notice the sunshine and the rippling water and the profile of the Houses of Parliament across the river. We wore our coats, but the sun was warm on our heads.

'Have you been on the London Eye?' asked Charlie. The set of his shoulders told me he was more upset than he was trying to sound.

Grace looked at him witheringly. 'We don't exactly need to pay for an aerial view of London.'

'Grace!' I murmured. 'That was rude.'

Charlie just laughed.

'You should come with us some time,' said Grace. I shot her a look, but she was looking out over the river.

'I would if I were a walker,' said Charlie.

'You just need practice,' said Grace, eyeing him speculatively. 'Will you come over and watch movies with me again? Soon? I hate school. Will you teach me to play the piano?'

Passersby might have thought we were a family. Grace and Charlie were deep in conversation about what she would have to do at school to win piano lessons from him. I dropped behind, deep in thought.

At first I thought about Charlie and his disabled brother. It was typical of what I knew of Charlie, that he would dedicate himself to a brother like this. But it was unnatural, too. Should I hold out hope? Could I cope with a disabled relative? It was a sobering thought. My instinct was that I would cope with anything if it meant I could have

Charlie. But that was too easy; and there was Grace to consider.

Then I was angry again: why would Charlie think I couldn't or wouldn't cope? Did I look like a lightweight — did I act like one? And that was a sobering thought, too.

And then I was too busy watching Charlie and Grace together to think about anything much except them. The two people I loved best in the world — *God, stop saying that!* — walking hand in hand, laughing into each other's faces, strolling down the river bank on a sunny afternoon. The scene shivered; the spirit of everything — buildings, blades of grass, people, water — shimmered, making every outline hazy and indefinite, sending dazzling rainbow colours into the air, mostly golds and pinks and blues. It was gorgeous.

And then it wasn't, because there was a counterbalance of something completely horrible going on at the same time. Mixing with the dazzle of the rainbow were terrible flashes of a different intensity. Black. Red.

Black for mystery and for hiding. Red for temper — and spiritual incontinence.

The pattern wasn't random; it was homing in on Grace and Charlie and me.

I ran forward and caught Charlie's hand in both of mine. I clung to it and he was instantly alert. 'What's wrong?'

'Don't let go of me. Keep Grace distracted.'

He returned his attention to Grace as if nothing had changed, but at the same time he twined his fingers firmly around mine.

There were five or six of them — I couldn't be quite sure. They hadn't popped; they were walking in the crowds around us, in our direction, and keeping close. I caught the eye of a youth in torn jeans. His eyes were bloodshot as if he hadn't slept for weeks; he smiled darkly at me. He didn't seem to mind at all that I'd spotted him stalking us. Ahead of us, on Grace's side, was a girl, tall, pretty, with a long stride and a brilliant red aura. She turned her head to smile at me with gleaming teeth. She too showed no sign of distress at having been noticed. From the corner of my eye I caught a shadow of deep black. There was no silver but it was, in every other respect, exactly like my nightmare.

My breathing hitched. This was it; he'd found me. My mother's killer had found me, on a brilliant sunlit day, out with my daughter and the man I loved. My whole life had been building up to this moment.

'Steady,' murmured Charlie. 'Tell me what you see.'

I was having difficulty keeping from crying out hysterically. It was bad enough being so scared, but having to hide my fear from Grace was worse. 'We're surrounded. I think there are five of them.'

'Mummy,' said Grace in her clear, calm voice. 'What are they doing?'

My stomach dropped to my knees, which buckled. Grace could see them. Of course Grace could see them. 'I don't know, darling,' I said cheerfully. 'I think we should ignore them.' I lowered my voice so only Charlie could hear. 'They haven't popped yet. Charlie, I think it's him.'

'Steady now. It isn't him,' murmured Charlie.

'I think it is.'

'Do you recognise him?'

I scanned the group again; and again. And then I relaxed. 'They're all young,' I breathed. 'They're all too young. Most of them are younger than me. It isn't him.'

This was the moment my knees chose to buckle; my relief was greater than my fear had been.

'Mummy,' cried Grace as I sank to the ground.

'Get up, Cora,' said Charlie between gritted teeth, yanking at my arm. 'Get up. We're not clear yet.'

'It's not him,' I said, and I was crying.

The stalkers were in a circle around us; the circle was closing tighter.

CHAPTER 31

'GET UP!' COMMANDED CHARLIE, and I did. 'They can't do anything out here. They're just trying to scare you.'

I looked up into the sky and there was my fear, and their activity, hanging in the air, an aurora borealis of spikes and sparks, black rimmed and red and the faintest, iciest yellow. It was a telltale cosmic symbol of what was happening on the ground.

I saw Charlie glance up nervously, and knew that, whether he could see it or not, he knew what would be showing up there.

'Remember what Raul said? They're deliberately attracting attention,' I breathed.

'They're wasting their time,' he said grimly, dragging me along by the hand.

I looked round him and tried to smile reassuringly at Grace; she was alert and concerned, but not scared.

We kept walking. They did not leave us. Charlie stayed resolutely calm and cheerful. He made us pause to watch a juggler, and then he turned us about and walked us back in the direction of the South Bank Centre. He kept up a flow of easy chatter, discussing details of the skyline, drawing Grace's attention to boats along the river. She was as distracted as I was by our menacing company; it was like being a general trapped within the iron cage of a Praetorian guard. Worse still, I could no longer get all of our unwanted companions in my eye-line; I could only sense their presence, and the recurrent tattoo of colour — red and black, red and black.

We turned onto a bridge and I thought we must lose them in the stream of bodies trickling into the narrow walkway across the river, but when we emerged by the Embankment tube station they materialised around us again. They seemed curiously relaxed, as if they had nothing better to do than follow us around, their Selfs pulsing like beacons through their skin. We walked up Villiers Street, past Charing Cross and St. Martin in the Fields into Trafalgar Square. Finally we lost them as we entered the National Gallery.

I pulled my hand out of Charlie's and flexed my fingers painfully. 'Sorry.'

'Don't be.' I put my hand back into his.

'Can you see them?'

Grace looked around. 'They've gone, Mum. Who were they?'

I leaned towards her. 'I can't tell you. I don't know. Are you okay?'

'Of course. Charlie wouldn't let go.'

At least Grace had the good sense to know she was safe with Charlie. He and I exchanged a long glance.

'While we're here,' said Charlie, and raised his eyebrows suggestively, inviting me to direct him.

'Room 45,' said Grace, and she headed for the stairs with a comical look of resignation.

'Van Gogh?' said Charlie as we entered a large, well-lit room lined with framed canvases.

'No,' said Grace eagerly. 'Not the Pissaros either. She likes this one.'

On the wall between a selection of well known Impressionist greats was a glorious story-book picture of a family group: a mother, a father, and a little girl who looked straight out from the picture into my eyes.

'On loan: *Picnic at Le Pouldu*. Maurice Denis,' read Grace with a studied air of casualness. 'Someone rich actually owns it.'

Charlie looked at me with surprise. 'Not what I was expecting. But I suppose I should have expected *that*, at least.' He turned back to the picture. 'It's like an illustration from a kids' book.'

'It's a memory,' I murmured. My heartbeat was still racing. I took a deep breath, pulled back my shoulders, gave a resolute smile and concentrated on the picture. 'See, the mother is giving the little girl a drink. It looks like wine. Daddy is watching. See how they *love* her. See how confident she is in that love; she doesn't even have to look at them. She takes it for granted. She's busy looking at us.' The familiarity of the scene acted like a balm on my senses; I'd thought I was going to die, and instead I was here, staring at my favourite picture.

'A memory?'

'A memory I would like to have,' I admitted. 'A memory I want Grace to have. Not the details. The feeling.'

We were still holding hands, the three of us. Charlie's thumb gently rubbed a path along the back of my knuckles. He didn't look at me again and I was grateful.

'Maurice Denis. Was he a walker?' he asked.

'I'm not sure.' I noted his swift look of disbelief. 'No really. I can't be sure because he deliberately hid himself.'

'How?'

'By insisting that no matter what a painting depicts, it's never anything more than a bunch of colours on a flat surface. It's okay, you're allowed to laugh.'

'Sorry. It's just that, in a room like this, surrounded by these astonishing paintings, that sounds sacrilegious. Although I can see how that approach would appeal to you — the insistent lack of mystique.'

'There's more,' I said. 'He also insisted that the source of all art is the character of the painter.'

Charlie paused with a frown to consider this. 'Is that such a surprise?'

'It depends on your point of view. What it does, however, is renounce any effort to reproduce the essential quality of an object. He hasn't painted a girl — his daughter by the way. He's painted how he feels about the girl.'

'So why can't you tell if he's a walker?'

'A walker would have reproduced some element of the *spirit* of his daughter in the picture. But she's completely absent. There's only him. And yet — it's such a strong impression of him, it's hard to believe he's not a walker.' I broke away from the mind-game the picture always provoked in me. 'It's like he's playing hide-and-seek.'

'But only with walkers,' said Charlie, amused.

'That's a point,' I said slowly. 'I never thought about that. Only a walker would understand the game.' I looked at Charlie bemused. 'I don't know whether to kiss you or thump you.'

My eyes inadvertently strayed to his mouth, and my body flooded with — it was lust. There was no other term for it. He was a magnet;

I almost fell forward into him. Instead, I took a resolute step backwards.

'Okay so that was a bit dim of me,' I mumbled, and then quickly added, 'I'm talking about the painting.'

He was grinning. 'Not dim. But curiously revealing, Cora. You've obviously spent so long wondering where the painter was coming from, you forgot where you were coming from. The answer isn't in what he was. It's in what you are.'

I gave him my best withering glance, a pale imitation of what Grace was capable of. 'Trying to give me a little life lesson?'

'Wouldn't dream of it. Could you reproduce this painting?'

'I'd struggle,' I conceded. 'For all the reasons I've described, it's virtually un-copiable unless you're the original artist.'

'I like this one better,' said Grace, pulling us towards Henri Rousseau's much more famous painting of a tiger in a forest. 'It's called *Surprise!*'

Charlie willingly played the stooge. 'What's the surprise?'

'It's supposed to be a tiger hunt, but the tiger's doing the hunting! Look at his expression.' Grace looked very pleased with herself. 'Tiger Tiger, burning bright, in the forest of the night,' she quoted. 'That's William Blake. I heard a woman telling her son William Blake wrote the poem after he'd seen this picture but that's wrong because Blake came first.'

'Clever clogs,' said Charlie.

Despite the sunshine outside, room 45 was full of people making pilgrimage to the tiger, or Van Gogh's *Sunflowers*, or Picasso's *Child with a Dove*. I didn't see the red girl come in, but a flash of red alerted me to her presence. I turned in a panic but she wasn't coming after us anymore. Instead, all of her attention — her desire, her fickle, momentary ambition — was focused on a middle-aged woman standing in front of the sunflowers. The woman was entranced. She wore thick, flesh-coloured tights and had on a tweedy skirt too heavy for the season. She had the weathered skin of Cezanne's woman with a rosary, which was hanging nearby, and was clearly overcome by Van Gogh's yellows and golds. There were tears on her cheeks; she was transfixed — she was *charmed*.

It happened in a moment. The woman popped and the red girl,

standing right beside her now, popped too. Two bodies, two Selfs — and then the red Self dived into the woman's body, leaving the red body precariously vacant, and the woman's Self blinking furiously from the ceiling.

'Good God!' said Charlie under his breath, staring at the ceiling. 'Did I just see what I think I saw?'

'Help her, Mummy,' said Grace, and then she screwed up her face and threw her hands to her ears as the dislocated Self began to scream. 'Help her, Mummy!' cried Grace.

Charlie made a grab for Grace's hand and, when she wouldn't — couldn't — take it away from her ears, he pulled her against his waist and put his whole arm around her head.

The peasant-like woman was beginning to walk calmly away from the sunflowers, heading for the exit. The red girl's body moved awkwardly in her wake, bound to the woman by a thin, scarcely visible silver thread.

Aaaahhh! wailed the Self from the ceiling, trying to move after them.

'We have to follow,' I said, urgently pulling Charlie and Grace along with me and wincing against the screams. There was a sudden restless shuffling around us; several people suddenly exited the room, as if on a whim.

'Can you hear it?' I asked Charlie, making an effort not to raise my voice over the screaming.

'Of course,' he said grimacing. 'It's pure emotion.'

Words couldn't penetrate the material world but pure emotion certainly could. I was worried the energy of her distress was going to start dislodging things in the room and cause a general panic — not to mention the potential for destruction. 'Charlie, I don't know what to do.'

'Nothing. Nothing. Cora, do nothing.' There was a tiny note of panic in his voice, the first I'd ever heard.

'I can't do nothing,' I said, and I popped.

Calm down! At least I could shout now. *Calm down and I will help you!*

The poor, unpractised Self obediently stopped wailing and fixed wide, astonished eyes on my face.

You've fainted. From the heat, I said, improvising madly. *This is a dream. In a minute you'll wake up, but first you have to stay calm and do as I say. Okay?*

The Self nodded.

Stay close to your body, and get right back inside it when I tell you to. Come with me.

We headed towards the woman's body, slowly, because this Self did not know what it was doing. The red girl's eyes gazed with unnatural fervour from out of the woman's weathered face. I flew practically into her face to make her stop, and then I pointed back at my body, smiling, miming an invitation.

The red girl widened her borrowed eyes, cracked an unnaturally broad smile, and popped. The woman's body fell in a heap on the floor, I shouted, *Now!* and after only a moment's hesitation her Self snapbacked into it.

The red girl's Self drifted close to mine. She looked back at my body, which was standing nearby, vacant but upright, flanked by Charlie and Grace, who were still also holding hands with each other, so that the three of us formed a little circle. The red girl looked pointedly at my hand, and her eyes followed the thread back to my body.

Impressive! she said without rancour. *Magda said you were a trembler. Magda? Did Magda send you?*

The girl looked at me laconically. *Nobody sends me anywhere. She suggested we might have some fun with you. It has been fun, although you're not what I was expecting. Is that your daughter?*

She's not a walker. I spoke too fast, sounded too earnest.

The red girl grinned. *Yeah, I'll bet she isn't. I suppose he isn't one either.* It wasn't a question.

What do you think? I said more coolly.

The red girl looked around her. *I love this room. You get more action here than most other places in the world. The Mona Lisa's good, too, of course. You get the random pictures that only send one or two people spinning, but you have to wait around for ages for anything to happen. I always think it's easier to come to the dead certs, don't you? Everyone loves an Impressionist.*

I don't see the fascination of preying on non-walkers.

You obviously haven't tried it, she said pleasantly. *Well, if you were a trembler, you're not one now. You've learned a few things.* She nodded at my silver thread, my standing body. *You're only a step or two away from invading waifs and strays yourself. How is our friend doing?*

The middle-aged woman was at the centre of a small crowd, sitting on a chair with her chin on her chest. An attendant was hovering with a glass of water and a clipboard.

I'll be seeing you, said the red girl, grinning. *You and your daughter.*

Tell my sister I want to see her, I called after her.

She snapbacked into her waiting body and walked quickly away.

'What were you thinking?' hissed Charlie fiercely the moment I snapbacked. 'That was ridiculous, Cora! What were you thinking!' He was shaking with fear and anger.

'It's all right,' I soothed. 'There was no danger.'

'And if she'd gone into you?'

'I'd have ejected her, like Joe did with Magda.'

'You haven't had enough practice! It's far too early for that!'

'I'm okay, Charlie. We're all okay. Even the woman.'

'I was watching your lips. You told her it was a dream,' giggled Grace.

I put my hands on her shoulders. 'You okay, Gracie?'

'Of course I am, Mum. You were cool.'

'Home,' said Charlie. 'Now.'

Chapter 32

NEXT DAY, JOE, REESE AND KEN were on the doorstep before I was out of bed — although, admittedly, I slept late that morning. I heard Amy let them in, and squeals from Grace that suggested she was being tossed between Joe and Reese.

'And Charlie stayed the night to protect us!' Grace was yelling as I came into the kitchen.

'Morning boys,' I said.

Raul was whispering in Amy's ear. 'Guest bedroom,' she replied pointedly, rolling her eyes.

Charlie was dressed and eating breakfast. I sat down without looking at him and he slid a mug of coffee towards me.

'Tell us everything,' instructed Joe.

Between us, Grace, Charlie and I recounted the previous day's adventures — the shadowing walkers, the red girl, the gallery.

'Unbelievable!' said Reese. 'In broad daylight!'

'Maybe we were wrong to concentrate on music,' mused Raul.

'What do you mean?' I asked.

'Music's what we know,' said Joe, 'so that's what we concentrate on. We patrol music events, but mostly at night. The hits are pretty random — nothing like what you've described.'

'It's all about the signal,' said Reese, stuffing a whole croissant in his mouth. 'When's Michael arriving, Charlie?'

'Shut up, Reese.'

'I'm just saying.'

'Well don't.'

'Saying what?' I asked.

'That Charlie's going to be tied up for a while,' said Joe.

****

The following afternoon I took a couple of blankets and a book and went outside into the May sunshine. There was nothing quite like summer in the city, I decided. Summers in Yorkshire were glorious, of course, but there was something intensely satisfying about the clean, gun-metal quality of sunshine among buildings and traffic, birdsong outside a dozen windows, green leaves fluttering over grey pavements. Most of all, it was the effect the sunshine had on the millions of inhabitants of the city that was so enervating; so many uplifted spirits in one relatively small geographical area.

The communal garden of Gregory Square was enclosed behind high metal railings. Each resident had a key to the rickety gate and the private world behind it. It had been planted and re-planted over at least two centuries, and was an enchanting series of tiny spaces screened from one another by groups of trees and shrubs. There were no walkways, only grass. The centre gave a 360-degree view of the top floor of all the buildings in the square.

I must have fallen asleep; the next thing I heard was Amy coming towards me, bearing mugs of tea.

'I've never sat out in a roundabout before,' she said.

'It's not a roundabout,' I objected, sitting up.

'It's surprisingly big, once you're in here. And private, now the trees have their leaves.' She handed me a mug and sat down beside me.

'Busy day?' I asked.

'Hmm.'

'Amy, did you know about Charlie's brother?' I asked her.

'Yes.' She took a sip of tea and pulled one of the blankets over her shoulders. 'Raul told me. Charlie's devoted to him.' She looked at me and said, very carefully, 'He never has serious girlfriends because of it.'

'So I hear.'

'I bet he'd make an exception for you.'

'Apparently not,' I said.

'Really? So what's he going to do then — give up his life to take care of his brother? That's very noble but it's not exactly realistic, is it?'

'Did Raul say whether the brother was — whether his disability was only physical?'

Amy shook her head. 'He didn't say.' She shuddered. 'God. Can you imagine being locked in a broken body and knowing exactly what's happening to you but not being able to talk or move?'

****

The best thing about having a child in the house — quite apart from how much I loved this particular child — was the way her demands superseded all other considerations. Too weary to get out of bed? The child needed breakfast and seeing off to school. Too fed up to work? The child needed food and clothing and a roof over her head. Too scared, too lovesick, too confused? Too bad; everything was subsumed to the domestic ritual of raising the child.

Which is why I felt calm when the doorbell rang the next morning and I found Magda on my doorstep.

'You're not in fancy dress,' I said pleasantly, holding back the door.

She grinned. 'I've come as myself.' She held out her arms, and I realised I was supposed to appreciate the fact that she was soberly dressed, for her, in a bottle-green velvet pinafore.

'Nice,' I said. 'Were you going to come in?'

She grinned again, and I felt myself wilting. There were people who could make you feel small just by breathing the same air as you, and Magda was one of them.

She took me by surprise by marching straight up to the first-floor living room.

'I know my way around,' she said, making herself comfortable in an armchair. 'I had a good look at your house last time I was here.'

'I believe you were wearing me on that occasion.'

'So I was. Well, I hear you've made progress. Sally told me what happened at the gallery. Not bad. We'll have you joining us any time now.'

'Us?'

'My gang,' she said.

I raised my eyebrows. 'Aren't you a little old to be hanging out in a gang?'

'Look who's calling the kettle black. Like you don't have a regular little walker gang of your own; I've met them, remember? Now then. I doubt you want to play at being sisters, and I certainly don't. I got your message. What did you want to talk about?'

The room — my much loved living room, filled with my books and my favourite pieces of furniture — receded and all I could see was Magda. 'I want to know why you came looking for me if ... if you dislike me so much.'

Magda threw back her head and laughed. When she'd recovered herself she smoothed her hair back with her hand. 'Dislike you?' She leaned forward and her tone changed. 'I hate you,' she said.

I shrank back; the intensity of her words hit me like a slap. 'Why?'

She leaned back again, as if she were settling in for a cosy chat. 'It must have been great for you, waltzing off to a life of privilege and safety in jolly old Yorkshire. All ponies and hockey and private school. Had a lovely time, did you?'

'I was six years old,' I said. 'I was in a strange country with strange people who told me my mother was dead and I could never go home again. I was an orphan with a new family, a foreigner with a strange accent, a walker forbidden to walk. How lovely do you think it was?'

'Oh, I think it was pretty nice. All things considered.'

I was knocked over by the ancient bitterness in her voice, a tangible thing, an extraordinarily potent negative energy. 'What happened to you?' I said, my voice barely louder than a whisper.

'I wasn't quite so lucky.' Magda examined her nails. 'The family I was sent to wasn't quite as — nice — as yours. No, wait, that's not quite true. The dad was very nice. He thought I was nice, too. He went out of his way to show me how much he liked me.'

I made a noise in my throat and she looked at me in disgust. 'Oh don't pretend to be sorry for me, Cora. You never gave me a thought, did you, as long as you were okay? I was eight years old, and completely defenceless, while that monster smiled and minced his way through my childhood.'

'Did you tell anyone?' I whispered.

'Of course,' she spat. 'Do you think they believed me? You have a very short memory. I was always Magda the liar, Magda the trouble-maker. You were the perfect child, not me.'

'What did you do?'

She calmed right down again. 'Ah well, you see, in a sense, that bastard was the saving of me. I walked.'

'You walked to escape him?'

'I couldn't escape him, you moron. He was legally my dad after Mum so casually handed me over to him. But I got my revenge. I walked, and guess who found me?'

Silver and black. Silver and black. 'Oh no...'

'Oh yes! Our mum's special fella himself! She was right, you know; I only had to walk once — just the once — and he found me.'

'But you're alive!'

'He didn't want to kill me, you fuck-wit. He never wanted to kill any of us.'

'Then why did he? Why did he kill Mum?'

Her expression changed; there was pity in her eyes. 'You really are clueless, aren't you. He didn't kill her, sister dear. She killed herself. Dear old Mum gave us away like used books and then she took a nice hot bath and slashed her wrists.'

'She did not.'

'Oh yes she did. I know. I found her in the bath. I pulled out the plug. I watched her drain away down the plughole.'

I couldn't see her anymore; I couldn't see anything and my voice was barely audible. 'What were you doing there? Where was I?'

'You, my dear, were safely in England. I'd run away, hadn't I? I ran away the first time my nice new daddy touched me. I ran home. But I was too late. Mum had already gone.'

'You're lying.'

She looked amused. 'You know I'm not.'

I was fascinated and repelled, as if this were some terrible story that had nothing to do with me. I felt that if I could only stay here, in the moment, I could avoid facing the reality of what she was saying. As long as she was here talking, it was all just words.

'So what happened then?' I tried to speak up, to get the tremor out of my voice; I was only partly successful.

'They took me back. To my new home. And when I had nothing left to lose, I walked. And that's what saved me. Magnus found me, you see. He was heartbroken over Mum. Don't look like that. He was fond of her.'

He had a name. The terror of my childhood — *silver and black* —

had a name. I licked my dry lips. 'He was called Magnus?'

'Magnus,' she said. She said it lovingly, like it was a mantra. 'He rescued me.' There was a craving, servile look on her face.

'How?'

She smiled. 'Let's see. First we took care of daddy dear.'

My eyes flew wide. 'How?'

'We drove him out of his mind.'

'You mean you drove him out of his body?'

She looked impressed. 'You're catching on! We did that next, yes. First we drove him mad, then we drove him out of his body, and then Magnus drowned him in the lake. It was fun! After that I was handed from one family to another.'

'Did anyone else die?'

'Look at you! All cold-blooded and curious! You could almost pass for my sister, you know.' Her eyes were blazing. 'We only hurt the people that hurt me. You can't imagine what it was like, having Magnus on my side. It didn't matter where they sent me, or who they put me with. Magnus always showed up and helped me out.'

I had an unnerving vision of the trail of chaos and disaster that must have followed in Magda's wake. Any minute now my flimsy detachment was going to crumble, and I would crumble with it. I swallowed hard. 'Lucky you,' I said.

'We looked for you,' she said. 'We searched and searched but you kept your word, didn't you? Not a single pop in twenty years. How did you do it? I'm impressed. I once stayed whole for a week, and it killed me. We had everyone looking out for you, you know. Magnus knows everyone. They were all searching. We never stopped. And then at last there was a sighting. At a hospital here in London. And that was it! Luckily I was already in England by then.'

'Well, clearly you found me,' I said. 'So where's Magnus?'

Her manner changed. She looked down into her lap. 'He'll be along,' she said.

'Why hasn't he come yet?' *Hold on. Hold on.*

I'd kept my Self silent; as it spoke to me now, an unnatural light sprang behind Magda's eyes. 'You're very keen all of a sudden,' she snarled. 'He'll show up. He just hasn't seen my messages yet. I'm going to send up the biggest flare you've ever seen. He'll come, you'll see. Even if he's locked up.'

Her self-control slipped. I saw her outlines blur and realised she was struggling not to pop. It was like a game of chicken: which of us would lose control first?

'Magnus is locked up? In prison? For how long?' It was imperative to get as much information as I possibly could while she was still talking.

She gave a nasty laugh. 'I didn't say he was in prison. I just haven't seen him for a while. But he'll come, you'll see. I'm just keeping you amused until he gets here. He'll be so proud of me.'

'And what will he do with me?'

She wasn't smiling now. 'Whatever he wants. I can't think why he's so bothered about you. I'd have given up on you years ago but he was insistent. We must find her, he said, your poor little sister! She's all alone out there!'

Her anger spurted out like a struck match and a book flew out of the shelf.

Good God, is she doing that whole? What can her Self do?

Another book flew across the room, and another, knocking a framed picture of Grace onto the floor; the glass splintered.

Magda calmed down as quickly as she'd lit up. 'I'm a much, much more skilled walker than you'll ever be, whatever progress you've made of late.' She stood up and looked around her. A vase smashed to the floor, and the curtains rose and fluttered into the room as if a sudden wind had come in through the closed window.

'What I'm doing now,' she said, 'is sending little jets of energy across the room to disturb physical objects.' A second photo of Grace crashed to the floor. 'It's quite advanced. I doubt your sanctimonious friends can show you how to do it. By the way, you can tell them they're welcome to patrol as much as they like. There are more of us' — she stood up — 'and nothing will stop us having fun.' She was out of the room and halfway down the stairs before she'd finished talking.

'Magda,' I called, following behind her at a run.

She stopped and turned to face me. 'Yes?'

'You're the only family I've got, and I'm the only family you've got—'

She stared at me as if I were mad. 'You want to play families? With me? Weren't you listening? I hate you! Always have. *Always* will!'

'I don't believe you,' I said desperately.

'Oh, you will.'

Chapter 33

GRACE WOKE ME THE NEXT MORNING by bouncing on my bed.

'Go away. It's too early.' I tried and failed to pull her under the covers with me for a cuddle. *She must never know how wretched I am.*

'Norway and I are ready for a parade,' she said, marching up and down on the bed and waving an invisible flag.

'What are you talking about. Norway?'

She dropped to her knees and shook me. 'It's Norway's national day. The parades have already started. Can we go?'

'What now? No. We haven't had breakfast.'

'I don't want breakfast. I want to see the marching bands. It's all friendly and happy,' she assured me. 'Feel it.'

With a little concentration I sensed what she had; a tide of excitement and celebration concentrated over a rocky, narrow strip of land to the north. How did she do it — pick out these random strands from the millions of events taking place all over the world?

I found myself sending up a silent prayer: *Please let it always be happy events she tunes into.*

'Breakfast,' I said.

'No parades?'

'No parades.'

'What *is* the point of being a walker if we never go anywhere *exotic*,' she sighed dramatically, and flounced off to get dressed.

'I'm not sure Norway's what you'd call exotic,' I called after her.

We had no plans and, because it was raining outside, we settled down to a quiet day at home. Grace persuaded Amy to show her around her make-up collection while I pretended to read.

For twenty-four hours now I'd been pretending nothing had happened. It was as if my body was storing the new information, but I was keeping it from my Self. I didn't want to know; I wished I'd never heard any of it. I knew I should tell Charlie and Joe — this was exactly what they'd told me I needed to find out. But first I had to make sense of it myself, and how could I do that when I could hardly even think about the things Magda told me?

Meantime, I'd cleared up the mess she made, and by the time Grace and Amy had come home, I was completely calm. I even slept that night, all night long, and woke up the next morning as if nothing had happened. And now I was pretending to read, sitting quietly in suspended animation, holding a book in front of my nose.

My mother hadn't been killed. She had chosen to leave. She had chosen to leave. She had chosen to leave.

Why would I want to process that information?

Later that afternoon Raul came over, with Reese and Joe. They looked gloomy.

'Michael's here,' they said. 'No more Charlie for a month or two.'

'Is it really like that?' I asked.

Joe looked at me. 'I'm sorry, baby. Don't go getting any ideas about trying to help him out. Charlie wouldn't like it.'

'So his brother arrives and Charlie vanishes off the face of the earth?'

'It's not that big of a deal,' drawled Raul. 'We're all used to it. Jeez, Joe, you make it sound like Charlie's a saint.'

'He is a saint,' said Reese. He looked drawn and tired; there were bags under his eyes. He was normally buoyant and upbeat, but he looked frankly depressed. 'I hate it when Michael comes to town. And I hate it that Charlie has to disappear.'

'He really won't let any of you help him out?'

'It isn't safe,' began Reese.

'Charlie doesn't like it,' said Joe, staring hard at Reese. 'He likes to keep it in the family. He's a proud man, you know?'

I looked at them all, Raul hanging round Amy's neck, Joe sitting at the table with Grace, Reese sitting tensely upright. They looked defeated.

'This is ridiculous,' I said. 'If Charlie wants to ruin his own life, that's fine, but he's not ruining mine. Amy, will you watch Grace?' I grabbed my jacket from the back of a chair.

'Leave it, Cora,' said Joe, running out after me.

I rounded on him. 'Joe, I love him. I love Charlie. I'm not going to stay out of his way just because he has a disabled brother. This is all nonsense. I'm going over there right now. I want to meet this brother of his.'

Reese was standing in the doorway watching us, fingering his silver hair. 'No,' he said. 'You really don't.'

'Well how bad can it be? Is he violent? He's not a monster, is he? Tell me!'

Reese put his hands on my shoulders and, short of actually picking me up, forced me back into the house.

Joe said, 'Stay away, Cora,' in a voice that made it clear why he was the natural leader of the group. And then he added, 'If Charlie wanted you, he'd have told you so.'

I ran from them, up the stairs to my room, and slammed the door, like a naughty schoolgirl.

****

But I wanted Charlie. Everything I'd always believed to be true was ... nonsense. The truth was more horrible than the horrors I'd imagined. My memory was faulty; the fears that had haunted my life were ... faulty. The only thing worse than my mother being killed was my mother killing herself; the only thing worse than the silver-haired man wanting to kill me was what he'd done for Magda — killing others.

I wanted Charlie. I sneaked out of the house and took a taxi through the busy London streets. I stared out of the window at the beautiful day, resolutely not planning what I was going to say when I turned up on his doorstep.

I paid the taxi fare, stood gazing up at Charlie's flat for a moment, and then pressed the buzzer by the door.

The speaker crackled. 'Who is it?'

'Charlie, it's me. Cora. Open up.'

There was a long delay. I began to think Charlie was going to pretend he didn't know me. But at last there was a buzzing noise and I pushed the door open and went up.

Charlie was at the door. 'What the fuck are you thinking of?' he demanded. There was no hint of welcome in his eyes, no friendliness at all, just a kind of astonishment. 'You've actually come to my door? Do you have a death wish?'

I took a step back as if he'd slapped me. 'Death wish?' I stammered. 'Because I want to see you?'

There was a noise from within his flat, more animal than human, an inarticulate yammering.

Compassion flooded my heart. 'I'm coming in, Charlie,' I said.

I must have taken him by surprise; he could have stopped me if he'd wanted but clearly he underestimated my tenacity. I was past him and in his flat.

Everything smelled different. Cleaning fluid, maybe; antiseptic. I didn't spot the wheelchair at first, because it was standing in a shady corner, but I felt an extraordinary presence, and a compelling need to keep stepping forward, to come deeper inside. I took a step further into the room and then I saw the wheelchair and the figure in it, and my spirit splintered.

It was as bad as it could get. Charlie's brother was hopelessly broken. He was large, a fully grown adult, supported by an exoskeleton of steel rods and hinges. A cushioned brace encased his head. He was strapped into his chair. As I drew nearer, he convulsed with that horrible, inhuman sound, and spit ran down his chin.

'Satisfied?' said Charlie. 'Would you like to stay? Eat with us, maybe? If you like, you can help me to bath him later.'

Michael was as big as Charlie, if not bigger. It would take at least three strong men to manhandle him into a bath. The idea of Charlie trying to manage alone was devastating.

'Michael,' I said, 'I'm Cora.'

I took a step forward but Charlie grabbed my arm.

'He's deaf,' said Charlie viciously. 'Blind too. He doesn't know you're there.'

Michael was convulsing more violently now, rattling around inside the steel cage that held him up. Charlie went to him and laid a hand on his head. He stroked his brother's hair. 'Get out of here, Cora,' he said.

Michael's eyes had been closed until now, but suddenly they snapped open. His eyes were brown, with no discernible pupil. They rolled madly, like a beast at an abattoir, as if he were struggling for vision. His feet were practically drumming on the footplate of his wheelchair.

'Get out of here!' spat Charlie.

It was monstrous; it was terrifying. I summoned every last ounce of compassion in me, and it wasn't enough to quash the bile rising in my throat at the sight of this appalling, pitiful creature in front of me.

But I felt something else too: an overwhelming desire to step forward, to touch him.

'Go! Now!' yelled Charlie. His eyes were flaming; he was holding onto Michael as if afraid his brother would fall out of his wheelchair. I turned and fled. A terrible wailing followed me out, like a dirge in an alien language.

At the doorway I ran headlong into Joe, who wrapped powerful arms around me.

'Let me go!' I screamed, struggling. 'I have to go back!'

'Walk away, Cora,' urged Joe. 'Charlie doesn't want you in there. There's nothing you can do to help him.'

Oblivious to my struggling, he forced me down the stairs and shoved me none-too-gently into his car. I stopped struggling. I put my face in my hands and wept. 'How does he stand it?' I sobbed. 'That poor creature. How does Charlie stand it, day after day? And how does he manage? He's ... Michael's ... huge. How does Charlie dress him and put him to bed?'

'He manages,' said Joe grimly, starting the engine.

I cried noisily for most of the journey. When Joe pulled up in Gregory Square, I couldn't find the energy to get out of the car.

'I don't think I can live with it,' I said.

'There's no shame in that,' said Joe.

'How does Charlie manage?'

'Just trust that he does.'

Reese must have been looking out for us. He came out and opened my door. When he saw the state I was in, he reached into the car and picked me up bodily.

'Put me down, Reese. I can walk.'

But he didn't. He held me like a baby, carried me into the house and sat down with me in his lap. I cried into his chest for several minutes and then I raised my head.

'I'm going back tomorrow,' I said.

'No, Cora, you aren't,' said Reese.

'Yes I am. I admit, I was taken by surprise. And it won't be a picnic. But I love Charlie. I love him more than ever, now I know what he's capable of.'

Joe was standing over us, arms folded. 'You know what you've just done?' he said in a voice that made me flinch. 'You've just handed yourself to him on a plate. After all this time.'

'And why wouldn't I?' I demanded. 'I love him, Joe. I have no pride left.'

'Charlie loves you and it's nothing to do with pride,' said Reese, looking up at Joe with a stark warning on his face.

Joe turned his back on us and stalked away.

I gave Reese a hug and then wriggled off his knee; he really was a huge man, like a bear. 'I'm not sure I can live without Charlie. I'm not sure I want to.'

Grace walked through the door at that precise moment, and I could have bitten out my tongue. But she came quietly and put an arm around my shoulder. 'Me neither,' she said.

****

On Monday morning Grace went off to school, Raul and Amy went off to work, and I went upstairs to finalise the shipping paperwork for *Above the Town*. I kept busy, but in my head I was busily plotting a strategy to get to Charlie. At just after two the couriers arrived. They spent an hour wrapping the canvas and getting it ready for transportation. When they left I rang Klaus, and then I cleaned up my studio and waited in the kitchen for Grace to come home. I always felt empty after finishing a commission, but on this occasion I barely registered it.

At four-fifteen the front door opened and Sue came in with one arm around Grace. She looked worried. 'I don't think she's well, Cora. The teacher said she fell asleep again at lunchtime.'

My eyes flew to Grace's face. 'I thought we agreed—' I stopped dead. Her eyes were closed. She was leaning against Sue as if she were going to fall. 'Grace?'

I supported her to the sofa and laid her down. She lay awkwardly, eyes firmly closed.

Sue glanced anxiously at her watch. 'I must go. I've left Ruth in the car and we're due at the dentist five minutes ago. Will you be okay?'

'Of course. Thanks Sue.'

I saw her out the door and hurried back to the sofa, kneeling beside Grace and laying a hand on her forehead. Her temperature felt normal. 'Grace, darling?' I leaned over to kiss her cheek as she opened her eyes.

And then I started screaming and fell back, banging myself on the coffee table. I righted myself and scrabbled backwards, over the table, into the sofa opposite, over the back of it, crouching away from Grace.

Grace lay on the sofa, gleaming eyes wide open, grinning maliciously.

She wasn't my daughter.

CHAPTER 34

I REVERSED MY PATH and flew back across the room, still shrieking, but with fury now, and I grasped Grace's shoulders and shook her hard. 'Where is she!' I screamed into her face. 'What have you done with her? You don't touch children! You don't touch children!'

I sank back as Grace started laughing. I was completely helpless; shaking Grace's body would only damage Grace in the end.

What on earth had made me think Magda would stick with the rules? There she sat grinning at me through Grace's face, flouting the great taboo, caring as little as if she'd stepped on a daisy in the grass.

You don't touch children. You don't touch children!

'Where is she?' I asked in a dead voice.

It was awful having to listen to the answer spoken in Grace's voice. 'She's safe enough.'

'Where?' I asked, my voice rising another octave. 'What have you done with her?'

'I told you. She's safe enough.'

'What do you want?'

'To punish you. To make you really miserable. And to send a signal no one could possibly resist. Although, I have to tell you, it's fabulous being eight again. If I'd known, I'd have tried this much sooner.' She stretched out Grace's limbs with a languid yawn. It was a terrible sight: the languor of an evil woman in my little girl's body.

I was practically rabid with fear and anger. I wanted to rip her eyes out; but they were Grace's eyes. I sat on my hands and closed my own eyes as they filled with tears of impotence. 'Where is she?' I roared helplessly. 'You can have me.' *Here, take me!*

'Take it easy. And snapback right now if you ever want Grace back again. I could choose to stay — it's really very comfortable in here. It could be our little secret. No one else would know, would they?' She giggled, stretching out Grace's arm and flexing Grace's little fingers. 'On the other hand, I might damage this body while I'm in it. I believe it would be very easy to do.' She took one of Grace's hands in the other and bent the wrist back to an alarming degree, wincing at the pain she had no choice but to feel, but grinning at the same time.

I snapbacked in time to run to the sink and vomit noisily to the accompaniment of Magda's giggles.

'Ugh. You really are disgusting, trembler. Your daughter loves you though, doesn't she?' This seemed to bother her.

'Stay out of her head!'

'Yeah. I'm really going to do that. *Mummy.*'

I wiped my mouth on a piece of paper towel and threw half a bottle of disinfectant down the sink. Bile rose to my throat again, but I swallowed it down, wincing. My mind was racing, looking for a way out, a way to evict Magda, to get Grace back.

'Relax, trembler. You might as well make dinner or whatever it is you usually do at this time of day. I'm starving and nothing's going to happen until I say so.'

I took a breath and tried to act calm, reasonable. 'What is it you want, Magda? I'm here. You can have me right now. You can *keep me*, Magda, I don't care. But let Grace go.'

Where were they keeping her? *How* were they keeping her? Wrong question. Who was keeping her? My heart almost failed me. *You don't touch children. Grace, where are you? What are they doing to you?*

'Relax.' Magda yawned again. 'I'll take you when I'm ready. And Cora? Don't even think about telling anybody else. Not that your creepy band of angels can help you now. But all the same, let's keep things simple, okay?'

I couldn't move. *Oh God. Make me stone so I don't have to feel this.*

'This is the perfect crime,' said Magda. 'I'm amazed I didn't think of it before. I've got your daughter and there's absolutely nothing you can do about it.'

'I could call—'

'Who? The police?' Magda gave a snorting laugh. 'Oh please, officer, my sister's kidnapped my daughter. Which daughter would that be, my good woman? Surely not the one that's sitting here in front of my eyes? Are you in the habit of wasting police time? Or, wait, let's see. You could call your freaky friends. Joe, Joe, Magda's stolen Grace. Oh well, honey, I don't think Magda's stupid enough to swap with me this time, and I'm far too stupid to charm her out. Who else. Can't think of anyone? Hmm. Me neither. Make my dinner, Cora. You wouldn't want to starve your daughter's body, would you? Although it's an idea... No. I'm hungry. Feed me. Now.'

I nodded and then, because I really couldn't think of anything else to do, I did as I was told. The idea of Magda hurting Grace's body made me so scared I could hardly lift the saucepans onto the stove, but I went through the well-practised domestic ritual of preparing food.

Would she ever leave? What did she want? What could I do? *Nothing. She's quite right: you can't do anything.*

It really was, in its way, the perfect crime. Charlie had asked me what would happen if you broke the taboo and interfered with a child. I didn't have the answer then, but I had it now. Nothing. Absolutely nothing would happen.

I laid my forehead against the kitchen counter and I cried.

'That's right. Cry. Call for Grace. Go on, call out her name, that's right! She's not coming. She's never coming back.' She was standing by my side, my own little girl, not my girl at all. 'That's how I cried, Cora, when Mum died. I stood by the bathtub and cried Mummy, Mummy, like a big fat cry-baby, but there was no one inside. Just a body. At least there's someone inside Grace's body. You're lucky I'm here. I could have left her empty.'

I raised my head and continued cooking. *God, make me stone. Grace!*

'You know,' said Magda, perching on a stool, 'it's not a bad idea to leave this body empty. Let's see. You could put her to bed. Or take her to the hospital. Ooh, I wonder what they'd do to her there? Hook her up to all sorts of things. Pump all kinds of things into her to try and wake her up. They might think she was dead.' She paused for a beat. 'They might try to bury her.'

'They wouldn't bury her,' I said. 'Her heart would still be beating.'

'True. Pretty tragic though, huh, to sleep away your entire childhood.'

My heart jarred; it hurt. 'You couldn't keep her that long.'

'I can keep her as long as I want. I can do whatever I want.'

I turned to look at her. 'Where is she? What have you done with her?'

'You mean why isn't she floating around hammering on her head to get back inside? I'm very, very clever, little sister. And I've got her safely tucked up in another body.'

We were way past tears. 'Yours?' I tried to sound interested, conversational.

'I really couldn't say. For all I know, they're playing pass the parcel with her right now.'

I ran to the sink and threw up again.

'That's disgusting,' said Magda. 'You better not get any of that in the food.' She closed her eyes. 'There's some interesting stuff in here. Except you're stamped all over every thought she's ever had.' She made a gagging sound.

'Get out of her head.'

'That's not nice, Mummy.'

I pinched my lips together and stirred the mess at the bottom of the saucepan.

There was the sound of a key in a latch, and then Amy's voice. 'I'm bushed!' she called, and then she came in and collapsed on the sofa. 'Hello you two. Dinner already? I'm starving.' She threw her head back on the sofa and then looked up at Magda. 'What, no kiss?'

Magda shot me a malicious look and went over to kiss Amy primly on the cheek.

'Is that it, you monkey? You think that'll do it, do you?' Amy grabbed her, pulling her back onto the sofa and tickling her belly, at the same time covering Grace's head and face with kisses.

'Get off me!' roared Magda, and Amy abruptly released her.

The breath caught in my throat. Magda's tone was all wrong; Amy must see something was wrong.

Amy sat back. 'Did I hurt you?' she demanded. When Magda didn't answer, Amy looked questioningly at me. I could see what she was thinking; if it really was Grace shouting at Amy like that, I'd have had her guts for garters. Grace got away with many things, but never rudeness. More to the point, Grace never was rude. Cheeky, occasionally sulky, but never unkind and never rude.

So why, Amy was wondering, wasn't I reacting appropriately?

Amy frowned at me. 'What's up?' And then as an afterthought, she added, 'You look awful, Cora. Have you two been *fighting*?'

'Something like that,' I said. I stared into Amy's eyes and then looked away. Even if I could communicate what was wrong, how could she help?

Magda was sprawling on the opposite sofa, watching us with interest.

Amy stood up. 'I'm going to change. You two need to calm down.' She dropped a light kiss on Grace's head. 'You know I'd never hurt you on purpose, kiddo.' Then she wrinkled her nose. 'Are you using a different shampoo? You smell funny.'

When she'd left the room Magda raised an eyebrow at me. 'Thick, but oddly perceptive, isn't she? Yuck. Grace loves her.'

'Why are you so interested in who Grace loves?'

'Children will do anything to protect the people they love.'

The penny dropped. 'You told Grace something bad would happen to me if she didn't stay with your … friends.'

'Something like that. Ooh look, we can threaten Charlie, too. Does this child of yours have no discernment? Seems she'll love anybody that's kind to her. I'll have her loving me next! Or maybe not. Since I won't be very kind.'

Precious, loyal little Grace. Stubborn, tenacious little Grace. She wouldn't relent for hours, if ever. *Stone stone stone.*

'Don't worry so much,' said Magda cheerfully. 'She's in a perfectly nice place with very respectable people. She's at my house. Imtiaz is with her, too, so she's not among strangers. And I believe the two of you have already met Sally. At the gallery?'

'How could I forget.' I was thinking: *Imtiaz?* Had it really come to this?

'He's not too happy about it, of course,' she said, as if reading my mind — again. 'But that's the thing with weak people. They're very easy to manipulate.'

I silently added pasta to the pan of boiling water, and put a can of tomatoes into the sauce. It would all taste of nothing, but I couldn't have cared less.

I was tempted to pop and find a way to warn Amy but several things stopped me: how could I warn her when she couldn't see my Self; what good would warning her do anyway; and what would Magda do to Grace's body if she caught me? I was, at last, ready to believe her capable of *anything*.

There was a series of resounding thuds from upstairs. I stared at the ceiling, perturbed. It sounded as if Amy was throwing things around the landing. Magda smiled at me knowingly.

Moments later Amy came downstairs. She'd changed into a tracksuit. I threw her a look I hoped would seem normal; no need to drag her into anything.

Amy looked directly at me and the breath caught in my throat.

'You — you — how could you?' I screamed at Magda.

CHAPTER 35

AMY SMILED AWKWARDLY. She was already dragged in. I don't know whose eyes looked out at me, but they weren't hers.

'She's not even a walker!' I spluttered. 'She'll be floundering around up there, terrified!'

'She'll find her way around eventually,' said Magda comfortably. 'Besides, Grace tells me' — she tapped the side of Grace's head — 'that she knows enough to work it all out pretty quickly.'

'You're unspeakable!' I screwed my eyes tight. 'Why don't you take me?' I begged. 'Take me, Magda.'

'Oh, I will. When I'm ready. Come on, Coralie. This is fun. Charlie will be here in about half an hour. Amy just called him.'

She and whoever was in Amy exchanged a smile. There was a flicker of something familiar about Amy now, something I recognised, and then the feeling was gone, drowned in panic.

Charlie. Oh no. No no no.

Magda tapped the side of Grace's head again.

'You're still the lucky one here,' she said in a changed tone. 'According to Grace there's about three people in the world that love you better than they love themselves. For God's sake. It's disgusting. What do they see in you, little trembler? It's Mum all over again. This world is made for the weak.' She curled Grace's mouth into a look of pain and disdain. For the smallest moment I felt sorry for her; the feeling didn't last.

I flicked my mobile phone off the counter and speed-dialled Charlie's number. It picked up immediately.

'Charlie, don't come! It's a trap. Run, Charlie, hide somewhere!'

His voice cut me off; it was the answer phone, clicking in immediately because Charlie was already on the phone.

'You're too late,' said Magda gleefully looking at her watch. 'We timed it all pretty well.'

Amy was sitting opposite Magda, sitting up straight, looking very confident and comfortable. Again, something flickered in my head.

'Who are you?' I demanded. 'I'm not going to call you Amy.'

'The name's Liam. We met on the Embankment that time. Well, we didn't meet exactly. But I was there.'

I closed my eyes.

'Told you I had a gang,' said Magda.

'So you're planning to kidnap all my friends?' I asked, trying and failing to sound scornful.

'Well at first I was only going to take Grace. But then I thought: why not really make it fun?'

'Dinner's ready,' I said in a monotone. 'Or do we wait for … Charlie?' I gritted my teeth to stop myself from crying out hysterically.

'We wait.'

I came to sit on the sofa. 'So where's your own body?' I asked Liam, trying to remember what he looked like, trying not to think of Amy's Self cowering somewhere upstairs, or what was happening to Charlie. Or Grace.

Liam watched me with interest.

'How did you get her out?' I asked, trying another tack. 'Amy isn't a walker.'

Magda giggled. 'A short sharp blast of paralysing fear. People don't like it when things start flying around — it tends to scare them out of themselves. Do you have any wine?'

'Fear's a key?' I asked, surprised, and at the same time I thought: *That won't work with Charlie because of what he can see*, and a tiny spark of hope rose in me. I took a bottle of red from the fridge and started to pour Magda a glass; it was only as I placed it into Grace's eight-year-old hand that I realised the incongruity of what I was doing.

'You can't have alcohol!' I withdrew the glass quickly. 'Her body can't take it.'

'Give me the bloody glass, Cora.'

I closed my eyes to steady myself, and then handed it over. 'So fear's a key?'

'It is the way I do it,' said Liam laconically. I felt the hair on the back of my neck start to rise.

There was nothing to do but sit and wait. I turned the gas down on the stove and sat at the table. I couldn't take my eyes off Magda; even though Grace wasn't home, as it were, at least I could see her body, and whilst that was safe, there was hope. But my heart was shrieking. I couldn't send Grace my Self, but I sent her my will, my love, my comfort. I prayed.

'Noisy bitch, isn't she?' said Liam, grinning at me.

Magda shrugged. 'I don't hear anything.'

Liam looked at her, disgusted. 'No, subtlety never was your strong point. I expect Magnus loved you for your faithful and obedient heart.' He ducked the book flying past his head, and began to pace around the room. He kicked the back of the sofa as he passed. 'You look quite good in that,' he said to Magda.

'I feel quite good.'

'Quite a risk, though.' He laughed. 'One of the few things I might not actually do myself.'

Magda wriggled with pride. 'What's to be scared of?' She sniffed with pleasure. 'What's the worst that can happen?'

'Who knows?'

'Maybe the police will arrest me,' said Magda. 'Ooh, I'm so frightened. This rubbish about children. It's superstitious nonsense. It's wonderful being a child again. All floaty and fresh. Very fresh.' She sniffed. 'Flowers. And milk. Really, I could get used to this.'

'Stay like that, then.'

Magda pouted. 'Magnus would miss me.'

Liam snorted. 'Yeah, if he ever shows up again.'

'You're jealous because you've never met him.'

'And you're full of it because you have. Magnus this, Magnus that. If he ever turns up — and I do mean if — he might not be happy about what you've been up to in his name.'

'Magnus trusts me,' snapped Magda. 'And anyway, when he comes — when — I don't have to tell him everything, do I?'

'Well if even half the stories about him are true, you wouldn't catch me not telling him stuff. All right, all right. I'm just saying. I thought he was interested in her for himself.' He jerked his head towards me.

'He's not interested in her except that she's my sister!' snapped Magda. 'Fuck off, Liam.'

I winced at those words coming out of Grace's mouth; I even opened my mouth to chide her, then snapped it shut.

'Oh cheer up, Magda,' said Liam carelessly. 'Enjoy the rush.'

'Well I can see that you are. You like women's bodies, don't you? Look at you, all long legs and blonde hair. Do you know, it suits you, the Barbie look. You've got a body to match your Self now.'

Liam threw himself at her and grappled her to the ground — Amy's body fighting Grace's body, pulling her hair, yanking her arms backwards — and then Magda pulled a fingernail down Amy's face and Liam threw himself backwards howling.

'You fucking retard! You made me bleed!'

'What do you care? It's not your face anyway.'

'Still bloody hurts. Bitch.'

'Oh settle down. Look in her head. See what's going on in there.'

Liam grimaced with distaste. 'She's in lurve. How sweet. Although' — he cocked her head — 'it's pretty interesting to see what *it's* like from a girl's point of view.' He began to smile, deep in Amy's thoughts.

Magda smiled too. 'You enjoy yourself, Liam.'

We sat in silence. Liam downed a glass of wine and helped himself to a second. When the doorbell rang, I jumped a mile.

'I'll get it,' said Magda enthusiastically.

I braced myself for a Charlie that wouldn't be Charlie, and didn't bother to look up as he came in.

'Hello, everyone,' he said. 'Looking good, Amy.'

I looked at him then and once again the breath caught in my throat; it's amazing I was breathing at all. I stared at him searchingly, especially his eyes. One would think … it was as if … could it really be *Charlie*?

Tears flooded my eyes and I looked away. Of course not.

'Don't be like that,' said Charlie, and he kissed the back of my head and snaked a suggestive arm around my waist.

He didn't fool me. It was him. It really was Charlie. I span around and caught the tiniest warning in his eyes.

'Get off me!' I snapped, a beat too late, but neither Magda nor Liam appeared to notice.

'Have any trouble, Danny boy?' asked Liam.

'Of course not,' said Charlie.

'Anyone else in the house with him?'

'Nah, just some poor bloke in a wheelchair.'

'Isn't this nice?' said Magda with satisfaction. 'Look, Cora, I've gathered everyone you love best. And everyone that loves you back. Grace, Amy and Charlie, all together. Let's eat, and then let's think of something really *fun* to do with each other.'

It was mesmerizingly horrible to hear Grace's voice ever so slightly blurry with alcohol. Magda stood and lurched towards the dinner table. 'This body really can't hold its liquor. Serve up, then, Mummy.'

I broke my frozen staring, and turned to the stove. I wished desperately that I could speak to Charlie without being overheard. Did he have a plan, or was he winging it? How had he got away from — Danny, was it? *Where are you, Grace? Hold on. I will come. I will.*

I carried the dishes to the table.

'How does he feel?' Magda asked Charlie.

'What?' He looked blank.

'Charlie. How does he feel?'

'Oh, great! He feels good. Good fit.'

'Stay out of his head,' I growled, hoping to give him a clue.

'Not much in there of interest.' He looked down and became very interested in his plate of food.

'You don't expect my sister to fall for someone seriously interesting, do you? Pass the salt, sister mine. I don't know what your cooking is usually like, but this is pretty poor.'

Good God, does everyone know how I feel about Charlie? I silently handed over the salt.

Liam wasn't saying much. I realised Charlie probably didn't know who was in Amy, so I said, 'Liam, would you pass the salt back here?'

'So,' said Charlie. 'What now?'

'We eat,' said Magda brightly. 'I tease Cora some more. Hell, I'm making it up as I go along.' She stroked a childish hand through Grace's brown curls. 'After we've eaten, I might even cut all my hair off. A razor, maybe. I like razors. I must get it from my mum.' She grinned at me provocatively.

'Cora likes razors?' said Liam.

'I wasn't talking about Cora. Keep up, Liam.'

'I want to move on,' he said. 'You might be having fun but I'm bored.'

'You said you'd help me.'

'I expected something a bit more original than some body-swapping and a sit-down dinner — which, I might add, is revolting.' He let a forkful of pasta slop back onto the plate, and pushed the plate away.

My heartbeat went into overdrive; if this was boring, what was Liam's idea of fun?

There was a ring at the door.

'Are you expecting anyone?' asked Magda, looking surprised.

I shook my head.

'Well go get it then! Impromptu is good, too.' She looked around and then picked up the telephone and dialled. Grace had no use yet for a telephone; I watched in fascination as her little fingers tapped out a number unknown to either her or me.

'Katy? You still out there? Get over here. We might have another body for you. No leave yours out there. On the grass, on the bench, what do I care? Move!' She slammed down the phone and turned to me. 'Answer the door!'

I felt Charlie's concern swirling around me and knew that if I didn't get out of the room he would give himself away. I walked, heavy-footed, into the hallway and opened the door.

'Coralie? You look awful.'

It was Rebecca.

CHAPTER 36

A S ALWAYS, REBECCA WAS MUMSY and managing in a Liberty-print shirt and bias-cut skirt. I laughed at the incongruity of her presence in this nightmare.

'Aren't you going to invite me in?' she asked primly.

'You don't usually wait to be asked, Rebecca. But it's not convenient right now.'

'Nonsense,' she retorted briskly. I don't know how she managed it — she didn't exactly push me — but seconds later she was through the door and had marched straight into the kitchen. She surveyed the room and then she saw Charlie. 'Who's this?' she demanded, as if he were the enemy.

She pulled up a chair and sat down, looking nosily into Grace's bowl. 'That doesn't look like one of your better concoctions, Cora. Is there anything fresh in there? So, Grace, how's school?'

'That's none of your business.' Magda winked at Liam and Charlie. 'Did Cora — I mean Mummy — invite you to sit down? Who are you?'

Rebecca looked at her in astonishment. 'Who am I? Who am I? I'm your Aunty Rebecca, you rude girl, and don't you forget it.' She gingerly sniffed the air between them. 'Cora, has she been *drinking?*'

I cast my eyes to the ceiling. *Give me strength.* 'Rebecca, this isn't a good time.'

'I'm beginning to think it's a very good time. And a very good job I came.'

'Ah,' said Magda. 'You're the other sister! I'm beginning to get the picture. Bossy, aren't you? Unattractive, too. That skirt! It takes genius to spend that much money and look that fat.'

'Grace!' exploded Rebecca, half-rising. 'Cora, are you going to allow her to speak to me like that!'

'I don't have much control over her these days,' I said truthfully.

'Is this your influence?' Rebecca glared at Charlie. 'Look Cora, look at what you've done. Exposing your daughter to strange men and I don't know what.'

Liam started to laugh.

'Amy, I thought better of you! I should have known you were unreliable when you didn't ring in the reports I asked for. Honestly Cora. What would Peter say?'

'Shut up, Rebecca!' I cried, as Liam and Magda fell about laughing, Charlie swiftly copying them. 'Nothing is what it looks like. This is *not* a good time for you to be here!'

'What do you mean not a good time?' Her eyes narrowed. 'Are you in trouble?'

Liam leaned forward. 'I'd like some of you,' he said in Amy's voice, but not her tone. 'I bet you're really something under that respectable middle-class Teflon-coating.'

'I beg your pardon, young lady?' Rebecca's voice was growing more clipped and icy with every passing moment.

Magda practically fell off her chair. 'Who speaks like that?' she shrieked in Grace's high-pitched voice. 'Ay beg yooah pahdon. Good God, Cora, did you grow up with people like this? I thought I had it bad!'

Rebecca sat down abruptly. 'What is going on?'

I looked at Magda, who held out Grace's hand, palm up, invitingly. 'Tell her, by all means.'

'No one is themselves today,' I said. 'All three of them — Grace, Amy and Charlie. There are other spirits inside their bodies. They've been invaded.' I began to giggle hysterically, as Rebecca's face darkened. *Oh dear God*. And then I was angry, because this messing about with Rebecca was only wasting time. 'You can believe me or not. It really doesn't matter, and you can't help, so there's no point in sticking around. This is one situation you really can't manage, Rebecca. They've kidnapped Grace. Do you understand?'

Rebecca looked pointedly at Grace and then back at me.

'That's not her,' I said. 'You're wasting time. Go away!'

'It looks like her.'

'It's only her body.'

Another Self drifted into the room.

'Kate! Join the party!' welcomed Magda.

Rebecca looked around as if everyone had gone mad. 'Who are you talking to, you rude, ill-disciplined child?'

For a moment I saw everything with Rebecca's eyes: Grace rising to her feet, a manic look in her eyes; Grace calmly picking up the kitchen knife from the counter; Grace holding it in front of Rebecca's disbelieving face and then touching the point against Rebecca's throat.

And Amy leaning back in her chair watching, with a gleam in her eyes and a quiet smile on her lips.

'This is the part where you become very, very frightened and we steal *your* body,' said Grace in a tone no eight-year-old had ever used.

Charlie made as if to jump up from his seat and for a fraction of a moment Rebecca quailed — the room balanced on the tip of that knife. And then Rebecca slapped Grace's arm away and stood up with a snort of disgust. 'Don't be so stupid, you ridiculous child. Cora you should be ashamed of yourself, letting your daughter get so out of hand.'

Even Magda was taken aback. 'What are you doing?'

'I'm going to make you a cup of coffee, you dreadful girl. I take it you have been allowed to get very drunk. Well, if you're old enough for alcohol, you're certainly old enough for caffeine. Now finish your dinner and I suppose I should take some comfort in the fact that you will very shortly have the worst headache of your young life.'

She stomped to put on the kettle, and then turned her back on us as she prepared a cup of coffee.

'She's brave!' said Liam with grudging admiration. 'It'll take more than a little fear to pop this one. Stick around, Kate. I'm sure we can think of something else.'

The new Self, Kate, looked bored, or drunk, or very tired; it was hard to keep track.

'I definitely want this one,' said Liam, staring hungrily at Rebecca. 'You can have mine, Kate — she's a little *compliant* for my taste. Older ones can be so much more interesting.'

'See? Another woman. You like being women,' accused Magda with a hard edge to her voice.

'I like being inside women,' corrected Liam.

Magda looked at Rebecca through narrowed eyes. 'Interesting or not, no one's going to have her if we don't think of a way to get her out. She's obviously tougher than she looks.'

Rebecca was paying them no attention whatsoever. She was either deaf or dense or very preoccupied.

'You're very quiet, Danny boy,' said Liam in a terrifyingly soft voice. My heart gave a jolt of fear as he appraised Charlie, but Charlie remained impassive.

'Passing out with boredom in here.'

'Got any ideas how to get her out?'

'Is she our priority now, then?'

'You know me.' Liam smiled. 'I like a challenge.'

'Aren't we wasting time?'

Liam looked at him in surprise and when he spoke again there was a dangerous drawl in his voice. 'Why? Do you have better things to be doing this evening?'

I willed Charlie to be more subservient; it seemed the safer option.

'I'm just saying,' said Charlie evenly.

'I'll decide when I'm done. Actually, it all got a lot more fun since she arrived.' He grinned at Rebecca.

Rebecca turned from the counter, a steaming mug in her hand. 'Now drink this down like a good girl,' she said to Magda in her best prefect voice.

'Fuck off,' said Magda.

'That's quite enough from you, young lady. Drink up.'

'I'm going to eat your heart out, witch!'

'And I'm going to scrub your mouth out with soap, brat.'

'I really don't think you're going to scare this one,' said Liam with amusement. Then his face changed again, and his tone of voice with it. 'What else works? I'm fed up waiting around. Where'd you leave your body, Kate?'

The new Self folded her arms and frowned at him.

Magda grinned. 'You left her all bruised last time, remember? In a ditch somewhere. It took her ages to find herself, and even longer to recover from that little adventure.'

'It wasn't a ditch. It was an abandoned car.'

'Not much better.'

'Nah, that was Kitty, not Kate.'

'You do get around.'

'And always dressed as a woman,' I said without thinking.

Magda snorted. 'Are you getting a sense of humour, sis? She's outside, Liam — Kate's body. I told her to leave it in that garden out there — we smashed the lock on the gate. But don't go yet. Kate, have a go at jumping into the battle-axe, will you?'

Kate pulled a face and shook her head vigorously.

'She's afraid,' murmured Liam.

'Go on, Kate,' encouraged Magda. 'Give it a go.'

Kate drifted up to Rebecca's face.

How can she not see her? I thought, but Rebecca didn't. She stood stony-faced looking down at Magda, who'd absently begun to sip the coffee Rebecca had forced into her hand.

Kate put her forehead to Rebecca's. Her mouth moved again but, of course, we couldn't hear her.

'Oh get on with it,' snapped Liam.

Kate tried to side-step into Rebecca; Rebecca looked around her, momentarily confused, and then shook her head, scratched her cheek and frowned at me. 'You should be very grateful I'm not one to gossip,' she said severely. 'Because this would cause a few raised eyebrows, I can tell you.'

I gave a weak sob. 'Rebecca, you're priceless,' I told her. 'You really need to leave.'

'Any time now,' said Rebecca comfortably. 'But not before I've told a few home truths to your friend here.' She turned to Charlie. 'Now listen to me, young man. This is a *nice* family. I'm sure you're a perfectly decent fellow, but you should stick with...' I worried that Charlie would feel obliged to answer her back, but he seemed to have switched off, as I had, because Magda's behaviour had changed, and suddenly we were all staring at her.

'What?' she slurred. 'What is it? What's everyone staring at?'

CHAPTER 37

'YOU SHOULD LIE DOWN NOW,' said Rebecca. 'Come along, Grace dear.'

Magda stood uncertainly and then collapsed into Rebecca's waiting arms.

'*What* are you doing now, Magda?' demanded Liam.

'Don't know whassup,' she complained.

'Give me a hand, Cora,' said Rebecca.

I rushed over to catch Grace's legs and we laid her on the sofa.

'Where is everybody?' mumbled Magda, trying and failing to lift her head.

Despite myself, I stroked the hair from her forehead. 'Rebecca, what did you give my daughter?' I hissed.

'You said she wasn't your daughter,' hissed back Rebecca.

'You believed me?'

'I have no idea what's going on, but someone had to do something.'

'So what did you do?'

'I put a Valium in her coffee. What? She'll be perfectly fine! You gave her alcohol!'

'What's going on,' said Liam suspiciously, breaking in on us.

'Time for you to be going, I think,' said Charlie, coming behind him and grabbing Amy's arm, forcing it up behind her back.

'You're very brave all of a sudden, Danny. Oy, that hurts!'

'I'm not Danny, and it's supposed to hurt.'

'You're not Danny?' The penny dropped. 'Well well. Not so stupid after all. Charlie, is it?'

'Inside and out.'

'And you're really going to break your friend's arm?' he taunted. But he couldn't help grimacing at the pain.

'If I have to,' said Charlie, and I could see that he really would.

Amy crumpled into Charlie's arms as Liam popped. He hovered for a moment and then smiled unpleasantly and said something to Kate. They turned simultaneously and disappeared through the wall.

'Wait!' I cried. 'Charlie, they can't go! Grace is at Magda's house but I don't know where that is. I'll never find her!' We froze for a second, my hands on his arms. Then I remembered. 'Kate's body is in the garden. Maybe I can get there first.'

I started to pop but Charlie cried, 'Wait!' and pulled a phone from his pocket. 'Ken? There's a body in the garden outside. A girl, if she's still there. Be quick, her Self's on its way. She might know where Grace is.' He gave me a poor attempt at a smile. 'Ken will find her, and Joe's outside the door. They're popping now. Go. Go and find Grace. Rebecca and I will keep Magda occupied.'

'Don't drug her again!' I cried, and popped.

Outside was the strangest sight I'd ever seen. If I hadn't been so focused, so bent on my urgent mission, I would have paused in wonder. The trees, the branches, the grass, the rooftops, the sky, even the air was laced with Selfs. I'd never seen so many in one place. The atmosphere was static, like an indrawn breath. These were witnesses, not invaders. I knew what they were here for.

You don't touch children.

No one spoke, but the words resounded like a communal thought. Perhaps there were consequences after all. I nodded grimly, and then Joe was at my side.

Charlie's in there? he demanded.

Yes.

Joe swore roughly. *How long has he been with you?*

We were heading into the garden. I didn't answer.

In the garden, a startlingly pretty young girl stood by one of the benches, feeling her own breasts and nodding her head. 'Wow!' said a female voice that was nevertheless disconcertingly and unmistakably Ken. 'These feel really nice!'

The address, snapped Joe.

'I'll show you,' said Ken. 'Yuck. There is — yuck — so much residue in her. She's going to have the worst kind of hangover in the morning.'

He popped and Kate's empty body slumped back onto the ground with a resounding thump.

Charlie's in there, said Joe, jerking his head back towards my house. *Where the hell is Michael?*

Reese should be there already, and Raul's on his way to help him, said Ken.

Joe swore again. *Reese? Reese is with Michael? He'll never manage!*

Focus! I screamed. *We have to get to Grace!*

She's right, said Ken.

Joe hesitated, then nodded, and then we were soaring over London, Ken leading the way.

We felt Magda's house before we saw it, and we saw it from a great distance — an ordinary terrace in a ubiquitous street in west London. It registered as a huge, dark trouble-spot, emanating an uneasy energy that tainted the air for several streets in every direction. There were Selfs mingling in the sky outside.

Ken, said Joe, *go help Reese. Now!*

My daughter had been kidnapped, her body and Self both taken. And Joe was throwing *three* of our only assets at Charlie's disabled brother? I'd have liked to punch out his lights, but I couldn't afford the distraction.

Within seconds Joe and I were in the house.

I don't know what I expected, but it wasn't a party. The house was full of bodies, animation and noise. There were people in the kitchen drinking and eating, people dancing in the living room, sitting and lying and touching on beds and on the floor. Bodies everywhere, doing — *everything*. The atmosphere was heavy with cigarette smoke and alcohol, and a certain tension I couldn't place until I looked more closely at people's faces. And then I noticed the common factor: wild eyes, too bright, that shifted with jerky, unnatural movements.

Joe said, *Damn. This could take a while.*

What's going on? My voice was high and frenzied. *Surely Grace can't be here?* What I really meant was: please, don't let her be here. Not here, among all these drunks and — well, who knew what else?

Start searching, ordered Joe, and when I didn't move he said, *They've all swapped, Cora. The bodies and Selfs are all mixed up. Grace could be anywhere.*

My Self disintegrated. Of course. The eyes. *You mean Grace could be inside one of these…?* Some of the bodies were drunk; some were drugged. Some were openly engaging in sex — there was a couple up against the wall, and a girl on her knees in front of a half-naked boy who could hardly stand. I began to scramble among the bodies, staring openly into faces. Everyone seemed to see me; most of them thought it was funny.

'Peep-oh!' said a girl, swatting at me with large, mannish hands.

'You looking for me?' asked another. 'Wanna swap?' He started to pop but gave it up as a bad job and lurched back into his borrowed hide.

It was hideous, knowing Grace could be here, inside anyone, doing anything. *Grace! Grace!* I shouted, again and again, and I heard Joe above the music and the babble of voices, calling her name, sifting through the rooms full of strangers.

We'd covered the ground floor, moved up to the second, taking in every figure on the staircase. Nothing here; we moved up to the top floor.

The music wasn't so loud here, and fewer people had made it this far up. There was a couple of Selfs halfway up the last flight. They were completely stationary, staring into the middle distance; they barely seemed to notice us. We left them fluttering in our wake. They were the first popped Selfs we'd seen inside the house.

There were two bedrooms here, and both doors were open. Inside one room there were tangled couples on the bed and on the floor.

She can't be in here! I wailed.

The second room was full of people, but they were not partying. They were waiting. Every head turned as we stood at the door.

They were waiting for us.

Chapter 38

MONGST THEM WAS IMTIAZ, doubled over on the floor. He lifted a pale green face to me. His eyes were bloodshot but, unlike most people in the house, he was entirely himself. 'I didn't mean—' he began, but someone kicked him viciously. He didn't cry out; he barely winced. But he said nothing more.

'Not bad,' said a pleasant voice I recognised. It was Sally, the girl from the gallery, but she was wearing a girl in her late teens whose face was cruelly marked by acne; not a first choice, I guessed. 'You got here quicker than I expected. Not quick enough, though!'

She held up a hand; there was a silver thread between her fingers.

Everything in the room seemed to slow down. It was as if nothing existed except the three of us: Sally, me, and whatever lay at the other end of the thread. My eyes travelled slowly along the strand, taking in its delicacy, the extraordinary grace and beauty of its line, the haunting silver colour, its silky texture belying its strength.

On the other end was Sally's body. She'd gained a tattoo since I'd last seen her, a tiny teardrop hanging off the end of her left eyebrow. She was slumped in a chair and appeared to be ill, or in distress; her fingers were making little jerky movements, and her eyes were rolling.

There was no mistaking the eyes.

Grace! I cried, and I flew to her. *Grace! Grace! It's me! You can come out. Come out, now, darling. Come out, Grace.*

The eyes turned to me. They were filmy and unfocused. 'Can't move,' mumbled the body. 'Want to go … home.'

Grace, I said, beginning to cry. *Grace, darling, come out. We'll go home.*

Sally tugged on the silver thread, jerking the arm of her body and Grace inside it. 'She can't hear you any more than I can,' she assured me. 'And I don't think she's going anywhere.'

I remembered how Joe had trapped Magda in his body, so long ago, in Charlie's flat. I remembered how horrible Magda had found it, being unable to move. Magda had been astonished at Joe's abilities; Sally, on the other hand, seemed to know exactly what she was doing.

Let her go, I begged. *I'll do anything. Anything at all. Just let her out.*

'She's begging!' Sally told her audience. 'Look at her face. I believe that's called motherly love.'

There was a murmur of amusement around the room.

Joe? I looked around wildly, but Joe was powerless. It took something physical to break the silver thread — and even then, a skilled Self could manipulate the thread even through a solid object, as Joe had showed me on Primrose Hill. There was little chance to discover how skilled Sally might be anyway, because Joe and I had left our bodies behind, and all the other bodies in the room had stood aside to create a clear passage between Sally and Grace.

Sally watched me as each successive realisation registered on my face. When I arrived again at hopeless, her borrowed, scarred face broke into a grin. 'Don't look so worried, love,' she said cheerfully. 'It's just a game! Magda's the only one round here that takes things seriously.'

'Silly cow,' said a voice.

'Well, yes,' said Sally. 'Although she's a bit of a dangerous silly cow now Magnus is back.'

There was a murmur around the room.

'Didn't you lot know?' said Sally, enjoying her moment. 'They've found him, at last. About ten minutes ago. He's out. Got himself a new body and everything.'

Fuck! said Joe. *Fucking shitting hell. Cora, I'm sorry. Oh fuck. Oh no.*

I hardly heard him; I was preoccupied with Grace. I blew gently on the alien face she inhabited, tried to force her to fix her eyes on me. *What have you done to her?*

Sally laughed. 'You can blame Imtiaz for the way she looks, not me. I only just got her; Imtiaz has had her for hours now.'

I was too preoccupied to look at Imtiaz but with some spare piece of my brain I promised myself revenge on him.

'Not strictly true, Sal,' said a boy's voice. 'Your own body is pretty messed up. I should know, I was just in there.'

A low laugh rippled around the room.

'I should have known,' said Sally. 'Come on then, own up. Who else has been in me?'

'Me,' admitted another boy.

'And me,' said another.

'Me, too.'

'I think Chris had a go, earlier.'

'All of you in one night? That would make little Grace here, what, at least the sixth visitor? No wonder she's not feeling too good.' Sally laughed again, inadvertently jerking the silver thread and Grace at the end of it.

Stop it! I shouted. *You're hurting her! Let her out! Grace, darling, everything will be okay.*

'We really can't hear you, you know,' said Sally peaceably.

Joe was engaged in a game of charades with a red-haired girl in a mini-dress. 'I think this one wants to join up,' the girl told Sally, appraising Joe critically. 'You don't look the type, mate. A bit old for this game. You need stamina.'

Joe mimed big muscles, and the girl and Sally laughed.

'We party hard,' said one.

'All night,' added another.

'And the rest,' scoffed the girl. 'I can go longer than all night.'

For once, even Joe looked blank. Sally laughed. 'You've surprised him, Roz. He hangs out with tremblers, remember?'

Joe pointed at Roz suggestively, and then back at himself, miming his desire to swap with her.

'Where's your body, then?' said Roz rudely. 'I'm not giving you mine until I've seen yours. Not that this one is mine anyway,' she added, carelessly shrugging her borrowed shoulders. 'I haven't seen my body for days. I don't even know if it's here tonight. I hope it's having a good time and isn't stuck in a dump somewhere with a headache.' She laughed noisily.

'You should be honoured, Roz,' said Sally. 'You're talking to one of the *patrollers*. You know, the good guys.' She sketched a bow at Joe as if he were royalty. 'I've seen you around, patroller. Anyway, you haven't brought a body to swap, so we're not interested.'

'I am,' said Imtiaz weakly. He was leaning against the wall, all but forgotten. His colour hadn't returned. He looked like a shadow, a green shadow against the chipboard wallpaper.

'You are what?' said Sally, and a boy standing nearby gave Imtiaz a swift kick with his boot. There were hoots of derision.

'The little coward speaks,' said Roz. 'The only thing worse than a trembler is a coward. Someone who thinks he's up for it but has a yellow belly.'

'I'm sick,' said Imtiaz, struggling to raise his head. 'Why don't you let him have me? See how he likes it. I don't mind if he doesn't have a swap.'

Roz started to say, 'No one wants to be you, you little—' but then she broke off and raised her finely pointed eyebrows. 'Fair point. What about it, big shot? Our first and last offer. You can take Imtiaz, weak and sick as he is, or you can float off back to wherever you came from and stop bothering us.'

Joe nodded vigorous assent.

'He'll feel like shit. I wouldn't do it.' I recognised the voice; it was Kate, whose body had recently been invaded by Ken and now lay out cold in Gregory Square garden. Her current body was much less pretty than her own.

'You'd do anyone, Kate,' said Roz sweetly. 'You! Coward! Out!'

Imtiaz popped with surprising speed considering his physical state. In the second before Joe snapped into his body, I saw the two of them exchange a look I did not understand.

Imtiaz hovered, weak and insubstantial, next to a large, care-worn wardrobe. Joe lifted Imtiaz's head experimentally. 'Ugh, you were right. He feels like shit.' He coughed noisily.

Roz, Sally and several others laughed gleefully. They watched closely as Joe appeared to try once again to raise Imtiaz's head. 'This feels weird. It's harder than it looks.' He lifted an arm and let it drop. It appeared to take him a full minute to gain any kind of control over Imtiaz's limbs. I couldn't tell if he was faking it.

Roz laughed with derision. 'Of course it is, idiot. For a trembler, at any rate.'

'Leave off the tough guy routine, Roz,' said Sally. 'It's bad enough when Magda does it. We really don't need it from you, too.'

'What do you think this is, a bleeding picnic in the park?' Roz took a threatening step towards Sally. 'We kidnapped a child, you stupid cow.'

'No we didn't. Magda did that. We're just looking after it.'

Roz raised her hand but there was a sudden noise, a new sound, at the window. No one had drawn the curtains — God knew how many days this party had been running for. I glanced up. The air outside was thick with Selfs. Several of them were pressed close against the window, peering in but not entering. The weight of their presence exerted a pressure against the glass. The sound was more than a tap, less than a crack; it was as if the glass shivered.

'What?' said Sally. 'Who are they?'

'Come on in!' shouted Roz. 'Enter, people! Especially if you've got bodies to trade!'

There was a change in the atmosphere of the room. Several people retreated quietly through the door. Those that remained seemed fixed on the presences outside the window, as if they'd never seen anything like this before.

'Bloody witnesses,' swore Roz.

'Aren't they pretty!' said Sally, approaching the window, lengthening the thread in her hand.

From the corner of my eye I saw that Joe had gained mastery of Imtiaz. As Sally stared delightedly at the Selfs outside the window, Joe stood up, was walking calmly towards the thread, was about to break the connection...

'So pretty!' said Sally reaching out to touch the glass.

'Got it,' said Joe, breasting the thread, which snapped with a tiny *ping!* of dispersed energy.

Grace! I cried. *Come out!*

There was an endless moment of slow-motion activity: Sally looked down at the broken thread in her hand; everyone else looked at Joe and then at Sally's body; and Grace slowly, slowly, slowly began to raise herself out into the air.

I leaned towards her. *Here, Grace, come to me, darling!*

And then there was a streak of corporeal silver and Grace emerged out of Sally in time to be sucked straight into the blackness that was —

'Magnus!' squeaked Sally.

Chapter 39

THERE WAS SILENCE. No one moved, and this time it wasn't my senses causing the apparent time lapse — literally, no one moved, and the seconds ticked by.

'Well,' said Magnus at last. 'A party. And not one of you thought to invite me.' He stood calmly in the centre of the crowd, several heads taller than everyone else. He was outstandingly ugly but sleek and immaculate, with silver hair hanging to his shoulders and a long rockstar jacket falling to his knees.

The height, the body, the hair — it was all Reese's. But the inhabitant was someone quite different. This was Magnus. This was my demon.

He threw a glance at the window where the Selfs still hung, peering in.

'It appears you have an audience,' he said. With a sudden movement he flicked the curtains closed. 'And you've taken a child.'

He looked around the room, holding one gaze after another as if committing faces to memory.

Where's Grace? I cried. *Where did she go?*

'Grace,' said Magnus, and there was a flicker of something on his face. 'Grace is the stolen child and where Grace is, Cora will follow.' He scanned the crowd and found me. His eyes lit up and he gave a small gasp of delight. 'You're here. At last. Don't worry — Grace is safe. I'm keeping her safe.' He patted his stomach as if he'd just eaten her for dinner.

Can he hear me? I asked Joe in disbelief.

'I can,' said Magnus, with a little flourish. He looked at the floor, still smiling, plainly considering something, and then he drew aside the curtain. 'I have the child,' he told the Selfs outside, in a deep, clear voice. 'I have rescued the child. There is no alarm.' He gave the smallest bow and closed the curtain again, but not before I'd seen the Selfs shrink back into the night.

'Well well,' he said again. His eyes roamed the room. His preternatural calm was terrifying. 'Sally, this wasn't your idea, was it?'

Sally shook her head miserably.

'And you — Roz, is it?'

'Course not.'

'Of course not. You're stupid enough to think of it but too stupid to pull it off. Well well. You lot were all teenagers when I last saw you. Look at you now. Bona fide junkies, with a bunch of new groupies!'

'Where have you been, Magnus,' said a voice; it was Liam, in a new body.

'I have been,' said Magnus coolly, 'in a very disagreeable place.' He looked straight at Joe. 'They thought they could keep me forever. Stupid children.' He looked at me again. 'Cora,' he said, and his voice was gentle. 'Cora, at last. You were nice to me when we met the other day. I do believe you suspected who I was.'

I looked between him and Joe; what was he talking about?

'Think about it, Cora. At Charlie's flat. That's right... The penny drops. I'm Charlie's ... now, what has he been calling me. His brother?' He paused for a beat while I stared at him, not taking it in. 'Look at you,' he said admiringly. 'It's so good to see you again. All grown up, too! Dear heart, I've been looking for you for a very long time.'

He looked around the room and suddenly his fists clenched and his voice rose to a fury. 'Who's responsible for this mess? Who took the child?' The window shook. And then he was instantly calm again. 'Was it you, Steve? Sarah? Ben?'

'It was Magda,' said a rough voice.

'Of course it was,' said Magnus, closing his eyes. 'And where is she?'

Without warning, Magda fell through the doorway into the room, as if she'd been pushed by several pairs of hands. I shrank back but Magnus barely spared her a glance. 'I don't want her body. I want her,' he said, and his lazy drawl turned steely.

She's at home, I said, staring at Magda's recently vacated body crumpled on the ground like a pile of dirty laundry. *She's at my house.*

Magnus looked at me again. 'Really? And what is she doing there?'

She's inside my daughter, I said, enunciating clearly, calmly, to belie my fear.

Magnus shook his head, a paragon of disapproval. 'Magda Magda Magda. What a fool that girl really is.' Another flash of temper flitted across his face. 'True, she created the diversion and signal I needed. But this time *they* might actually come, and sooner rather than later. Then again, an eyeblink and all that.'

I looked at Joe but he was staring at Magnus, as fascinated as everyone else in the room.

No. Not fascinated. Everyone else in the room was terrified.

'So,' resumed Magnus. 'I have rescued a stolen child. And I must give her back, of course.'

He smiled at me and if it hadn't been for the fact that Grace was inside him, I would have fled as far from him and that house as I could get.

'Give her back then,' said Joe.

Magnus swivelled his head towards Joe, still standing, with some effort, inside Imtiaz's body.

'I will give her back, patroller,' said Magnus politely. 'Of course I will.' He turned back to me and his eyes softened. 'Everybody out,' he said. 'And somebody take that with them.' He glanced at Magda with disdain.

He hadn't even raised his voice, but there was instant movement around us as many pairs of feet tried to leave the room at once. Magnus stood his ground. The hair that lay over his shoulders — Reese's silver hair — was stirred by the exodus, but no one came within a foot of him.

The flurry and noise continued for several minutes: shoving, pushing, feet on the staircase, doors banging. At last there was quiet in the house.

'I said everybody,' said Magnus.

From far away downstairs came the sound of tiptoes, and then the front door slammed shut. A few minutes more and even the street outside was quiet.

'I said everybody,' said Magnus.

We're not leaving, said Joe, who had left Imtiaz's body slumped on the floor. *Not without Grace.*

'You're leaving or you don't get Grace,' said Magnus.

I can't leave her, I said.

'You don't have to go, dear heart. He does.'

I turned to him. *Joe?*

Joe looked at me in astonishment. *Are you mad?* His voice was a shadow of itself.

I want Grace back. I'll do anything.

You might have to.

Magnus laughed. 'Don't be so melodramatic, patroller. Cora understands we have business to discuss. I need to ... apologise to her, for her sister's actions. Now get out.'

They might come. You said so. I can speak up for you, said Joe, holding his ground.

Who's coming? I demanded.

A slow smile spread across Magnus's face. 'You can string this out if you want to wait and find out. If you dare.' He watched Joe closely. 'Go ahead. Think it through. Though I wouldn't take too long if I were you. Personally I intend to be long gone before judgement arrives.'

What's he talking about? I said.

'And in the meantime,' said Magnus, and his voice dropped to a whisper, 'don't forget that I've got Grace inside me. Deep inside me. You might not want to prolong that experience.'

Joe threw me a desperate look and vanished. I was alone with Magnus.

I stared at him for a long moment, while he watched me quietly. 'How fortunate,' he said at last, in a voice like velvet, 'that you find me inside a body already blessed with my own personal calling card.' He brushed a hand through Reese's silver mane. 'Perhaps you recognise me? This one is a friend of yours, I think. Reese. I've been in him before — hence the hair. He's big, you see, and it takes a big body to hold me down. But this time I'm in control, not him.'

You had silver hair before ... when I was a girl. I faltered. *I don't understand.*

'I mess with people's heads,' said Magnus with fake modesty. 'It's my thing. Reese keeps his hair this way because he must. It's a little compulsion I left in his head, a thank-you gift for having once, um, housed me. I must say, I didn't expect to be back in him again, but here I am.'

Grace? I said tentatively.

'She can't hear you. Because she's asleep,' he said, raising a hand peaceably. 'It seemed best to let her rest. I won't hurt her, Cora. It's not her I want.'

You've got my daughter's Self with you inside Reese's body, I said slowly. *And you can hear me talking.*

'No need to worry,' Magnus assured me. 'Now then. Business.'

You're going to give me Grace and I'm going to take her home.

'Quite right,' said Magnus. 'To start with.'

To start with?

'Well yes. You'll do all that first.'

And then?

'It's not Grace I want, Cora. It's you. It was always you. The kidnapping of Grace has been a terrible mistake. Although, it did bring you to me, so perhaps I shouldn't be too hard on Magda.' He examined his nails. 'Come along now. Let's get Grace home and then you can climb back into your no doubt very fetching body and come to me.'

It took me a moment. *Come to you? You want my body?*

'I surely do,' said Magnus.

I closed my eyes. *What for?*

'Cora,' chided Magnus. 'It's a simple swap. A soul for a body. Or I could keep Grace, if you like, and you can keep your body. Your choice.'

Panic engulfed me. *You can't keep Grace. There's someone coming.*

Magnus smiled. 'You're brave. Gold star for effort. But you have no idea what's coming and you really shouldn't be wasting any more time. There's a very fine line between sleep and coma and Grace has already been through so much this evening. Make your choice.'

There wasn't one. He knew there wasn't one. My sun rose and set with Grace.

'Good girl,' said Magnus. His eyes caressed my face and I felt the appeal of his personality; it was powerful enough to have called to me from out of the broken body of Michael. 'Listen now, carefully. I'll have to carry Grace to your home because, with all due respect, you can't, and she won't manage herself. I'll drop her off and I will wait for you to get your body and join me. I could just take it, of course, but then I'd have to waste more time waiting for your Self, so it'll be much easier all round if you just come whole.' He smiled beatifically.

You said just my body. You want my Self too?

'My dear,' he said, 'I want you. All of you. I always have.' They were the words of a lover; he spoke them like a lover.

Let's go, I said.

'Splendid.' He pulled out a mobile, pressed speed-dial and said, 'Bring the car to the front.' He smiled again when he saw my expression. 'I have many skills but I can't fly, Cora. I have Reese's body to consider.' His mouth twisted. 'You, however, may fly if you wish. Go ahead. No? I guessed you'd want to stay with Grace. Although I wish you'd stay with me for my sake, Cora. Believe me, this isn't how I wanted it. I would much rather have wooed and won you.'

I looked at him in blank astonishment.

'You are so like your mother.' He shook his head humorously. He was walking downstairs, totally calm and at ease with himself.

Even my dreams couldn't have created a scene like this. And yet I was calm. Grace was close; I had made the bargain that would bring her home. Nothing else mattered.

CHAPTER 40

OUTSIDE, A SLEEK BLACK MERCEDES sat purring on the pavement. A liveried driver held the door open. Magnus slid in without a word, and I slid in beside him. The streets around us were silent and the air was empty of Selfs. There were no witnesses.

'Best not to talk,' murmured Magnus, as the driver came round to the front. 'It tends to distress the hired help.' He leaned towards me and added helpfully, 'He can't see you. He'll think I'm talking to thin air.'

So this was how it felt to know your life was coming to an end. No drama, no pain. It was peaceful, now I knew Grace would be safe. She was young enough to recover, and would go on without me. Charlie would take care of her.

Charlie. Panic nibbled away at the frayed edges of my mind, trying to claim my attention. I ignored it, and concentrated on Grace. I fast-forwarded to her future, to the wonderful woman she was going to become. She wouldn't grow up alone or dislocated from herself. The last few astonishing months had given me that, the gift of friends, including walkers, who would watch over her. Keep her safe.

Oh my God. History would repeat itself. Despite everything, she would grow up in hiding, in need of protection — just as I had.

Except for one thing: Magnus couldn't live forever. He looked young in Reese's body, but he had to be at least twenty years older than me, probably more...

Magnus broke in on my frenzied thoughts. He wanted my attention. I could feel his Self preening for me.

There was mercifully little traffic; it seemed to take no time at all to reach Gregory Square. The driver pulled up outside the house and Magnus insisted on waiting in the car while I went in to fetch my body; he wouldn't let me have Grace until then.

Why not? I wailed.

'Cora, sweetheart. I don't doubt your sincerity. But once you get home your friends might persuade you to challenge me and that will waste a lot of time. Although they ought to know better since they already know what I'm capable of.' He examined his nails. 'They've been with us all the time, by the way, did you know? Quite touching.'

I hadn't known; I was too focused on Grace. But sure enough, as I slid out of the car, there was Joe, and Reese had joined him; they must have flown above us the whole way home.

Reese! I said. *Are you okay?*

He was rage and misery, grey and diminished but with small sparks fizzing in him. *Cora. I'm so sorry. I couldn't hold him.*

Are you okay? Where's Grace? demanded Joe.

Come inside. I'll explain there.

I snapbacked the moment I was in the house, and found myself sitting on the sofa next to Grace's prone body. Charlie was a few steps away; I think he'd been pacing.

'Cora!' he cried as I raised my head.

Amy shook Grace's arm expectantly. 'Where's Grace?' she wailed.

I dropped to my knees and hugged Grace fiercely. She was empty — Magda was gone — and it was appalling how still she was, how limp and loose and yet so infinitely, endlessly precious, because she was Grace, my little girl, brown curls and smooth skin and thin arms that usually wound themselves around my neck.

'Grace is out in the car,' I said after a moment.

Then I looked around me, at Ken on the sofa opposite, Raul upright and alert on a stool, neither of them able to look me in the eye. Amy sat next to Grace, and Charlie stood frozen on the rug behind me. Joe had found his body and come into the house moments behind me.

And there was Reese, hovering in the doorway.

Still looking at the wall, Raul cleared his throat and said, 'We tried to contain him, Cora. We tried to keep Magnus in Michael, but without Charlie, we couldn't manage. He got out and took Reese's body.'

I flinched, imagining the scene. It would have taken significant power to separate Reese from his body; there would have been a fight.

'Are you okay?' I asked Reese again. Then I looked at Charlie. 'You should have told me.'

Charlie hadn't moved. 'I couldn't,' he said. 'I didn't know who you were, at first, and then I didn't want to know. How could I tell you that your mother's killer was my ... my brother?'

I shook my head tiredly. 'One of these days someone's going to have to explain to me how Magnus can possibly be your brother. Your father, maybe. But your brother? He's a generation older than you.'

'More than one generation,' began Joe.

I shook him away; he made no sense. 'And Magnus didn't kill my mother. She killed herself. To get away from him.' I shuddered.

A flicker of hope suddenly leapt into Charlie's face. 'He didn't kill her?'

'Apparently not.'

Joe was staring at Charlie, trying to read him, but Raul jumped up. 'Who cares about Cora's mother?'

I held up my hand to stop him. 'We don't have time to talk just now.'

'Why not?' said Ken.

I looked around at each face again. I felt so calm, and they all looked so still. It was a shame to have to rattle them up again. I wished there were some way to avoid it.

'Say it,' said Charlie, and he dropped a hand on my shoulder.

I took a deep breath. 'Magnus is carrying Grace. Inside him. Don't ask me how. He will give her back but I have to give him something in return.'

'We'll give him anything he wants,' said Amy vehemently.

It seemed to me then I'd always known that, in the end, my demon would own me, body and soul. 'He wants me.' There. Say it quickly and it's over.

There was an uproar. Only one person was silent. Charlie didn't say a word, but his fingers dug into my shoulder.

I turned to him with a flash of understanding. 'You knew!'

Charlie shook his head.

'You knew,' I said. I winced at the sudden noise in my head as random pieces clunked into place. 'You were always encouraging me to pop. You knew your brother wanted me. You let him out.' I stared at him in disbelief.

The room was silent. Everyone was staring at me; and then everyone was staring at Charlie.

He closed his eyes.

'Charlie?' said Amy.

'I didn't know,' he said. His voice was a shadow of itself. 'And when I found out you were the one he ... he'd always been looking for ... I wanted you to be stronger. You'll only withstand him as a ... a walker. He was always going to win, Cora.'

Reese had shot to Charlie's side. He was mouthing something and Raul popped for a moment to hear him. 'He says Charlie wasn't even there when Magnus escaped. He says it was his fault.'

'But you encouraged me to walk,' I repeated to Charlie.

He opened his eyes and looked at me with terrible regret. 'There's not much chance of escape if Magnus wants you. He's patient and you've both got time on your side. It was only a matter of how long we could delay it, and how strong you could become in the meantime. I just had to keep a clear head, to stay focused.' He passed a hand over his face. 'I didn't know it was you, at first. There were rumours, but you're not exactly what I was expecting. Even when you told me about your mother. It wasn't until later... But we had Magnus caged up inside Michael anyway. I thought we'd have plenty of time. And in the meantime, if you became a proficient walker, you'd have a chance of... And then your sister began interfering...'

He trailed off and I stared at him bleakly. I'd been suspicious; I'd doubted him. But I'd loved him from the first time we met, and I'd let that override the suspicion. And then I thought: *Magda came at me from one side, and Charlie from the other. One way or another, Magnus was always going to find me.* The inevitability somehow made Charlie less culpable, whatever his intentions.

I shook my head. 'I don't have time for this. Magnus is waiting.'

'What's he going to do to you?' wailed Amy. 'Would somebody please tell me what the hell is going on?'

I took a deep breath and kept my eyes on Grace's prone body. 'When I get into his car he'll release Grace.'

Amy began to panic. 'And what will he do to you?'

'I don't know.'

Practical, loving Amy was crying.

'I don't know and it doesn't matter,' I said resolutely. 'It's the only way I get Grace back so that's what's going to happen.' I looked up at Reese, who had faded to little more than a dark grey smudge. 'Reese? Whatever happens, it's just your body, it's not you. Do you understand? No one' — I looked around significantly — 'will ever blame you.'

Reese couldn't look at me.

'He thinks we're just going to let you walk out of here?' said Raul, rising from the stool, clenching his fists and his jaw.

'Sit down Raul. There's nothing we can do.' Even my heart sank at Joe's words, and I already knew they were true.

'Why not?' said Raul. 'Why can't we do anything?'

'Because he's got Grace inside him.'

'How is that even possible?' spluttered Amy.

'We'll ambush them on the way! We'll—'

'Sit down Raul! It's Magnus. This is Magnus we're talking about.'

'And what difference does that make?' demanded Raul.

It was Charlie that answered. 'It makes a difference.' I turned my head at last and saw Charlie exchange a glance with Joe. 'He'll hurt her. He won't hesitate. She's not ready—'

'Hurt her? He's going to kill her, and yet you'll sit here and let her go with him?' said Raul.

'I have to go,' I said, rising to my feet.

'No,' said Charlie, and he grabbed my arm.

'Charlie.'

He pulled me round to face him and for a moment there was no one else in the room.

'You can't go. I can't let you.' There was panic on his face and in his voice, and he was crying, too.

I put my hand on his cheek. 'I don't know what you've done. I don't know much about you at all. But I love you anyway.'

He pulled me into a fierce kiss but a car horn was sounding off outside, Magnus was getting impatient, and I pulled away. They all followed me to the door.

'Stay inside, don't watch. Don't. Just Joe — I need you to come out with me and help Grace. Don't watch. Please.'

'We're coming,' said Ken, and he sat down in the hallway, preparing to pop.

'No!' I cried. 'Don't you dare. None of you come, you hear me? I don't want you. Don't come. I'll be fine. Stay with Grace. Look after Grace.' I looked around pleadingly. 'I'm begging you. Let me go alone.'

I stumbled out of the door and Joe, who had popped immediately, came out with me.

Magnus was standing by the open back door of his car. 'I was getting worried,' he said cheerfully. 'Say all our goodbyes, did we? Get in the car, Cora.'

CHAPTER 41

MAGNUS HELD THE DOOR while I clambered in and belted up.

'Here you go, Joe.' Magnus put his hands to his stomach with a flamboyant gesture — he seemed to put his hands inside his own body — and he drew out Grace.

Joe, she said groggily, dropping against his waiting arms. I saw their Selfs mingle before Magnus slid in beside me, blocking the view.

'Drive!' he commanded.

I scrunched up into the corner of the seat, as far from him as I could get. He made no move to touch me, just gazed at me admiringly.

'How lovely you are, my Cora. You look exactly like your Self, just as you did when you were a child. How fortunate. Quite comfortable?'

'I'm fine.' I cleared my throat. 'I'm fine.'

'I won't hurt you, Cora.'

'Good.'

He laughed. 'And you've grown up with such spirit!'

'What do you know about my growing up?'

He smiled. 'The time for wooing is passed, dear heart. A shame, but you can thank your *sister* for that. The time left is for action. But that doesn't mean you shouldn't enjoy yourself.' He laughed. 'No one would blame you. Trust me, no one need even know. I'm not the baddie here.' He swung his silver hair. It was fascinating; with Reese's hair and face and body, he was nothing like Reese at all.

'You're not the baddie?' I would have liked to snort, like Amy, but I couldn't muster the required attitude.

He laughed quietly just the same. 'Of course not. You're the one, you know. Of course, I always knew the stories about your mother. But a newborn offspring — that's beyond hoping for in this day and age. Yet here you are.'

I stared at him. Was he mad? 'You know I have no idea what you're talking about.'

'Really?' He feigned surprise. 'Those patrollers haven't filled you in? Maybe they don't know. Charlie knows. Your mother never told you?'

'Told me what?'

'Ooh,' said Magnus. 'I get all the fun. Let's see — where shall we start. Who was your father, dear heart? No, not the salesman. Let me tell you. Your father was Bear — also known as Bjorn, sometimes Eimar. But usually just Bear. We're the watcher's children. We're the offspring.' He said it proudly.

'The watcher's children?' I said. 'You must think I'm stupid. No one believes those old stories.'

I was gratified to see a shadow of irritation flit across his face. 'Well, they'll soon think differently now I'm back. The others can hide if they choose, but I'm bored to the point of despair. Captivity has given me a taste for — let's call it adventure.'

'So you're a watcher's child. A nephilim.' I started to grin and when I saw that Magnus was even more irritated, I grinned more broadly.

'My forefathers were nephilim.' Magnus was struggling for self-control. 'I am offspring. That means I have a direct line back to the watchers, but I'm fifth generation. Your father, Bear, is second generation; he's a lot older than me.'

'I thought watchers mated with women way back when,' I said flippantly.

'Way, way back when,' agreed Magnus. 'Before recorded history.'

'So how old are you?' I asked.

'I was an accident of the middle ages. Your father, Bear, is one of the originals — an actual nephilim's son. He's several thousand years old.'

I hesitated, staggered by the sheer inventiveness of Magnus's stories, and then I said, 'If Bear is my father, that makes me offspring too.' And as the words slid off my lips, they became true and the world changed.

I was offspring. I had a direct line back to the watchers.

'Magda...?' I stammered.

He waved dismissively. 'A high-school accident. Your mother was an interesting woman with an unusual relationship trajectory. A student, a dreary businessman, then Bear, then me. Of course, I was only marking time with your mother, keeping you close, waiting for you to grow up.'

Magnus wanted me. Not my mother, not Magda. It was me. 'Don't walk,' my mother told me. 'Don't ever walk. He'll find you.'

There were a million things I wanted to know, but I needed to keep things practical, if only to stop my brain from exploding. I took a breath. 'So if you're a mighty offspring, how are you also Charlie's brother?'

'Ah,' said Magnus, and he looked disgruntled again. 'Charlie's family took up the burden of responsibility. The Tams have been acolytes for a century or more. We offspring always liked China; their myths *accommodate* us quite nicely, so we were generally well looked after there. Charlie started out with great promise but, honestly, modern western society is a very bad influence. No sense of tradition, no belief system or structure. Raised in this country, Charlie grew a very stupidly prosaic conscience, and he managed to infect his father along the way. Stopped walking and everything — can you imagine it?' He turned to me with a smile. 'Ah, of course you can. I forgot! Well he hasn't walked for a decade.' Understanding dawned on his face. 'You like him, don't you! Love him, even! Well well. It's lucky I'm not the jealous type. I'll deal with Charlie another time. I did not appreciate being Michael.'

'Who was Michael?' I wailed.

'Another of the Tams. Charlie's brother. He had an accident; should have died. Modern medicine has its drawbacks. The boy was gone but they kept on hammering away at his heart, and that's when Charlie decided he'd found a cage for me. He seemed to think I'd got out of hand.' He pulled a face. 'They call converts like Charlie *authentics*. All goodness and mercy but he nearly stole my girl, didn't he? I'll make him pay for that. You're mine.'

Listening to him was like running through fog, trying to catch up to someone that was too far ahead to even see. 'Are you going to kill me?' I asked.

He glanced at me sideways. 'We're not just walkers, beloved. We're offspring. I can kill your body, but I can't kill you. And why would I want to?'

I looked at him blankly. 'Then what do you want? Have you hunted me all these years so that we can play happy families again?'

Magnus gave a throaty chuckle. 'Happy families — now you're getting there! But don't imagine I want you for a daughter this time, or a sibling, dear heart. I had something more ... *romantic* in mind. The kind of thing that might lead to a happy family of our own, one day.'

My heart gave a massive leap of terror, leaving me faint and dizzy. I leaned my head back against the leather seat and closed my eyes.

'And a lovely added bonus is that we'll *really* piss off the watchers in the process,' continued Magnus. 'They could have freed me any time this last two years, and they didn't lift a...ah...a finger. Of course, it's never been done before. Offspring are always male. One of those irritating free will things; myths were always told by men so we always fulfilled the stories *as* men. But times have changed, and you're a woman, which is very original of you. And small, too — a total inversion! Honestly, I don't know for sure what the outcome will be. But darling, dear heart, my Cora. It was never just about the mating.' His voice suddenly grew deeper. 'Do you have any idea what it's like to live forever? The minute I meet someone interesting, they die. Everyone dies.'

He stretched languidly in his seat. 'Give in to me, Cora dear. We're going to be together for a very, very long time. And, as an extra bonus, we're going to cause no small amount of trouble.' He rubbed his hands together. 'A baby born of two offspring. Can you *imagine*? A super-offspring!' His laugh rang out, filled with joy.

A flicker of something very like hope sparked in my brain; I extinguished it quickly, for fear he would see it. Magnus thought he had everything worked out but there was something crucial he couldn't know... 'You want a child?'

'Why yes. Among other things. Isn't that what life-long companions usually do — make babies?'

I had stepped into a fairytale. Or a fairytale had burst into the real world; I really wasn't sure which way round it was. I knew, felt it in my Self, that Magnus wasn't lying; it's just that his version of the truth didn't tally with anything I was able to understand. There was too much to process. But this, at least, was becoming clear, even to my stunned brain: he wasn't going to kill me. Instead he wanted to play happy couples.

And make babies.

Of all the women he could have chosen for that particular task...

I had to keep him ... occupied ... to give the boys time to think of something, or for whatever it was Magnus was afraid of to arrive. To give *me* time to think of something. I closed my eyes at the thought of how long this might take, and what I might have to endure until then.

It didn't matter. All that mattered was the end of this tale. I wouldn't let Magnus overshadow the rest of my life or any of Grace's. I had to bring him to the end of his story.

Magnus was lost in his own happy thoughts beside me.

The car pulled up. The driver opened the door and I got out. We were in one of those short, discreet streets of townhouses that sheltered the outrageously wealthy. Every window locked and shuttered, and not a soul in sight. I glanced at the driver but there was no help there; his eyes were shuttered too.

Magnus tucked my hand into the crook of his elbow. 'Come along, my dear. Like my driver, my staff have been awaiting my return for a very long time. Everything should be prepared.'

He opened the front door, which was unlocked, and sailed in.

He was right. Inside, the house was illuminated, stretching away from us like a mansion, all marble and crystal. There were paintings on the walls, and potted orchids and bowls filled with exotic fruit on every gleaming surface. Everything sparkled.

'Oh,' said Magnus, 'Forgive me, I've always longed to do this.' He bowed with one hand extended towards me. 'Velcome to my home,' he said in a thick, central European accent, like Count Dracula in a bad film. Then he stood upright, laughing silently at himself. 'This way.'

He led me up a staircase and into a huge room. It was beautifully simple and completely unadorned. The only furniture was a sideboard with a tray of drinks, and a very, very large bed.

'Oh look,' said Magnus in mock amazement. 'A bed. Yes, a bed, dear heart, for us!' At my gasp of fear, he came and ran a finger down my cheek. 'Did you think I would take you over the back of a sofa? The floor perhaps?'

He stepped back and laughed. 'Oh relax. You look tired. We have plenty of time to get to know each other, first.'

'You think I'll ever lay down ... *for you?*' My incredulity came out in a squeal of defiance.

He began pouring something golden from a decanter into two small glasses. Then he came towards me, handing me a glass. His eyes were smoky. 'Lay down, stretch out, open wide. You might even beg, beloved. The second and third time.'

My insides turned to liquid. My heart failed me. I almost popped.

'Now, Cora.' His Self was vibrating, trying to reach me, to stroke me, kept in check only by the force of his will. 'You can run if you want to but you're really rather small and I'm not. It'll get you all panicked and sweaty. As will fighting. A little wrestling; well that's not always a bad thing, but perhaps not appropriate for now.'

I glanced at the door.

'Do you remember,' he went on, 'when you were a little girl, how long and *dark* staircases always looked when you were standing at the bottom? And then, halfway up, how someone always seemed to be following you? How you had to steel yourself to stay calm because once you started running the panic would suffocate you?'

My eyes shot to his face. 'How do you know?'

'It's a universal experience. I have not been spying on you, Cora. How could I spy on you before I'd even found you?'

'You didn't find me,' I reminded him. 'Magda did. The rest was just your luck, wasn't it?'

Magnus looked at me speculatively. 'What you're really asking me is whether Charlie helped me find you. You're not sure, are you?' He beamed. 'How exciting. The uncertainty, the tension. Ah yes: Magda. Well, I trained Magda to help me find you and she did, so perhaps I shouldn't be too rough on the girl. Not that I will need to be.' He smiled. 'I digress. Don't start running, that was my point. I strongly advise you against it, for your sake. This need not be terrifying and the outcome has never been in question, only the timing.'

I threw back the drink; it was whisky, the drink Charlie always gave me to calm my nerves. It was almost funny.

'Let's get on with it then,' I said. I laid myself down on the bed. 'Ready? Dive in.'

He was amused. 'So interested in the sex,' he chided. 'Your mother should have taught you a little modesty. I want so much more from you. Besides, you still have your clothes on.'

'So take them off,' I said.

But I couldn't keep it up. I meant to goad him, to call into question his manhood, to wrest some modicum of control out of this horror. But I couldn't do it. At the look on his face, I forgot every possible consequence; I popped and fled, leaving my body alone on the bed.

CHAPTER 42

I DIDN'T GET FAR. Charlie stopped me. He was standing, full-bodied, on the landing outside the bedroom.

'Cora,' he said when he saw me. 'Stop! Go back inside — I'm coming.'

What?

'Go back,' he urged. 'Trust me.'

Trust him. Trust Charlie, who was once an acolyte and was now a convert. Who had hated it when Joe told the stories, but lived his life right in the middle of them.

I snapbacked in time to hear Charlie banging on the locked door of the bedroom.

'Now who is that?' demanded Magnus. He cocked his head on one side to *sense* the air, just as Grace would have done. 'The authentic — my brother. Is that why you came back, Cora? How touching! You think he's going to change my mind?'

Magnus strolled to the door and unlocked it. 'Come in, brother dear!' he said, with a sweeping gesture of welcome. 'What can I do for you?'

'I've come to help you,' said Charlie. He was looking straight at Magnus; he hardly acknowledged that I was in the room, sprawling on the bed.

'Me?' said Magnus with exaggerated astonishment. Then his eyes narrowed. 'You've come to help me? Aren't you supposed to try to rescue the damsel?'

Charlie cracked a grin. 'Now what would be the point in that?'

'No point whatsoever,' agreed Magnus. 'Explain yourself.'

'Magnus,' said Charlie, and he came and sat on the edge of the bed and settled himself comfortably, warming to his theme. 'We've known each other a long time.'

'All your life,' agreed Magnus.

'This dream of yours, the mating of the offspring.'

'Why does everyone focus on the sex?' roared Magnus, and I shrank back on the bed. 'Anyone would think I was a monster! I want a companion, Charlie, a friend for life. For all of my life!' He leaned over Charlie. 'I bedded your great great *great* grandmother, Charlie Tam. It seems like only weeks ago, to me. Do you know what that's like — to lose *everybody*?'

'I understand,' said Charlie. He hadn't even flinched. 'I do. And so will Cora, eventually. But in the meantime, that body you're wearing. Reese. Cora has no feelings for Reese.'

Magnus was listening; Magnus was intrigued. 'I take your point,' he said. 'Your body, on the other hand...'

'Well,' said Charlie modestly. 'I think it might help things along. Just until things settle down.'

Magnus was all cool appraisal. 'And you'll just hand your body over to me, will you?'

'I will,' said Charlie pleasantly. 'For this purpose, you may have it.'

'And do you trust me to give it back afterwards?'

Charlie smiled. 'Come on, Magnus. I'm not as stupid as you think. Afterwards, as you put it, the whole world will have changed. The watchers aren't likely to stand idly by while you unleash a super-offspring into the world. I can't predict what will happen and neither can you. Let's not make promises for a future neither of us can foresee.'

I sat up; I stared from one of them to the other as they bargained over whose body would devour mine. And silently I willed Magnus to accept Charlie's offer. I didn't understand half of what was going on, but at this point I was willing to clutch at straws; if any of this had to happen, let it happen with Charlie's body. *Please, please.*

Magnus was studying Charlie's face. 'You haven't walked for years,' he said.

'I think I remember how.'

Magnus rallied and began strolling around the room. 'You know, it's really quite romantic of you. You're not stupid enough to try and save the girl, but you're willing to give up your body to spare her some initial discomfort. It'll still be me at the helm.' He smiled lasciviously.

'Believe me, Charlie, she'll *always* know it's me.'

'I don't doubt it,' said Charlie. His pleasant demeanour never dropped. 'But she'll prefer it this way, and you'll get what you want. And if we do this, Cora won't run away.' He turned to me. 'Because there's no point. Running will only get her or Grace hurt.'

My heart gave an unbearable lurch at this reminder of the potential danger to my daughter. I scanned Charlie's face for rescue, for some indication of how he was planning to save me. The answer was clear in his eyes: there is no rescue; this is the best I can do.

I turned away, tears blinding me. I didn't know if Charlie was trying to spare me, or very effectively serving me up on a platter.

'I am tired of the chase,' admitted Magnus. 'I don't really want to hurt her. Finding new bodies is so tiresome. The settling-in period can be a nuisance, especially the first time. As for me — well, one body is as good as another.' He looked Charlie up and down. 'I suppose Reese—'

Right here. Reese ghosted into the room.

'Of course you are,' said Magnus. 'And Michael?'

'His body died the moment you left it,' said Charlie. 'As you knew it would.' He stiffened, and I remembered that Michael had been his brother, his blood-brother.

'And I also suppose,' drawled Magnus — his arrogant nonchalance made me want to scream — 'that this is not a trap? Because, Charlie boy, I may have spared your father last time you trapped me, but I will not spare you, or that sweet little Grace you all dote on, if you try anything fancy this time. And I'll leave Reese a lot more than my hair to remember me by.' He turned a glacial stare on Reese, whose Self was blasted backwards against the wall.

'No tricks,' said Charlie, holding up a hand.

'And I will not hesitate to hurt her very badly indeed,' warned Magnus, looking at me. 'I may not be able to kill her, but I will do such things to her body that she'll wish I could.'

'I know that.'

'Very well then.'

'Very well then,' repeated Charlie and right there, before my eyes, he peered out of the top of his head and very slowly threaded his way out of his body, which sank back onto the bed.

With the speed of a striking scorpion, Magnus switched bodies, sending Reese's crashing to the floor and taking up Charlie's. A second later Reese had snapbacked into his own body and was picking himself up.

Horrified and fascinated, I stared at Charlie — the new, modified Charlie — to see what would happen next.

He sat up. He clicked his neck and wobbled his jaw, and then he stretched his hands out in front of his face and examined his nails. For a second, less than a second, hope leaped in my heart; and immediately died when Magnus began to speak.

'Not bad,' he said, with Charlie's lips and tongue.

'I thought you needed a big body,' I whispered.

'I'm in this body willingly,' said Magnus flamboyantly. 'A bigger model is required to imprison me, but not to accommodate me. Although,' he added as he stretched, 'I do generally prefer something with a little more leg room.'

I gazed around and found Charlie's Self hovering by the door. He might not have walked for years, but he knew what he was doing. His Self was clear and unwavering; he was in control. There were no ripples of tension coming from him, no colour changes or fluctuations.

Reese stood near him, whole, watching Magnus uncertainly.

'Go,' said Magnus, with an imperious flick of his hand. 'Both of you.'

They went, both of them. They had done what they could; this was as good as the rescue would be.

'Now then,' said Magnus. 'This is better, I think. I'm not unromantic, Cora dear. I've waited a long, long time for this, and on the whole I'm very pleased with how things are going. I'm so much happier if you're happy, my dear, and with Charlie's body involved, I suspect you will be very happy indeed. You can even pretend I'm Charlie, if that makes it better. I think you'll find I'm a much better lover, but then — oh!' He broke off with a look of happy surprise. 'My dear! I had no idea! You and he never... Well. Let me see.'

He put his hand inside his trousers and crudely manhandled his physical equipment. 'Yes, everything seems to work. I wonder what held him back?'

He closed his eyes and I could imagine him rummaging around in Charlie's head. 'He thought to stay away from you, to keep you safe from me,' he said with a smile. 'And that was even before he really knew who you were or what wonderful plans I had in store for us!'

'The offspring thing,' I said.

'Yes. The offspring thing.'

I tried to make conversation, to stave off the inevitable. 'So you're fifth generation?'

'I am.'

'And this Bear, my father, he was—'

'Second generation.'

'So I'm third generation. That makes me closer to the watchers than you.'

'You catch up fast,' he said; but he wasn't pleased.

'So what are my superpowers?' I said. 'If grandpa's a watcher, what can I do?'

'My dear,' said Magnus impatiently. 'You can live forever. What more do you want?'

I felt the blood draining from my face. 'What?'

'You see,' said Magnus, and he settled himself comfortably on the bed beside me. 'You can use the words, but your brain really hasn't caught up yet, has it? You believe me, you don't believe me. Don't worry. By the time you take your second or third body, you'll believe me completely.'

'I would never take another body.'

He looked amused. 'You will. You will, Cora. You won't mean to, at first. When that lovely body of yours dies, you'll stay silent and invisible, a spirit in a spirit world, unable to move away from the world of time and matter but unwilling to steal from a human. I'll give you a year, in human time. Maybe ten. I lasted twelve, but not everyone has my strength.' He laughed again at the sudden leap of hope in my eyes. 'Of course I tried to withstand it at first, dear heart! We all do! No one wishes to become a monster. But you'll soon learn.'

'What will I learn?' I said as defiantly as I could.

'That bodies are ripe for the picking,' he said complacently. 'You don't have to force anyone out. Unless you want to, of course.'

'You mean there are empty bodies just — what, walking about the place?'

'Yes, my dear, I mean exactly that. Apathy is the scourge of the world. Not hate or violence or any of those other *actions*. The rot begins and ends with apathy. An apathetic Self has little hold on the material world.' His eyes widened, as at a happy thought. 'Let's test-run my new body. Take off your clothes.'

'I thought it wasn't about the sex,' I said, trying desperately to disarm him.

'In the long run it isn't. Not at all. But I'm starved, my dear.' His eyes ran up and down my body. 'The magnetism between us! You must feel it. I concede that my use of Charlie's ... ah ... body probably helps. Clever Charlie.' He licked his lips. 'Let's play.'

There was red velvet wallpaper on the walls, and plush velvet curtains at the windows. I looked at Charlie, who wasn't Charlie, and my insides shrank.

'Let's talk,' I countered. 'Let's plan for the future.'

'Oh my dear, that's a conversation that could run and run.' He took hold of my white shirt and began undoing the buttons, gently at first, then more unsteadily.

'No,' I said. 'Please.'

'Listen to me,' said Magnus, pulling the shirt from my shoulders. 'Don't hide behind some misconceived notion of humanity, my love. You're not some hapless girl at the mercy of a callous rapist. You're offspring, the noble child of a nephilim, about to mate with one of your own kind. This is just the start. Look at me. Your eyes know this body but it's more than that. Admit it. Your Self recognises me. Admit it!'

I'd only known Peter. I'd dreamed of Charlie, but not like this. This was Charlie — and it wasn't. His hands, his lips and tongue and hips. His body moving over mine, into mine; his smell, his hair.

But not him. Not him at all, pulling and sucking and pushing, clawing at me and jerking my head backwards, hoisting me up, invading me, pounding in me, ripping and squeezing and flooding into my body.

And I couldn't pop to escape it because ... Magnus was right. I recognised him. I felt his desperate need for connection. In that rough coupling I took a world of loneliness and despair into my body, and was flooded with an overwhelming, earth-shattering compassion. I cried, and I cried out, but the tears weren't just for me. My human body might be limited, but a new way of being was conceived in my imagination.

Being Cora would never be the same again.

Afterwards we lay exhausted. And then Magnus raised Charlie's face to smile weakly into mine. 'I knew you'd understand,' he said, still panting.

I popped and fled.

CHAPTER 43

I HUNG OUTSIDE THE WINDOW of my house in Gregory Square. Grace was in bed under the covers, wrapped in Amy's arms; they were both fast asleep. Raul and Ken, in chairs placed on either side of the bed, sat like a pair of flanking angels. Reese stood behind Ken, moodily staring down. Charlie was nowhere to be seen.

I couldn't go in. I couldn't face them. Grace was safe, whole, wrapped up in love, flanked, protected — safe. Grace was safe. There wasn't anything more I could want. I vanished into the garden.

And Charlie was there.

I sprang back, wanting to hide myself, but he was as fast as me. I began to dissolve and he mirrored that action too.

Cora, he said. *Forgive me.*

I stared at him, and it was very clear why I'd always trusted him, despite everything: his Self was pure and true and untainted. I'd felt it through his body. It was why I loved him so much.

I stopped trying to escape.

Are you okay? he said. He reached out, but he didn't touch me. *I'm so sorry. There was nothing else I could do.*

We stared mutely at one another, as scenes of our intertwined bodies played in my mind — and his, for all I knew. He must have guessed what would happen.

Did you know what I was?

An offspring? He shook his head. *Not in time. But the more I heard of your story, the more I began to wonder. I tried to leave you alone. I meant to. It was already too late by the time I was certain. So then I tried to prepare you, to make you a stronger walker so that you'd have some chance of surviving him.*

You failed.

You're strong.

Do you believe it? All that offspring crap?

Charlie paused, then replied, *Do you?*

I don't know. He said I'm going to live forever. When Charlie didn't respond, I said, *Grace won't live forever. You won't. Why would I want to?*

It'll become different as time goes on. You'll change bodies. He was choosing his words very carefully, but he still got it wrong.

I will not! I cried, and the air around us went dark. *I will never take another body! And even if I did, what for? To live with Magnus? To be his mate for eternity?*

Charlie didn't answer. Instead, he raised a hand and placed it on my arm, and a look of pure delight crossed his face as his hand melted into me. *I'm touching you.*

Yes.

Really touching you.

Yes.

He'll never do that. Whatever he does to your body, it's not this. He put his hand into my chest, very, very carefully, and cupped it where my heart would be. *So for just a little time, let's just be together, like this. Okay?*

Until the watchers get here. That's what we're hoping for, right?

Until then.

As declarations of undying love went, this was original. Until now, I hadn't fully realised what Charlie had done for me: he'd given up his life. If the stories were true, sooner or later I would simply choose and take another body; I shuddered even as I thought this. Charlie, on the other hand, would simply die. I didn't know how long a walker could last without a body, but that's the risk Charlie had taken for me.

Cora, Charlie began. He licked his lips nervously. *If you ... if you have a baby ...* He was trying to be brave.

I won't have a baby, Charlie.

Hope leapt into his eyes. *He didn't...?*

Oh he did. My voice was rich with bitterness and guilt. *You know he did.*

Emotions were flitting across Charlie's face like moth wings. It was unbearable.

I sighed. *I can't have children, Charlie. I'm infertile. Barren. There's no chance of a baby.*

Charlie looked at me, puzzled, not understanding. *I'm sorry,* he said automatically.

No. I shook my head. *I've always known. Apparently I was born without eggs. That's partly why ... Peter didn't mind, you see. And he was older, with a good job and good sense, so it was easy for us to adopt Grace. I might have had to wait years for someone my own age to settle down. All I ever wanted was a daughter...* I was babbling. I hadn't told the whole story often, but it was hardly new, so there was no accounting for the despair in my voice and the grief pouring over me.

It was just so different saying these things to Charlie, with whom, in another life, another world, I would have longed to have children.

Charlie was crying. Spirit tears — I'd never seen that before. They shivered and sparkled on his cheek, tiny fragments of heartache. And then they were gone.

So you see, there's no risk of ... of a child ... with Magnus. He's already done his worst.

But you have Grace, said Charlie, and his voice was suddenly strong and unwavering.

Yes, I said, drawing on his strength. *Grace is my daughter.*

We smiled at each other and our eyes locked.

Darling, he murmured, sinking his hand against my cheek. *Thank God for Peter. He was better for you than I have been. I wish —*

I love you, I said. *I've always loved you.*

And I love you. I love you Cora.

Our smiles faded and we just stared, anguished, because we'd already missed everything we could ever have shared.

Charlie caught me into a strange kind of dance. *We've both spent far too long trying to escape from Magnus, living on the surface, not walking. Look at us now! We should celebrate, take what we can get.*

As we rose higher I saw Joe standing on the doorstep, gazing out at us, one hand shading his eyes. I hesitated and then waved, and he waved back.

Come on. Let's go in, said Charlie.

Shame engulfed me. *I can't. I can't face them.*

Everyone in there is terrified and it will help them to see you.

Any other argument to get me inside would have failed; he knew that. I could handle the role of comforter, as I couldn't have handled the role of victim. He knew that too.

We went into the house and everyone but Raul was in the hallway and had already popped to meet me.

Cora, said Joe, and touched his forehead against mine.

I'm so sorry, said Reese.

I frowned. *It's not your fault, Reese.*

I couldn't stop him. I couldn't help you.

You did help me, Reese. You all did. You still are helping me.

I couldn't help you, he repeated, and Ken laid a hand against his back. Reese seemed to lean back into it; huge Reese supported by the insubstantial Ken. Wonders never ceased.

'How's it going, flying boy?' Raul called quietly from the top of the stairs. He waved a hand at Charlie and me. 'Welcome home, Cora.' He jerked a thumb towards Grace's bedroom and went back to guard them.

I'm sorry we couldn't stop this, said Joe.

Joe, you did everything you could and more. Grace is safely upstairs asleep because of you — all of you. You saved her life.

So here we all were, bravely avoiding what I was, or what might happen next. I looked around me. *Don't leave her,* I said to them. *Whatever happens. Not ever.*

We won't.

Grace woke up. I was beside her in an instant.

'Mummy,' she said, yawning and stretching. 'Charlie, too! See, I knew you were a walker.'

Grace.

'Why have you *popped?* she asked, drifting out to meet me.

Go back in, Gracie darling. You shouldn't be popping now. We can talk later.

Her little spirit was as tired as her body; she leaned against me for support. *I love you.*

I love you too. Go on now.

'Night night. Fly awake, Mum.'

Night, love.

I settled back to watch over her, the love spilling out of me in a visible stream. Once, I glanced up and there was Charlie, watching over me, his love spilling over us both.

CHAPTER 44

I SNAPBACKED AS MAGNUS STIRRED.

'There you are,' he said, groggily. 'Been anywhere interesting?'

'Here and there.' I sat up and backed away from him, off the bed.

'I'm sorry,' he said. 'I really had meant to give you time.' He smoothed his silver hair and frowned. 'Although, my dear, I'm not sure I was entirely responsible for what happened. There was a very heady dose of Charlie behind all of that.' He looked troubled for a moment. 'I didn't know the boy had it in him.'

I felt a deep loathing stir in me. 'I never doubted Charlie's *passions*,' I said as crudely as I could.

'Oh, neither did I,' agreed Magnus. 'I was talking about the love.' He rose to his feet, stumbled and swore He was struggling to sound even vaguely civilised. 'I am so *tired*. It was exhausting being inside that crippled body all those months.'

He sat down again and put his head in his hands. 'You'll find food downstairs and any number of servants to prepare it for you. Go get something to eat. Or leave your body and go play somewhere. I don't care. You've got ... a couple of hours?' He waved a dismissive hand. 'Run along. Don't be late back. I believe I shall know where to find you, and you probably don't want me to go looking for you there.'

'I'm free to ... come and go?' I asked.

'Be gone,' he said, sinking back into the pillows.

****

It feels wonderful, sighed Charlie. *I never stopped walking in my dreams, but it's not a patch on the real thing.*

We were sitting on the top of Marble Arch watching the traffic swirling below us. The sound up here was only marginally less noisy than on the ground and, in this state, we could hear the swirling of the wind and the stars above us as well.

It's more like swimming when you dream about it.

He nodded and we both said, *Breast stroke,* and laughed.

I suppose we swim because we can't flap. I flapped my arms experimentally, and hovered in front of Charlie, who was sitting cross-legged on the blue-grey Carrara marble that gave off little sparks of the golden Tuscan sun it had absorbed over millennia.

He smiled and reached for me. *Little scraps of pink keep on shooting out of your mouth.* His eyes lingered on my lips.

I wonder if your experience of walking is the same as mine. Can you see much more clearly like this?

I see you.

I raised my hand to his and watched our energies merge. *Can't you see me better now than normal?*

You look the same as you always look.

I shook my head in wonder.

Do I look different to you? he asked.

I stared at him, thinking it over. *No,* I admitted at last, *although I didn't always see you this clearly. It might have been useful.*

Then I wish I'd been able to show you my Self before now and saved you some time.

Time. The one thing I apparently had loads of. The idea of time without Charlie and Grace: it was an aberration. It made the whole offspring thing impossible. It had to be impossible.

I'm so used to hiding, said Charlie. *It feels wonderful to just be who I am.*

Tell me why you stopped walking. Magnus said you and your family were acolytes. What does that mean, exactly?

We were a servant family, said Charlie, wrinkling his nose with distaste. *We served Magnus. It happens: walker families become enthralled by the offspring and fall into service without realising what's happening. It wouldn't be so bad if the offspring were reliable, helpful types.* He raised a sardonic eyebrow. *Most of them have given up the whole royal court thing these days, and keep a pretty low profile. Cloud and Bear tend to travel solo — I don't think most walkers would know them if they fell over them. Magnus is one of the few that likes to maintain an entourage.*

Cloud? I said. *Are you kidding? I thought Bear was odd enough.*

Charlie grinned. *You haven't heard the others' names yet. They used to change them to suit the prevailing culture, but most of them have reverted to their original elemental names.*

Magnus?

It means 'great'. Charlie rolled his eyes. *I don't think he'll be letting that name go any time soon.*

And how many of them are there?

Charlie looked at me steadily, as if he were trying to keep me calm by remote-control. *No one really knows. There hasn't been a new one for centuries. Before you, there's only been one since Magnus was born in 1548.*

Before me.

You'll get used to it, he said, still holding my gaze.

Would you? If it were you, would you get used to it?

You're forgetting that the offspring have been my reality all my life.

I stirred the air around me with my index finger. *Why don't these watchers do something?*

Charlie looked away at last. *The original sin was theirs. They don't exactly have the moral high ground.*

You said they were coming now.

Because of Grace. You don't take children. It's beyond the law — it's a fundamental principle of the universe. The watchers can't stand by. They'll be here.

And then they'll see what Magnus is attempting for his next party trick. Why don't they intervene before the trouble starts?

Charlie was surprised. *Free will, of course. They have to allow humans their free will. They can only react.*

So they would never come to stop one of their children causing mayhem?

Nope. Stupid, isn't it? But that's the way it goes. So we're lucky they're already coming because Magda stole Grace.

And you're sure they'll see what Magnus is up to?

Samyaza is very fond of Magnus, said Charlie. *He won't miss an opportunity to look in on him. He'll have to act.*

I feel faint.

Charlie laughed. He cupped his hand and sent a small ball of energy at me, knocking me off balance so that I had to flutter upwards to right myself.

Let's fly! said Charlie. *I've got some catching up to do.*

Being with Charlie at all was a thing of wonder; walking with him was nothing short of miraculous. We left Marble Arch and circled low over Gregory Square, looking down onto the treetops, and then took in the major landmarks — Piccadilly Circus, Trafalgar Square, the Houses of Parliament. We flew out to Kew, swooping low over the treetops where several Selfs sat peacefully gazing up at us. Charlie waved, but no one waved back.

The worst thing about not walking, said Charlie, *is being disconnected. Being an individual is hugely overrated. I wish everyone could see what they're missing by insisting on all this separateness.*

When did you last walk? Properly, I mean.

I stopped when I was fifteen. Come on. You show me your favourite places and I'll show you mine.

You're forgetting. I haven't walked properly since I was six. I don't have favourite places.

Then I'll show you mine. Have you ever seen the midnight sun?

You're kidding.

Why not?

He was floating away, dancing through the lovely day, a shimmer of white and pink, with edges of deep blue. I flew to his side.

Don't leave without me.

Look at the colours, Cora, he sighed, reaching out to me. *All this life!*

Below us, the city pulsed and flared with flames of colour and activity. The darkest sunglasses couldn't have begun to protect material eyes from this sight. It wasn't bright, exactly, but *vivid, actual, revealing.* All barriers were swept away to reveal the unique substance of everything — objects, emotions, intentions and sound, too. It wouldn't matter how many times I saw it; it would never be less than startling and new.

We flew to the coast, staying low most of the time, but picking up speed as we crossed the sea, heading north. It was exhilarating, swooping over the inky water, with the night sky wheeling above us. We gained altitude over Iceland, so I could see the whole island, cut across the tip of Greenland, and then we were in the northern territories of Canada, and the sun was sitting on the horizon, casting a luminous glow over lakes and mountains. We slowed down, drifting into a forest of Douglas fir. Pollen wafted gently on the air, love notes from male trees to unknown, distant mates. Further north still we saw a caribou peacefully grazing beside a glowing lake.

He was proud, showing me the things he loved; he was glad to have me with him as he revisited these favourite haunts. Beautiful as it all was, I knew that, by myself, the lake would just be a lake, each tree just a tree, magnificent in themselves but too far from home — from Grace, from my learned inclination to hide — to draw me. But now, with Charlie, everywhere felt like home. And everything was tinged with regret for the things I'd missed until now, nostalgia for a future I would never have. Perhaps beauty was like that, a double-edged gift, joy and yearning rolled into one.

I love you, Cora, said Charlie. *I would give this all up for you.*

****

I was back with Magnus inside the allotted time but he was in no mood to see me. 'Go,' he said, putting his hand in front of his eyes. 'Leave me.'

'You're kidding,' I said. I sat down in the chair in front of him.

He slowly lowered his hand and looked at me with Charlie's piercing eyes. 'What didn't you understand?'

'What I don't understand,' I said bitterly, 'is that you've spent a lifetime — at least, all of my lifetime — looking for me. And now I'm here and you're telling me to go. Again.'

A slow, nasty smile crept over his face. 'Would you rather I paid you some more close attention, my dear?'

'No thank you,' I said, as coolly as I could manage. 'But you promised me eternal companionship. Yet you don't seem able to stomach our first day together.'

'You've got me, my dear. You win. Off you go.'

I was alarmed, and more than a little scared. 'You're letting me go?' Was this a trick? I needed to know; I couldn't spend another twenty years looking over my shoulder.

'Oh yes,' he said sarcastically. 'After a lifetime of pursuing you, as you so eloquently reminded me, I'm just going to let you go. No, my eternal beloved. I'm telling you to go away for now. I have some thinking to do. Ah ah ah — not your body, obviously. That stays with me.'

There was something terribly wrong with this Magnus. My scalp prickled. 'Are you sick?' I ventured.

'Yes, of you. Go!' he suddenly roared.

I popped, leaving my body to slump back in the chair.

CHAPTER 45

THE BOYS WERE ACCOMPLISHED WALKERS. They knew when a Self was present; they knew when I was present. But on this occasion they were engrossed in conversation, and they didn't realise I was back.

'It'll be carnage,' said Joe. 'The offspring were bad enough in their day. A super-offspring? Can you imagine it?'

'But it will be Cora's baby,' said Reese. 'We can teach it.'

'You can't teach offspring,' growled Raul.

'We taught Cora a few things,' objected Reese. 'And she's always been as good as gold.'

They looked at one another. 'She's female,' said Raul at last.

'No,' said Joe. 'She's in her first life. You're forgetting the stories. The trouble begins when their first body dies and they start looking for a new one.'

'I still can't believe it,' said Ken, with more than a touch of excitement in his voice. 'Cora, an offspring. It doesn't seem possible. But I trust her. Completely.'

'So do I,' admitted Reese.

Joe sighed. 'Guys, I trust Cora as much as you do. But she's offspring. Make no mistake about it. The best case scenario is that we're all still around when her body dies, so that we can contain her.'

'You mean contain her like we contained Magnus in Michael?' said Raul, and even he looked horrified.

'Of course I don't mean that,' said Joe quickly. But it was hard to think what else he might have meant.

'So what do we do?' asked Ken. 'If the watchers don't do their job, and Cora comes back pregnant. We can't hurt Cora. I can't.'

There was a beat of silence and then Joe said, 'We kill the baby.'

I couldn't help it; I recoiled, and the kitchen door slammed shut. As a body, they turned towards me with guilty faces.

'Great,' said Reese. 'Because what we need right now is a baby Self running around without a body. It'll be an offspring, too, duh. You can't kill it.' He looked at me nervously and then quickly back at Joe again.

'It'll be a baby,' said Ken. 'Who kills babies?'

Joe half-rose to his feet. 'I didn't say I'd thought it through...' he began, with a supplicating gesture towards me.

Grace, who had been upstairs, chose that precise moment to come running down.

'Mummy mummy mummy *mummy*!' she purred, flinging her body onto Joe's lap and popping immediately to nestle against me. *I missed you so. Where have you been?*

I held Grace protectively against me and moved backwards. These boys, these men I thought I knew so well — they would have killed my baby. Forget that it would have been Magnus's baby too; forget that it would have been a super-offspring. It would have been my baby.

I stared them down, caution and mistrust on my face.

Cora... began Joe, popping. The others, too, popped, clearly anxious to make amends.

Tell me the story, cried Grace, oblivious. *Go on, Mum!*

I haven't thought of it for a long time, I said automatically. *Why don't you begin?*

You came looking for me, said Grace. *Remember? You came looking for me, and...*

I looked down at her and suddenly smiled. We might forget for months and years at a time, but the words were engraved in us.

I took up the lines. *I looked everywhere, and I saw dozens of children, but none of them was you. And I held on for you.*

Because you knew I was out there, said Grace.

Because I knew you were out there, and I knew I would find you. So I kept looking and waiting and hoping. And then, one day, Dad heard of a very special little girl who was living in...

...a terraced house in Leeds, said Grace.

So we drove to the house and there you were.

There I was.

Waiting for us.

And you knew me immediately.

I certainly did. Because I'd been looking for you for so long. A few weeks later, we took you home.

You sang me to sleep every night, said Grace.

I sang you the songs my mother used to sing to me, I said.

Grace giggled and began to chant a much-loved nursery rhyme in old French. *And you told me fairy stories.*

And you were the most precious child in the history of the world.

I am the most precious child in the history of the world. Grace smiled, her eyes closed. *We haven't done that in a while, Mum.*

You remembered all your lines, I said, leaning in to her.

It was so quiet in the kitchen that I raised my head to see if we were alone. We were not. Everyone was still there, silently staring at me.

Bed time, Grace, I told her.

Grace obediently snapbacked. Reese did the same and, without a word, took her hand and led her upstairs.

She's adopted? demanded Joe.

She's my daughter, I corrected him.

But not your birth daughter. Why did you adopt? There was a look on his face; I knew what it was. It was hope. In the middle of my own personal nightmare, perhaps I'd overlooked the magnitude of what its repercussion might have been. I saw a glimpse of it now, when I saw the birth of new hope in Joe's eyes at the very possibility that it might not happen.

Would it really have been so dreadful if I'd had a baby? Even if it would, it was a terrible thing to look at Joe's face and see the small, very private tragedy of my infertility look like the greatest favour I could do the world.

I stared at Joe with rebellion in my heart. He was strong and resolute and righteous. He would have put aside personal feeling and killed my baby. He would have trapped its little spirit as Grace had been trapped inside Magnus.

I wouldn't forgive him.

Why did you adopt? he repeated in a whisper.

Because I wanted Grace, I said, staring him down. Our energies were pulsing.

But you've had no other children, he said. *You birthed no children.*
No.
Cora, began Ken.
No, Ken, I interrupted him. *No! You may not ask any more questions.*
You — I looked at Joe — *deserve no answers.*

****

Charlie found me. I'd discovered my favourite place, at last, right down in the South Pole. In that white desert twilight, in the glow of the aurora australis, I found the purest energy imaginable. It was a place where you could be yourself unchallenged.

Joe told me you overheard him, said Charlie. He was almost invisible in the half-light; if I'd had to rely on my eyesight, I wouldn't have spotted him. *He says he's sorry.*

He would have killed my baby.

There was never going to be a baby, said Charlie.

He didn't know that.

He does now. Cora, Joe takes responsibility. You know this about him. He couldn't save you, but he's trying to make preparations for the future.

My hero, I said. *Preparing to save the world. By killing a baby. Can you imagine, Charlie? He'd have taken my baby's body and left the poor soul in the wilderness.*

He wasn't thinking clearly. And, again, there is no baby. Charlie was being brave; I knew that.

I still can't forgive him.

But you will.

I sighed. *Probably.*

We returned to Gregory Square. Everyone was waiting.

Cora, said Joe, coming forward. He wore an expression of abject apology, but there was defiance there, too. The apology was for having upset me; there was no apology for what he would have done had things been otherwise.

Save it, Joe, I said, but I put out my hand to touch him, so he would know we were okay — or at least, that we would be okay one day.

Thank God the danger is over, said Raul, and everyone turned on him at once.

For God's sake, Raul, began Charlie.

Fucking moron! said Reese, looking at him with contempt. *Magnus has still got Cora and Charlie, in case you'd forgotten.*

He mustn't know, said Joe. *Magnus mustn't know he'll never have a child with Cora.*

We should tell him, objected Raul. *Put an end to all this. He can't kill Cora. She's offspring.*

He can kill that body, said Charlie. *He can hurt her. More — he can hurt her much more than he is doing now.* He looked away, rigid and unhappy.

It's not just about the baby, for Magnus I began, but Ken interrupted me. *He can kill Charlie.*

My world stopped turning. I looked at Charlie, waiting for him to say that would never happen, that Magnus wouldn't ever kill him, they were practically family...

Charlie didn't say anything.

Joe said, *We have to wait for the watchers and hope Magnus doesn't find out. Cause even if it's not just about the baby, he is going to be seriously pissed. He might try and force you to change bodies.*

Joe! roared Charlie. *For God' sake!*

But I wasn't listening. I was thinking that I'd given myself to Magnus for Grace's sake, and now I would let him keep me for Charlie's sake.

Where are the fucking watchers? cried Reese. *Where are they? What are they doing?*

Ken tensed at the window, peering out. When he spoke, his voice trembled. *They're here.*

Chapter 46

JOE WAS INSTANTLY AT KEN'S SIDE. *Where?*

Watchers? said Raul, scrabbling to join them. *Really?*

This is what we've been waiting for? snorted Reese. *Like we should all be so scared. I thought they would be a little more exciting.*

It was hard to get even a little window-space to see what they were all seeing. When I did see, I immediately shrank back.

They were like walkers, the watchers, but ... *more.* They had draped themselves among the branches of a tree, but at that size they could scarcely encompass the energy they gave out — a dazzling, vibrant pulse I could hardly look at, even with spirit eyes. Their outline, crackling and pulsing with light, was indefinite — another sign that they could have chosen to be any size, any shape at all. The longer I looked, the more apparent it became that they were, most emphatically, not human.

I was exhilarated and terrified, just looking at them. I shivered. *Magnus was afraid.*

Magnus has reason to be afraid, said Raul.

They give me the creeps.

Those are your grandfathers, said Ken, and he gave me a big friendly grin.

They're late, said Raul.

Like time was ever their strong point, scoffed Reese. *They must be really pissed to send two.*

Lined up at the window, we were all taking care not to slip through the glass that was all that stood between the watchers and us. After a moment, Raul turned and snapbacked. He came back, whole, to stand beside us.

Coward, said Reese. But after a moment, he too snapbacked.

I realised that the glass was not enough for them; they wanted another layer of defence between themselves and the watchers; they wanted to be inside their bodies.

Ken just grinned at them. But Joe — Joe slipped straight through the glass.

Where's he going? I asked, panicked.

Someone has to talk to them, said Ken. *Don't worry Cora. There's nothing for us to be afraid of.*

I watched Joe and my resentment towards him fell away. He was small and wispy and completely vulnerable beside their electric whiteness. I could see from the colours that it was peaceful between them; peaceful, but not friendly.

I would not have gone outside to speak with them, grandfathers or not.

****

Joe returned.

Is it Samyaza? demanded Ken. He was deeply excited about the whole visitation thing.

Not yet, said Joe shortly. He looked at me. *We've got two. Two more have gone looking for Magnus.*

Define 'gone looking', I said. *Don't they know where Magnus lives?*

Magnus isn't there.

Well he was!

Well he isn't now. He put out a gentle hand. *Neither is your body, honey.*

Reese had popped again on Joe's return. He blew out in disgust. *He's got to be leaving signals a mile high out there. They can't track a bloody offspring?*

There are no signals precisely because he's offspring and knows exactly what he's doing, said Joe.

I must go! I cried. *He's got my body.*

No, said Joe quickly. *No. You're to stay here. Leave it to the watchers now.*

But he might hurt Charlie if I don't return.

Joe tried to calm me with his eyes. *Things are different now. The watchers are here. Leave it to them. You're to stay with us.*

I drifted to the window, staring blindly at the sky.

****

I felt Magda coming a mile off, saw her round the corner from Finn Street into Gregory Square. She stopped abruptly when she saw the watchers in the garden. I watched her freeze for a moment. When they didn't immediately respond, she hurried towards the house, pressing herself against the buildings as if hoping to become invisible.

She was pale and thin; even her hair seemed to have thinned. Her face was closed and pinched. She'd always dressed for attention, but today the clothes sat uncomfortably on her.

She rang the doorbell and Grace opened up before anyone could stop her. 'Hello, auntie,' she said, without expression.

'Hello Grace,' said Magda. 'Is your mother home?' There was no guilt in her manner, no remorse. She could have been talking to someone she'd never seen before.

Joe, Reese and I reared up beside Grace. Magda popped immediately, dropping her body on the doormat. *I just want Magnus,* she said. *Nothing else. Promise.*

Her voice made me wince. I'd always feared her exulting, teasing tone, but this new voice was worse; she sounded as if she were speaking from far away and long ago, from behind a brick wall.

Do you know where he is? she asked, pleading now.

Grace was watching us intently. She hesitated, as if thinking, and then she stepped calmly over Magda's body. She marched across the street and stood at the railings of the garden looking up into the trees where the watchers sat.

'It's her,' she announced loudly. 'Do you hear me? That's my aunt. The one that kidnapped me.'

I gave a strangled cry and flew to Grace's side. *Come away,* I urged. *Come away, my love.*

But Grace ignored me. 'Did you hear me?' she demanded, still looking up into the trees. 'You're here to protect my mother, aren't you? Do something!'

The watchers glowed, gentle and bright, and then they took off from the branches like two lazy eagles. One of them passed close enough to caress the top of Grace's head.

Magda was watching, wide-eyed, from the hallway. As one watcher approached she tried to dodge away but he was too fast for her. The other watcher raised her body and, between them, they slid Magda's Self smoothly back into her skin.

It was over in a second.

'What are you doing?' cried Magda, staring at their huge receding forms as they drifted back past Grace and I, who stood, fascinated, watching.

Reese and Joe were standing frozen in the hallway. 'Come and sit down,' said Joe gently, touching Magda's arm. Reese didn't move.

Magda turned to them. 'What?'

Grace hurried into the house with me at her side. 'Is it done?' she demanded.

'Is what done?' said Magda. She sounded slightly dazed, and panic-stricken. 'Where's Magnus. Where is he?'

Joe stepped past her and closed the front door. 'It's over,' he said.

'It'll never be over,' said Magda fiercely. 'I'll find him myself.' She made a strange leap forward, and stumbled against the closed door. 'No,' she whimpered. She stared through the glass in the doorway and head-butted it; there was a resounding crack. 'No,' she said again, more determinedly, and now she was flinging herself against the door again, and again, and again, straining like a bird against the pane, reaching for the light that shone dimly through the frosted glass.

She was trying to pop.

For a moment I was rigid with horror and pity, and then I tried to grab her, tried to wrap my insubstantial arms around her to comfort and stop her.

She no longer knew I was even there.

Joe took her instead. He wrapped his great arms firmly around her and held her back from the door. She struggled silently for a minute but he held her clear of the ground, pinioned against his chest, and at last she went limp, and he tentatively put her onto her feet and backed her onto the stairs.

'Where is he?' sobbed Magda, leaning clumsily into his chest. 'Please. I'm begging you. Where has he gone? He has to come back. Magnus always comes back for me.' She was sobbing openly, making no attempt to wipe her face or hide it.

'I don't know where he is,' said Joe in a gentler voice. He watched as Grace handed her aunt a tissue. 'No one can find him, not even the watchers.'

'Has he still got Cora's body with him?' She cried harder; it was difficult to make out the words. 'Oh no. I wanted it to be me. It was always Cora, but I wanted it to be me. I thought if I found her for him... Why does everyone always love her best?'

Reese still hadn't moved. Amy appeared and made Magda a cup of coffee. They sat with her until she'd finished crying.

And then she left. I watched her walk past the watchers that had grounded her, unaware that they lingered in the square. Her soul was no more than a lining now, permanently stitched to the inside of her body. It seemed impossible that I'd ever been afraid of her.

'Phew! What was that all about?' asked Amy. 'And what's wrong with you?' She gave Reese a shove and Reese sank slowly against the wall and slid to the floor.

Joe was white-lipped and shaking. 'Magda's been grounded.'

Raul had been hovering on the stairs. 'They really did it,' he said, shaking his head and following us all into the kitchen. 'I had no idea it was even possible. In front of us.' He shuddered.

Amy looked from one face to another, trying to read the scene in their eyes. 'You mean she can't walk anymore? Well hallelujah.'

'She didn't say sorry,' said Grace flatly.

Everyone turned to her.

'She had a choice,' said Grace. She didn't look or sound like an eight-year-old. She'd seen too much — and understood far, far more than I had. 'It could have gone differently but she wasn't sorry. She'd have done it all again to bring Magnus back to her.'

'Grace is right,' said Ken. I hadn't noticed him until now, sitting in a corner of the sofa. His voice was shaking and I realised he was crying. 'There was a moment ... just before they ... when Magda could have changed it.'

'Well,' said Amy, breaking the tension, trying to bring normal back into the house. She took bacon from the fridge and pulled out a frying pan. 'Even I know you don't touch children. Seems to me there are quite enough walkers in the world as it is.'

'And now there's going to be another one,' said Grace, beginning to slap butter onto slabs of white bread.

Again, we stared at Grace. 'What do you mean?' said Amy. 'What other one?'

Grace gave me a look of surprise, which quickly turned to confusion — and suddenly she was a child again, albeit a child with a special qualities. She stared at each of us in turn, frowning. 'Can't you see it?' she asked, as her gaze returned deliberately to Amy.

I followed her eyes, as we all did, and there it was, staring us in the face, except we'd all been too preoccupied to see it.

'Oh my God,' said Raul. He stood up awkwardly and took a step backwards.

'What?' cried Amy. 'What is it?'

Everyone waited for Raul to respond. 'Come with me,' he said at last, taking Amy by the hand and leading her from the room.

'Wow,' said Reese.

Joe sucked the breath in between his teeth. 'Ouch.'

'Why ouch?' said Grace. 'Won't they be happy? I'm happy.'

Did I miss something? said Charlie, coming quietly into the room. He'd missed everything. He was paler than ever and I was worried.

'Amy's having a baby,' sang Grace, taking over and laying rashers of bacon into the hot pan.

Of course she is, said Charlie. He glanced at me quickly. A lifetime of regret and apology was in that look.

Amy and Raul. Their love affair was playing out just as it should. Unlike ours. I gave Charlie the bravest smile I could manage.

Chapter 47

*G*RACE IS SLEEPING, I SAID, coming into the kitchen. *She still isn't talking about any of it. I'm getting worried.*

No need, said Joe. *Sleep is good. It will give her brain time to assimilate everything that's happened.*

I'm worried about how it's going to affect her. She's seen such things. I'm not sure how much she's even registered.

Kids have elastic minds, said Joe. *Ours snap if you push them too far, but theirs stretch and then ping back into place. She'll be fine.*

When did you become the expert? said Reese.

Just naturally gifted.

And then there's Rebecca, I sighed.

What a woman, agreed Charlie. *I don't think she believed a single thing she saw or heard the night she rescued Grace, and yet I suspect we couldn't have managed without her.*

Did you try to explain things, after I left?

She really didn't want to hear it. She left straight after you did.

What brought her here in the first place?

Charlie opened his arms to me and I drifted against him. It was alarming how little energy came from him. I edged myself into him, trying to give him some of mine; although my own wasn't what it used to be.

She appears to have made a promise to Peter, he said. *I have an idea that she already knew you were a spirit-walker.*

Peter told her that? I turned to look at him, frowning. *That's very unlikely. Peter didn't believe it himself.*

I wish I'd met your Peter, said Charlie. *I suspect he loved you rather more than you know. People generally do.* He paused, and then said, *Rebecca didn't really believe it either. Still, she came.*

But that's what I don't get. Why did she come? Why that evening?

She said she had a feeling you needed her.

I hovered protectively over Charlie. He'd been a long time without his body and he was getting thinner, somehow — translucent. Even so, I loved that our Selfs could mingle like this. I knew that everything would change when our bodies returned. As long as we remained in the spirit world, we could just about get away with pretending there were no physical realities to face up to.

That doesn't make any sense, I said.

He shrugged. *That's what she said.*

She came here, out of the blue, with Valium in her handbag, because she had a feeling I was in trouble? Rebecca doesn't have feelings like that. And if she did, she would dismiss them as nonsense.

And yet she came, said Joe, apparently amused by my amazement.

It doesn't make sense, Joe.

Not everything has to make sense, Cora.

Next you're going to tell me that the ghost of my dead husband prompted her to come and rescue me.

There was a second's silence — long enough to unnerve me — and then Joe gave a tight smile. *There's no such thing as ghosts.*

Ha ha. I wasn't amused.

I can answer for the Valium, said Charlie. *She says she's been taking the stuff for years. Always has it on her.*

Rebecca's on Valium? My sane, sensible, bossy sister — on Valium?

We all have our little problems, said Joe.

Grace came drifting in. *I had a dream,* she said, rubbing her eyes.

I looked at Charlie; here it comes. The bad stuff. The fall out. I was still haunted by the debauchery I'd seen in Magda's house that night, and Grace had been amongst it for hours by the time I arrived.

About what, baby? asked Joe.

A big cat, yawned Grace. *It was black with white paws. I cuddled it and it was so soft and cute. Mum, can we have a kitten? I'd feed it and everything.*

It was pathetic how grateful I felt for the reprieve. And yet, it didn't feel right to go on leaving serious things unsaid indefinitely.

Grace, I began.

Those people were freaks, Mum.

Yes they were.

They thought it was fun being inside other people. I thought it was horrid. She yawned again, completely in command of herself. *It felt dirty. And noisy. Imtiaz was alright. His body kept saying sorry to me, over and over again. It was okay but it got a bit boring. And Magnus!* She gave a grimace of contempt. *I didn't understand half of what was in his head.*

What was in his head? I asked, struggling to sound casual.

You know the kinds of films you don't let me watch?

Oh no. *Yes?*

Well now I know why you don't let me watch them.

His head was like that? I wailed. Of course it was; what else had I expected?

So I didn't watch, said Grace matter-of-factly. *I stayed out. I thought you wouldn't like it.*

Joe gave a shout of amusement, and shook his afro in Grace's face, making her giggle.

Good girl, I said faintly. *I wouldn't have liked it at all.*

Back to bed, darling, I said. *It's late. Come on, I'll take you.*

Grace hesitated and tilted her head in the characteristic way that made it look as if she were sniffing the air. *Honey, honey. The bees are making honey.* She turned to look at Joe. *Did you know it's made from nectar and spit? Bee spit? Yuck.*

****

And then everything changed. I was idly spying on the watchers in the early dawn light when one of them turned and beckoned.

Joe! I cried in panic. *The watchers are calling you!*

Joe was waiting. He left the house immediately and I saw him in animated conversation with the watchers. Then he returned.

We gathered around.

Well? I demanded. *Have they found him?*

No, baby, said Joe, very gently. *They've found you.*

Chapter 48

S O THIS WAS HOW IT NORMALLY WORKED: a walker died like anyone else. If the walker happened to be, well, *walking* when the body died, its Self behaved in all the normal ways: it shot upwards, straight into the sky.

But if *my* body were no longer breathing, I would still be here. Because I wasn't just a walker; I was offspring.

I could be dead. My body could be dead and I'd be none the wiser.

I couldn't face it; I stayed home. While the others, Charlie included, raced off to fetch me, I went to the South Pole instead, and watched the scientists there tracing neutrinos through the ice. Then I went back to the Canadian lake that was one of Charlie's favourite haunts.

Growing up, I'd kept my Self securely locked up and silent inside my body. Now, with just as much resolution, I was keeping it securely outside my body. There wasn't as much difference as one might think: either way, my body and my Self were entirely separated.

I had to come home to Gregory Square eventually. And there I was, sitting on the sofa downstairs, like a rag doll.

I hovered over myself.

Where's Grace? I murmured.

'We took her to stay with Rebecca,' said Reese. 'Ken will stay with her — just his Self, of course.'

Good, I said, and then I stared at him, alarmed. *You can hear me? You're whole, and you can hear me? What's going on?*

'Perhaps you're getting stronger,' said Joe. 'It's not surprising — now that you know.' He said it gently, kindly, but it didn't stop me from falling away from them, from my own body.

'It's all right,' said Reese, after a moment. 'You'll always be just Cora to us.'

'You look fine,' said Joe. 'Care to snapback?'

I looked around at their faces: Joe, Reese, Raul and Amy. *Where's Charlie?*

Joe answered. 'He's gone after Magnus.'

With the watchers?

'I think he's hoping he'll get there first. Now that you're safe...'

Of course, I said. *He needs his body.* There was something on Joe's face that I didn't like. *That's what he's gone for, right? He needs his body. Joe, he can't walk for much longer.*

'I'm sure that's what he's doing,' said Joe.

He can't help Magnus, I insisted, my voice rising so that a small wind whipped through Joe's afro. *It's too late for that and why — why would Charlie be trying to help Magnus?*

Joe was brave. He stood there calm and still, his expression telling me to my face that the man I loved had abandoned me not for his own sake, to save his own body and therefore his own life, but to try and rescue the creature that had destroyed my life.

I snapbacked. My body was exhausted, aching and sore, and desperately hungry.

'I want Charlie,' I said.

****

I didn't get Charlie. I got Magnus.

First there was a noise, as if there were a tornado moving around the ground floor. I went to stand at the door of my studio, looking down the stairs. 'Hello?' I called. My legs were trembling. The boys had all gone to try and find Charlie. Amy was taking spare clothes over to Rebecca's in case Grace had to stay there for any length of time.

I was alone. After all, there were two watchers at my door to guard me. Weren't there?

The tornado moved up a floor, first to my living room, and then up again to the bedrooms below me. I couldn't stand there waiting for it to reach me; I ran down the stairs towards the source of the noise.

Pictures were flying from the walls, rugs were lifting from the floors. There were books strewn across every room, and a never-ending stream of clothes, shoes and domestic detritus flowed from the bedrooms. I ran down through it to the ground floor. In the kitchen every gas burner was lit, while the cupboards and doors banged open and closed, open and closed.

'Stop it!' I shrieked.

Magnus was a blur, a whirling mass of pure, chaotic energy.

You have ruined everything! he screamed. His voice disappeared up through the ceiling.

I raced back upstairs to my studio. In the time it had taken me to run around the house, Armageddon had come and gone. The canvases were shredded, literally torn from their wooden frames and scattered everywhere, ribbons still flinging themselves against the walls and fluttering to the floor. There was paint on every surface, even on the glass window-panels in the ceiling. I stood staring at the mess, and then I burst into tears. A single canvas remained untouched, propped up on a shelf; I flung it to the ground and stamped on it, crying noisily.

Without warning, the watchers from the square came swooping in through the walls.

He is not here, one of them declared.

'Well he's certainly been here!' I shouted.

He must be nearby, said the other.

They vanished and I was left panting, torn between fury and panic. Panic, because this time I had heard voices in the spirit world even though I was fully embodied. Was it because they were watchers or because I was offspring?

A fresh wave of furious tears ripped through me. What was the point of the watchers if Magnus could waltz in and out of my house like this?

And what on earth was Magnus trying to achieve? Apart from chaos and confusion. And then I gave a panicky laugh at myself as I looked around; as if chaos and confusion weren't enough.

The watchers returned, dropping down through the ceiling.

We have scared him away.

'Couldn't you have stopped him?' I asked.

They ignored me. *He still has so much power left. You would think he'd have weakened by now.* They looked impressed.

'Will he come back?' There was an edge to my voice.

They turned to me and I realised my mistake; there was every reason to be afraid of them. There was a lot of them to be afraid of, for a start; close up they were huge, even bigger than they'd looked in the trees,

Biblically tall, white and thin. They stretched from floor to ceiling, and clearly felt cramped.

We don't know. We can't force him back.

One of them looked at me kindly. *Don't worry. Once he snapbacks — and he will; he must — he won't trouble you again.*

'Snapbacks into whose body this time?' I cried. 'I don't want him to keep Charlie.'

We'll keep good watch, said the other one.

'What's the point if you can't stop him?' I clenched my fists. 'I'm sorry. I don't understand what's going on.'

They were gone.

I looked at the destruction around me in despair, and then I started to clean up, waiting for the others to come home.

****

'We can't leave her if this is what happens,' said Reese.

'Yes, you can,' I said irritably. 'You have to find Charlie. There are watchers here, remember?'

Reese blew a raspberry in the general direction of the window.

'Is this the worst Magnus can do?' asked Amy, much later.

The question made us pause.

'I don't know,' I admitted. 'It's worse than I could do, but it's hard to see what else he could manage.'

I couldn't think straight, and it had been a relief when Amy had taken the lead and managed the clean-up operation.

'Bloody watchers,' said Reese loudly. 'I'll never see the point of them. Imagine letting Magnus get past them like this.'

'They have to want to catch Magnus,' said Raul. 'Don't forget whose line he is.'

'Guys,' said Joe. 'After what he's done, it doesn't matter whose line he is. Even Samyaza can't ignore this. Now get to work.'

'I'm working, I'm working,' grumbled Reese. I thought he minded being called upon like this to fix up my house, but when I suggested that he could stop any time he wanted to, he was genuinely offended. That was the thing about Reese; his heart was as big as his mouth. I knew that now.

Around two in the morning we ordered in a curry from an all-night restaurant on Finn Street, and went on clearing up until four, by which stage we could hardly lift a duster between us.

Everyone had appropriated a corner of the house. Joe had been spending nights in the single bed in what I'd already started thinking of as Amy's baby's bedroom, next door to Amy. Raul shared her room, of course. Reese camped out with Ken's body on the kitchen sofas, with blankets and cushions. Ken was still keeping guard over Grace.

'I'm sorry, Cora,' said Joe. 'Nothing's going quite according to plan.'

I tried to smile. 'There's a plan?'

Joe thought for a moment, then shook his head.

'Do you think Magnus will come back?'

He looked at me speculatively. 'I have no idea what's going on. Do you?'

I shrugged. 'Nope. Joe?' I tried to sound calm. 'Where's Charlie?'

He put an arm around me. 'Honey, if I knew that, I would have fetched him back already. We'll keep looking. One thing, though: if Magnus has been here, chances are Charlie isn't far behind.'

Before I climbed into bed, I peeked out of the curtains. The watchers had taken up guard duty again, but that was no longer a comfort. What if Magnus killed Charlie — what if Charlie was already dead?

What if Charlie had taken up his family trade; what if he was helping Magnus escape?

****

If it was hard living without Charlie, it was harder still living without Grace. We'd spent no normal time together since her kidnap; first I had no body, and now she was at Rebecca's. We had agreed that neither of us would walk, for now, so we spoke on the phone.

'Are you okay?' I asked. 'Is Aunt Rebecca feeding you well?'

'They eat junk food all the time,' said Grace, and I could hear the glee in her voice. 'She doesn't do any of that organic stuff she's always talking about.'

'Don't be disrespectful,' I said, and we both giggled.

'It's fun having Ken here,' said Grace. 'I've told the twins I have an invisible friend. Are you eating properly, Mum?'

'Of course.'

'Is Charlie home?'

'Not yet.'

'Let me talk to Aunt Rebecca, honey.'

A few moments later, Rebecca was on the line.

'I must say, your daughter's a credit to you,' she began immediately.

'Rebecca,' I said, 'about the other night —'

'No,' she said, and I felt her shudder down the phone line. 'I don't want to hear it. You can't persuade me to believe anything I don't want to believe.'

'But you saved us all.'

'I'm your sister,' she said primly. 'That's my job. Now, don't worry about Grace. She can stay as long as you like.'

'I love you, Rebecca.'

Rebecca harrumphed and hung up.

****

I went outside to clear my head. 'I have no idea what's going on,' I said out loud. I looked up at the trees, which had lost their earlier fluorescence and were becoming that deep shade of green that each year made me feel I could live on leaves and grass. 'Magnus caught me and threw me back. Which should be good. But now Charlie's gone.'

I glanced back at where the watchers still perched in the trees at the centre of Gregory Square. They paid me no attention at all.

After a few minutes, I returned home. Inside, I took the stairs two at a time.

And that's where I found Magnus, upstairs in my studio, hanging in a corner halfway up the wall, his head drooping down on his chest, his arms dangling loosely at his sides. He was long and thin like the watchers, but in every other respect he was nothing like them at all. I had only ever seen him in the bodies of my friends before, yet his Self was as familiar to me as my own.

A violent pulse of shock jolted through me, making bile rise in my throat. I saw Magnus at the end of a long tunnel. Then, as the world didn't end, and he didn't move, my vision began to clear, and I noticed that my studio was intact; nothing damaged, nothing disturbed. It was very quiet.

He was shadowy, not quite like a normal Self. Slowly, slowly he raised his head.

'Magnus?' My voice sounded as tiny and scared as I felt.

He stared without interest or hope.

'Magnus?' I said again. 'What are you doing?'

He didn't move. At all.

I turned and fled downstairs. I marched about the living room for a full minute, unsure what to do next, and then ran back upstairs to the studio. There he was, still hanging off the wall. His head was back on his chest.

What the hell are those watchers doing, letting him in here? I thought. And then another, horrible thought occurred to me: who were the watchers guarding?

I stamped my foot in frustration. 'Magnus, what am I supposed to do with you?'

I stared at him and, the more I stared, the less afraid I was. Something else took the place of fear. It was that awful compassion again.

That's ridiculous. This man has ruined my life. My past, my future, everything.

The funny thing was, although he was probably the least substantial Self I'd ever seen, his aura was still a shiny, tar-like black — which was, in itself, far more frightening than anything else about him. But I wasn't scared. I was ... sorry for him.

And then the front door opened and a voice I knew called, 'Cora?' A familiar step sprang up the stairs.

'Charlie! Charlie!' I cried, and I ran out onto the landing and hurtled down the stairs to greet him.

We met on the second-floor landing but before I could fling myself into his arms I stopped short and stared, eyes and mouth wide open.

It was unmistakably Charlie. He was really there, whole and safe. His warm eyes were flooded with love and concern, his arms were outstretched to catch me.

His hair was silver.

Chapter 49

'ARE YOU OKAY?' HE SAID, breathless from running. He reached out a hand to touch my arm, and withdrew it immediately as I flinched.

'I'm sorry — I'm sorry!' I said, and I reached out to touch him.

Very, very gently, he drew me into a hug. I wanted to bury myself into him; I wanted to run for dear life.

My confusion must have been obvious. 'It's okay,' he said, releasing me. There was a world of regret in his voice. 'This is going to take some time, Cora. Is he here?'

I had to clear my throat before I could answer. 'He's in my study.'

Charlie took my hand and we climbed the stairs. Magnus looked up as we entered the studio. A tremor went through him as if he were waking up and then, very slowly, he slid down the wall and came to rest on the floor in a crumpled heap.

I felt the tension ease out of Charlie. He dropped my hand and stepped towards Magnus. 'Are you okay?'

'Charlie,' I murmured cautiously. 'We don't know this isn't a trick.'

'It's not a trick,' said Charlie. 'The idiot's exhausted himself outmanoeuvring the watchers.'

The *idiot*? He might have been talking about a schoolboy caught in a prank. I reminded myself that he'd known Magnus all his life; they had, to all intents and purposes, been brothers.

I clenched my fists. 'Why is he here?' I asked.

Charlie was stooping over Magnus's fallen Self and I felt a blaze of possessive jealousy at the look on his face.

'It's complicated,' said Charlie.

'Then complicate me, Charlie.' There was an edge to my voice; Charlie heard it.

'He loves you,' he said.

'What?'

He stood up and looked at me. He understood I wasn't ready to have him close, so he kept his distance. 'You have to understand, Cora. He's been looking for you your whole life. He's been obsessed by you. He remembers every detail of you as a child. He used to quote the things you said and did. I ought to have recognised you the minute I met you, but you'd changed so much since he knew you... The years you were missing, he went crazy trying to find you. He was frantic about what might be happening to you, all alone out there.'

I stared at Charlie in disbelief. I believe my lower jaw dropped another inch. 'Are we talking about the same person?' I asked at last. 'Magnus, who drove my mother to suicide, ransomed my daughter and raped me? Can that possibly be the person you're talking about, Charlie? Because if it is ... if it is, I don't know you at all.'

I was trembling. I reached for a chair and sat in it, clumsy, not daring to even try and remain standing on my own legs.

'I didn't say he was doing it for the right reasons,' said Charlie. 'But they weren't all wrong reasons either. You can't be obsessed with someone for so long without some feelings developing.'

'Some feelings?' I spat. 'Are you joking?'

'Cora,' he said softly. 'It's not easy being offspring. You're going to live for a long, long time. If there were any chance of finding a companion for that journey, wouldn't you take it?'

I gaped.

'And then, he's been inside me for a while,' continued Charlie.

'What's that got to do with it?'

'I love you, Cora. Heart and soul. That's what he felt when he was using my body. He was already obsessed with you. Imagine what he felt when he was inside my body.'

'Oh I had quite a taste of how he felt when he was inside *my* body!' I spat.

Charlie winced. 'It's not all his fault,' he said. 'He can't help what he is.'

'So we'll just let him stay, then, shall we? Maybe he can move in. I'll introduce him properly to Grace.'

I was incandescently furious with Charlie. I completely forgot that just a moment ago I, too, had felt sorry for Magnus; or maybe that's what made me so angry, seeing my own weakness magnified in Charlie.

Charlie braced himself and put an arm around me.

I held myself stiff. 'You don't smell like you.'

He gave a small laugh. 'I haven't had a chance to change.'

'Where have you been?'

'Looking for Magnus. I wanted to get to him before the watchers did.'

'Why?' It was a wail.

He pulled back, keeping hold of my hand. 'I wish I could explain,' he said. 'My family has been tied to Magnus for generations. He's not that good, but he's not all bad. No, don't get angry, Cora. Very few things are black and white. Context counts. In this case, it counts a lot. Magnus is an idiot. He's dangerous and he's petulant and he's irresponsible. But he has a good heart, believe it or not.'

I threw off his hand.

'He'll be punished, Cora. Right now, he just wants to be with you. He knows what's coming.'

'What's coming? For God's sake, Charlie, the watchers have been here a while and nothing's changed!' In a whisper I added, 'Apart from Magda.'

He put his hand on my cheek and I turned my face into it and kissed his palm. He drew my head to his chest.

'I'm so tired,' I said.

'I know, love.'

I would have liked to stay like that for hours, not moving, not talking or thinking. 'Charlie?' I said at last. 'Why is your hair silver?'

He gave me a tight smile. 'It's the Magnus effect.'

'Will it stay that way?'

Magnus, who had been laying as if asleep, stirred. He might even have been laughing.

****

We left Magnus in the studio. Charlie raided some of Raul's clothes from Amy's room and went to take a shower, and I ran downstairs to make him a sandwich.

I heard him come into the kitchen behind me.

'I bet that feels better. I've made ham and cheese. You look like you haven't been eating properly. I made coffee too...'

I turned to him — and dropped the tray. Coffee and crockery and crumbs fell to the floor at my feet as I stared at Charlie, who was floating less than a foot away from his smiling body.

'No!' I screamed.

'Calm down,' said Magnus, enjoying the moment. 'It's not what it looks like.'

'You can't do this! You can't take him again!' and I popped. My body crumpled into a pile with the broken crockery.

Cora, relax, relax, said Charlie. *He didn't take me.*

Then what the crap is he doing inside your body?

I invited him in.

I looked at Charlie as if he were mad. *You did what?*

Calm down, love. It's okay.

I trusted you! I screamed. *I trusted you Charlie! Every step of the way, when there was no reason to believe in you, I did, I went on trusting you. What the fuck do you want with me?*

Cora! He was distressed. He tried to get close, but I wouldn't let him. *This isn't about you. He's hurting, Cora. I'm just giving him shelter, comfort ... until...*

Until the watchers get here? They're here, Charlie! They're here and they're doing nothing.

Magnus was lounging around my kitchen, watching us with amusement. He picked up the sandwich from the floor, dusted it off and took a bite. 'You have a lot to learn about watchers, my dear,' he said. 'A year is an eyeblink to them. Those two outside are just place markers until Dad gets here. And who knows how many eyeblinks that could take?'

Shut up, Magnus, said Charlie. *Sam will come. You know he will. He's winding you up, Cora.*

I hated it, this whole body-swapping thing. It was perverted. It was the worst use of spirit-walking I could possibly imagine. It turned something beautiful — miraculous — into an abomination.

I looked at Charlie's beautiful face, tainted by that waterfall of silver hair and inhabited by a monster, and then I looked at his Self. *I hate you!* I shouted at Charlie, and when he wouldn't respond I sent out my energy all around the house. I tore pictures off the walls and lifted the carpet off the staircase, ripping out the fastening nails, splintering the wood. Light fittings crashed to the ground, bulbs splintered. I slashed cushions and threw around the furniture. Magnus took his sandwich and sat calmly munching it under the kitchen table; I tore that to pieces and he simply dusted himself off, blew on his sandwich and took another bite. It was only when a flying shard caught him on the cheek — Charlie's cheek — ripping the skin and drawing blood, that I ceased.

Charlie had retreated to a corner of the room and floated there, sadly watching me.

How could you? I said. *I love you, yet you give it all away to help Magnus. Looking at you makes me glad I'm only half-human!*

'She's right,' said Magnus lightly. 'You've ruined everything, Charlie. Why couldn't you just hate me like she does?'

****

I displaced to the white darkness of the South Pole. I sat in the middle of the flags that mark the bottom of the world and I let my energy go. The flags ripped and pulled against the sudden wind, and the ice whirled into the air like tiny shards of glass. The southern lights poured down in sheets of ghostly green and gold.

It was hard to stay angry.

Cora, said Charlie.

Go away. This is my place.

I've come to ask you a favour.

A favour for you? Or a favour for Magnus. Because honestly, Charlie, I can't tell the difference between you anymore.

I thought I'd sent him away. I should have known better.

Cora, he said again.

I sighed. *What is it?*

Magnus is in real trouble. His punishment is coming. He paused.

Do you want me to cry?

He smiled and the wind around me died down. *No, love, I don't want you to cry.*

What do you want?

Come home. Come home and let him stay. Just until Sam gets here.

Who is this Sam and how long will he take?

Sam's his father. Well, not exactly. He's the watcher that sired Magnus's line. He adores Magnus, and Magnus has called him dad since his own father — never mind. That's another story. I don't think Sam will be long.

The stars were like headlights, pouring light out of the sky, the Milky Way was like a shining pavement, and there was the aurora, dancing up and down, humming its never-repeating song into the season's perpetual night. It was a song of great beauty, but it was also a song of loss and loneliness.

We'd never had a moment, Charlie and I. We'd never had a chance. The love between us had somehow become a commonplace, something to be bartered with before we'd had even a moment of privacy in which to enjoy it. I'd touched his spirit and I sure as hell knew his body, but I'd never held him, whole, as a lover. My relationship with Charlie was as fractured as my relationship with myself.

And if I come home, I said, *will you make him give you back your body?*

Charlie was very still. *He needs it.*

I sighed. *I don't understand you.*

Yes, you do.

All right. I understand you, but I could never do what you're doing. How can you forgive him?

Charlie shrugged. *It's the only way to win. When everything else is gone, the only thing I can do is ... be human.*

I winced. *But apparently I'm not.*

I believe that's your choice.

I was silent. Then I said, *I will come home. But when this is over — if this is ever over — I want you to move in with us. With Grace and me. We've come too far for half measures. Move in and be mine. Or go away and leave us alone completely.*

He didn't look at me and for an awful moment I thought I'd made a mistake. Then he said, *You'd have me, after all that's happened?* There were tears in his voice.

I want promises, I warned him. *You have to love Grace.*

I already do.

Then let's go home.

****

We took the long way home. Drawn by the howling winds that blew off the skeleton coast into the Atlantic Ocean, Charlie and I headed south to the African continent, corkscrewing with the grains of yellow sand that would have scoured our bodies, and skimming over the wild surf and in and out of the wrecked ships littering the shoreline. We went inland and traced the green thread of the Nile south through a brown landscape, plunging into the watery smoke of the Blue Nile Falls, and then chased the line of shadow separating night from day as it swept steadily westwards around the globe.

Charlie flew with the grace of an angel, hovering on the great line that split the globe longitudinally, his upper half in light and his lower half in shadow. Below us, the human population responded to the night in the best way it knew how — in their thousands and millions people turned on the lights, so that we left a glittering display of stars above and below in our wake. Occasionally there was only darkness, as we passed over the great wildernesses still left on the earth.

There were other Selfs out here, riding the nightline, drifting in the high-up currents that constituted the world's major weather systems. But it seemed to me there was a different code out here. They seemed intent on a purpose that wasn't mine, as if they had a job to do, whereas Charlie and I were merely spectating. Once, a spectacularly long, thin Self — a watcher, perhaps — saluted Charlie as he passed us at high speed. I thought the gesture had some meaning, but there were so many new things to take in that I didn't have time to think about it.

****

As we arrived in Gregory Square we saw a curious thing. The house was blazing with light. At first I wondered why on earth Amy and the boys would have every light turned on. And then I realised it wasn't electric light at all. It was a golden, liquid light. It came out at every window, and through the cracks between the bricks, giving the whole area a halo glow.

That'll be Sam, said Charlie.

CHAPTER 50

THERE WAS A WATCHER IN MY KITCHEN. He was huge, like the others, flickering and glowing as if there were a thousand candles inside him. Amy and Raul were nowhere to be seen, but Reese, Joe and Ken, too, were there. And Magnus.

Joe and Ken were more or less lost in dazed wonderment. Reese and Magnus looked unimpressed.

'Hello, Dad,' said Magnus in a lazy drawl.

Astoundingly, the watcher was struggling not to smile. *Magnus*, he said, and his voice sounded like a bell inside my head. *What have you been up to this time?*

This time? Did they think this was a game, these watchers and their cursed bloody offspring, messing around in the lives of humans as if we were toys?

I thought of Grace, marching over to the watchers in the trees, and I stepped forward. 'He stole my daughter,' I answered defiantly, trying to focus on the candescent figure whose feet hovered just above the ground and whose head touched the ceiling. 'He ransomed her for my body and then he raped me.'

I stopped dead in my tracks as the watcher swivelled his head to look at me. *Bear's child,* he said softly.

'I am not Bear's child,' I said. I ought to have been terrified of this figure, his extraordinary dimensions, his colour and, more than anything, the overwhelming aura of power around him. But I was suddenly angrier than I'd ever been in my life. 'I am my mother's child — I am Laura the walker's daughter. I refuse to be offspring. My father is nothing to me.'

The watcher smiled. *I understand,* he said.

'No,' I said. 'You really don't. Your children, if that's what they are, have brought nothing but chaos and grief to my family. This Bear person destroyed my mother's life. Your son or great grandson or whatever he is — Magnus — is responsible for her death, whether he killed her or not. He destroyed my sister's life, too.'

'Now that's not fair,' said Magnus, surprised. 'I protected Magda. Always.'

'You led her into as much trouble as you saved her from,' I said bitterly. 'You played to her worst nature, and in the end you've abandoned her as completely as Bear abandoned my mother.'

I turned back to the watcher. 'Thanks to Magnus I grew up separated from my Self. Perhaps you can't imagine how wretched that is for a human. Separate from my own being for my whole childhood. I thought walking was a sin. And then when I met Charlie and started walking, and had a chance of a normal life, Magnus came back and blasted it all to hell.'

Even Magnus looked upset. 'My dear,' he objected, 'have I been all bad?'

'Whose body are you wearing, Magnus?' I demanded. 'How do you think I feel about that?'

Ah yes, said the watcher, swivelling towards Charlie this time. *The authentic. Your family has served him well. Not always wisely, but you have done well to bring him to this point.*

It wasn't deliberate, said Charlie flatly. *Things just ran their course.*

I could hear Charlie, even though I was in my body and he was walking. 'What is that?' I said, and my alarm was clear in my suddenly shrill tone. 'Why can I still hear Charlie when I'm whole? These things keep happening.'

The watcher was amused. *In my presence, all things are possible,* he said kindly. And then he added, *But it is also a gift of your genesis. You are coming into your own.* He looked significantly at Joe, Ken and Reese.

Reese was still scowling, but he was also maintaining a safe distance from the watcher. Joe and Ken were backed up against the wall. I glanced back at the watcher and realised I might not have been showing the proper respect.

You are one of my children, he said, as if reading my mind. *You have the right to speak as you choose.*

'I'm a walker's daughter,' I insisted. 'Not an offspring's daughter and certainly not yours.'

Magnus laughed; it was a deep, happy sound. 'She was a pussy-cat when she was a child,' he assured the watcher. 'You can thank me for all this spirit.'

Back to the matter in hand, said the watcher. *I believe you called me, Magnus.*

Magnus suddenly looked a lot less happy. 'I was given no choice.'

'He called you?' said Reese 'You were waiting for an invitation?' His tone was full of derision, but he maintained his distance.

Of course I was waiting for an invitation, said the watcher. *Magnus has the same free will as any of you.*

I frowned. 'I thought you came because a child's body was broken into?'

Indeed, watchers were sent to deal with that. Watchers intervened.

Magda was grounded, Charlie reminded me.

'Sam,' I said to the watcher. 'Is that your name?'

Samyaza. He executed an elegant bow.

'Dad isn't any old watcher,' said Magnus in a bored voice.

'No,' said Reese. 'Samyaza's the ringleader — the one responsible for this whole sorry mess.'

Samyaza swivelled towards Reese and I felt my first leap of real fear. *You should learn respect,* said the watcher, and Reese's hair rippled gently at the force of his voice. *But you have shown loyalty. We will let it pass.*

'So you sent your minions to ground my sister, but you allowed your son to run riot until he chose to invite you here?' I tried to keep my voice neutral, to show neither respect nor disrespect, simply to state the truth.

Samyaza nodded and turned to Magnus. *But you have learned your lesson at last, son. What happened?*

Magnus grimaced. 'Charlie happened.'

Samyaza swivelled to Charlie. *I congratulate you, authentic.*

Charlie looked uncomfortable.

The watcher turned his beatific gaze back to Magnus. *Illuminate them, son,* he invited and, when Magnus simply stared at him, he said, *Now.*

'Oh all right,' said Magnus, rolling his shoulders irritably. 'Greater love. There, is that good enough?'

Joe looked confused. 'What's that?'

Magnus scowled. 'Oh for goodness sake. The law of greater love. Doesn't anyone read anymore?'

'Whose love for whom?' I demanded.

'Anyone's love,' said Ken softly, 'for anyone else. "Greater love hath no man than this: that he lay down his life for his friend."'

That is one interpretation, approved the watcher.

'It's the one that got me,' admitted Magnus, eyeing Charlie.

I stamped my foot. '*What* are you talking about?'

'Wait a minute,' said Joe. 'I get it.' He was frowning, as if he were trying to chase down a fleeing thought. 'It's one of the universal laws, isn't it? Charlie gave up his body for you, Magnus. You have to go.'

'I don't have to go,' said Magnus with some heat. 'I choose to go. Yes, all right, technically it's the law of greater love, but I don't have to go. If I wanted, I could choose to just disappear from your lives forever.'

Have a care, son, said the watcher. *You have walked a fine line on this earth. Do not fall away at this late hour.*

'It's my choice,' said Magnus stubbornly. 'You said it: I have free will.'

But now the truth is in your heart, warned his father. *Walk away and I cannot help you.*

I couldn't help noticing that the watcher's light had dimmed. He was afraid; he was afraid for Magnus.

'Calm down,' said Magnus in the voice of a sulky child. 'I'm not walking away. I called you, didn't I?'

Reese slumped to the ground. 'For God's sake,' he began, and then glanced nervously at Samyaza. 'For goodness sake. You're talking in riddles. My brain's going to explode.'

'Allow me?' said Ken.

By all means, said Samyaza, nodding.

Ken smiled. 'Greater love is one of the universal laws. But like everything else in the universe, it's governed by free will. Magnus experienced greater love. Once you understand what it is, and choose to take it into your heart, the law is activated. You can't walk away. Or at least, you can, but then ... well, there are consequences.'

'What, you mean you've crossed to the dark side?' mocked Reese.

There was a beat of silence before the watcher replied. *There is no corner of the universe that the Light cannot reach.* He spoke hesitantly, as if anxious to choose the right words. *But free will is absolute and some choices cannot easily be undone.*

A cosmic landscape of good and evil opened before me, but it was only a glimpse, and only for a moment, and then Magnus and the watcher filled my eyes again.

'So what brought you to this great change of heart?' I asked Magnus, trying to keep the sarcasm out of my voice.

'Charlie,' said Magnus. 'He gave me his body to protect you. At first, I thought he was just stupid. I thought he hadn't realised I might never return it. You would get pregnant, and together you and I would raise the offspring, and I would simply keep Charlie's body for this lifetime.'

Continue, said Samyaza.

'But nothing went quite as I planned it.' He looked at me significantly, and then he looked at Charlie. 'I quickly realised that the servant ... the authentic ... *Charlie* knew perfectly well he would never get his body back. But he gave it up anyway. For Cora.' He glared at me. 'You're a real pain in the neck. I hope you know that.'

'I wondered why you kept letting Cora come home,' admitted Joe.

'It alarmed me to realise that — ahem — that such love really was possible. I was hoping that would be an end to it. But it's insidious, this law. It grows. Eventually I realised I'd have to give Cora back to him. And then it seemed pointless not to give Charlie his body, too.'

Which is when you called me, said the watcher.

Magnus continued as if Samyaza hadn't spoken. 'So there I was, stuck with no body. I knew you'd take your own sweet time' — he raised an eyebrow at the watcher — 'so I came back to the only place I could think of.'

'Here?' I said, in disbelief. 'You couldn't have gone somewhere you'd actually be welcome?'

Magnus looked at me coolly. 'Wait till Charlie dies,' he said. 'Wait till Grace dies. And Amy and her child, and everyone you know. You'll think you'll never love again, but you will. And then they'll die, too. One day, sweet Cora, you'll know what loneliness is. And you'll remember what you've just said to me, and be sorry.'

I flushed and reached for Charlie.

'I came back to *you*,' continued Magnus. 'A bit angry, obviously. Sorry about that. Things have not gone as I planned.' He looked irritated again. 'And what does the wretched authentic do? He hammers his point home by offering me his body *again*. Honestly.' He glared at Charlie. 'You'll never last a whole lifetime at this rate.'

You have done well, authentic, the watcher told him.

Hang on, said Charlie. *Magnus was tired and I let him borrow my body for a while, that's all. I knew I would get it back.*

The watcher looked at him sceptically. *You are either dazzled by your family's generations of service, or a little foolish, Charlie Tam. Even I would not have been certain Magnus would give you back the body.*

'He hasn't yet,' I said. I inclined my head towards Magnus. 'You're still standing in it.'

'For goodness sake,' said Magnus. 'What happened to trust?' He grinned at Charlie who, astonishingly, grinned back.

It's time, said the watcher.

'And you're really going?' Reese asked Magnus sceptically. 'You're not just going to body-jump again like you usually do?'

'Haven't you been paying attention?' said Magnus. 'I'm bowing to the law. In return for Charlie's, um, gesture, I choose to go home.'

'You mean — die?'

Magnus glanced at Samyaza and laughed. 'You call it that. Why Cora, you look shocked. Will you miss me?'

'No,' I said. 'I won't miss you at all. I just don't think I believe you. You can live forever.'

'We all go, eventually, by choice,' said Magnus gently. 'I want to go. I don't know how many more times I can pop, and I wouldn't want to leave Charlie stranded.' My surprise must have shown on my face, because he gave me a twisted smile. 'I've done monstrous things, but I'm not a monster, Cora.'

'Yes you are,' said Reese, jumping to his feet. 'You're the exact definition of a monster.'

'You're always here, aren't you?' Magnus sneered at Reese. 'Don't you have a home of your own to go to?'

'There's never any food there,' retorted Reese. 'And it's nice here. It'll be nicer still once you've gone.'

'I still don't understand why you would choose to go,' I said.

Magnus came towards me and before I realised what he was intending, he put his arms around me and whispered in my ear. 'Try and have fun, Cora, while you can.' His lips — Charlie's lips — brushed across my cheek, my ear, my hair. 'I never meant to harm you. My love for you has been ... the best of my very long life.'

He pulled away and looked into my face. His eyes danced and his mouth curved into a self-mocking smile. He took my face between his hands and kissed me softly and sweetly. He took his time. Without thinking, my arms went around him.

And then he popped. For a moment Charlie's body sagged in my arms and I stumbled and then Charlie snapbacked and he was holding me up. Dazed, I pulled back.

Magnus and Samyaza were standing side by side.

Live a long and happy life with your authentic, said the watcher. *When your body is spent and you are in the wilderness, call me. I will help you. My foolish son* — he glanced fondly at Magnus — *always felt compelled to do everything alone. That's why he got into so much trouble. But I will help you, walker's daughter, any way I can. Call me, and I will come.*

'I'll never call you,' I said. 'When this body is spent, I'm dying with Charlie.'

The watcher smiled. *You have that choice, but you will not use it. Live well, walker's daughter.* He made it sound ironic — *walker's* daughter, like it was a joke.

The watcher's light was becoming unbearable. Everything was turning gold, then white, and I had to shut my eyes and turn away.

When I looked again, Magnus and Samyaza were gone.

'Is that it?' said Reese. 'I wanted to see him get his punishment. He's going to be punished, right? Right?'

Ken laid a hand on Reese's arm. 'He's learned his lesson.'

Reese snorted. 'He blackmailed Cora with Grace. He planned to sire a super-offspring. He's a monster. Sod the lesson. He should be annihilated.'

Ken shook his head. 'It doesn't work that way.'

'Well it bloody should! One small change of heart doesn't wipe out centuries of carnage.'

Ken began to laugh, very quietly, and then tears spilled down his cheeks. 'It wasn't a small change of heart,' he said. 'And yes, it wipes out everything that went before. Haven't you ever heard of the prodigal son?'

'No I bloody haven't,' said Reese. 'Fuck off. And stop ... are you crying?' He put a hand on Ken's shoulder, and then pulled him into an awkward embrace. 'Cry-baby,' he said, and put both arms around his friend.

I looked around the kitchen. Joe stood beside me, black as night, shaking his afro as if trying to dislodge dreams from his head. Ken withdrew to the sofa and sat staring into space, wiping his face. Charlie and Reese stood side by side, Reese huge and troll-like, indignant and benign, Charlie sleek and dark and beautiful to my eyes — both marked with that bolt of poker-straight silver hair that meant none of us would ever be allowed to forget that Magnus had been here.

I thought about Laura, my mother. It had taken Grace, Charlie, Joe, Reese, Ken, Raul, Amy and even Rebecca to help me navigate my way safely past Magnus. My mother had been on her own. She hadn't stood a chance. But by sending me away, and putting a ban on walking while I grew up, she'd saved me. And I'd saved Grace, and Charlie had saved Magnus.

That's what you do for the ones you love.

Amy and Raul came down the stairs, cautious and fearful. 'Is it over?' called Amy. 'You're so quiet down there, we were getting worried. Is it over?'

'It's over,' I told her, and I reached for the telephone. 'Rebecca? It's Cora. I'm coming for Grace.'

For Book Clubs

- Which relationship is key to the story: Cora and Grace? Cora and Charlie? Cora and Magda? Charlie and Magnus?

- Is there more than one walker's daughter in the story? Who could the title refer to?

- *The Walker's Daughter* deals with the separation of body and soul, and takes love and redemption as its themes. Would you describe this as an overtly religious story?

- Magda is arguably the most evil individual in the book. Do you agree?

- Cora grows up with a very selective idea of her identity, partly because key facts have been kept from her, and partly because she has suppressed certain memories. Does our understanding of our past shape the choices we make and who we become?

- Love saves Magnus in the end. Whose love — Charlie's? Cora's? Magnus's?

- The story ends quietly, despite Reese's expectation of a more retributive climax. Is this what you were expecting?

- If you could walk, would you?

JANET ALLISON BROWN is the author of dozens of children's picture books and editor of several volumes of academic papers. She has written explorer guides, restaurant reviews, and articles on a range of subjects including traditional Arabic ship-building and handicrafts, adoption, education, faith and ancient cave paintings. She was educated at Balliol College, Oxford, and lives by the sea with her husband, children and assorted refugee hedgehogs. She likes stories, and makes them up all the time.

A note from the author:

Would you write a review? Your opinion is gold dust to other book buyers, and helps writers enormously in finding new readers. If you've enjoyed *The Walker's Daughter* I'd love you to write a review, which you can do here:
UK: http://amzn.to/1l2MIy3
US: http://amzn.to/1jhZNzc

Before you go: When you reach the end of this novel on Kindle, you will probably see a 'Before You Go' page. This cool, clever Amazon technology lets you share that you've read *The Walker's Daughter* with your friends on Facebook and Twitter. It would be great if you could let others know about this book — it only takes a moment.

Finally, thank you so much for sharing Cora's story with me. May all your journeys be sweet.

Janet Allison Brown

Coming soon:
Tales of the Revolution

Janet Allison Brown

In the system known as Double Up, every life is a twenty-four hour life shared by two people: a nocturnal, and a diurnal.

IT'S A TALE AS OLD as time: Hana Takahashi loves the mysterious and charismatic nocturnal Head Boy, Rido Kitsu — she just doesn't know it yet. But time is a forgotten concept in the Eastern Cities, along with history, and freedom. And Hana Takahashi — diurnal, model schoolgirl, obedient citizen — knows everything.

Like: every life must be shared between two people to conserve resources. And: diurnals like herself *belong* in the daylight, and nocturnals like Suzy Hamasaki, with whom Hana shares her own life, *deserve* to live only by night. For all its rules and restrictions, its rationing and unexplained disappearances, the system of Double Up is for the Common Good and mustn't be questioned.

Hana's eyes are about to be opened. Her attraction to Rido drags her into a new way of thinking and a new danger — a thirst to live her own life, day *and* night, and a passion to give everyone else the same freedom. As the young revolutionaries pit their lives against the myths of Double Up, and create new myths in the process, they face the stark and terrifying question:

Is love enough to change the world?

Also available from Firedance Books

STILLNESS DANCING By Jae Erwin

LILLIANE HAS ALWAYS BEEN DRAWN by the desert — its emptiness, its eerie beauty and its people. When she takes the trip of a lifetime to a Bedu camp, she finds herself ensnared in a complex web of politics, blood feuds, terrorism and ancient spirits.

Karim is trying to find his path in the material world and to marry the girl of his dreams. But his soul cries out for the spiritual path of his fathers.

Lilliane's and Karim's stories collide in a forgotten, blood-soaked corner of Sinai. Brutalised, captive and bereft, they must find their own ways to survive.

A taut, unusual thriller set in the fascinating world of the modern Bedouin, *Stillness Dancing* shows us that the hardest paths can lead to the deepest wells.

"From *Stillness Dancing* I've learned that well-written books can truly suck you in. Erwin knows how to create characters and conversation, and she most definitely knows how to create a villain." Andrew Baker, *Fanboys Anonymous*

"A stunning book, filled with the mystery of the desert and the journeys of the spirit, plus blood, mayhem, and a truly nasty villain. Buy it, read it, tell people about it." Stephen Godden, Author

www.ingramcontent.com/pod-product-compliance
Lightning Source LLC
Chambersburg PA
CBHW030318200626
46816CB00006BA/1831